Robert Radcliffe is a pseudonym. The author lives in Suffolk and is himself an experienced pilot.

Praise for *Under an English Heaven*

'I love *Under an English Heaven* . . . I admired how lightly the author wears his knowledge — loads of research, but all so smoothly imparted, never holding up the action, never lessening the tension . . . I was almost sick with excitement' Margaret Forster

'[*Under an English Heaven*] really brings the past back to life. The feel of what the war was really like — for American airmen in Britain as well as for their British hosts and counterparts — is conveyed with an almost mesmeric confidence and exactitude . . . remarkable' John Bayley

'Radcliffe vividly describes the grim anticipation, chaos and occasional wild hilarity of aerial battle; he also movingly evokes the desperate camaraderie and the permanent threat of death . . . The tribute to courage and endurance remains memorable' *Sunday Times*

'A touching, real and evocative Second World War novel set in Suffolk . . . [Radcliffe's] story of an American bomber crew stationed in Suffolk in 1943, and the way their lives intertwine with those of English folk on the ground, is almost cruelly compelling . . . The whole thing might have been planned with a slide rule. Short scenes are artfully shuffled, almost every one primed with some revelation or shock, and the skill with which Radcliffe describes the nuts and bolts of flying a bomber is complemented by an equal facility at scene setting in the countryside below . . You will thoroughly enjoy it' *Daily Express*

'Crisply written, elegantly plotted and snappily paced . . . Each set-piece battle is artfully choreographed using details from actual events' *Scotsman*

'A rattling good yarn, the literary version of a Hollywood period blockbuster. The action sequences, in particular, are not only gripping, but provide an authentic sense of how terrifying it must have been to be at the controls of a Flying Fortress over Nazi-occupied Germany in broad daylight before there was sufficient fighter protection . . . *Under an English Heaven* has all the drama, action and romance you could possibly want' *New Statesman*

'The descriptions of air combat are first-class . . . humour and pathos are blended to superb effect. Radcliffe is not just a born storyteller, but one of those generous writers who look for the best in human nature . . . Will bring a glow to the most jaded cheeks' David Robson, *Sunday Telegraph*

'[A] meticulously accurate picture of life in wartime England . . . the simple doggedness of Radcliffe's theme is survival, which seems remarkable only with hindsight; at the time it was just something you did because there was no alternative. This matter-of-factness the author has captured flawlessly, and the result is enthralling. I loved it' *Daily Mail*

'Radcliffe has done his research . . . and the result, particularly in his description of life on board a bomber during combat, is often riveting' *The Times*

Under
an
English Heaven

ROBERT RADCLIFFE

For Stuart and June

An *Abacus* Book

First published in Great Britain
by Little, Brown in 2002
Reprinted 2002
This edition published by Abacus in 2003
Reprinted in 2003 (three times)

A CIP catalogue record for this book
is available from the British Library

ISBN 0 349 11503 6

Typeset in Perpetua by M Rules
Printed and bound in Great Britain
by Clays Ltd, St Ives plc

Abacus
An imprint of
Time Warner Books UK
Brettenham House
Lancaster Place
London WC2E 7EN

www.TimeWarnerBooks.co.uk

Acknowledgement

Wherever possible, details of specific combat operations are based upon first-hand accounts of real events. There is a wealth of published material available to the interested reader. Three books I can particularly recommend are: *B17s over Berlin* edited by Ian Hawkins (Maxwell MacMillan Pergamon, 1995), *A Wing and a Prayer* by Harry H. Crosby (Robson, 1996), and *With Crew #13* by Earl Benham (Earl Benham, 1990).

R. R., Suffolk, England

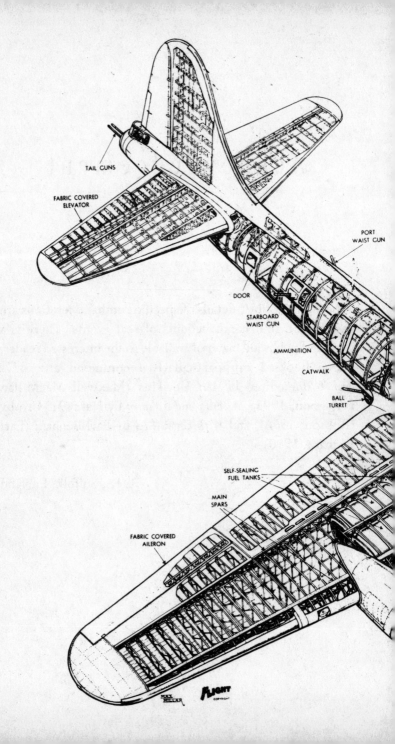

TAIL GUNS

FABRIC COVERED
ELEVATOR

PORT
WAIST GUN

DOOR

STARBOARD
WAIST GUN

AMMUNITION

CATWALK

BALL
TURRET

SELF-SEALING
FUEL TANKS

MAIN
SPARS

FABRIC COVERED
AILERON

FLIGHT

MAX
MILLAR

Boeing B17 Flying Fortress

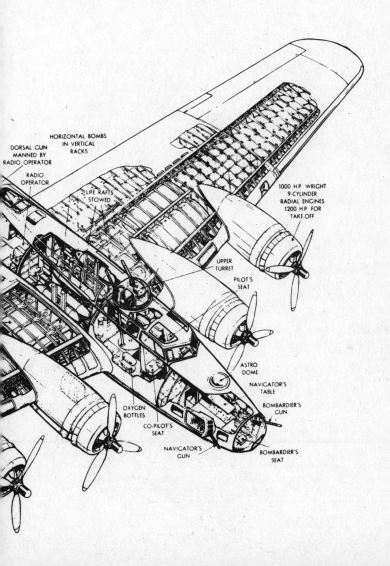

DORSAL GUN
MANNED BY
RADIO OPERATOR

HORIZONTAL BOMBS
IN VERTICAL
RACKS

RADIO
OPERATOR

LIFE RAFTS
STOWED

1000 H.P WRIGHT
9-CYLINDER
RADIAL ENGINES
1200 H.P. FOR
TAKE-OFF

UPPER
TURRET

PILOT'S
SEAT

ASTRO
DOME

NAVIGATOR'S
TABLE

OXYGEN
BOTTLES

BOMBARDIER'S
GUN

CO-PILOT'S
SEAT

NAVIGATOR'S
GUN

BOMBARDIER'S
SEAT

Prologue

The pounding, submerged beneath the hiss of heavy rain outside, summons her at last from restless, dream-filled sleep. She opens her eyes, blinking in confusion at the luminous dial of her alarm clock, while the shapeless faces, the fading echoes of her dreams, flee into the night through the blacked-out window. It is three o'clock. Someone is at the door.

She sits upright, reaches for the bedside light, sweeps hair from her face. It is him. It must be. She snatches up her dressing gown and runs for the landing. The cottage is in total darkness, the rain beating on to the roof a percussive tattoo. She reaches for the banister, swings on to the stairs, stumbles, recovers, hurries down to the hall. A candle and matches lie on the table by the door. She fumbles for them, the candle sputters, the knocking comes again. 'I'm coming!' she whispers frantically. Her hand reaches for the latch.

Behind him the whole lane gurgles, glistens, like a stream in spate, the rain falling to it in billowing silver curtains. Above it the sky is heaving, black and fathomless. He is standing in the open doorway, his cap, his tightly belted mackintosh darkly stained with rain. His face is drenched, the water flowing like tears down the pale skin of his nose and cheeks. His eyes, lowered, stare emptily, heavy with anguish. His hands are clasped as though in prayer.

'I killed a man.' He shudders, his voice cracked and hollow in the rain. 'Today. I murdered him. In cold blood. He was just a boy. I saw his face, saw him wave at me. I waved back, drew him nearer. Then I murdered him, as surely as if I put a gun to his head.'

'Please, come inside.'

He doesn't move, but slowly his eyes lift to hers. 'I'm so afraid.'

'I know.' She reaches for him then, takes his unresisting hand, draws him into the hallway, and leads him towards the stairs.

Chapter 1

'July second 1943. From milk-run to bloodbath in half a second.'

Major Finginger, nodding, quickly copied the words into his intelligence report folder. His pencil, slippery with sweat, stuttered across the page, his unique but infallible shorthand faultlessly recording every syllable. It was pure poetry. A guileless, unpremeditated nine-word grouping that effortlessly encapsulated the totality of the air war they waged. In the weeks and months that followed, it would return to him endlessly, settle and lodge in his subconscious, grow to become a part of who he was. Like the tiny flak fragment embedded in the skin of his left eyebrow that itched so infernally in the heat. There for the rest of his life. From milk-run to bloodbath in half a second. They should drill it into the new crews in basic training back home. They should splash it, weekly, across the front page of *Stars and Stripes*. They should paint it on signboards suspended above the entrance gate of every air base in East Anglia. It said it all.

It was just such a damn shame he never recorded which of the seven ashen-faced young men slumped around the table in his office that sultry July afternoon had actually said it.

And for a first mission, everything had been going so well for them.

Loren Spitzer said it.

It happened at eighteen thousand feet. The formation was on its way home, descending through the cloudless blue, duty done. The worst was over, behind them, and they were heading out across the Channel for home, somewhere over the Pas de Calais. The mission, Spitzer's first, his whole crew's first, bombing the railway marshalling yards at Rouen, had gone like a dream. Accomplished without a hitch and without loss. A milk-run. No fighters showed up, or if they did Spitzer never saw them. Some light 88mm anti-aircraft flak sprang up, as predicted, on the run-in to the target. But it never came near, and it looked so harmless, little smoky puffballs bursting in the sky high above them like silent firecrackers. A couple of aircraft in the high formation took flak hits. *Saucy Sue* lost an engine and *Snake Hips II* had eighteen inches of wingtip shot away. But both ships were still flying, still holding good, maintaining speed and tight in formation.

Spitzer could see them now as he peered straight up through the convex plastic astrodome set into the roof of his B17's nose compartment, his gloved hand shielding his eyes against the sun's glare. The high formation, forty bombers, winging its way steadily homewards a thousand feet above him. Forty silhouetted cruciforms glinting against a flawless milky blue. It was a beautiful, heart-stirring sight. A pencil-thin line of grey smoke trailing from one cruciform marked *Saucy Sue*'s position in the middle of the formation. He thought of the ten men on board, anxiously looking out at the smoking remains of their lifeless number three engine. But hopeful, comforted that they were safely among their friends and homeward bound. Anxious but hopeful. That's how he'd feel in their shoes, Spitzer reckoned.

But in his shoes he felt pleased and proud. If a little tired, and cold. He wiggled his toes in their fur-lined overboots, looking out at his own aircraft's wings. Huge, flat, green, slightly bowed, the control tabs drifting up and down as the pilot held position, the four massive engines, each with the power of a thousand horses, thundering on and on, spinning the propellers into whirling grey discs. Numbing the mind to jelly. He'd done it. Made the grade. Navigated a combat mission over enemy territory, attacked an important strategic installation, watched his aircraft's bombs tumble earthwards precisely on to the target. And come safely home again. So what that the actual navigating involved little more than following the aeroplane in front. So what that Bombardier Broman had simply released their bombs when signalled to do so by the lead aircraft. He was now a combat flyer. Nothing could take that away from him. He'd write home about it the minute he cleared debriefing.

A thousand feet below him flew the low formation, another flat layer of forty aircraft. He could see them too, crawling across the steel-blue sea beyond Dan Broman's hunched back. And, sandwiched protectively between the two layers, the middle formation. Their formation. It was the perfect defensive box, and *Misbehavin Martha*, their ship, was tucked right in the middle of it. The safest place of all. His tiny navigator's desk was neat and tidy, the navigator's thirty-calibre machine-gun that poked out through the window above it clean and unfired. His first mission. Number one, and straight out of the book. Twenty-four to go. It was a good omen. Nothing to it. A milk-run. Almost an anticlimax. Almost.

Spitzer tugged at the oxygen mask sucking at his face. His cheeks felt numb and chafed, his mouth was dry and tasted of rubber. Seven hours. Not long, not short; average. He stood at the astrodome, gazed out at the middle formation. There were Flying Fortresses in every direction. A gently undulating carpet of bombers. In front, behind and to the sides, each bristling with guns. Nothing could get past that and survive. The most powerfully defended flying force in the history of air warfare, Officer Commanding had reminded them at briefing that morning. He was right. Spitzer looked over at the nearest aircraft, *Appaloosa Lou*, flying to *Martha*'s right. On the way to the target they'd been so close their wingtips almost touched. Now, with the danger subsiding with every passing minute, pilots flew their formations a little more loosely. Yet she was still near enough for him to see the rivet lines showing through flaking green paintwork, oil streaks along the undersides of the wings. A couple of masked faces in the side windows. The little row of neatly stencilled bombs along the nose, each denoting a completed mission. Spitzer counted eight; this was *Appaloosa*'s ninth. Her navigator had his head in the astrodome too, and Spitzer could see the distant blue smudge of the Kent coast stretching across the horizon beyond him. Spitzer waved a thumbs-up, the man shook a thickly gloved fist in acknowledgement. *Lou* made it, the fist triumphed. Pulled off another one. Nine down. Sixteen to go.

Nine. It seemed a long way off. Spitzer's head turned once more in the dome, completing the semicircle, facing aft. Just two feet away rose *Misbehavin Martha*'s steeply raked windscreen and flight deck. Sticking up immediately behind it, the thumb-stub top of Lajowski's upper gun turret swivelled this way and that. Behind that the fuselage tapered from view until, thirty feet beyond Lajowski's turret, *Martha*'s huge tail-fin cleaved skyward. No wonder the Boeing people called the B17 the big-assed bird. Movement caught his eye nearby. He could see the heads of his pilot, Rudy Stoller, and co-pilot Irv Underwood moving behind the flight deck windscreen. They were half turned towards each other, nodding, gesturing, engrossed in discussion. Spitzer saw Rudy's hand raised, flat, as though demonstrating a flying aircraft. Irv nodding. Spitzer reached for his intercom switch.

'Navigator to pilot.'

Rudy's head came up. 'What is it, Spitz?'

'Kent coast off to starboard, estimated time of arrival back at base eleven minutes past the hour, just wondered if I could go aft and say hello to the guys back there.'

A chorus of groans and catcalls broke out over the intercom.

'Watch out, fellas, officer prowling.'

'Put your dick away, Greenbaum. Navigator don't want to see that itty thing.'

'Navigator couldn't find it anyways, not without a compass.'

'Up yours Ringwald, this is Kentucky prime, pure fifty-calibre.'

'Someone wake up tail gun. He still asleep back there?'

Spitzer's pilot shrugged at him through the windscreen, Irv Underwood grinning beside him. 'Be my guest.' Rudy's voice crackled over the headphones. Relaxed, amused. One down, twenty-four to go. 'We're descending through twenty thousand, be coming off oxygen in about fifteen minutes.'

Spitzer ducked down from the astrodome and began clipping his oxygen hose on to a portable walk-around cylinder. At the very front of the cramped nose compartment, the bombardier, Dan Broman, shifted on his seat. Despite the thickly muffled bulk of his fur-lined flying suit, his face looked pale and cold above the mask. He had his arms wrapped around his chest, gloved hands wedged under his armpits. He was staring sightlessly ahead through the huge curved plexiglas nose of the aircraft, his face expressionless.

'I'm going aft, okay, Dan?' Spitzer called, shuffling awkwardly into the crawlway beneath the flight deck. Broman said nothing, his eyes riveted to the burnished sheet-metal surface of the English Channel four miles below. But as Spitzer exited the nose compartment, something caught Broman's eye. A tiny black speck had appeared on the plexiglas. A squashed bug? An oil spot? But then it moved. A speck that moved?

'That isn't right,' he muttered to himself.

At last the truck appeared. Huge, open-backed, drab olive green, with a faded white star on its bonnet, it pulled up outside the school gate in a haze of blue exhaust, a grinding of gears and raucous honking of its horn.

'This is it!' Billy announced needlessly. 'Right, now then, everyone follow behind me.'

In an instant, a score of cheering fourteen-year-olds surged past him, sprinting full tilt across the playground towards the waiting truck like an army in rout. Billy, his round cheeks red with indignation, stared after them in disbelief. 'Hey! I said wait, didn't I? Come back 'ere. I fixed this, you've bloody well got to wait for me!'

'William,' his teacher said quietly. 'They're just excited. We all are. There's no need to swear.'

'But this is my outing. I organised it.'

'I know, and I'm sure we're all very grateful.'

But he was gone, stamping across the playground towards the truck where his classmates, assisted by two smiling servicemen in green fatigues, were already swarming over the tailgate. Billy ignored them, stepping up ostentatiously into the driver's cab. His teacher, Heather Garrett, looked on, then rose from the playground bench, discreetly plucked the damp back of her cotton dress away from her skin, lowered sunglasses to her eyes and followed.

They rode, high and riotous, through the village, intoxicated with excitement, like the unruly top deck of a works-outing charabanc, cheering and singing, waving and shouting at the bemused passers-by. Heather, limp with heat and languor, quickly relinquished any pretence at control. Instead, nodding and smiling indulgently, she just watched them, two swaying, elbow-jostling lines of chattering young people with no cares other than how to fill both the daily hollowness of their stomachs and the gaping void of the approaching summer holidays. A Yank tea on the base would deliver them, gloriously sick with sugary surfeit, from the first; the second yawned deliciously ahead, ripe with infinite possibility.

'Look, miss! Look, it's old Mr Howden.'

They were passing a row of cottages. An old man in string-tied trousers and faded waistcoat stood back from the verge, blinking at their passing. Hesitantly, he doffed his cap, as though to a liberating army. There was a renewed outbreak of cheering.

'Percy! Hey, Percy!'

'He's dotty, that one!' someone said. 'Lost his marbles working in them fields all those years.'

'No he ain't. He's just confused, my mum says.'

'Look, miss! There's the verger. On his bike, over there, look!'

Quickly through the village, the truck ground on, accelerating along winding lanes into open countryside, a welcome slipstream ruffling shirtsleeves and dresses, carrying the scent of hot soil and dog-rose. Beyond, in every direction, field upon field of sun-ripened corn stood waiting, brittle and dusty from weeks of heat and too little rain. They passed high above tangled hedgerows littered with poppies, busy with sparrows, then sank into the brief cool of the woods, where the smell was moist leaves, the light dappled, and the dank air filled suddenly with the shrieks of girls ducking their heads beneath low boughs.

And then, all at once, the truck rounded a bend, entered a tree-lined road and pulled up before a barrier. Beside the road a wooden signboard: '520th Bombardment Group, 8th

US Army Air Force. Bedenham.' Next to it a defused two-hundred-pound bomb had been painted bright yellow and upended into the ground. On it was written: 'Welcome to the 520th where missing is not an option.' Two military policemen in steel helmets stood at the barrier. They glanced cursorily at the truck, threw a lazy winking salute in Heather's direction, and waved them through.

With a closing speed of more than five hundred miles an hour, the single-seat Messerschmitt fighter flashed head-on through *Misbehavin Martha*'s middle formation of bombers in the twinkling of an eye. One instant it was nothing more than a distant, slow-moving speck on the windscreen; the next, it had turned in for the attack and was rapidly closing, rapidly growing. An instant after that it was upon them. A momentary glimpse of mottled grey paintwork, the flash of a clipped, compact profile, a black cross, a sparkling of cannon fire from a yellow-painted nose, and it was gone, scything through the formation virtually before anyone realised it had ever been there.

Loren Spitzer had just entered *Martha*'s rear fuselage area. It had taken him nearly five minutes to get there. Clutching his portable oxygen cylinder awkwardly to his chest, he had scrambled on hands and knees out of the nose compartment, squeezed with difficulty along the eight-inch walkway that ran the length of the empty bomb bay, and on through a bulkhead door into the radio operator's cabin. There, breathless, he paused only briefly. The radio operator, Gerry Via, was busy, headphones clamped to his head, a radio manual open on his desk. The two men exchanged a thumbs-ups before Spitzer opened a second bulkhead door at the rear of the radio room. Ahead stretched the tapering tubular rear section of the aircraft, *Martha*'s two waist gunners standing at their guns on either side, towards the back. He raised a hand in greeting. It was noisier here than in the rest of the aircraft, he noted. And colder. On the floor immediately in front of him, further impeding progress, the four-foot spherical ball turret hung in its socket in the floor. Squeezed into it, curled foetally like a chick in an egg and suspended in space beneath the aircraft, Eldon Ringwald, the youngest and smallest member of the crew, sat hunched over his gun sights, idly watching the French coast unravel behind them. Spitzer began to step awkwardly around the turret.

At that moment there was a muffled but audible clunk, as if someone had rapped on the outside of the fuselage with a spanner. Simultaneously, the right-hand waist gunner, Dave Greenbaum, jerked, as though from an electric shock, then doubled over sideways to the floor. At the same time there was a single long burst of machine-gun fire from the aircraft's tail gunner and the sensation that the bomber was tilting over slightly on to its side.

Spitzer and the other waist gunner, Marion Beans, stared down at Greenbaum's inert form. As they looked, a dark stain seeped from beneath him, quickly spreading across the floor of the fuselage.

'Dave? Greener?' Beans dropped to a crouch beside his friend.

Spitzer moved down the walkway. 'No. It's, ah, okay, Beans, stay at your gun, there may be more fighters. I'll see to him.'

12

Beans hesitated, his round face wide with confusion and disbelief. 'It's all right,' Spitzer went on, arriving beside Greenbaum's body. A gasp of pain escaped from behind the gunner's oxygen mask. Above it, his skin was deathly pale. 'It's all right, he's alive. Man your gun,' Spitzer repeated. Beans swallowed, then turned back to the machine-gun at his window.

'Greenbaum?' Spitzer plugged his intercom lead into a socket. Instantly his head was filled with confused shouts from all over the aircraft.

'Tail, this is radio, did you nail him? Did you get him, Tork?'

'You bet your sweet flight pay! Well, I didn't actually see hits, for sure, exactly. But I sure as hell gave it to him. Long and hard. Ball turret, did you see it?'

'I didn't see buckshit, he was through us so damn fast. I don't think anybody got near him.'

'I sure as hell did, didn't anyone else see? Waist? Waist, did you see anything?

'This is waist.' Beans' voice. 'Greenbaum's hit.'

A fractional pause. 'Shit. Is he okay?'

'Did someone say we got hit?'

'This is upper turret here. Can anyone hear me back there?'

'Greenbaum's hit. Jesus, is it bad?'

Spitzer slipped off his glove, easing a hand under Greenbaum's chest. The gunner's heavy flying jacket was soaked through already, the leather slick with blood. Spitzer probed gently with his fingers, but could find no tear, no sign of a hole. 'Greenbaum!' he hissed. 'Listen, can you hear me, Dave? Where are you hurt?'

'Er, look, this is Lajowski in the turret, can anyone hear me back there?'

The aircraft was still tilting, banked over ten or fifteen degrees to starboard, and it felt as though it was sliding downward. They were dropping out of formation, Spitzer realised, his mind numb suddenly with panic. And turning away from it. What if they were hit? Fatally damaged? What if they were crashing? Should they be bailing out? He tried breaking in over the shouts on the intercom. 'Navigator to pilot.' Nothing. He tried again. 'Co-pilot, this is Spitzer, I'm in the waist with an injured gunner, do you copy that? Irv?' Still nothing. Suddenly Greenbaum stirred, a long drawn-out groan of pain. Blood was everywhere. The knees of Spitzer's flying suit were soaked through with it. It slipped sticky warm between his fingers. He could even smell it, sickly sweet, through his mask. Helplessly he watched a huge puddle of it spreading in a brown stain over the fuselage floor. Yet still he couldn't see where it was all coming from. Gritting his teeth, he reached around the gunner with both arms and heaved him over on to his back. Greenbaum gasped, his eyes fluttering open. Blood spurted from a gaping rent in his flying suit, down between his legs, bubbling like a geyser. Spitzer leaned forward, peeled back shredded leather, saw a mess of torn fabric and purple flesh, a glimpse of white bone sinking beneath the welling blood. Wrenching at his neck, he unwrapped the scarf his mother had sent from Boise only a week before, bundled it into a ball and pressed it on to the gunner's groin. Still the voices went on.

'What's going on? Are we dropping out?'

'Where the hell is that fighter? Ball turret? Ringwald? Can you see any more out there?'

'No, I – no, there's no more that I can see. Did we get hit?'

'What was it? Focke-Wulf?'

'There's a B17 going down from the high squadron! A flamer. Jesus, look at that. No parachutes.'

'This isn't right.'

'Listen, this is upper turret, for God's sake can anyone hear me back there, we have a major emergency on the flight deck.'

'Did we get hit, you ask?' Beans was shouting, his voice almost hysterical. Spitzer could see him swinging his gun wildly back and forth through the left-hand waist aperture. 'Did we get hit?' He was yelling. 'Greenbaum's lying here in a goddamn ocean of blood, you asshole, of course we got hit!'

The balled scarf in Spitzer's fist was already soaked through. Gingerly he lifted it, peering forward over Greenbaum's body. Instantly blood welled once more, thick and dark, from the torn flesh of the gunner's inner thigh. The wound was shocking. Obscene. But it didn't look fatal. It was just the bleeding – they had to stop it. The skin of Greenbaum's forehead and cheeks above the mask was grey-white. His eyes stared up into Spitzer's, more in disbelief than in pain. Spitzer pressed down again hard with the sodden scarf. Again, the gunner groaned.

'Ah, listen up, everyone. This is navigator to crew. For God's—' Spitzer struggled to keep his voice calm. 'Listen, everyone, you've got to keep silence on the intercom. Radio, Gerry? Can you get back here, fast, with the big medical kit.'

Broman. The bombardier. Where the hell was Dan Broman? There was a momentary pause, then the voices flooded back, as if he'd never uttered.

'I know Greenbaum's hit, Beans, you piece of shit! I was asking about damage to the goddamn aircraft.'

'This is not right.'

'Turret to navigator. Spitzer, you'd better do something up here 'cos we're going—'

'Who the hell are you calling a piece of shit?'

'Shut-the-hell-up!' Spitzer roared, his voice cracking into a falsetto. 'Everyone! Right now!' Then, as an afterthought, 'That is an order.' Silence descended over the intercom at last. He could hear the incessant rumbling of the engines, the steady crescendo of the slipstream, the rattle and creak of the flexing airframe. His right hand and forearm were drenched. Blood trickled up to his elbow. 'Okay, now then. Ah, right, pilot, this is navigator, can you hear me?' Silence. 'Flight deck, pilot, co-pilot? Rudy? Irv? This is Spitz, can anyone hear me up there?' Still no response.

'Shit. Ah, okay, bombardier, this is navigator. Broman, can you hear me?'

A pause. 'I, uh, yes, this is bombardier.'

'Good, good. Listen, can you get up on to the flight deck right away. Upper turret says there's a problem and I can't raise the pilots on the intercom.' No response. 'Broman, did you get that?'

'Uh, right. I'm on it.'

'Fine.'

Gerry Via appeared at the radio-room door and began to move awkwardly towards him. He was carrying a medical box under one arm, bracing himself with the other against the increasingly pronounced tilting of the aeroplane. It was up to twenty degrees now. What the hell was going on? They were in a steepening descending turn. Dropping down and away from the protection of the formation. Easy meat.

'Ah, turret, this is navigator. Lieutenant Broman's coming up on to the flight deck now. Can you two assist the pilots as necessary and get a message to them that Greenbaum's hit bad. Try and get the intercom working up there.' The noise of the slipstream was rising, climbing steadily to a shriek as the aircraft accelerated into a diving spiral. Were they crashing? 'Uh, ask them if they need any assistance, or anything.'

Via lost his footing, skidding on blood. As he fell his hands wrenched open the medical box. Morphine phials, sulphur packs, splints, bandage rolls spilled out on to the wet floor. 'Jesus.' He scrabbled around on all fours, gathering the contents into his arms, his eyes, shocked, on the pulpy mess at Greenbaum's groin. 'Jesus, look at it. What the hell do we do?'

'I don't know.' Spitzer grabbed a compress and tore it open. 'I don't know. We have to stop the bleeding somehow. I think it's an artery got severed. Or something. In his thigh.' He glanced at Via. 'I thought you were the expert.'

Via stared down at the darkly glistening tangle of clothing and flesh. He had no idea, had only half listened as he daydreamed his way through a two-day course in basic first aid back in Riverdale. It all seemed so remote then, so far away, so unconnected with reality. This reality. Greenbaum, big, laughing Dave Greenbaum, the gentlest giant, with fists like hams and the heart of an ox, was staring up at them, his sparkling eyes dulling, while his big heart pumped the life out of him on to the floor.

'Get a sulphur pack open,' Spitzer suggested. 'And another compress. This one's useless.' He lifted a sodden wad of crimson gauze. Still the blood welled beneath it.

Via, on both knees, scrabbled through the contents of the medical box. His hands were shaking. He ripped open a sulphur pack, emptying it like a bag of icing sugar over Greenbaum's groin. He and Spitzer grabbed a compress each and covered the wound, pressing down together, four hands. He felt the compresses sinking, their hands sinking, into the flesh, the blood warm between his fingers. 'Jesus,' he said, over and over. 'Jesus, Jesus, Jesus.'

Spitzer looked up.

Broman.

Bombardier Dan Broman was standing, almost leaning, at the radio-room door. One hand reached up, fumbled at his oxygen mask, unhooked it, then hooked it up again. His intercom plug swung loose at his waist. He was wearing his life jacket. His chest parachute was clipped to his harness. His head was nodding, rapidly, and he was gesturing towards the front of the aeroplane.

'Broman?' Spitzer called. 'What? What is it?'

Broman pulled off his mask again. His cheeks were wet, his eyes wide. His mouth was working, his whole face. 'Not right!' he shouted, his voice cracking like a girl's. He waved in the direction of the flight deck again. 'That. Not right!'

Somewhat to Heather Garrett's surprise, Billy Street, up until that moment supremely cocksure, overstuffed in fact with impatient self-confidence, suddenly suffered an attack of stage fright. With his classmates arranged, at last, in a semi-respectful circle before him, the parked bomber at his back, he now stood in uneasy silence and obvious discomfort, wringing his hands and shifting his weight from one foot to the other. Apparently, having arrived at possibly the most eagerly awaited moment of his life thus far, he was like an Eskimo with a coconut. Completely at a loss as to how to enjoy it.

'Take your time, William,' she coaxed. One of the girls standing next to her stifled a giggle.

'Look, he's come over all shy.'

'When's tea, miss?' pestered another.

Still Billy said nothing, knitting and unknitting his chubby fingers, his mouth opening and closing like a beached cod.

Movement caught Heather's eye. Nearby, a sergeant mechanic in oil-stained overalls was sorting noisily through a trolley of tools parked in the shade beneath one of the aeroplane's huge wings. She could see he was trying to attract Billy's attention. Nodding minutely, he was touching a finger to the cap on his head. Billy licked his lips, reached behind him and pulled an identical green army cap from his back pocket. After a second's hesitation, he tugged it on to his head, tipped up the brim, American style, and launched into his speech.

'Um, right, well, now then, folks,' he began, in a sort of ghastly nasal cockney drawl. Heather inclined her head attentively, glancing at the same time at the mechanic. The name Knyper was stencilled on to his overalls. He winked at her then turned to watch Billy, leaning darkly haired forearms on to his trolley. Billy turned and smacked the flank of the aero-plane with the flat of his hand. 'So, um, this 'ere is the Boeing B17 Flying Fortress made by Boeing Aircraft Corporation of Seattle Washington America. It is called the Flying Fortress because of its dead impressive defensive armaments which is insisted of no fewer than five, um, six fifty-calibre machine-gun positions, those positions being positioned one poking out the back of the tail there, two sticking out the sides here, these are called the waist positions, one slung under 'ere in this ball-shaped thing which is called the ball turret, one called the upper turret up there just behind the cockpit, and one poking right out through the glass nose dome up there in the front. Also as well there's a thirty-calibre machine-gun the navigator can shoot poking out his side window in the front, and the radio operator has another one he can stick out the roof of his little radio operator's cubby hole, there, see?'

'Why's Billy talking all Yank funny like that, miss?'

'Where did you nick that hat from then, Bill?'

'Tell us more about the bombs and stuff.'

'How the hell do you get in and out that ball turret thing?'

'When's tea, miss?'

'Quietly, everyone. We'll do questions in a minute, and one at a time. Billy, please continue.'

'Right. Yes, well, as I was saying, the B17 has a wingspan of more than a hundred feet and is powered by four bloody great motors on the wings there called Wright Cyclones which have more than twelve hundred horsepower each which makes your dad's Austin Seven look a bit puny, Stanley Fisk.'

His confidence returning as he warmed to his theme, he

was soon conducting the group on a guided tour of the bomber, under the watchful eye of Sergeant Knyper. Heather followed behind, shepherding wayward classmates, nodding encouragingly as Billy paused to point out another important technical feature, or recite from his seemingly bottomless inventory of statistics, or pose beneath the flimsily clad and impossibly bosomed girl painted on the aeroplane's nose. She was a redhead, kneeling, coquettishly half turned, reaching behind her back to unfasten her brassiere. *Ginger Snap*, the aircraft was called. It was so innocent, Heather felt. So acutely boyish. So poignant. A pubescent sex-fantasyland reminder of the extreme youthfulness of the young men, some little older than Billy Street and his friends, who fought for their lives within these cramped steel tubes in the freezing and unbreathable air miles and miles above the earth.

It was unimaginable. She stopped to peer through a side window into the aeroplane's waist. Inside it was dark and spartan, just girders and guns, wires and bare metal walls. The stories. Although they tried to suppress them, they filtered through, floating quietly down to the villagers like flakes of winter snow in the woods. One boy she'd heard of recently, while queuing outside the greengrocer's. A new ball turret gunner, out on a long first mission. Sick with nerves, he'd been unable to relieve himself before take-off. Halfway into the mission, with the aircraft at twenty-four thousand feet and the air temperature at minus forty, he could hold on no longer and urinated in his clothes. The electrically heated elements woven into his flying suit were immediately shorted out, leaving him unprotected from the cold. He said nothing, too ashamed to speak, but sat, hanging in his icy turret in space, while the urine seeped down his legs and into his boots, where it froze. Four hours later they lifted him, tearful with shame and pain, from his turret and into an ambulance. Two days after that they amputated both his feet. Eighteen years old.

She started. The ringing clang of a spanner dropped on to concrete. The busy twitter of a skylark high overhead. Farther off in one of the hangars someone was hammering sheet metal. Along the perimeter track, a dust devil, borne of torpid mid-afternoon heat, whirled straw and cement dust into a swirling mist then wandered aimlessly away like a lost wraith. The smell was of dry grass, warm rubber, fuel oil, Knyper's cigarette. She stared round at the empty airfield. It really was unusually quiet; there were practically no aircraft to be seen anywhere. All but a couple of the concrete hard-standings where they parked the bombers were empty. It was as if the whole base was holding its breath. Nearly a quarter of a mile away squatted the box-like profile of the control tower. A Jeep was pulled up beneath it, figures were sprawling on the grass outside it, more lined the upstairs balconies. She looked at Knyper. He was gazing towards the eastern horizon.

'You've got aeroplanes out on a mission,' she said quietly to him. The children were clustered beneath one of the propellers, Billy holding sway in their midst. Knyper's eyes, china-blue beneath thick black eyebrows, met hers. His cheeks were darkly stubbled and an oil smear ran like a shadow beside his nose.

'Yes, ma'am. Due back any time.'

'It must be awful. This waiting.'

'Worst part, no doubt about it.'

'Thank you, Sergeant, for organising all this, for Billy. It's wonderful to see how enthusiastic and how knowledgeable he is about something. It really means a lot to him.'

'Bill? No problem. He's a good kid; practically part of the fixtures here.'

'Yes, well, he's certainly rather too rarely part of the fixtures at school these days, and I know he tends to get into more than his fair share of scrapes, but I'm inclined to agree with you. In any case, it really is very kind of you to give up so much of your time for the children. I'm quite sure you must have a thousand more important things to attend to.'

'No,' the sergeant said simply. 'If not for them, then who the hell is it all for?'

From then on, from the perspective of Lieutenant Loren Spitzer, twenty-five, formerly of Boise, Idaho, everything happened in extreme slow motion.

'Do what you can for him,' his voice said, low and slurred, to Gerry Via's blankly nodding face. His hand, slick with Greenbaum's blood, found Via's shoulder, gripped it hard. He hauled himself wearily to his feet, looked up the cabin. Broman was still there, sort of slumped against the radio-room door. But he was of no further use, Spitzer saw at once. Gone. Finished. He pushed past him without a word.

Back across the steeply canting bomb bay, the slipstream whistling around the airframe, the bomb bay doors rattling against their stops beneath his feet. Were they still turning? Were they still spinning towards the ocean like a dropped sycamore seed? Hard to tell any more; reality was a waking dream. He squeezed through the door to the forward cabin.

Ahead and below was the crawlway through to the nose compartment, and his home in the air, his tidy little desk, his astrodome, his bag of instruments, his Hershey bars and coffee flask. It seemed an age since he had left it, another place, another time. Maybe if he just crawled back there and sat at his little table, ruled out some lines on his map, maybe everything would return to normal.

No. Nothing would ever return to normal again.

There was a loud, piercing whistling coming from up in the cockpit. He stooped round the side of Lajowski's upper gun turret then hoisted himself on to the step-up to the flight deck. As he did so, his boot trod on something soft and slippery. The whistling was growing louder. He hauled himself up.

The first thing he saw was the horizon; sea and sky, shining wide, flat and blue through what was left of the windscreen. The horizon was canted over at twenty degrees and looked as if it was about five thousand feet below them. So he was right, they were still turning, and descending. But not, evidently, as badly as they had been before, not severely so. This, he guessed, was mostly due to the fact that *Misbehavin Martha*'s twenty-year-old upper turret gunner, Technical Sergeant Emmett Lajowski, was leaning across the erectly inert form of the co-pilot, Irv Underwood, and, despite the fact that Underwood's hands were gripping it too, was hauling back for all he was worth on the half-wheel of the co-pilot's control column.

In fact there were three pairs of hands on the flying controls. In the left-hand seat pilot Rudy Stoller also gripped his half-wheel, firmly, one fist on either side of it. Spitzer glanced at his commander, then, with a sort of clipped nod, added his two hands to the fray.

For about a minute the eight hands laboured with the aircraft's flight controls. Nobody spoke. The only sounds were the unfaltering, battering thunder of the four engines outside, the piercing shriek of wind rushing at two hundred and fifty miles an hour through the hole in the left-hand windscreen, and Lajowski's muffled grunts of effort. Then, after what seemed like an aeon, Spitzer saw that *Martha*'s wings were slowly beginning to roll level, and her nose was creeping back up the horizon. Finally, his limited flight experience told him that the bomber was more or less back on an even keel, flying straight and level once more. But he waited until he was quite sure, tightly holding the bomber in his hands, until both the grim nodding of Lajowski's sweat-streaked face and the needles on the blood-spattered flight instruments told him it was safe to let go.

Only then did he begin the difficult task of prising away the vice-like grip Rudy Stoller's fingers had on the control column.

'Here they come,' Knyper said quietly. Heather followed the direction of his pointing arm, but saw nothing save a hazy and irregular line of distant trees and buildings shimmering like a mirage beneath the cloudless sky. Then a small flat cross detached itself from the haze and began to climb from the horizon, then another, and another, a succession of silent crosses rising from the ground. Gradually they grew larger, shape and detail emerging, crawling across the sky towards them as though drawn in on invisible strings. Then came the

25

noise. A whispered low murmur at first, then a rumble like distant thunder. Finally the noise grew to the familiar pulsating roar of a hundred throbbing engines, until the whole sky seemed filled with it.

Knyper was counting. She could see the movement of his lips, the way his eyes searched methodically through the formation.

'How many?' Heather shouted above the din. The leading bombers were right overhead now. Dozens more followed. One or two of the girls had their hands clamped over their ears. The boys, feigning nonchalance, jumped up and down, punched each other on the arm, pointing excitedly.

'Looks pretty good!' Knyper called back, nodding to himself, cautiously satisfied. 'Thirty of ours went out, looks like most of them made it back.'

'Most?'

'Always get a couple of stragglers coming in late or diverting to other airfields. We won't get an exact head-count for a couple of hours yet.'

Overhead, one of the bombers banked steeply out from the formation and began to descend for landing. At the same time a burst of incandescence appeared at its cockpit window and a red flare flew out, spinning smoke.

'What's that?'

'It's the wounded-on-board signal. It'll come in to land first. Must have taken a hit. Aircraft looks okay from here, though.'

The aeroplane spiralled steeply down towards them, then banked away downwind. A minute later they saw it, wheels and flaps lowered, turning back towards the runway for landing. To Heather's untutored eye it appeared to be rocking rather a lot as it closed with the ground, as though the pilot was having difficulty with the controls. Knyper, hands on hips, was studying the approaching bomber.

'Problem?'

'Maybe.'

The aeroplane was descending too quickly to the runway, Heather could see that. She heard Knyper's sharp intake of breath as tyres struck concrete with an audible squeal of protest and twin puffs of smoke. The aeroplane bounced, rearing into the air again before settling unceremoniously to the ground once more, this time for good. She could see the rudder moving from side to side as the pilot struggled to keep straight on the runway. Finally, recovering, it began to slow. Reaching their end of the runway, it turned off towards them.

'He's coming past us. Better get the kids to stand back.'

Heather quickly gathered Billy's classmates together. Billy, his army cap still on his head, stood next to Sergeant Knyper. The aeroplane taxied ponderously around the perimeter track towards them, slowing as it came. Behind it others were lining up to land. In the distance, Heather could see a green van with a red cross racing along the track from the direction of the control tower.

Suddenly the aeroplane stopped. Without warning, right there on the perimeter track next to the clustered children. A moment later all four engines sputtered into silence. A moment after that the forward compartment hatch swung open and a heavily muffled figure dropped to the ground, picked itself up and set off across the concrete towards them.

A girl screamed. One hand on her mouth, she pointed with the other up at the aircraft's flight-deck window. Another joined in, pointing and screaming. Heather was transfixed by the figure striding towards her, still wearing his parachute harness, his life vest, his oxygen mask and leather helmet. 'Get 'em away!' Knyper was yelling suddenly. 'For God's sake get 'em away!'

Heather looked up to the window. Red smears.

'This is not right,' the walking flyer said. He walked straight up to her, his eyes fixed and staring, then past her without a pause, still walking, still shaking his head. 'No sir, not right.'

The screaming went on and on. One of the boys was vomiting on to the concrete at his feet. The aeroplane was called *Misbehavin Martha*. Something liquid, dark and oily, was dripping from the underside of its cabin. Up on top, the inside of its flight-deck window was smeared red. Almost completely obliterated, as though painted out. But not quite. A figure was slumped against it. Heather could clearly see its shoulder pressing against the glass, and, above it, a purple pulpy stump where its head should be.

Chapter 2

'William Street, if you are not dressed and downstairs in less than one minute I'm donating your breakfast to the chickens!' The accented voice floating up the stairs was brisk, shrill, businesslike. But distracted, lacking edge, as though the voice's owner was already thinking of something else. As though this was all just part of the daily routine. Which it was. There was the usual pause, then the usual follow-up. 'Did you hear me, Billy? And the same goes for you, Claire. Downstairs in the kitchen helping me, right now, young lady. At the double!'

He stirred, the warm constancy of the voice banishing into flight, as always, the pursuing chaos of the night. He opened his eyes, waiting for the trapped-bird flutter of his heart to subside. Directly above his head, wire-thin beams of bright sunlight pierced the moth-holes in the blackout pinned across his skylight. Drifting dust motes sparkled as they wandered unwarily into the rays, like night-fighters caught in search-lights. Fire. The usual dream. That and the running, and not knowing where to run. Then locked in the black hell of that cellar, for days, with no food.

Food. Billy's nose twitched. He was hungry. But then he was always hungry. This was nothing, not like the real hunger. Breakfast waited: mug of tea with powdered milk, no sugar. Two pieces of toast, possibly, just possibly spread with that delicious pork dripping, if there was any. If not, an invisible scrape of marge and a little dollop of Mrs Howden's black-currant jam. An egg on Sundays, though not today, from the ration book, or fresh if the chickens felt like it. He threw back his blankets, stretching lazily on the bed, his head turning to the familiar tapestry of sounds drifting through his small window. Twittering birds, the ever-present distant rumble of aero-engines on the base, the clucking of chickens in the yard and a clanging from the foundry. Ray must already be in there, bashing away at his horseshoes.

He breathed deeply. Another sunny day with lots to do. A bit of foraging first; business is business. Then perhaps a spot of fishing by the river with the lads. A visit up the airbase, of course. Maybe even a stroll in the woods, later, with Ruby Moody, if he could persuade her. Saturday. Holidays. Perfection. Creaking from below.

Quick as a cat, he rolled in a single movement off the bed and silently on to the planked wooden floor. Flattened almost to his stomach he then slithered, commando-style, on elbows and knees, across to the far end of his attic bedroom. There, entreating himself to silence, his round face screwed up with concentration, he slowly levered a six-inch section of floorboard from the joist underneath, thumb and forefinger tightly gripping the raised nail positioned there for the purpose.

His view of the bedroom below was partly obscured by the dusty floral lightshade suspended beneath the carefully enlarged crack through which he peered. A girl's room. A home-made wooden dressing table littered with cheap scent bottles and imitation jewellery from Woolworth's. Clothes strewn carelessly over a chair. A mostly hidden yet clearly overstuffed chest of drawers, half a tatty rag rug. And a bed by a window.

A girl was sitting on the edge of it, feet on the floor, head lowered, her brown hair thick about her head, tousled from sleep. She was seventeen. She sat there, hands flat at her sides, trance-like, for more than a minute, just staring sleepily at the floor. She was wearing a simple white cotton nightgown. The neck of it had slipped so that the pale skin of one shoulder was bared. Billy waited, breath held. Finally, the girl reached up, scratched under her armpit, then in a single movement hoisted the nightdress up and over her head, throwing it in a heap into the corner.

A floorboard squeaked at Billy's knee and he winced, heart bumping. She didn't hear. Her breasts were full and slightly pointed; he could clearly see the darker flesh of her nipples. The skin of her legs was pale and smooth. He could even see the fine golden hairs on her arm. But that was about all. She was leaning forward, her head and shoulders obscuring the thighs above her knees. Another few seconds later she yawned loudly, scrubbing fingers through her thick hair. Her breasts shook a bit as she did so. Quite appealingly, Billy thought. Then she stood suddenly and marched out of view. He knelt back on the floorboards, absently stroking his chin for non-existent stubble. Not bad, not good. Shoulders, tits, knees. Six out of ten.

Five minutes later his boots were clumping down the narrow stairway and on to the flagstoned floor of the kitchen. The back door was open. A cat, its tail flicking lazily, blinked up at him from a rectangle of sunlight flooding in from the yard.

'Oh, Billy. Good morning, dear. Did you sleep well?' Maggie Howden, a middle-aged woman in a striped butcher's apron, turned to him from the cooking range. She was short and round with big red arms and red cheeks and newly home-permed hair dyed the colour of polished conkers. It was piled up on top of her head, stiff and high at the front, like a sort of crown. She was smiling at him. Kindly. Almost anxiously. What? There was an egg at his place on the table. A boiled egg. And toast and dripping. And no ticking-off. Something was wrong.

'Yes, thanks, Mrs H. Pretty good.'

'Thank goodness,' said Maggie. 'No more bad dreams then?'

Dreams? He thought back, confused. Had she come to him again? Surely not.

The bomber! She meant the bomber. Three days ago. He'd completely forgotten. *Misbehavin Martha.* Blood dripping into puddles on the concrete, a dead gunner in the waist, and a pilot with his head blown off. Puking boys and hysterical screaming girls. The whole village had heard about it within hours. Those poor children, what a dreadful thing to have to witness. Dr Chillaman had been round to visit everyone. And the vicar. Be nice to them, they'd said to all the grown-ups. Go easy on the kids. Billy'd heard it himself, that night, listening on the stairs when Reverend Pindred came round to talk to Ray and Maggie. 'Billy will be devastated for a while, you understand. Go steady with him for a day or two, just until he finds his feet again.' The Howdens had murmured inaudibly in response, then the old vicar had come creaking up the stairs to the attic, smelling of sherry and mothballs, and they'd said the Our Father together, his bony claw resting on Billy's head.

'No. No dreams.' Billy sighed, his eyes falling to the scrubbed pine breakfast table. A teapot under a knitted cosy. A little doily with tassels over the milk jug. The dripping was melting into the toast, glistening like liquid gold. 'Well, a bit p'raps. You know, there was a lot of blood. And gore and that. Turned the stomach, it did.'

'Yes, quite. Do you think you might be able to manage an egg today? I know it's not Sunday, but the hens seem to be laying a little, and, well, I thought you could probably do with it.'

'I could try my best, Mrs H.'

'Good boy. Of course, if you can't, I can always give it to Claire. She'd have it in a trice. Where on earth is that blessed girl, by the way?'

'I'll try my best,' he repeated solemnly. He sat at the table, closed his eyes, sank teeth into warm, greasy toast.

A flurry of chickens outside signalled approaching heavy footsteps. The squeak of rusty wheels. A shadow fell across the open doorway. Billy opened his eyes once more, pork fat on his chin. An old man stood on the step. Thin, bent, wheezing, with wispy white hair, he was pushing an ancient wheeled shopping basket.

'Morning, Mr H.' Billy worked his tongue around the front of his teeth. The old man, breathing heavily, said nothing, his eyes narrowing on Billy's plate.

'Hello, Dad,' Said Maggie. 'Been out and about, have you, love?'

'Egg,' the old man said eventually, nodding at the plate. A moss sprig hung from his hair. He parked his basket and turned to leave. 'Going up the pub.'

'But Percy, love, it's barely seven. Wouldn't you like some breakfast?'

'Eh?' The old man looked around in bewilderment.

'Toast and dripping, Mr H. It's the best,' Billy said. But uncertainty still clouded the ancient grey eyes. Billy nodded encouragingly. 'And we are still on for the woods tonight, aren't we, Mr H? Pigeons, remember? You and me, like we said. Pigeons?'

At last, blinking, the old man nodded. 'Pigeons. Right. Got you.' He turned to the door once more. 'I'm going up the shed.' Moments later, renewed fussing from the chickens as he shuffled across the yard. 'Bugger all in the woods this morning,' he called back. 'Turnip in the basket. And a hare. Scrawny old bugger it is, though, not a scrap on it. Nothing else. Woods are empty, something's scaring the buggers off.'

'Lovely, Dad!' Maggie cast a critical glance over the corpse in the shopping basket, then wrinkled her nose at Billy. 'Dead for days,' she muttered.

After breakfast, she made him carry a mug of tea out to her

husband. Billy protested, desperate to be off and away. 'Got errands up the village, Mrs H,' he said. 'Promised Mrs Garrett I'd shift boxes for her, and then there's all the queuing at the butcher's and the greengrocer's and that.'

Ray Howden's blacksmith's shop was next door to the cottage. It was a large timber building overhung with trees at the back and with wide wooden doors that opened out on to the front lane. Inside it was dim, shadowy and hot. To Billy it was a hell-hole, a humourless, airless place of fire and fear and darkness. The old windowless walls, black with age and smuts, seemed to melt into infinite shadow at the back, where huge imaginary rats blinked out from indiscernible heaps of rusting iron and coal, sooty shelves and mildewed boxes. In the far corner an ancient foot-operated bellows fed wheezing lungfuls of air to a wide, brick forge that shimmered menacingly, white-hot, beneath a charred chimney. A man was bent over it, hammering rhythmically at an anvil. One big tap, followed by a small one.

'Mrs H said to bring you this.'

The tapping stopped. Ray Howden emerged from the shadows at the rear of the shop, accepted the tea with a nod, blew and sipped, his father's grey eyes on Billy. A pair of horses, big Suffolk Punches with legs the size of oak tree limbs, stood quietly outside, tethered to a post.

'I'd better be off then,' Billy said, turning to go.

'Just a minute.' Ray's Suffolk accent was softer than Maggie's, his voice measured and quiet. He was a slightly built man, in his late forties, but tough and strong, with sinewy arms and a thick neck. His hair was short, greying, the colour of his eyes. He wore a collarless shirt open at the throat with the sleeves rolled to the shoulder, a leather smith's apron, and what looked like Great War vintage army boots. 'Room tidied?'

'Yes, Mr Howden.' Billy looked round at the horseshoes stacked ready near the anvil, the boxes of nails, the rows of tools for gripping and shaping and filing and hammering. An ornately scrolled wrought-iron gate, thick with dust, stood forgotten against one wall beside a pile of scrap metal. A rusting bicycle wheel lay on top.

'Breakfast all cleared and washed up? Yard swept?'

'Yes, Mr Howden,' Billy repeated, adding: 'Managed the egg Mrs Howden kindly cooked me all right, too.'

Ray's eyes above the mug were fastened on his. 'You can spare me any of your clap-trap, boy. You and I both know there's nothing wrong with your appetite.'

'Can I go now, Mr Howden? Got errands to run, for Mrs Howden and that.'

'Mind you get straight to them, and straight back again. Know what I mean?'

''Course.' Despite the urge to go, Billy hesitated. 'Couldn't 'ave that, could I?' He gestured stiffly at the bicycle wheel on the scrap pile.

'What for?'

'Me and some of my mates, we're putting together a push-cart thing, you know, for riding down hills and stuff. We're short a wheel.'

Ray put down his mug and turned back to the forge. Picking up tongs, he withdrew a red-hot shoe and examined it closely, inches from his face, before returning it casually to the inferno. 'It may have escaped the notice of you and your "mates", Billy, but there's a war on. Some of your "mates'" older brothers are fighting in it. Some of them will die in it. Some already have. The Forces are crying out for lack of hardware, every town in every part of the country has a drive on for scrap metal for aeroplanes, ships and tanks. Don't you think, at your age, you and your "mates" could more usefully pass your time by helping collect the stuff together, rather than nicking it to build toy carts?'

Billy turned on his heel. 'Fair enough. I'll be on my—'

'One more thing.'

He was halfway to the light, the urge to run almost irresistible. Up the lane, Ray's father was limping slowly away from the house, once more wheeling his old wicker basket.

'I don't want you going up the airbase today. In fact, I don't want you going up there nearly so much from now on. You're getting far too pally with the Yanks. Do you hear me?'

'Right-oh then.' He began to edge forward once more. Out of the flames, into the light.

'They've got a job to do and so have we. Far better that we all leave one another alone and just get on with it.'

'Got you, Mr H. Better get going though. Errands and that.'

'Hello, dear. No news, I take it?'

'No. No news.' Heather Garrett leaned forward dutifully for a powdery kiss on the cheek, then held the door wide for her mother-in-law to pass, wafting into the house upon a swirl of lavender. As usual, she felt a familiar twinge of unease at the arrival. Unease and inadequacy. Rosamund Garrett's eyes missed nothing; her visits, no matter how closely woven the cloak of maternal affection they came wrapped in, were little more than spot checks. 'Inspection, surveillance and intelligence-gathering raids,' David used to call them. 'Comes of being married to a brigadier.'

'Good heavens, is that plasterwork on the cornice up there cracking already?' Rosamund deposited white gloves on a side table, her neat, silver-coiffed head ricocheting around the walls and ceiling. 'But I'm sure Gerald had that seen to only last year. What on earth have you been doing to the place? Never mind, it's probably the heat. I'll get him to send one of the men round to touch it up for you. Now then, dear, how are you coping? Bearing up, I trust? Come through here to the sitting room and let's talk. I have news. Gerald has had a letter back from the Ministry.'

Heather made tea, ransacked cupboards until she found an old packet of biscuits, shook the last three out on to a plate, and carried the tray through from the kitchen. Rosamund was dabbing at her nose from a compact, turning her head critically from side to side in the little mirror. 'Now then,' she began again, snapping the compact shut with a crack like a rifle shot. She dropped it into her handbag, folding long-fingered hands across her knee. David's fingers: pale, slender and delicate. 'Gerald's been pulling strings like mad and I've been writing to the International Red Cross again, twice this week, and guess what?'

Somehow she always made it sound like a thinly veiled admonishment for lack of purpose or resolve or activity on Heather's part. It was unfair. She wrote her letters too. Long, cheerful, news-filled pages that vanished, weekly, hopelessly, into the void. Never returned, never replied to. Yet she wrote them still, and tried to keep the unhappiness and uncertainty from emerging between the lines. She sipped her tea, eyebrows raised expectantly. Her mother-in-law, cool and fresh in powder-blue linen with white collar and cuffs, was arranged on the slightly threadbare striped armchair Heather kept by the window for reading. It was the one she'd bought herself for her little flat in Lincoln, the first piece of furniture she'd ever owned. Beyond it, an undisciplined but good-natured tangle of climbing roses scratched at the window outside. Lately, in the sultry still of the hot evenings, she'd throw the window wide, put Beethoven on the radiogram, slump into her chair and let the rose scent wash over her like ripples across a warm lake.

'Well, apparently, Gerald is assured, the Foreign Office is doing tremendous work behind the scenes, putting terrific pressure on the Japanese authorities, who have, in their infuriatingly roundabout way, nevertheless promised to look into the whole matter of our missing men and the prisoners of war. By astonishing coincidence, I was given almost exactly the same assurances by the International Red Cross. Now, what do you think of that?'

Seventeen months of silence. That's what she thought. Seventeen months since a husband of barely six months had held her in his arms, kissed her, marched cheerfully through the door, boarded a troopship for Singapore and vanished into thin air. Seventeen months. She had been separated almost three times as long as she had been married. She had been separated for longer than they had even known each other. For all anyone knew she might be a widow. Might have been for a year or more. Writing pointless weekly letters to a ghost. Nobody knew. Nobody knew anything. Yet still she wrote, every week, the words turning to gibberish on the paper before her, incomprehensible, incoherent, like a child's made-up language. 'My dearest, dearest darling . . .' Her eyes drifted to the gilt-framed photograph on the table by the fireplace. David, in subaltern's uniform, his humour-filled eyes beaming proudly from beneath the glossy peak of his cap. So certain, so assured, so visibly, tangibly alive.

'What on earth is that?' A rumble of feet on the ceiling.

'Oh, one of the children from school. He promised to help me clear up the spare bedroom. I thought I might paint it.'

'Paint it? Good heavens, what on earth for? It was only freshly papered a few years back. Simpsons, as I recall. Very costly.'

Floral, of course. Great scarlet blooms exploding around the walls. At night they looked like huge splashes of blood. 'White, I thought, might brighten it slightly. My parents, you see. I am hoping they might come down from Lincoln, stay for a week or so, later in the summer perhaps.'

'But my dear girl, you couldn't possibly ask your parents to stay here, it's far too small and cramped. And it can be the tiniest bit damp. What about your mother and her chest?' Heather opened her mouth, but Rosamund's hand was already raised, palm flat like a policeman's. 'I absolutely insist, if and when they come to Suffolk, they must stay up at the Grange with Gerald and me. It would be our pleasure. I say, what on earth *is* that noise?'

A peal of thunder broke on the stairs and a moment later

the door opened and Billy appeared, a large cardboard box in his arms.

'I say, miss, couldn't 'ave these, could I?'

'Oh, er, William, this is Mrs Garrett, my husband's mother, Brigadier Garrett's wife? At the Grange?'

'Bill, ma'am.'

'I beg your pardon, young man?'

'Folks call me Bill. Please to meet you, ma'am.'

'Rosamund, this is William Street, from my class at school.'

'Why does he speak so peculiarly? He sounds like one of the Americans.'

'William, Billy, here, lives at the Howdens'. You know, the blacksmith's cottage at the end of Bridge Lane?'

'Good heavens, yes. You're the evacuee, aren't you? From London. Tilbury, wasn't it?'

'Yes, ma'am.'

'And how do you like living here in Bedenham?'

'I love it,' he said simply. 'I love it best in the world.'

'Well, that's good. But you must miss your parents.'

'Um, dunno, missus.' Billy's American accent was slipping. He glanced towards Heather, hefting the box in his arms. 'S'pose.'

'Your father. Does he work in the East End? Or is he in the Forces?'

'He works on secret stuff, missus. 'Ush-'ush and that. Bank of England.'

'Goodness, how intriguing. And your mother?'

'Dead, missus. Blitz. Direct hit in the Balls Pond Road.'

'But how simply dreadful.' Rosamund looked in

astonishment from Billy to Heather and back. Heather, stifling a smile, was studying the interlaced fingers of her hands. 'And what is that you have there in the box, young man?'

'Just a, er, couple of old jigsaw puzzles and games, and stuff. And this old bashed-up clock.'

'But those are some of David's old things from school. Aren't they, Heather?'

'The games and puzzles all have pieces missing and the clock doesn't work. I'm sure David would have been pleased to know they were going, and going to an East London evacuee with barely a single possession to his name.' She hadn't meant to sound so hard. And a conditional perfect. Had she slipped in a conditional perfect? He would have been pleased. The past tense?

Rosamund hadn't noticed. 'Well, I don't know, I suppose so. Heather, was this one of the children who were with you the other day? When there was all that unpleasantness at the airbase?'

'Yes, Billy was there.'

Rosamund shook her head fretfully. 'Oh, I do think over-fraternisation between ourselves and the American servicemen is such a mistake. Especially with the children. The senior commissioned officers, well, that's quite a different matter, of course, but the flight crews, and mechanics and cooks and things, enlisted men, for goodness' sake, the children get exposed to such, well, unsavoury and unsuitable influences.'

Heather looked up at last. 'One of their bombers, Rosamund, ten young men, returned from a mission attacking German targets with casualties on board. Two of them were killed. They died for us, you know. Us. Here. Our country, our homes, our children. What on earth could be unsuitable, or unsavoury, about that?'

'Pssst. Len. Lennie! Can I come in? Where's your dad?'

'Down the Fleece. Get on in here quick.'

Billy slid through the door of his friend's garden shed, pulling it quickly to behind him. Len Savidge, a scrawny thirteen-year-old with a permanently running nose, scabby knees and a striped sleeveless sweater he wore year round irrespective of the weather, was emptying out the contents of a box on to a work-bench. 'What did you get?' Billy asked immediately. A couple of metal coat-hangers, a ball of wool, a rusting toy car and a badly dog-eared pack of playing cards fell on to the bench. 'What the hell is all that bloody old junk?' he asked, poking a finger into the pile.

'That's not junk, you idiot, that's all good stuff. Anyway, where's yours then, if you're so clever?'

'Stashed down the mill, of course. What about the bike?'

Lennie wiped his nose on his sleeve, a reflex action he performed a hundred times a day. 'I got this,' he announced proudly, pulling a circular mudguard reflector from his pocket. It lay, sparkling red, like a bejewelled coin, on the grime-stained skin of his palm. 'Found it in the gutter, down by Stan Fisk's.'

'Len. What is the bloody use of a mudguard reflector without a mudguard?'

'It'll come in, won't it! When we get the sodding mudguard. Anyway, what did you get, then?'

'Brakes. The rubbers, and the metal holders they go in.' He tossed them casually on to the bench.

'Blimey. Where did you get them from?'

'Off the verger's bike, queuing outside the greengrocer's. And I know where we can get a back wheel, complete with sprocket and all.'

They walked back through the village. It was spread out, with little evidence of planning or forethought, along a narrow, twisting street that meandered for more than a mile through the fields and woods of the flat Suffolk countryside. Clumps of houses, new and old together, had grown up along its length, apparently at random, like weeds sprouting from the undergrowth. Outside them, men, their brows pink with perspiration, struggled to turn forks through the baked soil, while the women picked early fruit from canes, or folded stiffly dry washing from the line. On the front step of one house, a puff-cheeked old woman sat fanning herself with a newspaper. On the next, a merchant sailor on leave lay sprawled on a deckchair, smoking his pipe and drinking beer from a bottle, his cap pushed back on his head, his uniform shirt-sleeves tightly rolled. 'All right, lads?' He waved to them cheerily. They waved back and walked on, the road smelling hot and dusty with blown soil and dried manure. After a while, a few more houses, the school, a garage, and a handful of shops: greengrocer, butcher, post office/general store, an incongruously located haberdashery. A noisy cluster of little children played hopscotch on the pavement near three old village women who talked knowingly, their tones hushed, their arms folded. As the boys drew near, the women fell silent, heads turning as one to follow their passing.

Ignoring them, Len and Billy walked on. Another quarter of a mile, another bend and they reached the village centre. A crossroads, a scattering of houses, a war memorial. The green – a patch of scrubby grass beside an evil-smelling duck-pond whose incumbents had long since been appropriated, without their consent, to the war effort. A fine Norman church set back deep among tall, brooding trees thick with rooks. An imposing Georgian rectory, a village hall, a scruffy-looking pub. At the crossroads they turned left, passed a collection of run-down farm buildings and crossed a narrow humped bridge over a dried-up stream. Next to the stream, alone, set back fifty yards from the road, stood a derelict black timber-clad building. After a brief pause to ensure the coast was clear, they ducked beneath strands of rusting wire and, bent double, sprinted towards it along an overgrown path smelling of warm grass, rustling with insects.

The mill by the stream had long since fallen into disuse. Although the giant waterwheel was still intact, its wooden paddles hung rotting and broken, sections of the timber-cladded walls were missing, and a portion of the roof had fallen in. Inside, it was damp, gloomy and vermin-infested. The giant cogs and spindles lay idle, thick with dust and swallow droppings. Near the ancient mill-wheel itself, a corner of floor had been roughly cleared, and in the centre of it a shed door laid over bricks served as a makeshift table, up-ended beer crates as stools. Three bicycle frames in various stages of dismemberment stood in a corner next to piles of scrap and Billy's boxes of salvage. Two boys were poking through them.

'You're late,' the taller of the two said, without looking up.

'Bollocks. Got the goods then?' Billy replied a little breathlessly.

'Yep.' The second boy produced a small sack and held it up. Something wriggled inside it. 'Got yours?'

Billy handed him a packet of ten cigarettes. 'Navy Cut, like you said.'

'Right. We're off. See you later. Coming, Len?'

'Wait. Aren't you coming up the base?'

'What for? It's miles of bloody walking, and when you get there the MPs just turf you off again. We're going up the riverbank, meet some of the girls. Shirley's coming, Dolly Makepeace said she might too. And Ruby Moody. Stan Bolsover's got a bottle of cider, so we'll have a wet and a smoke and maybe cop a feel off Shirley.'

'Ruby's coming?' Billy looked from one to the other, his round eyes glinting in the dusty light.

'Too right. You?'

'No . . .' He hesitated. 'No, got business. Anyway, what about the bikes? We said we was going to work on them today.'

'You work on them. We're off.' The three turned as one for the door.

'They sell for four quid apiece up the base!' he called after them. 'I ain't giving you any of it if you don't help fix them up.'

'Keep it.' A voice from outside. Retreating footsteps in the undergrowth, muffled laughter. 'You want to get out more, Bill Street! She fancies you, Ruby does. She said so.'

'Bill?' Lennie's fading voice piped. 'Catch you later then? Shower time up the land girls' hostel, all right?'

But it was already early evening, well past the land girls' shower time, when Billy slipped behind the big number two hangar and back into the woods beyond the base. Quickly, without pausing, he hurried along the familiar path, deeper and deeper into the woods, until the sounds of the airfield had fallen well behind. Only then did he stop, slumping breathlessly on to a lichen-covered tree stump, his forage cap perched on his head.

He still couldn't believe it. The best day ever. He'd sold the lot. Everything. But better than that, far better, most important of all in fact, was Hal Knyper's present. Billy took the bundle from under his arm and unrolled it on to the leaf-strewn ground. They were army green, of course, and second-hand, and slightly too big. But no matter, they were the real thing, real mechanic's overalls and, best of all, Hal had got his name stencilled on the chest. 'Street B. Pfc.' Bill Street, Private First Class.

He leaned forward, tracing the letters with his finger. It was fantastic. Like something official. At last. For what seemed like ages he just stared down at the overalls in amazed silence. A lone woodpigeon called out, unnoticed in the canopy above his head. A second replied, faintly, from far in the forest. One day, just maybe one day, he would own one of the flyer's leather jackets to wear over the top of the overalls. A2s they were called, mahogany brown, the softest leather; the flyers painted their names on the breast, and the names of their aircraft on the back, or pictures of wild stallions or pin-up girls. One day. Then something moved, deep in the woods, puncturing his reverie. With a deep sigh, he rolled up the overalls once more and began emptying his pockets.

Apart from the sticks of gum, candy bars and two slightly

47

squashed doughnuts, there was a total of eighteen shillings and threepence halfpenny in cash. He'd managed to get eight bob for the kitten he'd traded with Len's mate for the Players. One of Hal's trainee mechanics bought it. Next, he got a confirmed order for one of the bikes from a rookie gunner in hut six. Billy told him that demand for bicycles was high, which it was, and that the gunner, whose name was Boonebose, had to put down a deposit of five bob, which to Billy sounded about right. To his surprise, Boonebose paid up without a murmur, which meant that Bill could put the money towards buying tyres which were the most expensive part. Not only that, Boonebose's mate in the next bunk said he was interested in a bike too.

The rest of the stuff he sold piecemeal, wandering unchallenged from one hut to the next, his box tucked under his arm. The 'lucky' horseshoes he pinched from Ray's forge always went well; Bill had yet to meet an American who wasn't superstitious. He got a florin for Mrs Garrett's husband's alarm clock and another for the plaster crucifix he'd also put in the box but forgotten to tell her about. Holy stuff was always popular. The games and puzzles he did as a job lot to a technical sergeant in the catering block for three bob. He couldn't remember if he mentioned to the sergeant that there might be some pieces missing.

The only tricky bit had been the business of Lennie's playing cards, in hut twelve. By the time he got to the hut, his box was practically empty, only the real dross left. And, possibly because he'd been taken up with all the business things, deposits for bikes, orders for more kittens, getting people's change right and that, possibly he was just a little bit slow on the uptake. But whatever the reason, it wasn't until after he'd actually banged on the door and got in there, after he'd begun his sales pitch in fact, that he realised that the men in hut twelve, lying unusually quietly on their bunks, or sitting at a little table playing poker, were the ones from *Misbehavin Martha*.

'Good luck charms?' one of them interrupted incredulously halfway through Billy's spiel. 'Did he say good luck charms?' He was sitting on his bed, smoking a cigarette, his arms hugging his knees which were drawn up tightly to his chin. He was watching Billy closely, rocking backwards and forwards. The hut was a Quonset, like a soup tin sliced in half down the middle, as Hal Knyper would say. It could hold up to thirty enlisted men, but this one was more than half empty.

'Scram, kid,' another of them, a big fat gunner whose name turned out to be Beans, added. He too was on his bunk, reading a girlie magazine. 'We don't want any of it, and you shouldn't be in here anyways, so beat it before I call the MPs.'

'Take it easy, Beanman,' a third said. 'He ain't doing any harm.'

'Shove it up your ass, Tork. We don't want it, it's kids' junk.'

'Good luck charms. Now, I sure would like to see that,' the rocking man kept saying. His cigarette had finished, burned right up to his fingers. He immediately lit another. 'Do they work?'

Something about the man's voice, a calm, a chill, was not right. Billy turned to go. 'Listen, I'd better be off. Next time, see, I can bring more, um, goods and stuff.'

'No, wait!' The man sprang from his bed. 'Wait. I really want to take a look at the good luck charms.'

'Leave him be, Lajowski. He's just a kid,' one of the card players said quietly, a slender, darker-skinned man with jet-black hair slicked straight back over his head.

'Stay the hell out of this, Via. Now then, what have we here?' The man, Lajowski, tall, with a heavy jaw covered in thick black stubble, his cigarette wiggling between his lips, began to rummage through the box. 'Oh, well now, looky here. A little toy car, no wheels. That's lucky. Should work well against 88-millimetre flak, wouldn't you say? Oh, and here's a little kiddie's christening spoon. Stephen, it says on it. Lucky as hell that, Focke-Wulf one-nineties just hate those little baby-spoons. And, oh, here's a lucky deck of cards, or maybe it's a lucky half a deck, because there sure ain't fifty-two cards in here, are there, kid?' He waved them under Billy's nose. His breath smelled of stale cigarettes, his eyes were red and watery. 'What's your name?' he said, his voice deathly quiet.

'Bill, um, Billy, Street.'

'You see the thing is, Billy Street, I don't think it's very nice you coming in here, trying to sell us your garbage. That's profiteering. We're up there busting our asses, just to save yours, and all you want to do, all any of you want to do, in fact, is see just how much you can screw out of us before we go and get killed.'

'Emmett. It's enough now, let him go.' Gerry Via had stood up from the card table, was resting his hand lightly on Lajowski's shoulder.

'Take your hands off of me, Via.'

'Let the kid go, Polski,' the gunner with the girlie magazine, Beans, yawned from his bunk.

'And you can keep your fat ass the hell out of this.'

In an instant Beans had tossed the magazine aside and was on his feet. 'What did you say to me?'

'Let the kid go,' Via soothed. 'Emmett, it's okay. Ringwald, get the door.' The other card player, a youth, short, with a boy's face and fair hair, pushed back his chair, reaching for the door handle. Via took Billy's arm, pulling him away from Lajowski and round behind him. 'Go, now, Billy, it's okay, the guys are just a little tired right now. Go.' A moment later Billy found himself back in the open air, heart thudding, the door to hut twelve closing quietly in his face. Thirty seconds passed, not a sound came from within. At last he stood back, looking round uncertainly. Then, hefting his box under his arm once more, he set off back along the perimeter towards Hal Knyper's hangar.

Iken was more than an hour away from Bedenham by bicycle, but for Heather, setting off from the cottage into the early evening balm, her pencils and notebooks lying in the handlebar basket together with a sandwich and an apple, it was a much longed-for hour, brimming with rare and unexpected happiness.

At first she pedalled quickly, her head bent to the task of putting distance between her and the village. For no reason that she could easily define, it was important her departure was unobserved. That everyone seemed to know exactly what everyone else was doing, at any hour of the day or night, was a wearisome feature of village life that she had never grown accustomed to.

In no time, however, she found herself gliding clear of the last cottages and on, unnoticed, into open countryside. She slackened her pace, following by instinct the network of lanes that twisted between the corn-filled fields, her spirits lifting with each passing mile. She felt like a prisoner, released unexpectedly on compassionate leave, luxuriating almost guiltily in her unexpected freedom and the brief slipping of bonds. The sun was softening at last, its merciless, brassy afternoon glare fading, its light now a molten copper that touched the hedgerows with iridescent pinks and golds. The air that caressed her skin as she pedalled was soft and warm, like silk, and filled with evening fragrances, primrose, wild honeysuckle, drying hay. The only sounds were the shrill chatter of feeding martins on the wing, the hiss of her tyres on the tarmac and the brushing of the wind through her hair. She began to hum.

She cycled generally eastwards, bypassing the busy town of Framlingham and its own satellite bomber base close by at Parham. Soon she had moved out of the plain-like flatness of middle Suffolk and on into the softer contours of the coastal district where the North Sea, thick and grey, scoured against steep shifting shingle beaches and soft-soiled cliffs that melted into the encroaching sea like children's sandcastles. She paused briefly to sketch the churches at Stratford St Andrew and nearby Farnham, but conscious of the lengthening shadows thrown by their squat towers, and the sinking red orb at her back, she soon remounted, quickening her pace once more for the last few miles.

Iken was a village, little more than a hamlet, nestling amid a belt of marshy farmland three miles from the coast. When the winter easterlies blew in, its wide skies were filled with the tang of salt and the cries of both sea birds and river dwellers such as dunlin, curlew and shelduck. It existed in unnoticed seclusion, unremarkable and unassuming in every respect, except one. Its church was legendary. It stood alone on a little wooded hill, above the broad sweep of a wide river that curved back sharply beneath it to steep sandy cliffs thick with bracken and overhanging trees. Its origins, Heather knew, were Saxon at least, but almost certainly older. It was a place of pilgrimage, a place people felt compelled to return to. Something about its position, solitary, mystical, uniquely tranquil, together with a palpable air of timelessness, had been drawing the weary, the restless, the pained or the simply curious to the spot for much longer than any architectural history book could say.

Heather leaned the bicycle against a gate, plucked her notebook from the basket and wandered across the empty churchyard. The sun was setting over to her left, the air above her hung still and soft. She would never get back to Bedenham before dark, but she didn't care. The church stood before her, small, unfussy, perfectly proportioned, its thatched roof pale ochre in the failing light. She pulled the pencil from her notebook and pushed open the door.

A man was sitting, his back to her, in a pew near the front. She hesitated, momentarily uncertain, mildly irritated. He wasn't praying, evidently, just sitting. Perhaps she should wait outside until he was finished; perhaps she should carry on and ignore him.

But then he stirred, as though from sleep, turned, saw her and stood up quickly. He was an American. A flyer, a lieutenant in uniform, his cap in his hand. He had dark hair and eyes, and a sort of sad, apologetic smile.

'It's kind of difficult to make sense of man's apparently unending need to create war against his fellow man,' he said, 'when he is also able to create a place like this.'

Chapter 3

For John Hooper, sitting in the cool evening quiet of that church, the journey there begins, and ends, four weeks earlier, with the dawn rap of knuckles on door.

A click. Harsh light rudely severs the night's warm embrace. The Ops orderly's hand rocks his shoulder. 'Good morning, Lieutenant, it is four a.m. You are flying today.' Another mission, the same routine. It is take-off minus three hours.

The last vestiges of dreamless sleep slip from his grasp, he struggles from the warmth of his blankets, showers, shaves and dresses. Thermal underclothes first, then his uniform. Olive-green wool trousers and shirt, low-cut brown Oxford shoes, black wool tie. He likes to wear the short Eisenhower uniform jacket for flying. It is smart, comfortable, rides easily beneath the heavy flying suit, and if he gets shot down and has to spend the rest of the war in a POW camp, it's the one he wants with him.

A six-by-six truck pulls up. He goes outside, climbs up in back with the others, shivers. Dry mouth, head woollen from too little sleep, hollowness in his stomach. Low, murmured exchanges only; the day is too young, and they too pensive, for anything more. Around them, the Suffolk dawn looms pale and motionless, enshrouded within a dank mist. It is Sunday, he realises. Mid-June, the summer solstice barely a week away, yet their breath fogs the air at their heads.

The short ride to the mess hall. The two American Red Cross girls standing at the entrance smile beatifically. It is practically the middle of the night, yet there they are again, their hair fixed, their faces made, uniforms clean-pressed, seams straight, mission after mission, fresh and perfect. It does a man's heart good. 'Good morning, Lieutenant. Coffee?' A hint of scent as he passes them, an involuntary pang of lust; he averts his eyes. Susan's picture lies in the wallet at his chest. Mission breakfast: better coffee than usual, crisp Canadian bacon, pancakes, real eggs. He eats sparingly but savours the coffee. Not too much; it is a cold trek from the cockpit to the relief tube in the bomb bay. The hollowness fills out a little, people start to talk, a low, expectant hum rising around the mess hall.

Take-off minus two hours. It's getting light, the mist evaporating. Around the perimeter, ground crews are gathering at their aircraft to begin the pre-flight checks. He walks with the others to the briefing room, a large Quonset hut, big enough to hold everyone. Outside it, his black, leather-bound copy of the good book clasped in his hand, stands Saul Fetter, base chaplain. Everyone herds past. Saul smiles, offers a few words, touches an occasional arm. Some guys hate that, harbinger of death, but he is grateful when Saul touches him, reassured. Inside, grabbing for seats with your buddies, like kids in the school hall. Wide awake now, shoulder to shoulder, a buzz of nervous anticipation circulating beneath a pall of cigarette smoke. There's a cleared aisle down the middle of the hall, a raised dais at the front, like a stage. Two easels stand waiting upon it, left and right. The huge map of Europe on the wall at the back of the stage has been covered with black drapes. Added drama, as if added drama was needed. The hollowness has gone; in its place sits a small, tight ball.

Smack on time, the doors swing open at the back and the station adjutant's voice barks the hall to attention. Talking stops, everyone stands and pops raggedly to. The Group CO marches down the centre aisle together with Group Intelligence, Group Nav, meteorology officer and a couple of senior brasshats from HQ. One of them is Brigadier General Nathan Forrest III. Straight from Washington, West Point, career officer, pin-sharp grandson of the famous Confederate general of the same name. 'To win, git there fustest, with the mostest,' Grandpappy Forrest had said. Now his grandson is out to make fame of his own. He will not disappoint. Today is his big day. Everyone sits again, then without ado the Group Intelligence major steps up to the stage, pauses for effect, then peels the drape off the wall map.

'Gentlemen, today we go to Kiel,' he announces portentously. Pure Walter Cronkite cornball. And wrong anyway. The intelligence officer is a paddlefoot major, feet firmly on the ground beneath his desk. He's not going anywhere.

Around the room two hundred and fifty men draw breath. A long line of blood-red ribbon is pinned across the wall map behind Paddlefoot's pointing arm. It is their route to the target. It is longer than any of them have ever seen, longer than many would have believed possible. It strikes out north-east from Suffolk, crosses the Wash, and dog-legs right across the wide North Sea towards the distant Friesian Islands. Then, with almost casual effrontery, it parallels the full length of the German coastline before plunging inland towards Bremen, and on and on, deeper and deeper until finally turning north for Kiel.

There is a second's stunned silence in the hall, then a low groan, and instantly the buzz starts up. Muttered increduli-ties, low whistles, a few feeble wisecracks. It's insane. The distance. It's the deepest penetration of Germany ever attempted. They will be over enemy territory, in broad day-light, for hours and hours. There's worse. It's too far for their fighters, the little Mustangs and Thunderbolts, to escort them. For a large part of the distance, the most dangerous part, they will be on their own. And Kiel. Germany's precious shipyards. Kiel will be defended to the teeth. Around him the hubbub swirls like a river in spate. But he says noth-ing, his eyes still fastened to the wall map, following the line of a second ribbon and a different, but equally lengthy, and dangerous, route home. Home. Briefly his thoughts stray there. The river, that final night of his final leave, walking its moonlit banks, arm and arm with Susan. The press of her head against his shoulder, the smell of her hair, the warmth of her hand in his. Then Paddlefoot shushes everyone down again and the briefing proper gets under way.

Take off minus one. The six-by-six drops them at the air-plane. On the way they stop at Equipment to collect the heated leather flying suits, fur-lined overboots, Mae West life vests, parachutes and harnesses. Out at the hardstand the B17 sits heavy on its tyres, visibly overloaded. The ground crew are there, still fussing around it, pecking at it like chickens. Pulling the props through, screwing down inspection hatches, checking and rechecking everything one last time. They are uncharacteristically attentive to the flight crew's needs, serious and helpful, their voices low and reasonable. They know you don't rile up a flight crew before a mission. Airmen can kid around if they want to, crack jokes, goof about. But not the ground crews. Not until after the fliers get back. It's a question of respect.

While the others board, he makes his walk-around inspection, Altman, his crew chief, at his side. It's a needless formality, the walk-around, Altman's the best, but it's time-honoured, a ritual handing over of the ship from engineer to pilot. He checks that the control locks are out and that the wheel chocks are in. He inspects damage repairs, runs a finger under a tightened oil line, kicks a tyre. On board the others are settling in. As he circles the ship he sees the bombardier and navigator through the nose bubble, unpacking equipment, talking quietly. The navigator looks pale and nervous. Above them the co-pilot, Pete Kosters, is settling himself into his seat. Further aft, radio grins out of his little side window, holding his thumb and middle finger up in a circle. At the back, babyface Bowling, the tail gunner, waves as they pass, plugging in his oxygen, intercom, power supplies. And all the while the thin metal hull echoes with the rattle of ammunition belts, the snap of firing pins and the ratchet cocking and uncocking of machine-guns as the others check their weapons. The ball in his stomach tightens a little more. He's back at the nose hatch.

He sucks in deeply one last time, eyes closing, just catches the scent of dew drying on the grass, the shrill morning call of a blackbird. Then, on the far side of the field, an engine shatters the peace, sputtering noisily to life. Then another. It is time. 'Good work, chief. Ship looks swell.' He signs Altman's clipboard, and shakes his hand, his own little ritual, swings up through the hatch and locks it shut behind him.

Lieutenant John Hooper was wrenched to wakefulness upon the perspiration-drenched sheets of his hospital bed by the agonised cries of his dead tail gunner. It was not the first time he had heard them, he pondered, blinking back a watery blur. A white-painted room was emerging: a chair, a window, two more beds, one of them occupied. In a moment the eternal pounding at the back of his head resumed, exactly as it always did. He tried to swallow, but his mouth was too dry, his throat parched. Carefully, he adjusted his neck on the pillow. Pain flared there like bushfire, before slowly dying back. Not the first time. The gunner's screams. He heard them constantly, in his waking dreams, in the long, still watches of the night, in the echoing cries of the other patients around the hospital. But this time was different, he was forced to concede. Now, for the first time, he could remember why he heard them. And who they belonged to. And how they got there. His eyes had been wet when he'd woken. Maybe it was a good sign.

'It's a good sign, John,' Brent Wallis said, shining a flashlight into Hooper's left eye an hour later. Hooper stifled a gasp, the beam like the probing of a red-hot needle. After an eternity, the doctor grunted non-committally, then thumbed back the other eyelid and blasted hot light into his skull once more. Hooper recoiled, his body rigid on the bed. At last the probing heat was withdrawn. Wallis sat back, apparently satisfied. 'What else do you remember?'

'Not much,' Hooper replied selectively. Terror. The overwhelming need to escape. Sorrow beyond bearing. Guilt. He pressed a hand to his forehead, which felt cold and clammy. 'Running. Quite a bit of that. Soft ground, misty light, gasoline fumes. Then a big bang. Then nothing, until waking up in the base hospital two days later.'

'Five days, as it happens. The mission? The crash?' Wallis, eyes closed, was steering a stethoscope through the dark hair of Hooper's chest. 'Deep breath, now.'

Hooper exhaled, shaking his head. 'Sorry, Major, not a thing.'

'No matter, it'll come, it's already starting to.' Wallis gathered his instruments together. 'You're in pretty good shape, John, physically, all things considered. But I'd like to talk to you again later, in my office. Feel like getting up?'

It took him the best part of an hour and the patient assistance of two nurses. Under the empty gaze of his room-mate, they helped him shuffle sideways on the bed until his feet, two dangling strangers far beneath him, were planted on the floor. They then helped him, without ceremony or fuss, out of his pyjamas and into his clothes. Then they hauled him upright where at last he stood, swaying, an embarrassed smile pasted on to his face, a nurse on each arm, like a drunk at a party. Finally, after a couple of experimental laps of the room, they gave him a wheelchair and a stick, and with strict instructions not to push his luck left him to get on with it.

He spent the rest of the morning making use of both to explore his surroundings, sometimes wheeling, sometimes tottering from room to room on his stick like a confused centenarian. It was a small hospital, more like a nursing home in fact, set in secluded leafy grounds. Near the town of Beccles, he learned during the course of his wanderings, about twenty miles from the base. There were half a dozen small rooms like his on the second floor. Two or three beds in each, mostly occupied. Downstairs on the first floor were two larger wards of twelve beds. On the ground floor were the examination rooms, offices and a lofty wood-panelled reception area that opened out through swing doors on to gravel paths and neatly tended lawns. He sat outside on a bench for a while, immersing himself in the clean air, the smell of pine resin and lawn cuttings and the feel of the sun-beams that played on to his upturned face through the branches of a vast cypress tree. The hospital was very quiet. There were few medical staff, no operating theatres, no X-ray facilities, no fancy treatment rooms. It was a place of convalescence, evidently, he concluded. Or something like that.

'It's a neurological unit, officially,' Wallis explained later in his office, an elegant panelled room with glass-fronted book-cases. 'You know, nervous systems, their disorders, all that hokum. Unofficially, it's just where they send all the head cases.' Hooper shifted on his chair, unnerved by the doctor's apparent indifference. Is that why I'm here? he wondered. Across from him, Wallis sat at a leather-topped mahogany partners' desk set in front of tall sash windows. He was leaning back, hands linked behind his head. His eyes were locked on to Hooper's.

'You know, the field MOs on the bases can work wonders with the worst physical injuries imaginable. Really, I've seen them put men back together from nothing but shattered pieces. I once watched a surgeon at the 490th over at Eye sew a man's entire face and arm back on. Unbelievably skilful. Technically. But that's as far as it goes. The minute an airman starts acting funny, or reports sick when there's nothing visibly wrong with him, or won't get off his bunk one morning, base MOs send them here – and fast. There ain't nothing more infectious than a flyer with a dose of the jitters.'

'I see.' Is it why they sent me here? Hooper dragged his gaze from the crisp cumulus cloud moving slowly across the sky beyond the window. It was hard white, so incandescently bright that it hurt his eyes. Is it a crack-up? he wondered. His head was aching again. Wallis leaned forward. He was about fifty, bespectacled, hawkish, with a turned-down mouth and jutting chin. He wore a white coat over his uniform. He clasped his hands together on the desk before him. A buff document file lay beneath them.

'So, we get the whole bag here, anything and everything, in other words, that can't be fixed with a sticking plaster. The confused, the unstable, the delusional and the suicidal. The neurotic, the manic, the melancholic. The amnesiac, of course – that's you, John.' He was counting off on his fingers. 'The insomniac, the euphoric and the catatonic. Those that don't sleep, don't eat, don't talk. Those that don't even move, sometimes.'

'Don't or won't?' Hooper broke in quietly. It was enough. He'd seen them that morning, during his tour of the hospital. Rolling his wheelchair past the rows of motionless humps upstairs. The hunched bodies, the pale, listless faces, the tear-stained pillows. He'd tried talking to a few. But his gentle enquiries had been met with incomprehension or hostility or just wide-eyed silence. One man had simply burst into tears.

'Same difference in my view. Do you know what the Brits call combat fatigue, John? When a pilot of His Majesty's Royal Air Force can't or won't fly any more because his nerves are shot to hell?' Hooper shook his head. 'Get this, they call it "lack of moral fibre". Can you believe that?'

'What happens to them?'

Wallis shrugged. 'In the last war they got stood up in front of a firing squad. Now, I believe they just get removed, fast. Court-martialled, dishonourable discharge maybe, or sidelined into a desk job in another theatre of operations. Or just quietly demobilised and sent back into the world without a word.'

'And what happens to ours?' A blood-red ribbon, stretching for ever across a wall map.

Wallis' eyes came up, narrowing on Hooper's. 'I'd like to think we treat our war-weary a little better than that.'

'I don't have combat fatigue, Major. I know I don't. I want to get back into it.'

'Yes, I believe that.' Wallis picked up the file at last. 'Trouble is, John, you don't remember what or where the hell "it" is.' He studied the file, one hand plucking at the slack skin of his neck.

'Okay. John Alden Hooper, born Harrisburg, Pennsylvania, October six nineteen sixteen. Father, Alden

Buford Hooper, college lecturer, mother, Catherine, née Danneker, salvationist. One sister, Jo-Beth, born January twelve nineteen twenty-four. Upstanding, God-fearing members of the community, it seems, John. You attended Capital High, got good steady A grades, keen sportsman, pianist too, went on to major in American literature at college where you also played football quite seriously.' He lowered the file, peering at Hooper over the lenses of his spectacles. 'Let me see, no way you were quarterback material.'

'Wide receiver. Listen, Major, if it's any help, I don't have any difficulty remembering my childhood.'

'Then tell me about it.'

They talked for over an hour. Despite a casual, almost dismissive façade, Hooper soon realised that Brent Wallis was an adept and patient talker, and a skilled listener. After a hesitant start, Hooper found that he could recall with comparative ease details of his early life in Pennsylvania. Yet as he spoke, of his relationship with his father, a man whom he felt sure he loved, yet scarcely knew and had never embraced, and his mother who loved him too, but whose unswerving devotion to the Lord came first and to her husband second, which left little for him and his estranged younger sister, it felt as though he was discussing another John Hooper. Someone with whom he had once enjoyed a fleeting acquaintance. Someone he barely knew at all.

'You married, John?' Wallis asked at one point.

'Engaged. Susan.' He'd known her since high school, been dating since college. But had he? Had he really known her? He broke off, a frown of concentration narrowing his dark eyes.

Petite, fair hair, freckles, a nervous giggle. But that was Susan the schoolgirl. What about Susan the young woman? The fog began to descend. And as the discussion moved on to more recent events, it quickly thickened.

'Says here you joined the Air Corps straight after Pearl Harbor. Why flying?'

'I, uh, I'd done a little, with a friend from law school. It seemed to come naturally to me. Also, I suppose it was vanity. Like everyone who joined the Air Corps, I assumed I would be immediately trained as a fighter pilot, and sent straight to the Pacific to take on the Japanese one to one. Heroically naive, I know.'

'Nothing wrong with that.' Wallis turned pages. 'But instead of going to the Pacific you end up here in the ETO. How did that happen?'

Hooper rubbed at the back of his neck. His head was pounding like a trip hammer. 'Ah, Santa Ana, first. Cadet training.' Marching, shots, psych tests, more marching, hikes, a little more marching. 'I passed out okay and was assigned to pilot training, but on bombers not fighters, that was where the main need was then. From Santa Ana I was sent to Rapid City, South Dakota. It was there that the ten-man crews were put together and we first started flying as a team in B17s.' He braced himself.

'Tell me about your crew.' Wallis stepped in, casually but predictably.

He screwed his eyes, a chill sweat breaking on his brow. But the fog was like soup. It was a happy time, that much he knew. Despite the hardships and deprivations at Rapid City, the tar-paper huts, cold food and freezing rain. Despite the steepness of the learning curve, the confusion, the foul-ups and the near misses. Despite the accidents. He could clearly remember one of the crews they trained alongside flying smack into a hillside on a navigation exercise. Ten dead. Another, about a week later, messed up the approach on a night exercise and cartwheeled down the runway in a ball of flame. Ten more dead. It was hard, it was exhausting, it was shocking. Yet somehow it was exhilarating too. There, right there in the midst of it all, was Hoop and his crew. He recalled warmth, humour, a fun-loving disorderliness. Ten young men, strangers, completely unknown to each other, thrown together like a bag of pick-and-mix, yet growing daily in stature and confidence, consolidating, fusing into a single smooth-functioning unit. He had belonged to them, quickly grown fond of them, and they of each other. They bonded, became a team, an entity. A family. Now, faceless, shapeless. Gone. He shook his head, something leaden, like dread, turning over in his stomach. 'Sorry, Major,' he murmured.

'No matter, John, leave it for now. Go on. After Rapid City?'

'Ah, after Rapid, it was Kearney, Nebraska, for final combat training and OFW, outfitting for war. Oh, and that's right, we got a final leave home.' Two days staring out at the rain-swept continent through steamed-up train windows. Two more spent drifting restlessly around the house in Harrisburg, feeling like a stranger and waiting for the farewells. Susan first. Love pledges, chaste kisses and strained silences in the car on the moonlit banks of the Susquehanna. Then, later that night, his mother knocking softly on the door to his room, speechless, tearful. In the morning, the whole family, hands joined across the breakfast table, praying for his safe deliverance and return. After that, a ten-minute man-to-man with Alden, pacing the carpet in his musty-smelling study. Alden expressed moral and intellectual misgivings about America's involvement in the war, shook his son's hand and said he was proud nevertheless, his eyes all the while on the floor. It was not enough, Hooper's heart yearning for so much more. But it was all there was. At last the cab drew up in the street outside and it was over. He threw in his bags, slammed the door and sat back, his eyes fixed rigidly ahead. Then a young girl's shout, and Jo-Beth, his unknown little sister, eighteen, suddenly beautiful, sprinting to the sidewalk. She throws her arms about his neck through the cab window. 'I love you, John. Write me. Properly. Write me.'

Wallis dropped the file to his desk. 'And at Kearney you were assigned to the European Theatre of Operations and the 95th Bombardment Group, based firstly at Alconbury, where you arrived with your crew in the delivery aircraft in March of this year, then Framlingham here in Suffolk, then finally a few miles on to the 95th's permanent home up the road at Horham. Which way did you fly the Atlantic crossing, by the way? North about, was it? Gander, then Greenland, Iceland, Scotland?'

'Yes, uh, yes it was, north about, that's correct.'

'What else? Can you remember anything else?' There was an edge to Wallis' voice now.

But there was nothing. After arriving in England the fog was a wall. He stumbled blindly against it, head pounding. Fumbling in vain for the slenderest finger-hold, searching for a landmark, a fragment of memory, any slight detail. There were none. Except one.

'There was an explosion. A huge one. At Alconbury. One afternoon, shortly after we arrived. I remember that. A B17 blew up on the ground.' It was fully laden, armed, bombed and fuelled to the gills. Its ground crew were still working on it when without warning it simply vanished, taking them all with it. There was nothing left but a huge hole in the ground, a drifting smoke pall, and a steady fall of debris that rained down from the sky for minutes. The magnitude of the blast was such that shock waves rippled out all over the airfield. Aircraft deployed around the perimeter folded up like paper. Sixteen were completely destroyed or damaged almost beyond repair. Nineteen men died, some in eerie circumstances. Hoop, together with some engineers, ran to the aid of a fallen ordnance officer some distance from the blast. The officer was completely unmarked, without a scratch, yet stone dead. Another man, standing in a group elsewhere on the field, fell down, apparently in a faint. Yet he too was dead, while those standing with him were completely unhurt. A flight crew, lazing in the grass near their aircraft, felt the force of the blast from the other side of the field. They were all lying at the time, except one, their navigator, who was sitting upright. The nine on the ground were unscathed, the navigator died. Their aeroplane folded itself in half down the middle, dividing into two separate sections.

'Yes, I heard about that.' Wallis was jotting on a notepad. 'You were there?'

'Yes. I . . . well, I believe so. It sort of stuck in my memory.'

'Uh-huh. Anything else?'

'No. Sorry. That's it.'

There was a long pause while Wallis resumed his note-taking. A nurse passed the window outside pushing a hunched, blanket-wrapped figure in a wheelchair. At last Wallis looked up. 'Do you know what sodium pentothal is, John?'

'No.' Hooper swallowed.

'It's a drug. Sometimes known as the truth drug. It gets a bad press because criminals, like, you know, murder suspects and so on, are given it. To make them talk, see if they're lying. But we find it quite effective, in certain cases, in trying to help people who are suffering amnesia. It can be very help-ful in that respect.'

'I don't want it.'

'It's nothing to be afraid of, John. It can help break down a log-jam, and the side-effects are negligible. Some patients say the effect is really quite pleasant. Like a mild narcotic.'

'I don't want it. Major, the amnesia is getting better, you said so yourself. I just need a little time. A few days.'

Wallis tore the page off the pad and slid it across the desk. 'I'm sending you to the 101st RCD, John. A flak-shack, in other words. It's a quiet little country house not far from here that the 8th Air Force uses for officers in need of a break. I want you to go there, get some R&R, relax, take walks, see the sights, get strong and then come back here and we'll talk again.'

Hooper took the note and rose from the chair. 'Thank you, Major.' He turned for the door.

'John. I can only give you a week. There's a spare Jeep outside.'

'Yes, sir.'

'One more thing you should know, Lieutenant. Two, in fact. Firstly, you did not fly your aircraft across the Atlantic north about, you came south about: West Palm Beach, Natal, Dakar, Morocco then St Eval, Cornwall. And that explosion you mentioned at Alconbury. On that date, according to your record, you were on a precision-flying course in Catterick. Hundreds of miles away.'

Brigadier General Nathan Forrest's master strategy for instant entry into the history books was a four-pronged affair. The first prong was the Kiel mission itself. An unbelievably daring plan to plunge three bomber groups deep into the heart of enemy territory, it would have warmed the heart of Grandpappy Forrest himself. The second prong involved the introduction of a new oil for the B17s' machine-guns. The search for a gun lubricant that wouldn't clog up firing and ejection mechanisms at high altitude and low temperature had been going on for months. Nathan Forrest had found one, a viscous, evil-smelling compound, and all crews were instructed to use it henceforth. The third prong was his crowning glory. Somehow, Nathan Forrest persuaded the highest echelons of the 8th US Army Air Force to abandon the defensive three-layered box formations so beloved of the crews that flew them. Instead, he argued, a flat formation, with the aircraft spread out in groups of six across a horizontal plane, would somehow provide a more effective field of fire. Despite problems with the formation in training, and increasing numbers of voices raised in doubt, the new formation, together with the new oil, would be tried out on the mission to Kiel. And to prove just how robust his confidence was in the probable success of all three, Forrest produced his fourth prong. He would lead the mission. Personally. From the front. Flying shotgun in the lead aeroplane.

It was a catastrophe.

Hooper and his crew took off, together with twenty-four other aircraft of the 95th Bomb Group, a little after 7 a.m. At first, all went as planned. They climbed to the rendezvous point, a radio beacon over Diss known as Splasher Six. There they formed up with aircraft from the 94th and 96th groups, and headed out over the North Sea, spread across the sky in their new, flat formation.

The first German fighters appeared before they'd even reached the enemy coast. Until that day, the pilots that flew the tiny Focke-Wulf and Messerschmitt fighters against the formidable defensive box formations had but one main tactic at their disposal. Try to dive straight down through the middle of the box in the hope of breaking it up; a courageous but dangerous and often futile manoeuvre. Now, to their surprise, they found that there was no box, no protective layer above and below, no withering crossfire coming at them from three dimensions. Circling at a safe distance, they studied the approaching bomber stream, swiftly modified strategy and began to attack head-on, with lethal effect. Within minutes Fortresses were falling. And as the formations droned steadily deeper into their airspace, the German pilots, emboldened by their success, began calling up their friends, summoning more and more fighters up to the fray.

'Jesus. They're like gnats around a camel's ass,' a lone voice broke in soberly over the radio. Hooper and his co-pilot stared out in awe. The air above and ahead of them was thick with fast-moving specks. Many more, they knew, circled to the rear.

'Keep it quiet, keep it tight, cover your backs.' That was the lead aircraft, General Forrest's, breaking radio silence to steady nerves and bring the formations in tighter. Tighter? Hooper, perspiring within his heavy flight suit, wrestled with the controls in the turbulent air. They were too close already, his wingtip just yards from that of the airplane to his right, and he could clearly see the tail gunner's face staring out from the one ahead. It was too close, pilots were expending all their effort and concentration just holding position.

'Here they come!' His co-pilot, Pete Kosters, pointed ahead through the windscreen. In silence they watched four fighters peel down from above and slice through the formation at enormous speed. Mesmerised by the twinkle of machine-guns along their wings, and the puff of cannon fire from their blunt noses, Hooper could do nothing but hold position and duck. Instantly, a Fortress to their left reared slowly upwards, rolled over on to its back, flames pouring from its belly, and dropped away towards the sea. Far out to the right another took a direct hit in the bomb bay and simply exploded, leaving nothing but a trail of falling wreckage from an ugly brown cloud staining the sky. Seconds later the next pair of fighters flashed through, half rolling on to their backs as they fired. 'Hoop,' Kosters was buckling on a steel flak helmet, 'we are in a whole heap of trouble.'

The bombers kept doggedly onward. The fighters kept coming at them, relentlessly. Striking, breaking away, circling, peeling off and striking again. They bit deeper and deeper into the formation, cutting out and picking off stragglers like wolves about a doomed flock of sheep. 'I can't get a bead!' one of Hooper's gunners yelled in exasperation at one point. 'The formation, it's too goddamn tight, I can't get a clear shot at them without hitting the ship in front.' A few minutes later, another gunner, left waist, stopped firing. His gun was jamming.

Still the disintegrating formations kept on towards the target. As they drew nearer to it, flak, ground-based anti-aircraft shells, began to explode in the sky around them. Bursts of dirty orange amid puffs of black smoke, sporadic and inaccurate at first, then growing in intensity and accuracy as the gunners on the ground found range and distance. A bomber rolled over, a whole wing torn from it by an exploding shell. Hooper followed its fall, saw it spinning like a leaf. No parachutes. Another, close by him to the left, took a direct hit and burst into flames, somewhere in the midsection just aft of the bomb bay. They all watched in horror as it flew on and on, straight and level, its pilot apparently oblivious of the inferno raging behind him. 'Get out,' one of Hooper's crew pleaded quietly, over and over on the intercom. 'Come on, you guys, get out of there.' The doomed bomber flew on, flames pouring from it like a blowtorch, the pilots unmoving at the controls. 'For God's sake get out!' Then with agonised slowness it began to turn, and roll, over on to its back, then sink down and away from them. Falling, slowly, almost gracefully, with its rear half completely engulfed, trailing a hundred feet of flame and smoke behind it like a dying comet. A second later it blew up, disappearing in a silent ball of red. No parachutes. At the same moment a shell exploded not far beneath

Hooper's Fortress. The aircraft bucked, flak splinters rattling against its undersides. Teeth gritted, Hooper wrestled it back on to an even keel and flew on, his eyes fixed on the bomber ahead. He glanced at Kosters. The co-pilot was gripping the sides of his seat, staring out in disbelief. 'This is madness.'

All around them the carnage went on. Nobody thought to call off the attack, nobody even broke radio silence to query the wisdom of continuing. Nobody turned and fled. They just went on, deeper and deeper into the teeth of the storm, for hours, a waking nightmare of thunder and flames, panicked shouts, exploding skies and falling airplanes.

Then, almost without realising it, they were at the IP, the Initial Point, and turning in at last for the bomb run. Somehow, impossibly, it got worse. Hooper switched on the autopilot, handing over control of the airplane to the bombardier lying prone in the glass nose-dome beneath his feet. Now there was nothing to do except sit in numb helplessness, and wait and pray. The air was thick with flak now, an intense, furious barrage flung up at them by hundreds of anti-aircraft guns, completely filling the sky with exploding clouds of white-hot hail that tore through the flimsy skins of the bombers like paper, riddling them with holes, smashing controls and instruments, snapping wires and fuel lines, shredding flesh.

Forrest's aircraft got hit. Right in the middle of the bomb run. Hooper saw it, far out in front, set upon by two fighters simultaneously. Flying one down each side, they raked it with fire from end to end. Straight away it flopped over and dropped away. 'Is that the lead airplane going down?' a voice asked over the headphones. A hand grabbed suddenly at

Hooper's shoulder, and he jumped, turned in alarm. The hand was a bloody mess, the fingernails torn and bleeding. It was Galba, Joey Galba, his soft-voiced upper turret gunner from Iowa.

'Joey, Jesus, are you hit?' Hooper shouted. Galba shook his head. There were tears in his eyes from the pain and cold. His guns had both frozen up. The charging handles, seizing solid, had snapped off in his hands. He'd torn off his gloves and been trying to charge them with his bare fingers. He hadn't been able to fire a single round. The new oil.

And then there was an almighty thump from behind, like a two-fisted punch to the back. At the same instant the aircraft bucked, then it staggered, its chin nodding groundward as though tripped to its knees, like an elephant dropped on a game shoot. Thick, acrid smoke filled the cockpit; someone was shouting over the intercom. A bloody hand still gripped his shoulder. But Hooper just sat in stunned silence, watching in detached fascination while the ground, a kaleidoscope spiral of fields and buildings and shipyards and trees, swirled nearer and nearer.

'Something happened. On the Kiel mission. Something bad. Didn't it?'

'Lieutenant, I trust you are not expecting me to discuss mission details over an open telephone line,' Brent Wallis replied formally. Yet there was no mistaking the flicker of interest in his voice.

'I . . . no. Sorry.' Eyes squeezed shut, Hooper pressed fingers, pincer-like, into his temples and tried to force himself further into the corner of the little office. In doing so, he dragged the heavy black telephone right to the edge of the desk. The telephone's owner, a stout, middle-aged nurse from the American Red Cross sitting not more than three feet from him, busily shuffled papers, her face a study of composed indifference. 'Major,' Hooper pleaded, his voice little more than a whisper. 'Please, can't you tell me anything?'

It had woken him in the night. Kiel. It was the fifth night of his stay at the 'flak-shack', a well-appointed, comfortable, yet unaccountably cheerless former country guest house. One moment he had been resting in comparative peace between the clean sheets and warm blankets of his private bedroom, his mind plodding through the darkness like a slow goods train, the next, the night was split by a man's scream and instantly he was sitting upright, a trembling arm reaching for the bedside light. The shout, unearthly, blood-chilling, echoed through his head, the hairs pricking on his neck. Was it his? One of the other guests? Or Bowling, yet again? Young Danny Bowling, his baby-faced dead tail gunner. And he *was* dead. That much was certain.

Kiel. Hooper had hoisted himself up in the bed, his chest damp with perspiration. He reached for his water tumbler, drank greedily. Slowly his breathing eased, the blood-roar receding in his head. Silence gathered cautiously about him once more. Beyond the blackout an owl hooted once in the trees. He definitely remembered Kiel. Some of it. Being woken, the dawn, breakfast, the briefing, taking off, forming up. Then the nightmare, the fighters, the twinkling guns, the flak, Fortresses falling all about him like flaming leaves. Then a bang. Then the fog. They'd been hit. An 88mm flak hit, right over the target. But what then? Had they crashed? Bailed out?

Ditched in the ocean? No, he was home. Concussed but alive, back in England. They'd got back, they must have. Wallis was talking.

'John. Don't you see? That's why we need you to tell us.'

'You mean you don't know.'

Fractional hesitation. 'No. I mean, if I tell you, anything, then it defeats the whole damn object of the exercise. My job is to help you recover your memory yourself, not hand it back to you on a platter. That would be pointless. Listen. You've still got my Jeep, right? Why don't you come over this afternoon and we can discuss it here?'

He opened his eyes. Outside, the Jeep stood untouched on the gravel where he'd parked it five days ago, a layer of brown dust coating its faded green paintwork. Sodium pentothal. The prick of the needle, cold flowing into his veins, engulfing blackness. Then what?

'Am I in some kind of trouble, Major? Am I in disgrace?'

'John. The sooner we get your memory back, the sooner we can get this whole thing cleared up. Just come on over. There's nothing to be fearful of.'

Hooper put down the telephone.

He left the flak-shack thirty minutes later. It was a warm morning, cloudless and still. Saturday, he noted, checking his diary. He dropped his bag into the back of the Jeep, climbed behind the wheel and thumbed the starter. There was a map in a side pocket; Wallis had given it to him together with directions. He found the base on it, Horham, home of the 95th; it could only be forty minutes' drive. He'd go there, find the guys, get to the bottom of this once and for all.

Halfway there, he wrenched the Jeep on to a grass verge and braked to a stop. Maybe not the base. His thoughts were coming in wild batches; a mad rush, a pause, a regroup. The base, maybe not such a good idea. Technically he was still hospitalised. Under Brent Wallis' guardianship. Or custody? The MPs on the gate at Horham, would they be suspicious? 'Hi, Lieutenant, good to see you, thought you were still in the hospital. Got your discharge papers handy?' Yet he needed to speak to someone, anyone, who might know something. He checked his watch. Eleven, Saturday morning. If there was no mission they'd be there. Hanging out in the messes, lounging outside the huts, putting baseball games together, taking it easy.

He drove on, mind in turmoil. After a while he came to a small town and ground down through the gears, creeping through narrow streets until he came to a triangle of shops and houses, pulled up beneath a clock tower and switched off. The place was busy, locals queuing, as ever, for goods at the butcher's, the fishmonger's, the grocery store. Old men sat on benches in the sun, kids careered to and fro. He picked out uniformed servicemen moving more slowly among the townsfolk: some grey-blue RAF, half a dozen khaki, quite a few olive-green American.

'Yes, Lieutenant?' The woman behind the counter at the post office beamed, her eyes brazenly on his. He straightened his tie self-consciously, feeling a tug at the hem of his jacket.

A child's voice squeaked at his side. 'Got any gum chum?'

'Oh, uh, no, honey, I'm real sorry.' The little girl was about three, a round smiling face with wayward ringlets tied in an untidy bow. Her cheeks were dirty. He turned back to the woman at the counter. 'Yes, uh, I need to use a telephone, if possible.'

'There's a queue.' The woman gestured towards a booth at the back of the post office. 'Is it an emergency?'

'I . . . no, I guess not. I can wait my turn.'

The squeaking persisted. 'Got any gum chum?'

It took twenty minutes. Finally his turn came, and he gave the operator the number and waited. Eventually, a series of clicks and she put him through.

'95th Bomb Group, station adjutant,' an American voice said.

Suddenly he didn't know what to do.

'Got any gum chum?'

It was the fog that did it. It began to appear beneath them about halfway back across the sea. Scattered patches at first, little islands of mist dotting the blue-grey. Then the islands began to enlarge and cohere, until a tattered blanket was formed, through which the sea's surface was only occasionally glimpsed. Finally, as they began at last to draw near to the coast, the blanket hardened, coagulating into a thick, white crust that completely obscured the surface in every direction. Hoop stared pensively down at it through his side window, the stricken bomber's flying controls shuddering in his fist. To his right, Pete Kosters was also gazing at it. The others as well, Hooper instinctively knew. All inactive now, all quiet, the intercom silent for the first time in more than an hour. They'd done everything there was to do. Fought as hard and as bravely as any men could be expected to. Now, all they could do was wait, sitting or standing at their positions, wrapped within their own thoughts, their own worlds, watching the fog crawl menacingly by just five hundred feet beneath them. It was the last straw.

After the flak shell hit them, Hooper had eventually regained control of the plummeting aircraft at three thousand feet. Fearful of further hits, and stray bombs falling from above, he banked steeply away from the smoke-enshrouded target, turning roughly west. Then he took stock. One propeller, the port outer, was windmilling uselessly. Quickly he feathered it. There were flak holes all along the wings and fuselage, a large section of rudder was missing, two of the fuel tanks had been holed. The controls shook in his hands, and beneath his feet the rudders felt slack and unresponsive.

'Pilot to navigator?'

'Here, pilot.'

'Pilot to bombardier?'

'Here.' He called up the crew, all of them, one at a time over the intercom. And one at a time, they reported back to him. All nine. All alive. It was scarcely believable. The airplane riddled with flak holes, a colander with wings, yet no one killed, not one. He and Kosters exchanged relieved glances, then without further ado he levelled the airplane, opened the throttles on the three remaining engines as wide as he dared, and with the wall-map ribbon still fixed in his mind's eye turned on to the heading for home.

Fortune favoured them a while longer, their escape from enemy airspace, by a miracle, going largely undetected. There were a few poorly ranged flak shots, but the ground gunners were concentrating on targets fifteen thousand feet higher. As for fighters, Hoop knew his bomber was the perfect target. Alone, unescorted, unprotected, flying low, slow and damaged. He waited, his whole body rigid at the controls, for the warning shout over the headphones, the stutter of the Fortress's machine-guns, the sickening thud of cannon shells tearing into the fuselage. Yet none came, the minutes ticked by, and slowly, incredibly, they stole unnoticed from the field of battle.

But then the tide changed against them. Soon it became evident that the damage to the bomber was much worse than previously thought. Within half an hour the number three engine, the starboard inner, began to overheat, boiling oil streaming from beneath its cowling and back over the wing. Hoop used its dying minutes, together with the remaining two good engines, to hoist the bomber to eight thousand feet. But there the streaming oil turned to smoke, the temperature gauge needle slid off the dial and the seizing engine began to shudder violently in its mountings. He shut it down before it tore the wing off. From that moment on, heading out over the wide North Sea on just the two remaining engines, they began to lose height.

And so they jettisoned everything. They tore the oxygen bottles from their fixings, gathered the spent ammunition from the hoppers, unbolted equipment from floors, ceilings, bulkheads. They manhandled the Norden bomb-sight from the nose, ditched the spare radios, the spare jockey seats, the spare tools. The moment they were out of range of fighters they began unhooking their machine-guns and tossing them overboard. They even hoisted the ball turret gunner from his seat beneath the airplane, unbolted the whole turret from its supports and watched it plummet silently into the sea below.

Still they lost height and soon there was nothing left to ditch. Almost nothing. There was one more item of unwanted extra weight, the heaviest item of all. They'd all avoided it, at Hooper's instruction, since it was first discovered minutes after the flak hit. Above the Fortress's gaping bomb doors, lodged at a slight angle in its rack, nestled a single bomb. It weighed a massive five hundred pounds. When the bombardier had toggled the bomb release switches over the target, all except one had dropped from the racks. This one. The biggest. It was fully armed, ready to go. The two waist gunners offered to go try to kick it free, but Hooper forbade anyone to go near it.

And now, finally, the fog. His plan — overfly the English coast, order the crew to bail out, turn the deserted airplane to face back out to sea, then follow the crew over the side — was now seriously compromised. Firstly the coast, together with the sea, the land, everything below them in fact, had vanished. They had little means of knowing whether safety was ten miles ahead, or twenty. Or thirty. Secondly, with every passing minute the doomed aircraft sank lower and lower. Within just a few minutes it would be too low for anyone to bail out and thus any choice in the matter would be gone. They would be crash-landing into the sea, or on to the land. In zero visibility. With a live five-hundred-pound bomb on board. He reached for his intercom switch.

In a fumbled moment of intuition, he asked the station adjutant to put him through to the maintenance section. Ground crews know everything there is to know. Rumour Control. So it was Altman who told him, as much as he could. His trusted crew chief. Marooned in the telephone booth in the crowded post office, a little girl tugging at his sleeve, a curious teller eyeing him from behind the counter, a steady flow of people eddying by, he listened in silence and let the words fall like tears.

'They're gone, Hoop, buddy,' Altman said simply, towards the end. 'Didn't they tell you that in the hospital?'

'Gone? All of them? But it isn't possible.'

'One of the coastal batteries near Orford, I think it was. They reported hearing a lone B17 coming in very low over the coast at around three that afternoon. A while later there were a couple of local people, kids, I think, thought they heard a crash-landing on farmland somewhere in the neighbour-hood. Then a confirmed report of an explosion, some time later.'

The bail-out bell. He felt sure he remembered hitting it. Felt sure he'd watched them jump clear, one by one, watched as their parachutes streamed then blossomed, watched them, alone in his cockpit, drifting down towards the fog layer. A flooding sense of relief, tinged with an acute loneliness.

'You were found a hundred yards from the wreck.' Altman was still talking. 'Unconscious. Severe concussion, we were told later. There was the remains of one body found in the debris. Danny Bowling's tags on it, tail gunner. The rest turned up over the next few days.'

'Turned up?' A flicker of confused hope. The little girl had stopped pulling on his hand, and was just holding it, standing right there next to him in the open booth, thumb in mouth. Her Yank.

'On the beach. It took a week or so, but their bodies all washed up in the end. Much better that way, wouldn't you say, buddy? At least we got them back and they got to be sent home to their families. Pete Kosters was last. We'd just about given up on him. Then we heard he was found down the coast a ways, only a couple of days ago.'

He left the post office and wandered back to the Jeep. After a while he started the motor and began to drive, at random to begin with, then with purpose. Altman had given him what details he had of the location. He drove to the coast, following directions until he found Orford, then asked at a pub down near a river jetty. The landlord pointed him to the police station. There, eventually, the desk sergeant found the paperwork and gave him further directions to the site. He was able to drive partway, but was soon forced to abandon the Jeep by a gate and continue on foot, tramping through fields waist-high with rasping yellow corn, the perspiration breaking on his brow, the sound of his own laboured breathing, skylarks and crickets filling his head.

By the time he found the site it was early evening. The salvage crews had done their usual thorough job. There was nothing left except a wide circle of scorched crops, a slight depression in the ground, and a few missed fragments. In a few weeks, after the harvest, and the plough, there would be nothing at all. As if the aircraft and the ten men that crewed it had never existed. As if the whole adventure, the training, the pressure, the excitement, the danger, Rapid City, Kearney, the flight across the Atlantic, Suffolk, the first missions, as if it was all nothing but a dream. Except him. His was the reality. And the legacy. He stood in the centre of the crash site, stooped to pick up a twisted shard of fuselage skin. He'd killed them all.

He began to walk. Slowly, away from the site, skirting fields. Following tracks, crossing ditches, the river on his right. He climbed a steep bank and saw it flowing brown and slow, with wide mudflats that glistened in the setting sun like burnished copper. Birds, waders and river-dwellers of all kinds, fed at the edges, the air echoing to their mournful piccolo calls. He kept walking, following the bank. In the distance a low, tree-covered hill jutted into the river, a small church tower peeking through above.

He'd killed them all. It was what Wallis wanted to know. How? How on earth could it possibly happen that nine members of a ten-man crew perished, yet one, their leader, escaped with a bump on the head? Hoop was right, they didn't know. And they needed to. They needed to hear it from him, the sole survivor. Even though the details were still not clear to him, even though, in truth, he could not recall the exact final events, and perhaps never would, he didn't need to. He knew enough. He'd ordered them to bail out before they crossed the coast and thus dumped them into the freezing waves miles from shore where they all drowned. All but Danny Bowling who, for reasons unknown, crash-landed with him into the cornfield. Then he'd abandoned him too, left him, trapped, injured perhaps, in his battered turret. And with Danny's anguished cries ringing in his head, he'd scrambled through the cockpit window, dropped to the ground and fled into the mist. Then the bomb went off.

The church was small, still and cool. It was deserted. He went in and sat on a pew at the front. Prayer, an integral component of his consciousness since his earliest memories, eluded him. It would have been an obscenity, a desecration. Deity, faith, forgiveness had no part to play in this, his unholy shame. He thought of his family, of how he could possibly begin to tell them, try to help them understand. It was not possible. And the harder he imagined, the more insubstantial, the more unreal they became to him. The crew. They were his real family, and now they too were lost to him. He was alone. It was as it should be.

After a while, ten minutes, an hour, he had no idea, he stirred in his pew. The church was in semi-darkness, filled with deep shadows and centuries-old silences. Outside, the gentlest of breezes sighed through the trees. It was getting late. He stood and turned to leave, and then he heard movement, a discreet cough. A young woman was standing in the arched doorway, the last of the evening light throwing her body into soft silhouette.

Chapter 4

'Spam casserole?' Claire Howden poked at the watery lumps on her plate, wrinkling her nose distastefully. 'I can't possibly eat this.'

'I can!' Billy's arm reached over. Instantly, Maggie's hand shot out, slapping his wrist.

'You keep your thieving hands off, William Street, and as for you, young lady, you'll eat what you're given and jolly lucky to have it. There's tens of thousands of folk all over the country going without a crumb for their dinner.'

'Are there?'

'Yes there are!' Maggie's voice was emphatic but her expression was a flustered furrow of uncertainty. A lock of chestnut-brown hair from a collapsing home perm was drooping across one eye, and she puffed at it from the corner of her mouth, dabbing her brow with the back of a wrist. Finally she sat down at the kitchen table, eyeing her own plate forlornly.

A sheen of perspiration lay on her flushed cheeks, like dew. Beyond the door the afternoon air hung humid and heavy.

'It's fine, Mags, love,' Ray soothed, patting her hand. Four heads lowered as one. 'Billy? Mind you do it proper now.'

'What about recede truly thankful amen.'

They began to eat, except Maggie who looked as though she might burst into tears. 'It's not blooming fair. My poor dad. He'd turn in his grave, he would. Betty and me, daughters to the finest butcher in Halesworth. Give us a scrap of meat and there isn't a single thing we couldn't do with it. Now look what it's come to.'

'It's fine, love. Eat up.' Ray looked up. A moment later a tiny warning tinkle of shaking cutlery was followed by the whoosh of a heavy slipstream and the deafening thunder of passing engines. Instinctively they all ducked. Ten seconds later they felt the house shudder again as a second aircraft passed. 'That's a bit bloody low, isn't it?' Ray scowled, brushing flakes of plaster from his shoulders.

'Got an ME tomorrow, they have,' Billy sputtered through bulging cheeks. 'Got to get everything up.'

'Blasting about the sky ten feet above the trees like that. They're nothing more than a bunch of bloody spivs.'

'Ray, language, the children. What's an ME then, Billy?' Maggie asked.

'Maximum Effort. It means that all the bombers from all the bases will be joining in and everyone's got to pull out all the stops to get all the ships flying.'

'Yes, but Billy, dear, isn't that supposed to be secret? I mean, how on earth do you know these things?'

'This is that dreadful powdered mash potato muck, isn't it?'

Claire interjected, gesturing accusingly at her plate. 'Why can't we have real mash like the old days? This tastes like Lux flakes.'

'Oi, that's enough, you.' Ray shot his daughter a warning glance. 'You know well enough there are no potatoes just now, they won't come in until the autumn. Just eat your lunch and stop your complaining and that's an end to it.'

'I like the powdered stuff, me.' Billy's plate was already half empty, one arm, as always, crooked jealously round it.

Claire watched, straight-backed beside him, the corners of her mouth turned down in disgust. 'You are an animal, you know that? Is there anything you won't eat?' Billy, munching steadily, cocked his head, eyes narrowed in consideration.

'And where *is* Percy?' Maggie fretted, her lunch still untouched. They all looked to his place at the table. As if on cue the cat jumped on to his chair, and Ray swatted it away.

'He'll be along in his own time. Don't worry yourself.'

'Of course I worry. He's old, and . . . confused. And I didn't hear him come in last night. I think he might be sleeping out again.'

'Well, what if he is? If it's what he wants. Weather's mild enough.'

'Sprouts. That's summat I won't eat. Hate the squishy little beggars.'

'It's not right, man of his years sleeping rough like that. Where does he go?'

'Down the woods, back of the base mainly,' Billy said. 'I seen him there.'

'All right if I pop into Ipswich tonight, Mum?' Claire said lightly. 'Me and the girls at the shop thought we'd go in on the bus. To the flicks.'

'No. If I've told you once I've told you a hundred times, you are not going into Ipswich night-times until you're eighteen. And especially not with that Dot and that Vi. They're a lot older than you, and nothing but trouble.'

'But Mum, that's not fair. Deirdre Fisk's allowed in, by herself, and she's nearly a month younger than me.'

'The Fisks don't come from round here. They moved here from Yarmouth before the last war. Townies. Don't hold with it myself, but they do things different.'

'I can get real spuds,' Billy offered. He nodded round the table, his fork gripped tightly in his fist, like a baby with a spoon. Nobody spoke. 'Tinned fruit and veg and stuff too. I can, you know, if you want it.'

Maggie stole a sidelong look at her husband. He was shaking his head. 'We don't,' he said doggedly. 'I told you before. We don't need Yank charity. We don't need Yank spuds or Yank tinned fruit, or Yank anything else for that matter.'

'Ray. Love. Billy says the boys up there on the base will pay five bob a week, each, just for a bit of laundry. What's the harm in him bringing a couple of loads of it back here and me adding it to the Monday wash? It would make no difference to me, and you know we could do with it, what with the forge being a bit quiet right now.'

'That's right, Mr H. And guess what else? Bikes! They're totally desperate for 'em. I've been thinking, perhaps we could turn over a bit of the forge, like. To a cycle repair place. Do 'em up and flog 'em. Like a little shop. We'd sell hundreds.'

'We don't need it!' With a crack like a gunshot, the flat of Ray's hand struck the table. They all jumped. The cat, startled, fled through the open back door to the yard. In the sudden silence that followed there was a discreet knock at the window. Claire leapt to her feet.

'Postman. I'll get it.' A moment later she returned, dropping the pile to the table. 'Just bills and boring things.'

'We do not need hand-outs, not from the Yanks, not from anyone.' Ray's voice was very quiet. As he spoke, his head moved from side to side, but his eyes remained fixed on the table. 'Yes, I know the forge is slow just now, but come the autumn when ploughing and drilling and top-dressing starts up, it will be busy again. It is always busy then, and it always will be. As for bicycles, I am a blacksmith. I shoe horses, I fix farm machinery, I don't—'

'It's another one, look,' Maggie said softly. She was holding a printed letter, peering at it at arm's length. 'Like the last one. Isn't it? From the Ministry—'

'So you can just forget all about bicycles, and taking in Yank laundry—'

'Yes, look, Albert Harold Crossley. Something about a census of unregistered evacuee placements. They're missing one, an Albert Harold Crossley. Writing to registered evacuee placements in the area asking if we have any information on his whereabouts. I'm sure we had a letter about him a while back.' She looked around the table. 'Didn't we?'

Unusually, John Hooper's papers were double-checked at the Horham entrance gate. He waited, cap in hand, while an earlier, half-remembered anxiety nibbled at his subconscious: Sorry, Lieutenant, can't let you in, you don't belong here any more. But it didn't happen. The MPs merely explained that the base was on high alert, and thus they were under standing orders to be extra careful. They disappeared into their hut to telephone. And while he waited, looking out over the wide expanse of his old airfield, the smell of high-octane gasoline drifting through the humid afternoon air about him, a semi-submerged tapestry of sound began to tug, surfacing like missing wreckage on to the flotsam-strewn shores of his memory. Mechanical sounds. Heavy-duty machinery sounds. Industrial aviation sounds. The deeply ingrained music of an airbase gearing up to a high state of readiness. Engines being tested, running slowly up in a crescendo, from humming idle to roaring full power, the massive propellers straining at their mountings while the aeroplanes pushed at their chocks, their tailwheels hopping skittishly in the slipstreams. Other bombers, taxiing out for air tests, their four unsynchronised engines throbbing unrhythmically. Heavy trucks, fuel bowsers, low loaders, buzzing to and fro between depots and hardstands, carrying gasoline, ammunition and bombs to the loaders, armourers and fuellers swarming busily around the waiting aeroplanes, like ants at a picnic. Beneath it all, the percussive ring of hammering, drilling, cutting and panel-beating rising like drums in a jungle from the cavernous bellies of the huge domed hangars.

'Come in, John.' Papers in hand, Colonel LeBrock, Hooper's Group Officer Commanding, ushered him into his cluttered office. Cheap wooden furniture, steel filing cabinets, calendars and maps on the wall, a desk sinking beneath stacks of files, three telephones. 'Sorry about all the confusion at the gate. Got an ME on tomorrow, huge one, more than a dozen bomber groups involved. Everyone running around like their tails are on fire.' He pulled up a chair for Hooper in front of his desk. 'Between you and me, though, there's a good chance the mission will get scrubbed. Lot of thunderstorm activity expected in the target area, apparently.'

It was a confidence, a big one, telling him about the ME. In all probability less than half a dozen out of the three thousand people on base would know there was a possibility of weather cancelling the mission. Instead of putting him at his ease, however, somehow the knowledge just made him feel more tense. Something bad was coming. Hooper sat across the desk from his colonel, damp palms pressed between his knees.

'I see here you had the full third degree from Brent Wallis,' LeBrock said, flicking through the file. 'Quite a guy, huh? Folks here call him Dr Frankenstein the way he screws around inside your head. But don't tell him I said so, for God's sake.' Another confidence. 'So, John, in your own words. How do you feel?'

'Good, Colonel. Some residual symptoms from the concussion, odd headaches and so on, but Major Wallis said they're normal and will wear off in time.'

'Excellent.' LeBrock hesitated, unsure, momentarily, how to proceed. He was barely forty, a career fighting man, a soldier, a born organiser and leader. And one of the best. Hooper, in common with most of LeBrock's men, trusted and respected him. Yet, as with so many of his kind, dealing on a personal, one-to-one basis with the tragic, the unfortunate or simply the awkward was a skill he lacked, his normal sure-footedness and unshakeable confidence abandoning him. 'I guess Brent told you about your crew,' he said clumsily.

'No sir, I kind of figured it out for myself.' That was a test. Hooper had the line well rehearsed.

'Bad business, John. I was real sorry to hear about it. About them. About all of them. That whole day.' His gaze wandered to the window. 'Kiel.'

'Yes, sir.' An uneasy silence descended. In the office next door, telephones rang, typewriters clacked. LeBrock's time, especially today, was precious.

'What do you want to do, John?'

'I want to get back in the war, sir. Finish my tour of duty.'

'Are you sure you feel up to it? You took a hard knock to the head. Wallis says there's still some neurological problems, some amnesia.' Unresolved crisis, in fact, was how Wallis had put it. Hooper was an unknown, a time-bomb. 'You did good, the best you could. There's nothing dishonourable about a medical discharge, you know.'

'Sir, I came into this thing, we, my crew and me, came into this thing, to fly our twenty-five combat missions. It's all I want to do. It's something I need to do. For me, and for my crew. Otherwise, what was it all for?'

LeBrock nodded, studying the file. Finally he got to his feet, paced to the window. 'Things have . . . kind of changed around here in the weeks since Kiel, you know. That mission, well, up until then, although I won't say we had it easy, it is true to say that Kiel was the 95th's coming of age. We took a bad beating, lost a lot of men and we lost a lot of aircraft. We're back up to strength now, almost, which is good. But it's not the same. We've changed. Grown up, moved on. Different people, different culture, different ways of doing things, do you know what I mean?'

'I think so, sir.' He doesn't want me here.

'Do you know, John, that same night, after Kiel, Colonel Le May telephoned here from 3rd Air Division HQ, over at Bury St Edmunds. He wanted to know how many serviceable aircraft and crew we could put up the next day. We told him the truth, we had one ship, and one crew, that was it. He said fine, you're on alert to fly and I'll be over early in the morning to fly with you.' LeBrock turned to Hooper. 'And he was, too. Needless to say, we didn't fly that day. But he was here and ready to go, and so were we. One ship and one crew. Quite something, huh? It was a turning point for the 95th.'

'Yes, sir.'

'I've got a proposition for you, John.'

He walked across the wide apron towards his old hut, scurrying vehicles dodging round him as though he were a rock in a stream. To his relief the hut was deserted. He opened the door, sniffing the unfamiliar air like a dog. Tobacco, leather, someone else's shaving lotion. There were four beds in his room. All had new owners, he noted, his included. Kiel had cleaned it out. His bags and possessions had been brought out from stores, left in a tidy heap behind the door. It was a small gesture of humanity. When a crew was overdue, they were generally only permitted a few hours before all their belongings were removed and stored. Dead men's personal effects lying about a barracks were bad for morale. Quite often their beds, the beds they'd woken up in that morning, were occupied by their replacements that very night. Hoop knew a pilot who crash-landed his flak-riddled bomber on to the Sussex coast after a particularly tough mission. He and half his crew escaped without serious injury, but three were wounded, and two were dead. By the time the pilot had arranged for collection of his dead, seen his injured to the hospital, and organised transportation for the rest of them back to Suffolk, it was already late. When he got back on to base it was gone midnight. Pushing open the door to his hut he found his possessions all cleared out and another man in his bunk. Without a word, he removed the hapless replacement at the point of his service automatic, flopped fully clothed on to the still-warm blankets and passed out. He too was dead now, Hooper reflected, looking round the room. After all that. Shot down and killed. Kiel.

Running footsteps outside, the door bursting open, a youthful face appearing, red hair, freckles. 'Oh, hi. Sorry, ah, I didn't know anyone—'

'It's okay, come on in. I was just dropping by.'

'Oh, right. Moving in?' the young man replied, confused at Hooper's baggage. He was a navigator, Hooper noticed from his wings. Straight out of training, fresh and neat, just like his uniform. One of the 95th's many new replacements. The boy was holding out his hand. 'Jack Meeley, pleased to meet you.'

'John Hooper. And no, not moving in, moving out.'

'Oh, right,' he said again. Calculating. Hoop could see the boy was putting it together, adding it up. Hooper? Wasn't there a Lieutenant Hooper managed to get back from Kiel, then dumped his entire crew in the ocean or something, ended up over at Frankenstein's place on some kind of a breakdown? 'Shipping home?' Meeley asked.

'No. Got a transfer to the 520th over at Bedenham. Rookie crew there lost a pilot, I'm his replacement.'

'But you were based here, isn't that right?'

It was time to go. 'Once I was. A while back. Good luck, Jack.'

He picked up his bags and walked outside. A Jeep was waiting, engine idling, its driver leaning on the wheel. LeBrock had sent it, to take him to Bedenham. A kindness? Or a precaution? He wanted him off the base. They all did. As soon as possible. An unsettling old presence amid the new order, like a medieval ghost turning up in a brand-new hotel. He threw in his bags and climbed in.

'How many, sir?' he'd asked Colonel LeBrock at the end of their interview. He needed to know. 'If you don't mind me asking, how many did we lose at Kiel?'

LeBrock studied him. Maybe it was one confidence too far, but Hooper had the right; he'd earned it. 'A hundred and two killed or missing from Horham alone.'

'I see. General Forrest?'

'KIA. Shot down. He didn't make it.'

'The flat formation?'

LeBrock turned once more to the window. 'We went back to the old one.'

Somehow, even after all these weeks, Loren Spitzer managed to take a wrong turning somewhere among the spidery network of lanes that surrounded the base. Soon he was lost. Muttering furiously, he pulled over for the third time, hauled around and set off once more in the opposite direction, his head bent to the handlebars, his legs pumping. In the end, breathless and sweating, he pedalled into Bedenham village from an unfamiliar direction. He passed a short row of cottages, then a blacksmith's house and shop on his left, then the cottages ran out and he was back in open country. Or so it seemed. He cursed roundly under snatched breaths, but pedalled on. Around the next bend some more cottages hove into view, then a broken-down water mill on his right, then suddenly he was up and over a narrow bridge and on to the village green. The pub was on the far side. He pedalled to it, threw the bicycle against the wall and pushed open the door.

Inside it was dim suddenly after the hazy brightness outside, and stuffy and thick with smoke. The walls were uneven, bowed and roughly rendered, once white paintwork now stained yellow and dripping with rivulets of brown, the ceiling low, studded with ancient and sticky tar-black beams. The floor was flagstoned and dirty, puddled with slopped dregs. The smell was appalling: stale beer, sweat, old men and bad tobacco. Blinking against the darkness, Spitzer peered round, still panting from his exertions. There were only men in there, he noted, and most of those were elderly. They sucked wetly on empty pipes, eyeing him with only casual interest, as if he was a vaguely unusual sheep. One or two turned and nodded to each other.

'Is this . . .' Spitzer coughed, leaning to the nearest, a toothless ancient with wispy white hair and a broken-down shopping basket on wheels. 'Excuse me, sir, is this the Fleece pub?'

'Up the woods, son.' The old man nodded meaningfully. ''S where he is.'

'The Fleece? That it is, lad.' The landlord appeared behind

the bar. He was fat, and bald, and wearing a grime-stained string vest. 'Take no notice of old Percy, he means no harm. You'll be the Yank, come for your mate, I'll be bound.'

'Yes, er, yes sir, that is correct.' Spitzer looked anxiously around once more. 'Is he still here?'

'Good bloomin' job you turned up then, isn't it? We was about to call out the MPs. Then where'd he be?'

'Yes, sir, I appreciate it, we both do.'

''E's been in here since opening time, completely cleaned us out of Scotch, bought the lads here a couple of rounds of mild, which was thoughtful of him, then he began to get a bit out of order.' A ripple of wheezy tittering broke out around the bar.

'Please, sir, is he still here?'

'In the gents.' The landlord jerked his head. 'Out back.'

It wasn't hard to find; the smell led him, and the flies. It was little more than a small wooden shack with a single blocked and overflowing urinal and a door through to a lavatory. The shed was windowless and airless, even darker than the bar. The lavatory door was shut.

'Irv? You in there? It's me, Spitz.' Silence. 'Irv, come on now, open up.' Muffled movement from within, then Spitzer thought he heard a clunk of heavy metal. 'Irv, what the hell are you doing? Open the damn door, for God's sake!'

'Go away.' A second later an unmistakable ratchet click. Spitzer took one pace back, raised his foot and kicked the door in.

Martha's co-pilot, Irving Underwood, sat hunched on the dirt next to the bowl. He'd been sick down his uniform. As Spitzer looked, Underwood's face, staring up at him from the floor, pale with anguish in the dim shadows, began to collapse, his shoulders to jerk, his eyes to blur. He was holding his service-issue Colt automatic pistol to his head.

'Okay, that's it, I've had it, I'm getting out of here.' Beans rolled off his bed and clumped towards the hut door. 'Any of you guys coming?'

'Too right, Beaner, count me in.' Emmett Lajowski ground his cigarette underfoot and made to follow.

Gerry Via looked up from the card table. 'Ho, now, just wait a minute, fellas. It may have escaped your attention, but there's a flag flying, the whole place is on full alert, there's an ME tomorrow, and no one but no one is allowed off base.'

'Wrong, Geraldo.' Beans, heavy hands resting on wide hips, leaned over the table. Around it Gerry Via, Eldon Ringwald and three other hut members from a different crew instinctively held their cards to their chests. 'You are wrong in one detail. You see, I don't care. Everyone else may be on alert to fly, but we in good old Crew 19 are not. In case you hadn't noticed, we haven't been on alert to fly since Rudy Stoller got his head blown off, since Dave Greenbaum bled to death in the waist' – he paused fractionally, his eyes on Via's – 'and since Lieutenant Broman went AWOL. We're not on alert, we're not supernumerary, we're not even on standby. We are stood down, remember? We don't exist. Nobody gives a damn, nobody knows, nobody wants to know. Dawn tomorrow the rest of these guys in here are getting up to go to war while we lie in bed fiddling with our dicks. And I just can't be doing with it any more, so I'm going to Ipswich, tonight, to get drunk. Now are you with me or not?'

There was a brief stand-off. Ringwald, the youngest, turned from one to the other, awaiting a cue. Via checked his card-hand. The other hut members looked embarrassed. Then Al Tork, Crew 19's softly spoken tail gunner, rose quietly from his bunk in the corner. He picked up his jacket, heading for the door.

'Let's go.'

They took the bus. They had to walk the first three miles to the bus stop on the main Ipswich road, five solitary figures hunched into their A2 jackets, tramping wordlessly along the quiet lanes in the gathering dusk. Occasionally a vehicle appeared and they scurried into the undergrowth like startled rabbits. But after a while, as they drew further from the base, they stopped hiding.

Ipswich was crowded, as always. Long queues snaked from the restaurants, dance halls and movie theatres, pubs overflowed on to pavements thick with wandering servicemen, strolling couples, giggling girls and cruising streetwalkers. There were uniforms everywhere. Maintenance crews in RAF blue from the fighter stations at Ipswich and Martlesham mingled with khaki-clad engineers from the shore batteries at nearby Felixstowe. Packs of Royal Navy ratings on shore leave from three corvettes moored in the docks roamed restlessly from one bar to the next. Americans, as always, by the hundred, in their greens and browns. And among them all, threading their way invisibly through the sluggish streams like hungry pike, lone pairs of beat policemen and military police prowled, and watched, and waited.

Misbehavin Martha's five surviving enlisted crewmen drifted, rudderless, through the throng for a while, borne upon the eddying currents like leaves in a stream. They queued for twenty minutes at one bar only to find it had run dry an hour earlier. They queued at another to be told it was off-limits to Americans. Then, in gathering darkness, they joined a line down among tall, brooding grain warehouses on the docks to eat a tasteless tinned-ham supper in a stuffy Red Cross canteen, before eventually elbowing their way into a pub near the bus terminal. It was tall and Victorian, a single large smoky room with a long bar and high ceilings. It was hot and steamy, dimly lit, inadequately blacked out, and packed to the rafters.

'So, how's Cheryl?' Lajowski blew a plume of smoke, his voice raised against the din. He drank deeply, pulled a grimace. 'Boy, I am never going to get used to this gnat's-piss beer they drink over here. It tastes like ditchwater, don't it? Do you think they water it down for the GIs?'

Beans was leaning heavily over the bar. 'She's lonesome, same as a million other wives back home. She hates living on her own in the trailer park, hates Oklahoma City, doesn't understand about the war, just keeps writing and writing, asking when I'm ever going to get home.'

'I thought you were farm people?'

'We are. Was. Grew up on a big sprawl of a place with my folks and brothers. Outside of Supulpa. Beautiful country. You know it?'

Lajowski, third-generation Brooklyn, shook his head. Further along the bar, Tork, Via and Ringwald were chatting to three English girls. Gerry Via, brown eyes glinting mischievously, was murmuring in the tallest girl's ear, one hand resting on her arm. A moment later she broke away, laughing.

Tork, less interested in his girl evidently, nodded inattentively as she spoke. Eldon Ringwald, his hairless cheeks blushing visibly, was standing nervously next to a young girl with round eyes and thick brown hair. They both looked uneasy, Lajowski thought. And absurdly young beside the others. '. . . then after we got married, we decided to give the city a shot. Cheryl's idea. Big mistake. Moved into the trailer park, I had work doing auto repairs at a gas station nearby, then before we knew it I got called up.' Beans broke off, picking sodden shreds from a beer mat. 'I miss the farm. I miss Cheryl. Haven't seen each other since Rapid City. Lousy way to run a marriage.'

'You said it.' Lajowski glanced at the curve of Beans' broad back hunching over the bar, then drained his glass, patting pockets for cigarettes. Gerry Via was leading his group over towards them, his girl in hand. Three English sailors in ratings' uniforms followed unseen in their wake. Over on the far side of the room a commotion was starting up.

'Do you think we'll ever get out of here, Emmett?' Beans' voice was barely audible above the growing din.

'Sure. You'll see. We'll all get reassigned to other crews, next few days probably, be back on the flight line before you know it. Give it six months and we'll have finished our tours and be home free.'

'Lajowski? Beaner? I'd like to introduce you to some friends of mine. This beautiful young lady here is Dot, this is her friend Vi, she's had a little to drink, and young Kid Ringwald here is standing next to the lovely Claire. Ladies, this here is Technical Sergeants Marion Beans and Emmett Lajowski.'

'Excuse me, Yank. These three was with us.' One of the sailors was tapping on Via's shoulder, the two others crowding in behind. Via froze, his back to the sailors, his eyes on Lajowski's. Lajowski shook his head minutely. Beans straightened from the bar. The commotion by the door was getting louder. There was a shout, the shattering of a dropped glass.

'Okay, Navy, let's just take it easy, okay?' Al Tork said quietly to the leading sailor. 'MPs are everywhere, nobody wants any trouble now, do they?'

'We *was* with you.' Vi gestured blearily at the leading sailor. Gin and lemon slopped from her drink on to her wrist. Her face was flushed, eyes glassy. 'But now we're with them, see. So shove off out of it.'

'Come on, buddy, why don't we all get a drink and—'

'I am not your buddy!' The sailor shrugged Tork's hand away. He leaned his face to Vi's. 'You bloody slags. Happy enough to take drinks off us all evening, then as soon as the sodding Yanks show up—'

'Eldon.' Claire was tugging at Ringwald's sleeve.

'Say, perhaps you'd better watch your mouth in front of the ladies.' Beans began to push forward. Lajowski and Via were still watching each other.

'Eldon, come on!' Claire dragged at Ringwald's arm. 'Come on, let's go!'

'You bloody Yanks. You come over here all flash, with your free candy bars and your free cigarettes and your free nylons. You ponce about in your fancy uniforms and your fancy aeroplanes, helping yourselves to our beer and our rations, and our women. But when it comes down to the real fighting—'

He got no further. Beans' fist landed squarely between his

eyes. He staggered back into the arms of his comrades, disbelief on his face, one hand to his streaming nose. Simultaneously there was a woman's scream over near the door, renewed men's shouting, the splintering crash of a breaking window. The sailors lunged forward as one, Via ducked down to his boots, Lajowski, head down, barrelled forward. Then all the lights went out.

The night's heavy torpor dragged Heather from a troubled sleep long before dawn. She lay, alone on the big bed, naked save for a single limp sheet, one hand resting on the soft skin of her lower belly, and waited for sleep to enfold her once more. But instead it eluded her, slipping from her grasp like a barely formed idea. For a while she pursued it, tossing and turning on the mattress, listening to the unearthly infant-like mewling of a vixen far away on the other side of the village, blinking up at pale shadows cast by a hazy half-moon. But the air about the room lay thick and oppressive, restlessness overcame her languor and her mind began, inevitably, to ponder the prosaic uncertainties of her situation. A missing brother, domineering in-laws, an unwell mother, an absent husband. David. In a final desperate bid for sleep, she even allowed herself, her fingers sinking lower and lower on her abdomen, to replay the few brief nights of passion they had shared before his departure. Or preferred versions of them that had evolved, almost imperceptibly, in her imagination over the intervening months. But in a trice, as she knew it would, David's face, fair-haired and smiling boyishly, disappeared from her mind's eye and dark-haired strangers invaded. They came silently, anonymously, pressing down rudely on to her imagination, pinning her helplessly, driving hard into her with an urgency that both shocked her and aroused her deeply.

She threw back the sheet and padded barefoot to the kitchen to boil water for tea. As she waited for the kettle's asthmatic wheeze, she detected another sound: a far-off low murmur, like the rumble of distant thunder. She went to the kitchen window and threw it wide, inhaling the pre-dawn freshness. A hint of pink suffused the grey horizon to the east. The noise grew. It was a sound she recognised, as famil- iar now to the Suffolk dawn as iron-shod hooves ringing on cobbles or cattle lowing to the sheds. The warming up of aero-engines. A hundred or more. After only momentary hesitation, she flicked off the gas beneath the kettle and ran upstairs.

Three-quarters of a mile away Billy Street was lobbing gravel at a window. Stones struck glass with a noise that to him sounded like machine-gun fire. He ducked into the bushes. Nothing happened. He stepped back out, frowning up at the window in the fading moonlight, and threw yet more. Again a deafening rattle, again no result. Finally, after an entire handful which he was convinced the whole village must have heard, the blackout curtain beyond the glass twitched and a face appeared, pale and round, the whispered voice thick with sleep.

'Billy? Billy Street? Is that you?'

'Ruby,' he hissed. 'Ruby, it's me. Get on down here, quick.'

'Why, for goodness' sake? It's the middle of the blooming night.'

'No. It's getting light. Get dressed and come down.

There's something I've got to show you. Please. It's dead important.'

He waited, hopping from one foot to the other in the lane beside her cottage. After an age he heard the click of a gate latch, the soft fall of her foot on gravel.

'What?' she hissed in his ear, her anger tinged with excitement. He could smell her hair, the warmth of her body from bed. She was wearing someone else's too-large jacket over a simple floral dress, her school gym shoes on her feet. 'What is it, Billy?'

'Come on.' He grasped her hand and pulled. They began to run, slowly at first, then faster and faster.

'You're mad, you are, Billy Street!' Sprinting through the empty lanes, full tilt, two night sprites pursued by the gathering dawn. And as they ran, the noise of engines grew louder.

Finally she dragged him to a breathless halt. The noise was a deep throbbing rumble now, so loud, so powerful, she could feel it as well as hear it. It filled her head, shook the ground beneath her feet, made a peculiar vibrating sensation deep in her stomach. 'Where are we going, Bill?' she gasped. 'We're not going on the base, are we? It's not allowed. What's happening? You're scaring me.'

'Don't be scared, Rube. It's all right, we're not on the base. Look, here's the fence, we're on the perimeter.' He led her round a tree-lined bend in the lane and suddenly they were in the open, the sky arching unbroken overhead like a vast grey-blue dome, pinpricked with dying starlight. The terrain ahead of them stretched flat and treeless in every direction. The light was coming. 'It's all right, see? Look,

108

there's the end of the runway just over there. They'll all be along it in a minute.'

'Who will? What's going on?'

He pulled her to his side. After a brief, awkward hesitation he placed his arm round her shoulder. Immediately, and with a thrill like electricity, he felt her draw closer. A mile away at the far end of the dark stripe of the runway, a single green flare popped like a distant firework.

'What's that?'

'It's the most fantastic thing in the world, Rube, and I wanted to show it you. It's an ME. Right this very instant, all the bombers on all the bases all over Suffolk are getting ready. Hundreds of 'em. They're going to take off and form up into one huge formation in the sky, like an enormous, kind of . . .'

'Armada?'

'Armada, that's it. And our base, Rube, the 520th, is joining in with it.' Suddenly at the far end of the runway a hum detached itself from the background rumble, and rose quickly to a roar. They could see nothing but the roar grew louder and louder until it was deafening, a high-pitched throbbing snarl. Ruby clapped her hands to her ears; Billy was making little jumps at her side. 'Here they come!' His yell was exultant.

A huge black shape materialised suddenly, hurtling, head on, straight at them from the grey shadows beyond the runway, thundering, shaking, shrieking furiously like some madly charging animal. Ruby's terrified scream was plucked, unheard, from her lips and vanished into the fury like leaves in a hurricane. She was going to die now, she knew, rooted rabbit-like to the spot, part in fascination, part in raw terror, certain beyond doubt that the monster would plough straight through them and smash them to bloody ribbons. But as she watched, open-mouthed, at the very last instant it detached itself from the ground, skewed slightly sideways on its precarious cushion of air, steadied, then thundered over their heads with a noise like the end of the world. A moment later she felt the heat of its passing, hot exhaust, a kind of eerie whirlwind of slipstream vortices, then silence. Thirty seconds later, the next bomber was thundering down the runway towards them. Then the next.

Twenty yards away Heather stood in the shadows by the trees and watched the bombers lifting off, felt each one as it strained impossibly skywards, passing through her like a welcome violation. As she watched she could see the two figures silhouetted against the pale dawn sky ahead. It took her a while to identify them, Billy Street's roundly gesticulating profile first, the slighter, donkey-jacketed outline of Ruby Moody rather later. She smiled, left them in peace and, as the last bomber clawed its way into the sky above her, turned and started back for the cottage.

A quarter of a mile away further round the fence, Crew 19 lay sprawled on the dew-soaked grass. 'Twenty-seven,' Eldon Ringwald said, tearing weeds from the ground. 'That's not bad.'

'Not bad? Twenty-seven airborne out of twenty-nine possibles? It's a goddamn miracle,' Beans replied. The five of them were lying in a row, like corpses at a battle site. Al Tork, despite the noise, had fallen asleep. Above and behind them the rumble of the departing bombers had receded to a hum.

'Twenty-nine? Which is the twenty-ninth?' Lajowski asked.

'*Up and at 'em.* Don Cleaver's ship. She's in the shed with that busted undercarriage leg, remember? Maintenance couldn't get it fixed in time for the ME.'

'Oh, yeah.' They fell quiet, each submerged in his own thoughts. On the far side of the airfield, a single empty bomber, theirs, stood alone on its hardstand.

'Do you think we're ever going to get back into this war?'

Chapter 5

Lt J A Hooper 520th BG

Dear Mother and Father,

A great many thanks for all your mail. I can't tell you how much of a boon it is to hear that life continues as normal back home. Sometimes 'home', Harrisburg, life there, friends, even family, can seem altogether like another existence, another reality. Does that make any sense? I expect not. Thank you also, Mother, by the way, for the little book of the Psalms. It is a real treasure.

I'm sorry for my slowness in replying, but a great deal has happened in the past few weeks. Some, as usual, I am at liberty to tell you about, some I am not. I suppose the most important news from my perspective is a switch of groups. For operational reasons, I have transferred to a new group (the 520th) on a base about thirty miles from the old one, near a little village called Bedenham. I moved in here a few days ago. It sure is a pretty spot, the village is very quaint and 'English' although I have yet to meet many of its inhabitants. I hear they are typically friendly and hospitable.

I should also add that I have transferred crews. My job is to train up a new crew here that lost its pilot. I am greatly looking forward to that challenge, as you can imagine. I hope to meet them all, along with my new squadron commander, tomorrow. I hear they are a fine bunch of guys.

I forgot to mention that I suffered a slight injury on my last mission with the old crew. It is nothing to be concerned about, the injury was superficial, I passed a week or so in the hospital and am now completely recovered, thank the Lord. But as a whole, the mission was only partially successful. My crew, the one I trained with back in Rapid City,

. . . is gone. All dead. Hooper stared down at the page, then tore it from the pad, screwed it into a ball and dropped it on to the growing heap on the floor beside him. The occupant of the bed next to his stirred, rolling on to his back with a loud smacking of lips. After a minute he began to snore once more. Hooper sank his face into his hands, elbows propped on the little table. It was very late, the hut in almost total darkness. Hopeless. There was nothing to say, and no form of words in which to say it. What was the point? He stared down at the blank pad. After a moment he took up his pen and began again.

Dear Jo-Beth . . .

'Billy! Billy love. For goodness' sake, what on earth is it?'

He fights, struggles, drowning, suffocating, towards the surface, but a great weight presses down on to his chest, pinning him to the floor, squeezing the last drops of air from him until there is no more left. And the surface is so far off. The more he struggles, the further away it gets, a tiny receding light at the end of a cavernous smoke-filled tunnel. And all the while the flames crackle nearer, and louder. He can feel their heat. He begins to try to scream.

Someone is shaking him. 'Billy, stop struggling, wake up now!'

The fire dream. The disused warehouse down by the river at Southwark. Night-time, the whole site deserted, just he, Ron and Jimmy Cagney, whose real name is Canning but everyone at the home calls Cagney, like the American gangster bloke at the flicks. Freezing cold, February, jet-black sky, harsh sliver of moon. Slip through the corrugated-iron fencing, No Trespassing, dash across the piles of brick rubble to the smashed door, duck inside. Then running, up and up, thumping up stairwells, splashing through puddled floors, hobnail boots ringing around the huge empty caverns. Excited young boys' voices echoing off dripping walls, rusting girders, vaulted roofs lost in shadow. Then panting to an exhausted halt at the top. The startled clap-clapping of pigeons' wings, the mournful blare of a barge way down on the oily-black river, Jimmy Cagney's breathless giggles. 'Christ, it's cold!' Their shivering laughter fogs the crisp night air. Blacked-out London spread out far below them in the moonlight like magic, a darkened fairyland, a night-time toytown. 'I know,' says Ron. 'Let's get a little fire going.'

Maggie is shaking him, but still he can't breathe. A fire is going all right, going crazy. Flickering shadows glow at the end of the smoke-filled cavern. So far away, while all the time the flames rush nearer, cracking and snapping all around him. Hungry, angry. Everywhere. 'Ron? Jimmy! Where are you?' But he is alone, and they are gone. For ever.

His chest bursts at last like a dam, a gasping sob racks him and he opens his eyes. A single yellow flame dances on his chair by the bed. 'Billy, what is it?' He can see its reflection in her eyes. Mrs H. She pulls him close, holding him tight. Like a mother. Like the Irish nurse at the home, Sally Corrigan. 'We'll get you out of here, Bertie boy, don't you fret.' As she rocks him, holds him, he can feel the comforting swell of her chest, smell her warm night smells. Someone else is standing in the shadows by the door. 'Mum? What's happening? What's the matter with him?' Still his lungs feel as if great straps of steel are bound around them. His breaths come in harsh shallow rasps.

'It's all right, Claire, go back to bed, dear. He's having one of his turns.'

Then at last the steel bands are easing and he's sinking limply against her. Flopping, shaking, his heart banging in his chest. His face is hot and flushed, his eyes wet.

'Steady. Steady does it. A bit better now, love?'

'Yes.' He gasps, hugging her to him. 'Yes.'

'Perhaps we'll get Dr Chillaman round to check you over in the morning,' she said a few minutes later, handing him a cup of tepid squash. He drank greedily, propped up on his pillow, his pyjama top damp against his skin. Maggie's eyes were wandering the darkened attic. 'That asthma again, I'll be bound. And I suppose it is a bit musty up here.'

'It's all right.' He wheezed. 'I feel better now.'

Her fingers combed hair from his forehead. 'Hmm. Your poor mum, what would she have said?'

Billy sipped his squash.

'Did you always suffer with your chest, then? As a little boy?'

'Um, dunno. S'pose.'

'You must miss her so. And your dad. Perhaps we could organise a visit. Up to London. Go and see him, your dad. Would you like that?' Eight months and not a word. In the eight months since Billy'd arrived in the village, together with the others, he'd not received a single word. Not a letter, not a card. Nothing.

She was watching him; he could feel her eyes on his. Switching from side to side. 'It's all right, Mrs H. I feel a bit better now.'

Maggie said nothing, patting his leg through the blankets.

He'd arrived, one rainy afternoon the previous November, with two other evacuees. Little girls, twin sisters. And a bossy local co-ordinator from the Ministry ticking off names on a clipboard. Ray had been dead against the idea of an evacuee, of course. 'What the hell do we need with yet another mouth to feed? And where's the little so-and-so going to sleep?' The two little girls went off with the local co-ordinator to the Bolsovers' farm over towards Dennington. Billy stayed with the Howdens. It was his third billeting. Somewhere near Felixstowe had been first, she thought. Something had gone wrong there, Billy said. They didn't like him, accused him of pilfering, locked him in the cellar, fed him dog scraps out of a bowl. So he was moved to another family, an elderly couple, on the coast, Bawdsey way. That was all right, he said, he liked it there. But then the Ministry decreed it was too dangerous billeting evacuees near the coast, what with the beaches being mined, and the air attacks on the shore batteries, and scare stories about German night-raiding parties. All evacuees were to be billeted at least ten miles inland. So he came to Bedenham to be billeted bang next door to the huge American bomber base being built there. It made no sense at all, Ray said. The Yanks were a prime target. There had already been hit-and-run attacks by German night fighters, and there were sure to be more. The Ministry must be off its head.

But Ray had come round in the end. War effort, Maggie had reminded him. It always worked; he was very conscientious about doing their bit. Anyway, she went on, as an evacuee Billy came with a ration card, a few shillings a week from the Ministry and an extra pair of hands to help about the house. Maybe Ray could even train him up to help out in the forge. And he could sleep in the attic. Tidy it up a bit, clear away some of the old things. Her eyes wandered to the corner once more. The stacked boxes, the battered suitcase. She'd hoped it might even be good for Ray. Bring him out of himself a bit. And what with Billy being a boy, too.

'You mustn't mind him, you know, Billy, love,' she murmured. 'Ray. He comes over all gruff sometimes, but deep down he has a golden heart.' She turned her face to the blacked window, the light from Billy's night candle soft yellow on her cheek. His breathing was steadying and he was beginning to feel sleepy again. He liked it when she called him 'love'.

'He lost two brothers, you know. In the first war. Did I ever tell you? He was the youngest of the three, they all joined up at the same time. Took the bus from Halesworth to Norwich and signed on for the infantry together. I watched them go.' Scarcely seventeen, standing on the step outside her parents' butcher's shop, waving a little flag on a stick. Ray, marching in his Sunday best up to the bus stop with the others. Eighteen years old, bursting with it. 'I'll be back,' he called out to her. It was all planned: he would finish his apprenticeship, then they could marry, and he would set up a forge on his own. Not doing horse-shoeing and ordinary smithing work, but designing, crafting, making the fanciest, most intricate wrought ironwork for all the nobs' houses, the public gardens, the royal parks even. He had the skill, the eye. And he had the will. 'I'll be back, Maggie Cowell, you see.' But when the nightmare finally ended four years later, he came home with the stuffing gone out of him, his iron will crushed, his dreams shattered. Dashed into the mud, together with the blood of his brothers and a million others.

'We had a little boy before, once, you see,' she was saying very softly. 'Long time ago, about four years before Claire was born. Stephen, we called him.' She nodded towards the boxes in the corner. 'Those are what's left of his things. Baby clothes, his christening spoon, that sort of thing. I don't know why we keep them. He died when he was very little. In that fearful winter of twenty-three. Pneumonia, the doctor said. I think that was the last straw, as far as Ray was concerned.'

'Hi. Crew 19 in here?' Mid-western drawl. A square-jawed face had appeared around the door of hut twelve. Fifteen pairs of eyes looked up.

'That's us. Among others,' Gerry Via murmured, the draught from the door fluttering the playing cards at his table. 'Who wants to know?'

The door opened wide and a tall, gangly youth of about

twenty entered carrying an A3 canvas kitbag on his shoulder. Close-cropped tufts of dark ginger hair sprouted above a long, lopsidedly smiling face. He held out a hand to Via. 'Herman Keissling. I'm your replacement waist gunner.'

Lajowski's head came up. Via and Keissling shook hands. 'Gerry Via. Radio operator. Well, er, Herman, good to have you aboard. Play poker?'

'Sure, deal me in. Uh, where do I bunk?'

'There's a spare down here.' Tork, hitching his trousers, rose from a writing table at the far end of the hut. 'I'm Al Tork, tail gun. Over there is Lajowski, we call him Polecat, he's upper turret. Kid Ringwald, ball turret, is outside somewhere. That lard-assed s.o.b. lying over there is Beans.' It felt good, introducing Crew 19 to a replacement. That meant they weren't going to break it up. They were putting it back together.

'Is that left or right waist gun?' Beans' voice was muffled. He was on his bed, eating from an open tin of peaches balanced on his chest.

'I trained mostly on the left, but I ain't fussed.'

'Well, *I* shoot left waist. You get the right, and mind you stay out of my way.'

'Sure.' Keissling shrugged. 'Whatever you say.'

'Keissling,' Lajowski was muttering thoughtfully. He was in his habitual position, hunched on his bed, knees tucked up to his chin, cigarette between lips. 'Keissling. Herman Keissling. Ah, excuse me for asking, this, Herman, but what in the hell kind of a name is Herman Keissling anyways? I mean, are you sure you're on the right side?'

'Jesus, Lajowski, give the guy a break, for God's sake.'

'Easy, Torky, I was only asking if Herman the German here—'

The door flew wide suddenly, banging against its stop. Cards fluttered like leaves to the floor. Via cursed. Billy burst in. 'The spoon!' he sputtered breathlessly. He waved his arm towards Keissling's bunk. 'The man on that bed. I sold him the spoon. Where is he?'

'Hey, look, it's lucky charm kid again! So what did you bring us this time, lucky charm kid? No, hold it, let me guess . . .'

Billy stared around the hut in panic. Keissling looked bemused, the others exchanged shrugs. 'The gunner! From *Appaloosa Lou*. He was there, right there on that bed! He followed me outside, to the hangar. He bought the spoon for a bob. Where is he?'

'Steve Kolarik, you mean?' Beans said, folding his hands behind his head. 'He's dead, kid. *Appaloosa Lou* went down on the ME. Flamed in, on the run-in to the target. No 'chutes.'

Lajowski lit another cigarette. 'Guess that old spoon you sold him just wasn't quite lucky enough, was it?'

'*Appaloo*— Gone? But I've got to find it, got to get it back, don't you see—' Billy broke off.

For a third time the door to the hut swung wide. Via's hand slapped down on to the cards. 'Jesus, Ringwald, will you just shut the goddamn door!'

The distant burble of engines was drifting into the hut. 'It's *Martha*!' Eldon Ringwald, wide-eyed, was pointing outside. 'Quick! Knyper and the ground crew're prepping her. For flight. Someone's going to fly her!'

Half a mile away, Hooper's Jeep, tyres squealing, raced

120

around the perimeter towards the distant bomber. He held on grimly, knuckles white on the rim of the windshield, while the driver, his new squadron commander Gene Englehardt, a sodden cigar-stub clamped between his teeth, weaved around potholes, skidded between parked vehicles and dodged slow-moving pedestrians.

'Get out the way, dummy!' Englehardt roared as a sergeant wobbled past on a bicycle. 'Idiot!' He winked at Hooper. 'So now then, John, here's the score. We got the four squadrons here on base that make up the 520th. Each squadron should have seven, eight ships apiece, but usually flies with average of six, on account of crew shortages, or ships grounded for maintenance. That means that the 520th generally puts up anything between twenty and thirty ships at a time, you got that?'

'Got it, Major.' Hooper had to raise his voice over the clatter of the Jeep's engine. A moment later they both leaned over, puppet-like, as Englehardt sped into a corner.

'Call me Gene. We don't stand for any boot-camp chicken-crap in my squadron, John.'

'Hoop.'

'Hoop, right. Mighty glad to have you with us!' To Hooper's horror, Englehardt, grinning widely, took his hand off the wheel and reached across to shake. He was the classic dashing bomber-jockey. Early thirties, non-regulation haircut, pencil-thin Errol Flynn moustache, deliberately crumpled uniform cap, weather-worn flying jacket. Round-faced, bright-eyed, tough, supremely cocky, contagiously confident. Hoop had met them before, at Horham and elsewhere. Often they failed to live up to their carefully cultivated images of

121

themselves. Sometimes they failed to live long enough to cultivate them properly in the first place. There are old pilots, the ancient saying went, and there are bold pilots. But there are no old, bold pilots. Yet Englehardt's enthusiasm was irrepressible. And invigorating, like a blast of fresh air up an airless mineshaft. 'Mighty glad, I don't mind telling you. We've been hurting, sometimes just three or four serviceable ships in the squadron. Pitiful.'

'I see.' They passed two B17s, parked, empty, on their hardstands. Then a third hove into view. Hooper could see ground crew and refuelling vehicles clustered around it. Its two inner engines were running. A distantly familiar knot, deep in his stomach, drew a little tighter. This had to go right, it just had to. Englehardt was still shouting.

'There's *Martha*! She's a part of my squadron. Or was. Thing is, she hasn't flown since Rudy Stoller got killed.'

'Oh, yes. How so?'

Englehardt was slowing as they drew nearer to the bomber. Timing his arrival. There was more he had to say. 'Two reasons. First, Operations stood the crew down while the pen-pushers decided what the hell to do with them.' He glanced at Hooper. 'They're basically good kids, Hoop, but their morale's shot, they never had a chance to settle into the job. And there's been some . . . trouble among the enlisted guys.'

'Trouble?'

'Yeah, well, you know, bickering, in-fighting, that kind of thing. And they've been slipping on and off base without passes. There was a minor incident last week with some Brit sailors in a bar in Ipswich. MPs picked them up. It's nothing serious, Hoop, we've been trying to cut them some slack. They just need to get back on the job. Tough break losing three members of the crew on their first mission like that.'

'Three? I thought it was the pilot and one waist gunner?'

'The bombardier. Broman. He walked off the ship when it landed and went AWOL. Colonel Lassiter, our Group CO, finally gave up on him and assigned a new one. A Lieutenant Holland, you'll meet him later. Regular guy.'

'I see. And the other officers?'

'Spitzer's pure gold, straight, positive and reliable, although as a navigating officer he's completely green, of course. You'll need to work on that. Irv Underwood, he's your co-pilot. He, well, he was in the cockpit when Stoller got hit. He, uh, he's been calling in sick most days since.'

The 520th has a rookie crew for you, John, LeBrock had said. Great team, eager as hell, terrific opportunity . . . Hooper should have known. 'What's the second reason?' he asked.

'What's that, buddy?'

'You said there were two reasons *Martha* hasn't flown since Stoller died.'

'Oh, yeah.' Englehardt nodded towards the waiting bomber. 'Well, Hal Knyper, the clear-up crews, they all did the best they could cleaning up the ship. But it was one hell of a mess on the flight deck. As you can imagine. Twenty-millimetre cannon shell straight to the head like that. Nobody really wanted to go near it. One evening last week, a mechanic went on board, just to run engine checks. Came running straight off again like a startled rabbit, yelling there was, like, pieces of . . . tissue, you know, human remains, on the throttle quadrant. Once a ship gets a reputation, jinxed, like that . . . Well, it's all horseshit, we both know that. That's partly the reason we're out here now. To fly this mother and blow away all the horseshit jinx crap.'

The Jeep slewed to a halt fifty yards short of the parked bomber. Hooper watched, the knot in his stomach a little tighter, while the two idling engines sputtered to a stop. An unlucky pilot, a screwed-up crew, now a jinxed ship. It was hardly auspicious. The ground crew were standing to one side now, waiting, the refuelling vehicle reversing away from the hardstand. They were ready. 'Partly?' he asked, although he already knew.

'Yep, Hoop. Partly.' Englehardt turned to him in the Jeep, his voice quiet suddenly, one hand cupping a lighter to his cigar stub. 'I heard all the stories. About what happened to you, and to your crew. After Kiel. Colonel Lassiter briefed me on the stuff that Frankenstein Wallis and Colonel LeBrock sent through from the 95th. Frankly, it don't interest me one jot. Or Lassiter. He just told me to check out your flying, and that's all I care about. If you can fly this ship okay, which you will, then me, the 520th, and those boys watching over there in hut twelve, can sure use you. If you can't, then Lassiter will have you off this base and on your way home with an honourable medical discharge by nightfall. Do we have an understanding?'

Hooper nodded, his eyes on the waiting bomber. There was still a choice, even now. A line of retreat, a last way out. Turn us around, Gene, I want to go home. Home. Mum, Dad, Susan. Jo-Beth. A hero's welcome and no awkward questions. Safety, with honour. Nobody would ever know.

'I'd like to think we treat our war-weary a little better,' Brent Wallis had said. The knot had solidified, crystallising to a hard singularity. But within it flickered a tiny spark. Like rebellion. Everyone was waiting. It couldn't get any worse; it was already as bad as it could get. He found he was smiling, at himself.

'Let's get to it, Gene.'

It is all right. Better than all right. They park up and walk over to the ship. Immediately Englehardt swings himself up through the nose hatch and disappears on to the flight deck, shouting to come up and join him when he's ready. It's a nice touch: give the man a few minutes on his own. He begins a walk-around. It feels good, everything looks familiar, exactly as it should, he can remember it all. But something isn't quite right. The crew chief is watching, from a distance, having a quiet smoke with his boys. Hoop beckons him over. His name is Hal Knyper. They shake. I like to do the walk-around with my crew chief, if that's okay with you, Hal. No problem, Knyper shrugs. He is shorter than Altman, dark and hairy, but with straight-talking china-blue eyes, and a listening smile. During the walk-around Knyper points out a few modifications and repairs, cautions him about a niggling supercharger runaway problem on number three engine, shows him the neat patch where the cannon shell tore into the fuselage beside the waist gunner's position. He has a quiet, methodical approach to his job, and his responsibilities. Listening to him is like listening to soothing music. There's nothing wrong with this ship, Lieutenant, he says at the end of the walk-around, his china-blue eyes on

Hoop's. She just needs to get back in the war, that's all. Like her crew.

He signs Knyper's clipboard and swings up through the hatch, nose twitching as the smells prick at his subconscious like snatches of half-forgotten dreams. Gasoline, gun-oil, cordite, rubber, leather, sweat. Fresh paint. He clambers up to the flight deck. The left-hand windscreen is brand new, completely unscratched. There is a card on a string, hanging over his pilot's control column. Handwritten. 'Pull back to go up,' it says, with a big black arrow pointing skywards. 'Push forward to go down.' Very funny. Knyper's boys. Another nice touch. In the right-hand seat, Englehardt's face is expressionless, his head down, scribbling on a notepad. Hoop lifts the card off the controls, hangs it on the bulkhead behind him and settles into the seat.

'Start-up checks,' he calls.

'Fuel transfer valves and switches,' Englehardt replies straight away. He had the checklist ready, waiting on his knee.

'Off.'

'Intercoolers.'

'Cold.'

'Gyros.'

'Uncaged.'

Fifteen minutes later he's taxiing the big aeroplane slowly around the perimeter track towards the runway threshold. Englehardt is looking out of the side window, a study of nonchalant indifference. From the corner of his eye, Hoop sees binoculars glinting from the control tower. There's a crowd on the balcony there. Elsewhere, airmen are trickling from their huts, or pausing on their way across the apron.

Mechanics wander to the front of the huge domed hangars, drivers pull up their vehicles. The buzz has gone round. Is that *Martha* taxiing out? Hey, look at that, someone's taking up Stoller's old ship. Say, isn't that Englehardt? I hear he's checking out *Martha*'s new pilot.

'Looks like you've got yourself an audience, Hoop.' Gene chuckles over the headphones.

'Here's hoping I don't give them anything to see.'

'Hmm. Maybe.' Englehardt grunts. A green flare pops from the control tower. 'Then again, maybe not. There's your green.'

Cleared to go. Sweet and steady. Do it sweet and steady, right by the numbers. The control column feels solid and heavy in his hands, strange yet familiar, the pedals bouncing slightly beneath his feet as *Martha* lurches to the threshold. He touches the brakes with his left boot, easing up the power on the two right-hand engines, turning the lumbering bird left on to the runway. He lets her creep forward, prodding his right pedal to straighten her up and tidy up the tailwheel, gives a final little wiggle with his feet to make sure. Ahead the runway stretches to infinity, wide and grey, tapering to a point more than a mile away in the far-off distant trees. He's ready. Now.

'Say, Hoop,' Englehardt pipes up. Headphones are squashed down over his battered cap, they're wearing throat microphones, no oxygen masks. No need, they won't be going high. Englehardt is grinning. 'Tell me, did you ever slow-roll a B17?'

Although her brother Richard hotly denied it, Heather Stonybrook's first meeting with David Garrett was a set-up.

A wedding, in Holt, Norfolk, a bone-jarring two-hour trek in Richard's battered little Austin from her flat in Lincoln. He, Richard, was a subaltern in the Royal Norfolk Regiment, one of his closest friends was getting married, Richard was best man. 'You've absolutely got to come, old thing,' he insisted. 'I can't possibly pitch up without an escort. Battalion CO's coming, plus you've got to hear me do my speech – it's taken three weeks to write.' He blinked at her plaintively, like a soppy spaniel, exactly as he always had as a child. And, as always, she found him impossible to refuse. Two weeks later, against her better instincts, and wearing a hastily modified dress borrowed from a friend at the primary school where she worked, Heather found herself in the passenger seat of his little car, lurching up the drive of a grand country manor. Despite her reservations, and an inherent fear of formal social gatherings, she was none the less unable to deny the visceral thrill of anticipation that fluttered like a bird in her stomach. Had her capitulation been too willing? Had she agreed because, deep down, she hoped to encounter an indefinable presence, to fill an intangible absence? In the months and years that followed, the question would return to her again and again.

Why? It made no sense. She lacked for nothing. Her life was completely filled, meticulously organised, deeply satisfying. She had everything she wanted, much more, indeed, than many would have believed possible for a young woman of her years and modest background. At just twenty-five, when most of her contemporaries had already long since embraced domesticity, marriage and children, Heather had her profession, her flat and, most important of all, her hard-won and jealously guarded independence. It was this self-sufficiency that she valued above all else, and justifiably so, for in those pre-war years of institutionalised inequality and spiralling unemployment, she'd had to work hard for it. Empowered by a versatile and questioning intellect, encouraged by impecunious but far-sighted parents, and baffled by her peers' endless obsession with men and matters matrimonial, she forwent teenage parties and proto-romances in favour of study, qualification and self-betterment, naively optimistic that having attained the latter, the rest would surely follow.

But it didn't happen quite like that. She'd achieved much, through sheer hard work and determination. Her teaching was respected, valued work that she loved greatly. Her flat, although rented, and rather small, was nevertheless comfortable, centrally located and, best of all, hers alone. Beyond its door she filled her leisure hours with wide and varied interests and activities. She studied the piano, wandered the bookshops and galleries of the old city, went to recitals at the cathedral, attended evening classes in architecture and painting and literature. She compiled notes for a pamphlet she hoped to publish on Saxon churches.

She had gentlemen friends. Two of the earnest young teachers at school were regular callers. There was a brief dalliance with a literature professor at evening class. Another with an arty student type she met at a concert. Nothing perilous, of course, nothing too serious. Nothing lasting. She broke off with the literature professor the evening he confessed he was married. The art student turned out to be quite incapable of controlling his ardour and he too had to be dropped. And when one of the likeable young teachers from school became bothersome, mooning around her flat wringing his hands and begging tearfully to be allowed to 'penetrate the fortress of her heart and beyond', she found, almost regretfully, that it was painless to propose they see less of each other.

It was not that she didn't want more. Not that she didn't seek excitement, intimacy and risk, or have urges in that other, physical direction. It was just that all too quickly, and with depressing inevitability, relationships changed from exciting and intimate to onerous and isolating. Invariably she found herself looking forward to the return of her solitary but treasured independence. Yet the irony was it was the joy her independence brought her that she longed to share with someone else.

She was dithering, in other words. She knew it. And slipping into acceptance. Her life had everything but passion, and that was all there was to it. Its absence gaped, void-like, ahead of her, like a crevasse blocking a path. And then, just at the point where resignation began to settle about her like a comfortable old overcoat, her brother, sensing her growing isolation and with characteristic guilelessness, stepped in and introduced her to David Garrett.

That was 1940. A sudden lurch jolted her to the present. Something was wrong with her bicycle. It felt distinctly wobbly, as though the back wheel was loose. She braked to a halt and dismounted.

The back wheel *was* loose. In fact the frame was broken, one fork completely sheared from the weld under the rear mudguard. It was a miracle the whole thing hadn't collapsed beneath her. She fingered the break, calculating, a moist breeze plucking at the sleeve of her blouse. Something tiny rustled in the grass beside her, then a harvest mouse dropped to the dust and scurried across to the far side of the lane. It was about half a mile back to the cottage. The bicycle was unrideable, yet the back wheel still turned, albeit drunkenly, and the shopping basket on the handlebars was full. She'd just have to walk. She straightened up and began to push. As she did so she heard the endless distant crescendo of a bomber's engines.

The whole day of that Norfolk wedding, the next six months in fact, passed by her in a blur. Richard's friend's marriage was a full military affair; guard of honour, crossed swords, dress uniforms, gold braid and medals. There was even a fly-past, a lone Hurricane fighter swooping low over the skyward-pointing guests. Heather had never encountered so many dashingly handsome young men beneath one roof in her life. And they were all so polite, so gallant, so winningly attentive. But even amongst so many, David stood out from the crowd. Indeed, the crowd stood around David. She noticed him immediately, fair cheeks, hair the colour of ripe corn, a wide, smiling mouth, eyes that sparkled as he laughed. He was at the centre of a noisy group which included the bridegroom, the bridesmaids, the maid of honour and several others, all of whom, she noted, including the groom, seemed to be hanging on his every word.

'Come on, you, no wallflowering allowed.' Richard gripped her arm and steered her purposefully through the guests towards David's group. A moment later, his blue eyes gleaming like warm pools, he was stooping to kiss her hand.

Although she tried to ask, once or twice in the ensuing weeks, bemused and flattered at the intensity of his attention, she never did really find out what it was that drove him to want her so badly. On one of their few genuinely relaxed and undisturbed afternoons together, David, in rare reflective mood, his head lying in her lap amongst the wreckage of a picnic by the river, allowed her to feed him apple slices while he attempted to explain. It was something to do with the way she held herself, he said, munching pensively. Held herself in. And back. And apart. Her apartness.

'Sounds rather uncomfortable,' she teased. 'Like a contortionist.' But he was being serious, just for a second.

'You see, most of the girls I tended to socialise with, well, I wouldn't say they were necessarily forward, exactly, but sometimes they do, well, gush, rather. Do you know what I mean?' She did. She'd seen them. At the wedding and on more than one occasion since. Like moths at a candle.

'But you don't. Poise. That's the word. Poise. And grace. You've got it in spades, old girl, and that's what I love about you.' He reached up, caressing her cheek. 'Your poise. That and your neck, of course. Oh and your hair, and that darling little nose, and those lips.' He pulled her down to kiss him.

'Marry me?' he pleaded, for the tenth time that day.

Heather smiled, cupping his apple-smooth face in her hand. Madness. Utter madness, everywhere. The whole world going insane. And everything happening too fast. It was autumn, 1940. Months of phoney war had ended. First the sudden horror of Dunkirk, now total catastrophe lay waiting just across the English Channel. For weeks the flawless summer skies above them had raged with desperate conflict as Luftwaffe pilots struggled to wrench aerial dominance from their beleaguered RAF counterparts. Preparatory, everyone knew, to the inevitable German invasion. The word was on everyone's lips. Eastern Europe had fallen, Scandinavia, then even mighty France. Now there was nothing left except Britain, and no one to help. So, live for the day and damn the consequences. It had become the mantra of millions. Seize what little happiness you can, while you can, for disaster looms barely twenty miles over the horizon. 'Marry me, Heather, sweetheart. Please. I adore you. And only God knows how little time we may have left.'

It was folly, it was without logic, it flew in the face of everything she understood and believed in. She gazed down into his eyes. Those warm, liquid-blue pools. And she dived in.

It was almost two years ago. A Jeep pulled up beside her.

'May I help you, ma'am?' It was Finginger. A moment later he was lifting the bicycle into the back of the Jeep. Brushing the dirt from his hands, he clambered in beside her. 'We're all set,' he chirped, thumbing the starter.

'This really is too kind of you, um, Major,' Heather replied. 'But hardly necessary; I was practically home.'

'I know.' Finginger winked. He sped off in the direction of her cottage, one or two heads turning, she noted resignedly, as they passed. What do you know? Mrs Garrett, riding in a Jeep. With a Yank off the base. The word would spread quicker than flu in school.

'You do?'

'Yep. You're Heather Garrett, schoolteacher, of Walnut Tree Cottage, Dennington Road.'

'That's very impressive, Major, but, well, I'm afraid you have me at a disadvantage.'

'Scott, ma'am. Scott Finginger. And it's my job to find out things. I work in intelligence. I was on my way to visit you.'

Heather glanced across at the major. He was slender, about thirty-five, thinning grey hair above a cheerful, angular face. A small scar, white, worm-like, curled above his left eye. They were crossing the village green, forking right on to Dennington Road. Two old men were sitting outside the Fleece, waiting for it to open.

'You see, there's a dance, next Saturday week. On base. We're inviting several local dignitaries. I wondered whether you might like to come. As a guest of the 520th. And as my guest.'

Heather laughed. 'Well, Major, I'm obviously delighted, very honoured, to be thought of as a "dignitary", although I hardly feel I fit the part, and I'm really deeply flattered that you wanted to ask me, but—'

She broke off. Gerald Garrett's car was sitting outside her cottage. She could see Gerald at the wheel. Rosamund was standing by the front gate, looking up at the empty house. As the Jeep drew up the hill Rosamund turned towards them.

'You're married. I know that too. To Brigadier Garrett's son, an officer in the infantry. He's MIA, isn't he? Missing in action. Pacific Theatre. You have my sincerest condolences and best wishes for his safe return. And it goes without saying that you also have my complete assurance that you have nothing to fear, Mrs Garrett. I am an honourable man.'

'I believe that, Major, um, Scott.' The Jeep lurched to a halt outside the cottage. Finginger leapt out and began unloading the bicycle. The drone of approaching engines was growing louder.

'Well, ah, good afternoon, then, dear,' Rosamund blustered, standing to one side. Finginger wheeled the bicycle past her. 'We only popped by to see how you— I say, what has happened? You haven't crashed, I hope?'

'Nothing has happened of any consequence at all. My bicycle has broken and Major Finginger here kindly gave me a lift home.'

'Well, ask him to put it in the boot of Gerald's car, for goodness' sake. We'll have one of the men see to its repair.'

'No, I'll see to its repair. You do far too much for me as it is.'

'Oh. Well, yes, of course. As you wish.' Rosamund blinked at her, twin spots of pink colouring her cheeks.

'Major Finginger here has invited me to a dance next Saturday. On the base. Isn't that a kind thought?'

'A dance? Well, yes, but Heather—'

At that instant *Misbehavin Martha* rocketed over their heads like a flung thunderbolt, so fast that they felt the ground shake beneath their feet, and so low even Finginger ducked. Rosamund screeched inaudibly, her face contorted with terror. Gerald's mustachioed face, puce, strained at the window of his car. Finginger and Heather, the bomber's slipstream plucking at their sleeves, turned as one to follow its passing. As they all stared, *Martha*, tail on to them, rose slightly, paused, then, with agonising yet majestic slowness, began to roll. Tilting, further and further on to its side, until the wings were vertical, and yet still the vast machine rolled, impossibly, slowly, right over on to its back, then still on, without stopping, in one smooth, slow rotation until it was upright again. A second later it vanished behind a clump of trees.

'What the bloody hell does that lunatic think he is doing?' Gerald was hauling himself from his car.

'Didn't know a B17 could do that.' Fininger whistled, hands on hips.

'It's an absolute outrage. Somebody could have been killed.'

'Who was that, Scott?'

'That was Major Eugene Englehardt. He's checking out the new pilot for Crew 19 today.' The bomber reappeared in the middle distance, banking steeply to the south, wheels lowered for landing. 'I guess he passed.'

'Got you this.' Billy produced the small paper-wrapped package from his pocket and placed it quietly on the kitchen table.

'What's that then, dear?' Maggie turned from the sink. The package was stained with blood. She wiped her hands on her apron and began to unwrap. Outside the light was failing, a chill breeze stirred last year's leaves in the corner of the yard, the chickens fretted half-heartedly in their hutch. In the fields, man and machine worked on. Harvest was coming in at last, the corn flowing in an unstoppable flood, like a spate river to the sea, until it was done. At his chair by the range, his feet encased in ancient slippers, hands hanging limp at his sides, Percy snored softly, his white head nodding on his chest, his cat curled on his lap.

'Pork! Good heavens, pork chops? But, Billy, where on earth did you get them? We've had the meat this week. It's not Friday, is it?' Maggie stared down at the two pale cuts lying in her hand, her face a mix of suspicion and wonderment. She sniffed them quickly, inhaling, eyes closed, like a wine-taster nosing the glass. 'These are Bert Day's chops, from up the road here. I'd know them anywhere.' She gazed down at them lovingly, then her face hardened. 'All right. Where did you get them then? Please tell me you didn't pinch these, Billy.'

'No, Mrs H. Honest I didn't. They're a present, like. For you and Mr H. For your tea.' His voice was unusually subdued, eyes down. His fingers picked pine splinters from the edge of the table. 'I got them off the ration.'

'The ration? But how?'

He looked up at last, the ghost of a glimmer in his eyes. 'Easy, Mrs H. Old Mr Day, his eyesight's dodgy, and 'e never looks that close at the ration book anyhow. Also, he uses pencil when he cancels the coupons. You can rub it out with a school rubber, then go back again a few days after, late on – when the light's going's best – and use the same coupon again.'

'But Billy, that's dishonest. You shouldn't be doing it.'

'Why not? Lennie's mum does it, and the Frys. Fisks too, I'll bet.'

'The Frys? Doris Fry fiddles her coupons? Are you sure?'

Heavy footsteps were crossing the yard. A moment later two figures appeared at the back door: Americans, in uniform, shirts and ties, polished shoes. Billy, with a start, recognised them. Two of the crew from *Misbehavin Martha* – from hut twelve: the tall one with the Polish name who always picked on him, and the little blond ball turret gunner, Ringwald.

'Good evening, ma'am,' said Lajowski, bowing towards Maggie. They were wearing the little rectangular uniform caps that perched at an angle on their heads. 'We're real sorry to disturb you, we were looking for Mr and Mrs Howden's place. Would this be it?'

'Oh, er, well, yes it would be,' Maggie stammered, still clutching the chops. 'It is, yes.'

'What's up, lads?' Ray Howden squeezed past them into the kitchen with barely a glance. He went to the sink, rolling his shirtsleeves. There was a polite knock at the front door. 'Just saw your teacher coming up the lane, Billy. Expect that'll be her. Well go on, boy, run and let her in. What you got there then, Mag?'

'Oh, it's, er, nothing, I . . . Ray, love, these two young men were looking for us.' She nodded pointedly towards the doorway. At last Ray turned to them, as though noticing them for the first time. He looked them up and down, drying his hands on a dishcloth.

'And what can we do for you two lads?'

'Well, sir, my name is Emmett Lajowski, and this here is Kid, I mean Eldon, Ringwald.' The two of them, Ringwald a foot shorter than Lajowski and visibly nervous, stood shoulder to shoulder in the open doorway. 'We're here to see lucky charm, ah, that is, young Billy. Well, I am, anyhows.'

'Are you indeed,' Ray said flatly. He turned to Ringwald. 'And who are you here to see?'

Heather appeared, following Billy into the kitchen. 'Oh, goodness, please excuse me. I'm so sorry to trouble you.'

'Mrs Garrett! Well, this is a nice surprise.' Maggie hurried forward, began pulling out chairs from the table, the bloody paper package still in her hand. 'Look, why don't we all sit down. I'll put the kettle on.'

'No, Mrs Howden, that's most terribly kind, but you have visitors. I just popped by to ask your husband whether he could possibly take a look at my bicycle. The frame's broken and I'm afraid it needs welding. Billy here said that your husband does cycle repairs, so I thought I'd drop it in. I'm so sorry, did I say something . . .'

Percy's snores seemed much louder in the sudden hush. Heather, confused, looked from one face to the other. They were all, Billy and the Howdens, staring at the taller of the two Americans standing in the doorway. Looking at his hand. He was holding a child's silver spoon between finger and thumb.

'Tracked it down for you, kid. Kind of a peace offering, know what I mean?'

There was a crash at the front door and Claire burst in. 'Old Vic's frying!' she cried breathlessly, then her hand flew to her mouth. 'Eldon!'

Maggie and Ray exchanged glances. 'Eldon?'

'Did summun say old Vic's frying?' Percy, hacking loudly, was already hauling himself from his chair. 'We'd better get going then, 'fore he runs out.'

'Vic? Opening the chip shop? Are you sure, love? I mean, how?'

'His son, Bobby,' Claire sputtered. 'He's on the boats at

Lowestoft, dropped a load of cod and skate in this afternoon, on the quiet. Plaice too, Deirdre says. She said Vic's been hoarding stocks of old lard for months, greengrocer managed to get hold of half a sack of spuds off the base, so Vic's opening the shop, just for tonight. Well come on then! What are we waiting for? Fish and chips!'

T/Sgt Eldon Ringwald 520th BG

Dear Mom and Pop,

Well what a day! First off, we got assigned a new pilot at last, Lt John A. Hooper, to replace poor old Rudy. We didn't get to meet Lt Hooper yet but our Squadron Commander Major Ingelhard checked him out good in the ship and so tomorrow we all get to go back on ops training together. Can't tell you how good THAT feels at last, though you can imagine, me and the guys are raring to go! Tonight, me and Polecat Lajowski had a truly amazing time. Get this, we ate REAL English fish and chips. No kidding. We had to go into the village to see some of the village folk about some things, anyway there daughter, whos a real respectable girl name of Clare, comes in hollering about fish and chips and so we all hurry like crazy down to the fish and chips place together. It was all done in secret like, what with the blackout and all the rationing and so on, but when we got there, the entire damn village was out on the street, all talking and laughing together in hush voices. Everyone, even the village policeman, and the pastor, mothers with babies, everyone, the old and the young. The fish and chips place was just this old guy's back door and we had to bring our own newspapers to carry it in which is what they do with fish and chips. I tell you, I NEVER ate anything quite like it. Kind of greasy, a little, and the fish was a little too rare for my liking and kind of bony, but the chips were what we call fries only bigger and kind of softer but I swear they were practically the best things I ever ate in my whole life. The best thing I ever ate over here, that's for sure.

It was truly magical, all the village people just standing out in the road eating their fish and chips in the moonlight together, smiling and laughing, even singing some, in hush voices. It was like there was no war, no hardship, no rationing, like they had no cares in the whole world. Just for a few minutes. I felt real privileged to be invited along. Emmett too. A little homesick as well I don't mind admitting tho' I'm not sure why. We walked back to base together hardly talking. Clare's a fine girl, youd like her.

Well that's all for now, I'll write again soon. Write me. Your loving son, Eldon.

Chapter 6

'Navigator to pilot.'

'Go ahead, navigator.'

'Turn left, heading two three zero degrees.'

'Two three zero? Are you quite sure about that?'

'Ah, yes, pilot, pretty sure.'

'You're pretty sure.'

'Well, yes.'

'Okay. Turning left on to two three zero.' Raising eyebrows at his co-pilot, Irv Underwood, Hooper reached out to the instrument panel, twirled the heading knob on the direction indicator on to the revised bearing, then hauled the bomber over into a steep left turn, rolling her nose level exactly on the new course. Within seconds another familiar voice came over his headphones.

'Say, Captain?'

'What is it now, Beans?'

'I thought we was supposed to be heading for Scotland, sir.'

'We are, Sergeant. Now could you please just keep it quiet on the intercom. Important messages only.'

'You got it, Cap. Sorry about that. Only enquiring.'

Silence descended once more, for about a minute. Hooper waited.

'Navigator to pilot.'

'Yes, Spitz, go ahead.'

'I, ah, when I said two three zero, I might have meant three two zero.'

'You might have meant.'

'Yes. No, well I guess I did mean three two zero. I must have made a mistake reading the heading off the plot. Sorry about that.'

A chorus of groans floated over the intercom. Somebody unidentifiable blew a raspberry.

'Holy shit,' muttered another.

'Told you we was lost,' said a third.

'Right, now you can all just cut it out back there!' Hooper snapped. 'Any more spurious intercom chatter and there's going to be serious trouble, okay? Now then, pilot to navigator.'

'Navigator here. Look, pilot, sorry about that. I must have just gotten in a mess reading off—'

'It's okay, Spitzer, forget it. Here's what I want you to do. Take your time, go back through the plot, double check your position, then verify it with a beacon fix from Sergeant Via in radio. Then I want you to plot a fresh course for the Moray gunnery range, in your own time, and when you're ready, pass it on to me. In the meantime, I'll just take up the old heading. Now have you got that?'

143

'Got it. Thanks, pilot.'

'Radio here. Did somebody call me?'

'No, Via, you idiot, pilot was talking to navigator. Don't you ever listen?'

'Why don't you just mind your goddamn business, Tork! I thought the lieutenant was calling me on the intercom.'

'No, ah, radio, it's okay, pilot here. Navigator will be calling you in a while for a beacon fix, that's all.'

'Okay, got it, pilot. See, Tork? He *was* calling me, you asshole.'

'You come down here to the tail and say that.'

'That's enough, everybody! Quiet down now.'

Another silence. Another minute.

'Upper turret to pilot.'

Hooper sighed. 'What is it now, Lajowski?'

'Sir, what does spurious mean?'

And so it went on. After another hour, nearly four into the training mission, Crew 19's third within a week, *Martha*, descending cautiously, broke through a thin undercast. To Loren Spitzer's audible relief, two thousand feet below them lay the slate-grey waters of the Moray Firth. With it came the plaudits.

'Way to go, Spitz, baby, right on the money!' Tork.

'Well it's about time, if you don't mind me saying so.' Via.

'I told you we wasn't lost. I did. Didn't I tell you that?' Beans.

'Ball turret to pilot. Sorry about this, sir, but I gotta use the pee tube.' Ringwald.

'God's sakes, Ringwald, didn't I tell you to go before?' Lajowski.

'Be quiet! Everyone. Right now!' Hooper waited until silence settled once more. 'Okay, now, right then. There it is. Good work, navigator, we got here in the end. Now listen up everyone, here's the drill. The drogue target will be coming by in a few minutes. The drogue is a large oblong canvas banner, painted white. It is towed through the air on a wire a thousand yards behind the towing aircraft. You can't miss it. The towing aircraft will bring it by at fifteen hundred feet, flying straight and level, north to south. We will make two head-on passes on it, one down either side, so that everyone gets to practise their shooting. Do *not* shoot until the towing aircraft is safely past us. Remember to deflect your firing well ahead of the target, keep your bursts short and controlled. Okay, now, does anyone have any—'

'There it is! Jesus, right over there, look, look, three o'clock!' Immediately, the road-drill rattle of machine-gun fire hammered over the open intercom. Long, wild bursts from at least three of *Martha*'s eight firing positions. Simultaneously, everyone began shouting. Hooper, completely unable to break in over the mayhem, the gloved fingers of one hand rubbing tiredly at the bridge of his nose, waited for the frenzy to subside. But it never did. Beneath his feet the bomber's airframe trembled on and on from the guns' recoil. Finally, gesturing angrily to Underwood to take over the controls, he tore off his headphones and clambered from his seat.

Emmett Lajowski, standing in his upper turret directly behind and above the pilots, was still shooting. Hooper punched him hard in the thigh as he passed. There was a muffled yelp and the shooting stopped. Hooper continued aft without pause, climbing through into the bomb bay, *Martha*'s four dummy two-hundred-pound bombs rattling in their racks. Beyond the bomb bay, in the radio room, Gerry Via was standing at his gun-slit in the roof. There were spent shell cases in the hopper beside him, but he had stopped firing. 'Couldn't see a damn thing!' He shrugged sheepishly.

'Then what the hell were you firing at!' Hooper pushed past the radio operator and on through the bulkhead door into the aircraft's waist. A heavy vibration beneath his feet signalled another burst of firing. Ringwald, sealed into his ball turret under the bomber, was still shooting. Hooper snatched a fire-axe from the bulkhead, and with a dull clang, like a muffled church bell, brought the wooden handle down hard on the turret's curved lid. The shooting stopped.

That just left Beans. He was at the left-hand waist window, leaning right through it, wrenching at the charging handle of his machine-gun, which appeared to be jammed. Empty shell-cases swirled at his feet in a thick brassy carpet. Behind him, the new right-hand waist gunner, Keissling, a toothpick between his lips, watched, arms folded, as Beans, cursing furiously, attacked his lifeless weapon. Keissling looked up as Hooper entered. Hesitantly, he stepped forward, tapping Beans on the shoulder.

Beans turned. 'Goddamn son of a bitch's jammed, God damn it!' He caught sight of Hooper's expression. 'Uh, the gun, sir. You see. It's jammed. You see. Sir.'

'Correction, Sergeant. The gun is empty. And in any case the gun's breech has almost certainly seized up through excessive heat. Both these matters are directly attributable to the fact that somehow you have managed to expend your entire ammunition allowance, that is enough rounds of fifty calibre, I would remind you, to last an eight-hour mission over enemy territory, in a little over five minutes. As a consequence, the gun has suffered severe heat damage, is probably beyond repair, and will almost certainly have to be scrapped.'

There was less talking over the intercom on the way home. Hooper stayed in the nose for much of the flight, crouched next to Loren Spitzer as the navigator plotted a fresh route back from Scotland. Then he stood at the shoulder of Crew 19's new bombardier, John Holland, while, hunched into *Martha*'s plexiglas nose dome, he peered down through the viewfinder of his Norden bombsight, guiding the bomber towards their practice target. Suddenly, seconds before bomb-release, he straightened up from the bombsight, pulled a paper sack from his pocket and vomited into it. To Hooper's astonishment, he then resumed his position, smiling sheepishly, and toggled the electrical switches to release their dummy bombs. Nothing happened. *Martha* flew on, her bombs firmly locked in their racks above her gaping bomb bay doors. Holland, face perplexed, stared down through the viewfinder, then up at the switch panel at his side. Then, idiotically, back down through the viewfinder, as though the bombs might yet magically appear. Seconds ticked by.

'Master release?' Hooper prompted at last. He rubbed tiredly at his face.

'Master release! Forgot the damn master release.' Immediately the bombardier threw the switch and toggled the release buttons once more, watching through the viewfinder with a satisfied 'There they go!' as the four bombs tumbled earthwards, to impact at least two miles beyond the practice target marked out on the Essex mudflats eight thousand feet below.

At last, seven hours after *Martha*'s wheels had left the runway at Bedenham, Hooper clambered back on to the flight deck preparatory for landing. Irving Underwood, his face pale and perspiring, seemed relieved to see him.

'Everything okay, Irv?' Hooper began strapping himself into his seat.

'Uh, fine, fine, thanks. Would you like to take the controls now?'

'No. I think I'd like you to bring us in today. Come in overhead the airfield at eight hundred feet in the normal way, then peel off into a left-hand circuit and then straight in for landing. Take your time, everything by the numbers. I'll call the checklist for you.'

'I, uh, if it's okay with you, Captain, I'd rather not bring her in. Not today.'

'No? How so?'

'I . . . well, I didn't feel so good when I got up this morning. Kind of a bad headache, migraine, I reckon, or neuralgia maybe. Probably nothing, but perhaps it would be best if you land the ship. Wouldn't want to bend anything, would I?' He forced a sickly smile. Hooper, adjusting his seat straps, regarded his co-pilot. In their three flights together so far, Underwood had only ever handled *Martha* in level flight. He had yet to perform a take-off, or a landing. It occurred to Hooper that he probably hadn't done so since *Martha*'s ill-fated first mission when, caked from head to foot in his pilot's flesh and blood, and shocked beyond all capacity for reason, he'd had to be forcibly coaxed from the flight deck and into the waiting ambulance.

A navigator who couldn't navigate. An air-sick bombardier who could barely bomb. Undisciplined, wildly trigger-happy gunners who couldn't hit fish in a barrel. Now a co-pilot who couldn't fly. It was hopeless. Was never going to work, not in a million years. 'You guys are flying supernumerary today,' Gene Englehardt had told him that morning. 'You can head off on your practice mission after we've formed up.' Supernumerary. It meant that they took off with all the rest of the bombers. But at the back of the line, like the class dunce. Then they followed them as far as the RP, the rendezvous point, off Clacton, ready to slot into the formation in case anyone had to turn back with a mechanical problem. Mercifully, none did, and the formation set out across the sea to Hanover without them. Hooper was lucky, he knew; supernumeraries were quite often called upon to fly the mission.

'They're just not ready, Gene,' he'd protested at the briefing.

'Sorry, Hoop,' Englehardt had replied. 'They've got to be.'

For a moment, just for a second, his mind, unbidden, drifted to another time, another bomber, another crew. His first crew. Smooth, tight-knit, harmonised, efficient. Completely in tune with their work, their aircraft and each other. Like a single, well-oiled machine. A cold wave of long-ing, a dragging undertow of loss, swept over him suddenly, and with unexpected force, like a rogue wave from an icy sea. Its power shocked him. He struggled from it, almost reluc-tantly, and was left feeling numb, and full of dread. It was hopeless. Couldn't be done. He should have taken the medical discharge. He reached for the control column. 'Okay, Irv,' he said quietly. 'I'll bring her in today. We can talk about this later.' Underwood's hands fell from the controls without a word. He turned his face away to his side window.

A moment later a voice came over the intercom.

'Radio to pilot.'

Hooper drew a long breath. 'Yes, Via, this is pilot. What is it?'

'Well, uh, fighting, sir. In the waist.'

'What's that? Via? What are you talking about?'

'Well, sir, Sergeant Tork came up from the tail position, to use the pee tube, sir. And on his way back something must have happened between Sergeant Tork and Sergeant Beans. And now, well, sir, they're fighting. Sir. On the floor. In the waist.'

'Ray, Raymond? I brought your tea, love.' Maggie peered into the gaping maw of the shop. Ray was right at the back, sweeping up. She looked around. It was unusually quiet inside, and tidy, and empty. And something smelled different. Fire, she realised. There was no fire in the forge. No face-prickling heat, no acrid tang of coal-smoke, no hot iron the colour of ripe cherries. The forge's brick hearth lay neatly swept, cold and bare. It was the first time she could remember it like that in months. 'Having a clear out, then?' she enquired lightly.

Ray took the mug, parking his broom against a wall. Heather Garrett's bicycle, its broken fork unmended, stood discarded behind a door. 'Yes, well, what with business not being so bright just now, thought I'd take the chance to clean up a bit before the autumn rush sets in.'

Maggie nodded, hugging a thin cotton cardigan closer to her shoulders. She shifted on her feet. A gravel chip, entering through the split instep of her shoe, had lodged uncomfortably beneath her heel. Overhead, densely leaved branches of a huge elm hissed and swung in the breeze. 'I hear there's a big new foundry opened up at Walter Skeet's garage in Framlingham. Taking in a lot of the agricultural machines repair work, I suppose.'

'What of it?'

'Nothing, love, just heard it, that's all.'

'It doesn't matter. Folk round here still like the old ways. There's always been a blacksmith's shop in this village – two, once upon a time. There always will be. It's part of the way of things.'

'Ray. The way of things, it can change, you know. Quicker than we realise. This war, it's changing everything. Fields don't lie fallow any more, Ministry wants every scrap of spare land ploughed up and planted, year in and round. And quick too. There's subsidies to be had on tractors, Jean Bolsover told me. Their horses are going, she said, her Ted says one tractor can do the work of three horse-teams and twice as fast. Soon they'll all be gone, he says.'

'Ted Bolsover's a bloody fool then. There'll always be horses. Always have been, always will be.'

'Ray, just because there's always been something—' She broke off, a wave of dizzy nausea sweeping over her suddenly. She felt icy cold, then hot. She closed her eyes until it passed. The flushes, Dr Chillaman said. Perfectly normal for a woman at her time of life. But it wasn't fair. She wasn't ready for 'her time of life' yet. It was too much. Everything was coming apart, just when it needed to be staying closest together. Claire, sullen and secretive, hardly spoke to them any more. Percy grew more unreachable by the day; Ray, too. Hurting and distant. Now Billy. A minute ago, standing alone by the sink in the kitchen, she'd burst into tears, for no reason at all. And every reason under the sun.

'Mag? Maggie? You all right, girl?' She felt his hand on her arm.

She nodded, forced a wan smile. 'Ray, love. Billy—'

The hand left her, reaching for the broom once more. 'He's got to go, Mag. I can't be doing with it any more. He's thieving, lying, deceiving. He skips school, swindles the ration, runs black-market fiddles up the base. And God knows what else he gets up to that we don't know about. He's a bad lot and he's got to go back.'

'Back? But back where?'

'Back home, of course. To his rich dad, the big house in the city and that hush-hush job at the Bank of England he keeps telling us about.'

'But you don't really believe any of that, do you?'

''Course not! That's the whole point. He can't be trusted. That's why he's got to go.'

'It's just, like, his way of coping. He just wants to be some-one. He desperately needs to belong.'

'Not to us, he doesn't. And that's just it. He's not ours, so he's not our problem. Sorry, Mag, but he's had every chance and my mind's made up. I've already been on to that blasted local evacuee co-ordinator woman; she can sort him out. Send him back home or find him another billet. But he's not staying here.'

Anger flashed in her brown eyes, suddenly, like fire in summer bracken. 'All right then! Do it! Send him away, if that's what you want, and I hope it makes you happy. But don't blame me if your life is all the emptier for it. And don't blame him neither. It's not his fault, don't you see? Not his fault there's a bloody war on. Not his fault that your poor brothers died in the trenches, that your mum passed away of a broken heart and that we lost little Stephen. It's not his fault your dad's losing his mind and you're losing a daughter that don't hardly speak to us no more. It's not Billy's fault your business is going under, though God knows if only you'd listen to him sometimes, he's got more of a nose for it than the rest of us put together. All right, he makes up fibs and pinches things and fiddles the ration and God knows what else. He's just making do, the same as the rest of us. Surviving, as best he can. Because that's all he understands.' She was crying now, big rolling tears spilling on to her cheeks. 'You had it once, Ray. A fire like his in your belly. Ambition. You were going to take on the world.' She gestured towards the dust-covered wrought-iron gate propped against the wall. 'That's why I loved you. Why I married you. There wasn't nothing we couldn't do, you said. Nothing. And I believed you.'

'This one.'

'Um, let's see. It's signed – I can't read it properly, the writing's terrible – Belly? No, it can't be. Betty! That's it. It's from someone called Betty. It says dear Maggie, hope you are keeping well. What did the doctor have. To say. Oh, I get it. What did the doctor have to say? About your turns. Bob and me are doing fine—'

Billy snatched the letter away, returning it carefully to its envelope. 'It's all right. Betty is Mrs H's sister. What about this one?' He handed her another letter. Ruby took it, eyeing him doubtfully. They were in the old mill, sitting side by side on up-ended beer crates. He was wearing his Yank mechanic's overalls, the ones with his name on, and his army baseball hat, as usual. On the door-table before them, a water-filled Spam can steamed gently above a mess-tin cooker. 'What do you want to know for anyway, Billy?'

'Never mind that. It's, um, it's secret, like. To do with intelligence, that's what. Military intelligence. Go on, Rube, read it.'

Ruby tilted the letter towards the cobweb-covered window, quickly scanning the lines. 'It's from the Electric. Some guff about interruptions to services. Why don't you read them yourself, if it's all so bloomin' 'ush-'ush?'

'I told you, Rube. Eyesight, remember? I've got dodgy eyesight.'

'Doesn't seem to stop you playing football. And you can spot one of your bloomin' bombers from ten miles away.'

'It's only dodgy for the reading, like. I told you. We couldn't afford the specs, back home.'

'I thought you said you was rich.'

'We are! Was. That is, we were, before.'

'Before your mum and dad got killed by them bombs, you mean.'

She watched him nod, his eyes falling to the Howdens' letters on the table. Above them a pair of house martins flitted tirelessly in and out of their fortress nest high in the mill's rotting roof timbers. Billy'd been unusually quiet the last few days, Ruby reflected. Subdued. Tentatively, she reached out a hand to his knee. 'It's all right,' she soothed. But he just went on nodding and staring. 'Bill? Shall we go up the woods for a bit? Would you like that?'

He walked along the lane beside her in pensive silence. Passing the Howdens' cottage, and checking briefly that the coast was clear, he stuffed their mail back through the letter box. The house was deserted, the big barn doors to the blacksmith's shop closed and padlocked. There was no sign of Ray or Maggie. A little further on, Ruby slipped her hand into his. It felt limp and lifeless.

'What about that Claire then?' she asked cheerfully.

'What about her?'

'Is she having it off with that Yank then? That little blond tail gunner from your plane, what's it called, *Misbehaving Mary*?'

His hand pulled away. 'It's *Martha*, Rube. And it's Technical Sergeant Ringwald, and he's not the tail gunner, he's the ball turret gunner. And, while you're at it, you don't never call them planes, it ain't done. They're airplanes, or aeroplanes, or they're aircraft. Never, ever planes, see? And as for Claire bloomin' Howden, how the hell should I know what she gets up to? She don't tell me nothing.' She hardly spoke to him at all any more in fact. Wolfed her breakfast and pedalled straight off to work at the hardware store in Fram. And in the mornings, through the floorboards, she just threw back the sheets and scampered straight out of view, clutching her nightgown to her chest. As if she knew.

'Sorry. Only asking.' They walked on. On both sides of the lane, visible for miles in every direction between gaps in the tall hedgerow, pointed corn-stooks stood waiting in the newly cut stubble, like villages of Indian tepees. After half a mile the field on their right ended abruptly at a wall of trees. A narrow track beside the lane led into the woods. As they turned on to it, the ceaseless rumbling of the airfield in the distance grew nearer.

'I got to pop on base,' he said. 'Little bit of business to tend to. It's all right, you can come too, there won't be any trouble.'

'As you please.' He seemed to have forgotten their wood-land tryst. He seemed to have forgotten everything. They trudged deeper into the woods, the air dank and still. Some of the leaves were beginning to turn, she saw.

'And what about your mates?' she went on, to break the silence. 'You don't seem to mess about with them so much these days.'

They were wasters, mostly, Billy had long since concluded. Lennie excepted. A bunch of useless dullards. Never wanted to do anything. Anything useful, that is. Anything that might require a little bit of effort. Or organising. Or work. All they wanted to do was hang about the back door of the Fleece, drinking beer dregs from the empties and cadging soggy Woodbine butts off the old farts as they traipsed back and forth to the privy. Or spend an entire afternoon throwing stones in the river. Or try and cop a sixpenny feel off Shirley Fry out in the Frys' Anderson shelter. Or, worse still, try and cop a feel off Ruby Moody. Hesitantly, his fingers found her hand once more, circled it, squeezed, a little.

'Rube—'

'What was that! Billy! Did you hear it? That noise, what the hell was it?'

'What noise?' She was pulling him to her, and for a moment he thought she was having him on, that she was suddenly going to plant one of her sloppy kisses on him. But her eyes were wide with fright, alert, switching about, searching the woods like a startled doe's. She was moving behind him, pressing against his back.

'That! That rustling noise. It's coming from over there somewhere, in them bushes. What is it?'

Billy heard it, thirty yards away, movement in the bushes. 'It's nothing, Rube. Probably just a badger, or rabbits or something. Don't worry about it. Ow!' Her fingers were pinching the skin of his arms beneath the fatigues; he could hear her breathing, fast and shallow, on his neck. 'Shall I go have a look?'

'No! Don't you dare go leaving me, Billy Street. Come on, let's get going. I hate this place. How far is it to the bloomin' base?'

They ran, crashing headlong through the undergrowth like hunted deer. Ten minutes later, breathless and bedraggled, giggling nervously like children after a dare, they emerged behind a hangar and stepped on to the base.

Ruby was amazed at the transformation in him. In the space of just a few seconds he changed completely. He seemed to grow taller, and older, stand straighter, his head higher. He took longer strides as he walked, so that she had to hurry to keep up with him as he marched around the perimeter track towards a row of huts. Americans spoke to him, said hello as they passed, as though he was an old friend. As though he belonged there.

'Say, Bill, how you doing?'

'Billy! Good to see you.'

'Hey, Private Street, aren't you going to introduce us to the beautiful young lady?'

'Bill, there you are, I need to see you. Catch you later?'

'Wait here,' he said, pausing outside one of the huts. The number eight was stencilled on the door. He disappeared behind it. A moment later he was back, striding purposefully towards the next. 'Dogs. They all want dogs. God knows why, when they just run away again. But then that's the good part.'

'It is?'

'Yeah, dogs are a doddle. You see, they're not supposed to keep pets in the huts, although they do, there's hundreds of 'em. But when one goes missing they can't report it. I'm forever finding the buggers, wandering in the woods, or scrounging for scraps. I just keep rounding them up and selling them to the next bloke.'

'But don't they know?'

'Rube, look at the size of this place.' He gestured around at the airfield. 'It's huge. Hal Knyper says there's more than three thousand people living here. There's bars and shops and canteens and things. A hospital, libraries and stuff. They've even got a cinema and a kind of concert hall place. Nobody gives a toss about a few mangy mongrels.' They'd arrived at another hut. This time he held the door open for her to pass. 'I've sold one dog five times, so far.'

'Bill!' A young man was at a table. He stood up when he saw Ruby, hastily pulling a forage cap from his head. He had curly black hair. 'You made it, great.'

'Sergeant, um, Clark, isn't it? What can I do for you? Hal said it was urgent.'

'Not urgent, but, well, delicate. Kind of. There's this girl. She works in the village. In the post office stores. I don't know her name, but she's kind of brunette, real pretty . . .'

Billy held up a hand. 'See what I can do. Got the Strikes?' Two packets of cigarettes changed hands, and a moment later he and Ruby were outside once more.

Ruby looked perplexed. 'That's Madge you were talking about with that man. Madge Bolton.'

'I know that.'

'But what about her?'

'Look. He fancies her, right? And wants to meet her. So, I go and tell her and, if she wants to, I fix it up for them.'

'But she's engaged to that farm labourer bloke over Stradbroke way.'

'I know that too. But that's her business. My business is just to tell her that one of Hal's mechanics thinks she's pretty and wants to meet her. That's all I do, and it's worth two packs of Lucky Strikes. If she says yes, it's worth two more.'

'But you don't smoke!'

'Neither does he.' He stopped suddenly. 'Ruby, girl. You don't get it, do you? This isn't for me, this is for business. A puppy dog'll fetch five bob which'll get you an inner tube for a bike, a large catering tin of peas, a stack of girly mags, a photo of Jesus or even one of them poncey gramophone records by that deaf German bloke.'

'Beethoven?'

'That's him. A bit scratched of course, but otherwise in good enough nick. Two packs of Strikes'll go a bomb in the village, especially down the Fleece of a Saturday night. The old boys are gasping for 'em, they just can't get decent cigs any more. It's how it goes, Rube. People need something, I trade with 'em to help them get it.' He broke off. They'd arrived at the next hut, number six. A scruffy-looking bicycle was parked outside. Billy fingered it. 'That's a bit peculiar.'

The hut was long and narrow, like all the others, a dozen beds down both sides. Men lounged on a few of them. Reading, playing cards, writing letters. Several others were empty, yet littered above and below with their owners' unmade bedding, clothes, magazines, baseball mitts, candy wrappers, every square inch of wall behind them papered with family photos, letters and pin-up girls. But towards the far end, one row of six beds stood empty, freshly made, their blankets neatly tucked, clean white linen on the pillows, the walls behind them bare, the floor beneath swept spotless. Clean, aseptic, devoid of all signs of human occupation. Ready. Like an empty hospital ward, Ruby thought. Nearby, two airmen were feeding papers into a flaming pot-bellied stove set on a concrete plinth in the middle of the floor. They looked up as she and Billy entered. Then went back to burning their papers.

'Where's Sergeant Boonebose?' Billy asked.

'Hanover,' one of the men murmured, his eyes flickering orange.

'What? All of them? Everyone from *Goin' South*?'

'Crashed and burned. Ten minutes short of the IP. No 'chutes.'

The two men didn't even look up. None of the men in the hut did, their carefully composed expressions of casual indifference inadequately concealing their shock, grief and fear. Silence, save for the crackle of dead men's papers, fell over them all. Nobody seemed to know what to do, or say, like poorly rehearsed actors abandoned on a stage.

Billy, too, was disbelieving. 'But, well, that's my bike. Outside. Sergeant Boonebose hasn't finished paying me for it.'

'Take it.'

Billy was staring at the floor six feet in front of him, jaw set, eyes fixed in a slight frown. Ruby, bewildered, standing at his side, could see that his fists were tightly clenched. She plucked lightly at his sleeve. 'Billy?'

'No,' he said, turning for the door. 'You take it. I don't want it.'

That Saturday evening, Scott Finginger was outside Heather's cottage precisely at eight. He peeled off his cap and stood back, tugging down the hem of his Eisenhower uniform jacket, wiping dust from his fiercely polished shoes on to the back of his trousers, feeling for the smooth fold of his tie where it tucked inside his shirt between the regulation third and fourth buttons. Through the door, he heard the muffled thump of feet on stairs.

Heather hurried down into the hall, stretching fingers into white cotton gloves purchased especially, and at considerable expense, from Mrs Campbell's haberdashery that morning. They felt strange: tight, formal, old-fashioned. Dignitary-like, she hoped. She stopped by the hall table to collect her handbag, her eye catching her face in the mirror. Her hair was down, curling loose about her shoulders but fastened at the side with a tortoiseshell clip. She'd applied make-up, a little, for that was all there was in the drawer, to her eyes and lips, and a tiny dab of ancient, dubious-smelling scent to her throat. She wore a knee-length yellow summer dress with little matching shoes, a white woollen cardigan with the silver butterfly brooch David had given her pinned to it. Her legs were bare, her only pair of stockings holed beyond salvation. It was not quite the desired effect, she concluded. Whatever that was. But it would just have to do. 'Local dignitary,' she muttered, reaching for the door.

She needn't have worried. The venue, a large wooden hall on the base, gaily decorated with paper streamers, posters and flags, was packed to the seams. A band on a stage at the far end of the hall was already in full swing, arm-waving couples gyrating energetically on the floor in front of it. Long trestle tables had been set up down the full length of one wall. They bowed visibly beneath crates of beer, vast tureens of raspberry-red punch, and platters of meats: chicken, ham, mutton, even beef. Pastries, rolls and sandwiches, cakes, jellies and trifles, a huge and ornately decorated cake with the numerals 520 iced on it. Heather gaped. It was almost beyond comprehension, more food and drink spread out along one table than the imagination could grasp.

'Here you go.' Finginger was wading towards her through the crowd, a glass of punch in either hand. 'Watch out for this stuff. You never know with these guys, probably spiked with anti-freeze. But at least it'll keep the cold off. Come on, let me introduce you to some of the brass.'

With his hand at her elbow, he steered her back and forth through the growing throng. She met Finginger's boss, a bespectacled lieutenant-colonel called Stracey, then Stracey's boss, everyone's boss in fact, the Group CO, a willowy, softly spoken full colonel called Lassiter. Then she met a succession of majors whom Finginger introduced as Joe, Operations, Deke, Meteorology, Conrad, Maps, and a wildly enthusiastic red-faced one who gabbled non-stop and turned out to be Pete, Public Relations.

'Dance?' Finginger shouted suddenly above the growing din. 'Day-ance', it sounded like. The little white scar above his eyebrow was turning pink.

'No, I, well, Scott, really I don't think . . .'

Relieving her of her glass, he took her hand and led her to the front of the hall. The music was much louder there, the floor packed with hot, swaying bodies. They found a spot close by the stage, and there she danced, for hours, it seemed. For her whole life. Modestly at first, politely, and with what she hoped was restraint appropriate for a local dignitary. But soon the other dancers, the smoke, the urging rhythms of the band, the body-heat smells, released in her more fundamental responses and movements. Finginger was slightly shorter than she, and a little off-time, but it didn't matter; he bobbed and swung with gusto, and then, within a minute it seemed, one of the many other majors appeared and politely butted in. Then another, and another, until their smiling faces, their twanging, flattering voices, their swaying bodies, melted before her into a single warm, homogeneous presence. And as she danced, the torpor of months began to fall from her shoulders, like a sloughed skin. She felt a great weight lifting from her, releasing her from its burden. Felt herself being borne up, re-energised, revitalised, re-emerging from herself, as though from the claustrophobically dark confines of a cocoon, or a prison. She felt unburdened and renewed. For the first time in as long as she could remember, she felt alive.

She felt dizzy. Finally, breathless and perspiring, she stopped. The band had fallen still. A moment later its drummer rattled out a brisk roll on the snare and Major Pete of Public Relations sprang on to the stage.

'Ladies and gentlemen.' He gestured theatrically towards the trestle tables. 'Let the food be served.'

It was at that moment that she caught sight of John Hooper.

He was standing across the room, side on to her, hands propped on his lower back, his head bent towards one of the majors that Finginger had introduced her to earlier. The one with the Errol Flynn moustache. Englehardt. Englehardt was doing the talking while Hooper, his eyes narrowed with concentration, listened, nodding. It took her a second or two to place him as the man she'd seen in Iken church. He seemed taller, fuller, less gaunt than the brief shadowy figure of her memory. But the eyes were the same, unmistakable, deep and dark, and as she watched he smiled briefly at Englehardt, the same modest, gentle smile he'd given her, so apologetically, weeks ago in the church.

'Who's that?' she found herself asking.

'That? With Gene Englehardt? That's Hooper. Crew 19's new pilot. The one who nearly took your roof off barrel-rolling *Misbehavin Martha* last week. Why, do you want to meet him?'

Englehardt, laughing, still talking, was punching Hooper lightly on the shoulder. Jokingly, repeatedly, as though for punctuation. Slowly, and with a wry shake of the head, Hooper's smile spread out into a shy grin. Then he looked up and their eyes met.

'No,' Heather said at last. She tore her gaze from his, began moving towards the food tables. 'I already have.'

Half a mile away, *Martha*, silhouetted against an ink-black sky, stood parked on its concrete hardstand. Aboard, on the cold, unyieldingly hard and downward-sloping floor of the aeroplane's waist, their bodies intertwined, their arms tightly wrapped, lay Claire Howden and Eldon Ringwald.

Their faces were so close that their noses touched when they spoke. Claire could taste the warmth of his breath. She pursed her lips in the darkness, felt them brush against his, pushed out the tip of her tongue until they parted. A moment later their mouths were sealed once more, and she felt the thrilling tightening of his arms about her neck.

'Eldon,' she murmured, at length. She reached down, found his hand, drew it upwards between them, placed it on the thin cotton of her dress over her breast, felt her body shiver involuntarily at the chill air and the touch of his fingers. 'Do you want to?' Her voice was a hoarse whisper.

'Sure,' he whispered back. His thumb found the rise of her nipple through the cotton, began rubbing slowly at it until it swelled, hardened to a stub, until she sighed, grew breathless, and her lips sought his once more. He felt her hand sliding down between them, her palm pressing against the excruciating discomfort of his hardness. She squeezed, and he broke away suddenly.

'What? Eldon, what's the matter?'

'Not like this.' He sat up in the darkness, pushed away from her until he felt the cool curve of the fuselage against his back, pulled his knees to his chin. 'I don't want to do it like this.'

'But why? Why not? Don't you want to do it with me?' She shuffled towards him on hands and knees, turned to sit beside him, her shoulder against his.

'Of course I do! It's just that, well, I really like you, Claire, I like you more than I can say right now, and, well, I just don't want it to be like this.'

'Like what?'

'Like . . . the whores, you know, in London, the Piccadilly commandos. We heard about them. Up against a wall, or down among the trash in some back alleyway. It ain't dignified. It ain't nice. Anyhow . . .'

'Anyhow what?'

'Anyhow, well, nice girls don't. That's all. Not where I come from anyhow.'

'Are you saying I'm not a nice girl!' Claire's voice rang, indignantly loud suddenly in the metallic darkness.

'Say, Kid, could you guys just keep it the hell quiet back there!' A muffled voice floated from behind the closed door of the radio room.

'Sorry, Gerry.'

'Appreciate it.'

'Well, are you?' Claire hissed.

'No! Heck no, of course not. It's just that, look, it's kind of public here, don't you see, what with Via and Dot next door in radio, and Lajowski somewhere up in the nose with his date. And it's cold and cramped and, well, I just don't want it to be like this, for us.' He hesitated. 'I love you too much.'

She stiffened beside him. 'You do? Really?'

'Yes. Yes I do.' He slipped his arm around her shoulder, drew her close. They sat in silence, listening to the distant thump of the dance band drifting to them across the empty airfield. Then he heard her giggle.

'I'm glad, too, Eldon. I didn't want it to be like this either.'

He kissed the top of her head and they fell quiet once more.

'Are you flying a mission tomorrow?' she whispered eventually.

'You know I can't tell you that.'

'No. But are you, though?'

He wasn't supposed to say. Either way. Court-martial offence. 'No we're not.' What the hell. The way things were going, they never would fly a mission. Super, that's the closest they ever got. Super-goddamn-numerary. Worse yet, a brand-new crew, Lieutenant Dickinson's, in a brand-new ship called *Looky Looky*, had beaten them to it. A bunch of wet-behind-the-ears replacements flown in barely a week earlier, slotting straight into the middle of Englehardt's squadron while *Martha*, squadron flunkey, squadron standing joke, tagged along behind, like a lame dog.

It was a bitter disappointment to the entire crew. That very morning they'd followed the formation out to the RP, as usual, only to be sent back home, as usual, to fly yet another practice mission, or do machine-gun practice in the butts, or weapons maintenance, or evasive manoeuvring or bomb-aiming or radio navigation. *Looky Looky* had come home later in the day, taxied right past *Martha*, its crew thumbing noses and pulling faces through the windows. One mission in the bag. Twenty-four to go.

'What's he like?'

'Who?'

'Your new captain.'

'He's okay, I guess.' Ringwald shifted his weight on the unyielding floor. It was getting late. He'd have to smuggle Claire off the base somehow. Again. Suddenly, a crash as Gerry Via's boot kicked the radio-room door wide.

'No he ain't, he's a goddamn perfectionist ball-breaking son of a bitch.'

That they should meet, Heather sensed, that they should touch, was as inevitable as the coming dawn. It was late; suddenly tired, feeling deflated after too much food and excitement, and the brief euphoric release of her dancing, she was ready for Scott to take her home. He set off to find her cardigan and arrange a Jeep. 'Here,' he said, grabbing an arm from the crowd as he went. 'This is John Hooper. Talk to him while I'm gone, he doesn't know too many people here either.'

Then there he was. Standing before her, that shy smile on his lips, his eyes searching hers, as though struggling to recall something.

'Hello. Again,' she said, taking his proffered hand. It was absurd. She could actually feel her heart moving the collar of her dress.

'Again?'

'The church? At Iken. One evening a few weeks ago?'

'Ah. Sorry.'

'You don't remember?'

'Not exactly. Kind of a murky time.' He smiled, looking away, embarrassed. On the stage the band were playing a final number. Slowly. A little raggedly. But sweetly. Jerome Kern. 'The way you look tonight'. She said yes almost without realising it. His hand soft yet firm in hers as they walked, together, as though in slow motion, across to the dance floor. There, in a single movement, they turned to one another, moved closer, her hand falling naturally to his shoulder, his palm spreading, fingers outstretched against the small of her back. They began to move, together. Hold me, the saxophone sang. Never let me go. Time stood still, the other couples melting from awareness. Englehardt, waiting, glancing at his watch. Finginger too, standing at the edge of the dance floor, holding her cardigan up in his hand. They didn't exist. Nothing existed. She inhaled deeply, lifting her chin, her eyes, until they were directly on his. They were waiting for her. Their bodies were close, barely moving. The music was winding to a climax, the saxophonist, eyes closed, soaring to a finish. Because I love you. Just the way you look tonight.

They stopped. Scattered applause broke out. The saxophonist nodded. The spell broke. Gently, he lifted her hand from his shoulder, held it, then brought it to his lips and, his eyes still on hers, lightly kissed the slender gold band on her finger.

'This has to be goodbye,' he said and led her from the floor.

Chapter 7

Hooper's eyes blinked rapidly in the blackness. Had he cried out? Had he? The roaring in his ears was deafening, like breaking surf, his throat was dry, his head pounded a storm. He swallowed, struggling through the surf towards the softer rhythms of the breathing men around him, the patter of fine rain on the hut's roof. All asleep? Please God. 'Hoop?' But a lone voice was floating across the darkness to him. 'Hoop, are you okay?'

Jesus. Please not. 'Sure, Spitz. I'm fine, get back to sleep.'

Had he shouted? Shouts still echoed in his head. But from his lips, or his dream? His endless nightmare. About Danny Bowling, the tail gunner from his first ship. They were shouting the psalm together, the twenty-third, 'The Lord is my shepherd, therefore shall I lack nothing.' Ringing through his skull like the shriek of the bail-out bell. 'Surely, goodness and mercy will follow me, all the days of my life.' The two of them, close together, face to face, arms gripped, shouting out the psalm together. It was claustrophobically cramped, a tube, maybe, or a tunnel, with the smell of blood, and smoke and dizzying oceans of pain. Whose? 'Stay with me, please don't leave me alone.' Danny had begged, over and over. 'Did I do good? Please tell me I did good. Stay, please, pray with me. For the love of God, don't go.' And all the while the desperate need to slither free. To get out in the open. And run. And lie down in green pastures.

Hooper stared up at the shadowy curve of the hut's tin roof, forcing his breathing to slow, his heart to steady. It was just the old dream, he told himself, the old reality. Bowling was gone. He knew that. The new crew, *Martha*, the first mission they'd flown together that very day, these were what counted, these were the new reality. He must be more careful. Suddenly, with a shiver he thought of Heather.

He'd gone to her house. After they'd landed. Turned on his heel, put his back to the crew, to the ship, and walked off base just like that. Walked and walked, his head full to bursting. Then he was sitting there, in her front room, having English tea, of all the insanities. Trying to act rational, appear half normal, sitting with a little china teacup between his fingers, rattling on its saucer like castanets, and his head flying apart at the seams. Good God, how he'd talked. Spurted. Like a crack in a dam.

For minutes? Hours? He had no idea. Arriving at her door like some mad mumbling drunk, she'd had to drag him in off the street, pull him inside, steer him into an armchair by a window. Then she sat down opposite, folded her legs up beneath her and said not a word, just listened and listened, trying not to look shocked and pretending to ignore the drunken fumbling, the clacking castanets, while his head split open and the words poured unstoppably from his lips, like sand through fingers.

And why? Why the dam-burst? Why now?

And why Heather?

It was the mission. Their first. At last.

But the mission had been a milk-run.

'Good morning, Lieutenant Holland, it is five a.m. You are flying today.'

Dutch had risen from his bed the second the orderly's hand left his shoulder. He was already wide awake, yet dizzy with sleeplessness. Lying, rigid with anticipation, listening to the ceaseless rumble of the loaders' trucks, and the fuellers', and then the armourers, then the ground crews. Zigzagging endlessly back and forth through the night, like ships on a darkened sea. To and fro, back and forth: the hangars, the hardstands, the fuel dumps, the bomb dumps, the hardstands again, the equipment sheds, the spares sheds, the ammunition stores, again the hardstands. Fetching and carrying, loading, arming, fuelling. Filling the Forts to brimming. Prepping them, priming them: gasoline, oil, hydraulic fluid, oxygen. Bombs and ammunition. Back and forth, all night, loading and loading, heavier and heavier, until the ships groaned and sagged on their wheels like bent old men with too much baggage.

The other fellows in his hut were struggling wearily from their beds. Dutch laced on his shoes then reached for his uniform jacket, discreetly patting pockets for his secret spectacles. There was a story doing the rounds about over-laden bombers. Dutch had heard it from the ground crew, as usual. Rumour Control. But this one turned out to be true. Apparently an over-zealous operations officer at one of the bases nearby – the 390th maybe, down the road at Framlingham, or the 100th over at Thorpe Abbotts, or one of the others, nobody was quite sure; it was a big hush-up. Anyhow, this operations officer was out to make a name for himself with the top brass at Bury St Edmunds. He devised a series of experiments, loading three B17s to maximum take-off weight. Filling them to the gunwales. Then he began adding more weight. And more, to see just how much the poor old Forts could actually stagger into the air with. Final test, the three bombers are on the runway threshold, full fuel, full crews, full bomb load, everything, packed to the roof. And then some. To each he'd added another full two thousand pounds of extra ballast. Over and above maximum take-off weight. Just think! Another two thousand pounds. If a Fort could carry that much extra load, it could transform the way operations were planned and executed. They'd be able to fly much longer missions, and carry bigger bomb loads. It might even alter the outcome of the war. He'd be famous. So he sends all three ships lumbering down the runway. Not one at a time, to see what happens. But all three in a line, at thirty-second intervals, like a mission take-off. Off they go, creaking and groaning down the runway like three sick old men. Slowly, too slowly, they pick up speed. Then at last, with their sweating pilots fast running out of runway, the poor guys haul them desperately into the air where they hang for a few seconds, engines screaming, wings bowing from the strain, airborne but not flying, three doomed birds. Then they stall and crash, exploding, one after the other, into a stubble field beyond the perimeter. Thirty dead. Three whole crews. Thirty pointlessly slaughtered, charred, mangled young men's bodies scattered among the stubble like so much carrion. Their shrivelled claw-hands grasping nothing, their blackened stretch-lipped mouths twisted into frozen, soundless screams. Thirty. And then what? Thirty lying, killed-in-action letters of condolence. Thirty all-expenses-paid funerals with full military honours. Thirty folded flags for thirty grief-stricken mothers. And then everything hushed up again, covered over, closed down, like a lid, as if it never happened. Harvest of a quiet eye.

But it had happened. Dutch glanced around at the seven other beds in his hut. Their occupants were up now, donning their flying gear in sleepy silence. Irv Underwood was sitting on the edge of his bed, hair awry, pulling on his electric underwear slowly, clumsily, like a kindergarten kid trying to dress himself for school. Irv was the only other one of *Martha*'s four officers who lived in Dutch's hut. Spitzer and Hooper bunked in the hut next door. Irv looked drugged, his face grey and pasty. The others around the hut too seemed oblivious, still sealed within their own slowly waking worlds.

All clear. Dutch fished under his bed for his bombardier's flight bag, began rummaging through. His checklists and signals books, his weight and balance charts, his load calculation tables, slide rule and notebooks. Then his .45 service automatic pistol and spare clip. Carry it always, orders dictated. Don't carry it, many of the older hands advised. You get shot down over Germany wearing that thing, likely as not the locals will shoot you with it. And who could blame them? Dutch compromised. He took it with him, but tucked in a corner of his bag. The same corner as the packets of dried biscuits, the barley-sugar candy, the little bottle of motion-sickness pills and the canteen of water. He glanced around the room then dug into a side pocket. Four grocery sacks, the stout little brown-paper ones from the PX. Checked and counted. Nobody outside Crew 19 knew about them, or the hours aloft he spent vomiting into them, the crippling stomach spasms that completely incapacitated him, doubled him over. The dehydration and the dizziness. The stink and the shame. He snapped the flight bag shut and rose for the door.

He and Irv met Spitz and Hooper at breakfast. He still couldn't say he knew any of them very well. Irv, the oldest of the four, was silent and withdrawn. Little Loren Spitzer, 'Thumbs-up', the gunners called him, ever the optimist, raring to go. Hoop was good, the ideal commander, a gently joshing joke or two, a reassuring smile, a kind word. Today was the day, but don't sweat it, he seemed to be saying. We got a good team and a good ship. Plenty of time, just concentrate on your job, concentrate on doing it right, as well as you can, and everything will go fine. Dutch nodded, wanting to believe. He ate, but only a little; what was the point? He already felt nauseous. Then they all walked to the briefing room together. Quiet, thoughtful, but determined too. It was their first real mission. Together. Not supernumerary, not training, not following dumbly on behind in case anyone had to turn back. But the real thing at last. Flying number two in Englehardt's high squadron. They walked into the crowded briefing hall. Dickinson was there, scowling at them. Englehardt had bumped his ship down to supernumerary, so that *Martha* could fly the mission. Dickinson looked pissed about it. Then the doors banged open and Colonel Lassiter, Group CO, strode in followed by his team. The S-2 intelligence major stepped up, the curtain was pulled back, the briefing began. After that, there were separate briefings for the navigators and the bombardiers. So Irv and Hoop went on ahead to meet up with the gunners out at the ship. Finally, Dutch and Spitz were through with their briefings and clambering back up on to the six-by-six for the long ride out to join them. It was a grey day, windy. A little chilly. The Forts sat waiting, heavy on their wheels. Crows paced about on the stubble fields. Dutch held his flight bag close to his chest as he rode.

At *Martha*'s hardstand, Hooper and Underwood, arms laden, clumsy in their heavy flying suits, jumped down from their truck's tailgate, watching it speed off in a blue haze towards the next bomber. They picked up their parachutes and bags. *Martha*, the morning dew still wet on her wings, stood ready before them. 'Go ahead, there, Irv.' Hoop patted his co-pilot's back. 'Get aboard and make yourself at home. No need to rush, we got plenty of time before engine-start.' Underwood was visibly nervous, Hooper could see. Right on the ragged edge. But then so was every one of the two hundred and forty airmen arriving at the twenty-four aircraft parked, fuelled, armed and ready on their hardstands around the field. Hooper, all things considered, he concluded, felt all right.

Prepared, focused. Set. He'd been here before, some vestigial fragment of remembered experience told him. It was something he'd been able to do and do well. He could do it again. He began undoing some of the thirty-six feet of zippers that held his flying suit together. He was already too hot and it would be hours before they were climbing into the freezing layers above twenty thousand feet. Don't sweat it on the ground, someone had advised him once, an aeon ago. When the temperature hits minus thirty, sweaty suits make for seriously unpleasant flying.

Twenty-four ships. Three squadrons of seven, plus the usual three supernumeraries, one for each squadron. *Martha* was in Englehardt's squadron, the high layer. The other two squadrons would fly the middle and bottom layers, the whole making up the classic three-layered defensive box. Gene had briefed Hoop to slot *Martha* into the number two position, right next to his ship which was called *Shack Time*. Their formation would fly like the five spread fingers of a left hand, plus two tucked in behind. *Shack Time* would be the leading middle finger, *Martha* wedding finger, behind a little and to its left. Dickinson's ship, *Looky Looky*, to his disgust, was designated mission supernumerary, and would follow the seven only as far as the RP, the Rendezvous Point.

Knyper came over, wiping oily hands on a rag pulled from his back pocket. Hooper dumped his bag and parachute by the nose hatch. 'Okay, chief?' Knyper nodded and they began a walk-around together. Inside *Martha* all was business, the gunners completely immersed, for once, in the job at hand. Swivelling their guns on the mounts, checking the ammunition feed trays, the charging handles, the sights, the firing mechanisms. Then checking them again. And again. Another truck pulled up: Dutch Holland and Thumbs-up Spitzer clambered out. Hooper waved to them, continuing his walk-around.

Then it was time for him to board and start up. He swung up through the nose hatch, locked it shut, clambered awkwardly up on to the flight deck, stowed his parachute in the rack behind his seat. The ground crew's little sign still hung on the bulkhead there. Pull back to go up, push forward to go down. Underwood turned to him, his face a fearful, sickly mask.

'Okay, Irv,' Hoop said lightly. 'Let's have those pre-start-up checks.'

Then everything went blank. Everything. Just like that. He couldn't do it. Ten minutes later, as all around the field twenty-three other pilots cranked ninety-two sputtering engines to life, Hooper, his mind reeling, could do nothing but stare incredulously at the meaningless battery of knobs, levers and dials arranged before him. He couldn't do it. It wasn't fear, it wasn't nerves. It was erasure. As if a switch had been thrown in his head and wiped out everything he knew about flying B17s. As if he had never sat in an aeroplane before in his life. It was a meaningless environment, alien, completely unknown to him. Underwood, his voice perplexed, the checklist trembling in his hand, kept calling the start checks. Hoop, head shaking in disbelief, kept trying to go through the motions. But each time he got to hitting the start and mesh buttons, the number one engine just cranked and cranked, turning over and over, yet stubbornly refusing to start.

'What's happening?' Dutch whispered, down in the nose, to Spitzer. But Spitzer just shrugged, eyes wide with confusion. Behind the flight deck Lajowski, perching on his upper turret platform, ducked down to peer into the cockpit. He could see the two pilots' backs, Hooper's hands moving over the controls, see the number one propeller clunking over and over, see, from the corner of his eye, that all the other bombers, their engines running, were starting to taxi away around the perimeter track towards the runway. But not *Martha*. Nothing. Lifeless. No engine start. Not so much as a cough. Further aft, Gerry Via swung open the radio-room door. Ringwald, legs dangling, was sitting on the floor, ready to drop down into his ball turret as soon as they were airborne. Beans and Keissling, bundled up in their fur-lined suits, stood waiting beside their guns.

'What the goddamn hell's going on?' Beans hissed, gloved fists bunched on his hips. They all looked at one another. Via spread his hands, pulling a Latin grimace. At that moment the intercom crackled to life in their headphones. Hooper came on.

'Okay, uh, crew, this is pilot. I, well, sorry about this, but I seem to be having a problem starting the engines. Turret, could you get the nose hatch open and ask Sergeant Knyper to come on board as quickly as you can, please.'

Beside him, Underwood turned his face to the window. They weren't going to make it. The other twenty-three bombers were already nearing the runway threshold, right at the far end of the field, forming a queue for take-off. *Martha* wasn't going to make it. The relief, to his shame, flooded through him like the unexpected kiss of warm winter sun. In the nose, Dutch Holland, swallowing bile, exchanged glances with Spitzer. 'What? What did he say?' But Spitzer, bewildered, just shook his head and turned back to his desk.

In the waist, Beans, scowling in disgust, slumped, arms folded, over his gun. From the floor, Eldon Ringwald's boy-like face swung questioningly from Keissling to Via, to Beans, then back to Keissling. Tork's hiss floated up from the tail. 'Hey, guys. Did I get that right? Did I hear that?'

'Yup.' Via double-checked his intercom switch was off. 'Seems our brave and capable captain plum forgot where to poke the match in the hole.'

'Jesus Christ!' fumed Beans. 'I just knew the guy was a dead-beat no-hoper. I just knew it.'

'Maybe not.' Keissling shrugged. 'Maybe there's just some kinda, I don't know, technical problem up there.' Ringwald nodded in agreement.

'Technical problem! The technical problem is in Hooper's goddamn head. Keissling, I tell you, the guy's a total screwball.'

There was another crackle on the headphones. Hooper's intercom was still on. Knyper was aboard, Hooper was talking to him. Nine pairs of ears strained to listen.

'Sergeant. Thanks for coming up. Listen. As you know, ah, this is our first combat mission, together, that is, in this ship. And I know that I'm feeling a little spiky, I don't mind admitting it. Clearly I am doing something wrong during the engine-start procedures. I wonder if we could just run through them together, see if we can't get these damn fires lit.'

Fifteen minutes later, with all four engines burbling

contentedly, *Martha*, lurching inelegantly on her wheels, was hurrying around the airfield perimeter towards the runway. She was alone, the airfield empty. All the others had gone, exactly on schedule. In the nose compartment, Holland and Spitzer braced themselves against the rocking, Spitzer's pencils clattering to the floor from his little table. The questions hung unanswered between them. Had Hooper left *Martha*'s intercom open deliberately? Or was it just yet another in the worrying sequence of errors? Was his public admission that he was so damn nervous he couldn't remember what to do accidental or calculated? Yet he was man enough to admit it to the whole crew. That took guts. So maybe he was human after all. Somehow it made Dutch feel a little less anxious. Through the nose dome, the concrete sped by six feet under his feet. You had to admire the man, a little. He swivelled on his seat, managed a half-grin at Spitzer, who returned it with a hesitant thumbs-up.

And the intercom was still on. Above them, in the cockpit, Irv Underwood was clearing his throat, staring glassy-eyed through the windscreen at the distant treeline at the far end of the runway. 'Um, what are we doing, Hoop?'

'We're going after them. Call the take-off checks.'

'But they're long gone, we'll never catch them. Anyway, the supernumerary will be in our slot by now.'

'Supers don't get to take the slots until the rendezvous point. We'll head them off, beat them to it. Call the checks.' But there was no more time for checks. As Underwood fumbled for the list, Hooper swung the bomber on to the runway, wiggled the tail straight and pushed the throttles to the stops.

'You're not cleared! Hooper, the control tower, look! They're firing a red! Jesus, you're not cleared to go!'

'We're already gone.' Hooper held his right hand hard against the four throttles, the buzzing engine note rising swiftly to a harsh, four-part snarl. Immediately *Martha* strained forwards, accelerating swiftly down the runway. Hooper, one eye on the indicator needle, waiting for the speed to build, nudged the bomber straight on the runway with his feet on the rudders. 'Come on, sweetheart.' He pushed forwards slightly on the control column, lifting the tail, and suddenly *Martha* was transformed. From ungainly to majestic, reluctant to eager. From a wheelbarrow with wings into a spreading eagle. Streamlined, balanced, racing flat out down the blurring black strip. Seconds more and she was ready, skipping, the wheels off, then on, then off again. He eased back, lifting her clear, then held her down low, just feet above the ground, let the speed keep building, faster and faster. The ground flashed by beneath, then a road, then stubble, then trees, a glinting metallic twist of the river. Only then did he haul back, pointing her glass-domed nose towards the waiting clouds.

'Wheels up, flaps up, throttles to max climb. Come on, Irv! Work to do! Let's have the after-take-off checks and get her settled in the climb. Pilot to navigator.'

Below, Spitzer fumbled for his intercom switch. 'Er, yes, yes, pilot, this is navigator here.'

'Spitz, where's the RP today?'

'The rendezvous point today is off Harwich.' But he must already know that, surely?

'Correct. But the formation is currently climbing up to

height over the Splasher Six beacon at Diss, isn't that right?'

'Splasher Six, yes sir, that's right.' He was going to leave them. Leave them all there at the radio beacon circling laboriously up through the clouds. Cut across country direct to Harwich, get to the RP before them.

'We'll stay low for the moment. I'll need headings and position information soon as you can get them to me. Have you got that?'

'Yes. Yes I have. Ah, give me thirty seconds, pilot, I'll get you there.' He began scrabbling for rulers, fumbling for his pencils, then broke off. Dutch, both hands gripping the sides of his seat, which was visibly shuddering from the vibration of the four thundering engines, was watching him. Spitz wondered if he was about to throw up, but his expression, although tense, looked almost tranquil. And there was a gleam in his eyes, like excitement. No, not excitement. Triumph. 'Go, Spitz,' he said simply.

Thirty minutes later *Misbehavin Martha* intercepted Gene Englehardt's formation as it was approaching Harwich at fourteen thousand feet. Hooper drew up alongside the seven tightly bunched aircraft. Dickinson's ship, *Looky Looky*, was already slotted in next to Englehardt's. Hooper edged *Martha* closer to it, right alongside, wingtip to wingtip. Looking across, he could see Dickinson's masked face at the controls. His ungloved fist was at the window, middle finger extended upward.

'That's not very polite,' Underwood murmured. 'I guess we're too late.'

'We'll see about that.'

Back in the waist, Keissling, Beans and Ringwald were

crowded around Keissling's window. Their opposite numbers in *Looky Looky* were similarly positioned, gesturing rudely, waving them away.

'Sons of bitches are giving us the bird! Did you see that?'

'That's Walter Passmore, the asshole, just wait till I get to him tonight.'

'Yeah, but what do we do now? Throw peanuts?'

There was a click in their headphones.

'Dickinson. This is Hooper. Listen to me.'

Everyone froze. He was on the radio. Not the intercom, the high-frequency radio. Hooper was breaking radio silence. Against every rule in the book. Everybody could hear: Dickinson, Englehardt, the whole squadron. The whole group. Everyone back at Bedenham, the Ops controllers, tower chief, even Colonel Lassiter with his loudspeaker relay on the wall of his office. And beyond. Every single radio operator in the entire 8th United States Army Air Force, every RAF controller at every plotting board in south-east England. Listening to a quietly spoken American breaking radio silence.

'Here it is. You know as well as I do that supers don't get the slot until the RP. So either you move that ugly-looking bag of scrap out of my way right now, or I'm coming down over the top and will not hesitate to knock the living shit out of you.'

Dickinson, his body erect with disbelief at his window, stared out at Hooper, then turned to look over at Englehardt flying on his right. Then back to Hooper. Then, at last, after what seemed like an eternity, he slowly pulled *Looky Looky* up and out of the formation and banked steeply for home.

Hooper slid *Martha* into position next to Englehardt's ship. For several minutes the formation flew on, exactly as if nothing had happened. Englehardt's eyes stayed fixed, motionless, on the sky ahead. Then at last he turned towards *Martha*. He was shaking his head. He was laughing.

'Tail to pilot.'

'Yes, Tork, what is it?'

'Well. Sir. Well, hot damn. That's all.'

She'd heard it all. From start to finish. Every detail. Every last word. All about not being able to get the aeroplane's motors running, then being left behind by the others, rushing frantically to get to the, what did he call it, the rendezvous point. Breaking radio silence. Everything. He'd told her the lot.

And she still couldn't believe it. Even twenty-four hours later, watching clouds of seagulls following the first dark furrows of the plough through the window in the back of Gerald Garrett's car, Hooper's image, the whole bizarre episode in fact, still crowded to the forefront of her mind. Like a frantic traveller, rudely displacing other thoughts and preoccupations, jostling and pushing all else aside. The intensity of it, the sheer power. The way his eyes had clamped on to hers and stayed there. She'd felt like a rabbit caught in headlights. The way he spoke. Low, quiet, yet quick and urgent. Insisting, almost imploring her to understand.

The car lurched. 'Now then, dear.' Rosamund swivelled to her from the passenger seat. They had entered the northern outskirts of Ipswich, row upon row of those new box-like semi-detached houses. 'Sir Richard is a fine man and doing his best under trying circumstances, but it is absolutely essential that we keep up the pressure. So I've arranged for a private chat with him after the meeting, to ask that he personally intervene on behalf of the boys. Of course, you'll want to be there too.'

'Of course.' She tore her gaze from the window, forced her mind to the present. But there was no present. Nor a past. Nor even a foreseeable future. Her life was on hold, waiting, in limbo. Scarcely even real. She lived out her days trapped within some surreal repeating loop. A dream-like non-existence.

'Rosamund?' she found herself asking. Gerald's chin lifted in the rear-view mirror, watching her quizzically. 'Isn't that a little unfair on all the other families? I mean, there are thousands and thousands of missing men. It doesn't seem right that we should be asking for special treatment.'

'Right? What on earth has right got to do with it? I don't think it's right that the Japanese have been holding David and Richard prisoner for more than a year without allowing them so much as a single word for their families. And as far as special treatment goes, I am only doing exactly what any son's mother would do in the same circumstances. Lying awake all night trying to think of any slightest thing I can do to help him.'

'You're quite sure about that, aren't you?'

'What?'

'That they are alive. Being held prisoner. You really do believe it.'

Rosamund hesitated. Just for a second. 'I have to. It is the only way I can cope with it. Don't you?'

186

She turned back to the window. 'I don't know that I am coping with it.'

The meeting was at the Corn Exchange in Ipswich, a capacious hall off the main town square. Oblivious of the frustrated gesticulations of an arm-banded traffic policeman, Gerald parked directly in front of the building. The pavement outside its doors was already thick with friends and relatives of missing men, together with reporters and photographers from the *Eastern Daily Press* and *East Anglian Daily Times*. As the Garretts dismounted to the pavement, the journalists, instinctively sensing the presence of authority, or at least the presumption of it, clustered closer.

'Brigadier Gerald and Mrs Rosamund Garrett,' Rosamund enunciated loudly, like a party greeter. She jabbed a finger at the nearest reporter's notebook. 'President and Honorary Secretary of the RNRCC – that's the Royal Norfolk Regiment Comforts Committee. And that's Garrett with two Ts, young man. This is my daughter-in-law, Mrs David Garrett. Both her husband and her brother are captains in the 5th Battalion Royal Norfolks. We're here to attend the Comforts Committee regional meeting and listen to the address by Sir Richard Howard Vyse. We shall also be holding private talks with Sir Richard afterwards, to demand that more strenuous efforts be made on behalf of our missing men by the Prisoners of War Departments of the British Red Cross and the War Office. Frankly, it's just not good enough. Be sure to put that in your newspaper. Photograph? By all means, dear boy.' A moment later Heather found herself backed against a wall amid a cheerfully resolute covey of women, blinking at the flashbulbs popping in her eyes. There seemed to be a plethora of tweed skirts and sensible shoes gathered there on the pavement, she noted, hers, at Rosamund's insistence, among them.

But once inside and seated, and all too soon, it seemed to her, the tweed offensive began to falter before an increasingly abject barrage of bad news. Standing rather forlornly on the stage of the hall, Sir Richard Howard Vyse, Chairman of the Red Cross's POW Department, spoke to the packed audience quietly, unsparingly and at length. He was a tall, diffident, tired-looking, slightly rumpled man in his late sixties, with a white Edwardian moustache, an ancient broken nose and a pipe sticking out of his top jacket pocket. As he spoke, of the endless diplomatic wrangles, the behind-the-scenes negotiations, the implacability, insensitivity and, frankly, the blatant dishonesty of the Japanese authorities, a funereal gloom began to settle over his audience like a pall.

'But the good news is that we're starting to get some mail back at last,' he cajoled, sensing their growing despondency. 'One or two of you may already have received a card from a loved one. Of course, it is, regrettably, just a trickle at this stage, and sadly there is little evidence that your letters or our Red Cross parcels are getting through to them in return. But we're confident that they will, and it is a start. Also, the lists of missing are now beginning to be processed, albeit slowly, by the Japanese, and each week a slightly clearer picture of the numbers of survivors, and more importantly their whereabouts, is emerging.'

But a pitifully bleak picture it turned out to be. Less than ten per cent of the missing had been identified as having been captured alive. In other words, more than a year and a half after they had left home, ninety per cent of the soldiers who had sailed for Singapore were still completely unaccounted for.

'Hopeless!' Rosamund hissed angrily at Heather's side. She was jotting notes into a little book. On Heather's other side, a young woman, no more than twenty, thin and pinched, poorly dressed, strained forward in her seat, struggling to follow proceedings. 'Jack,' she kept muttering. 'What about my poor Jack?'

The last-ditch defence and fall of Singapore was, to a great extent, an East Anglian affair. Part of the 18th Infantry Division, David and Richard had sailed from the Clyde in November 1941, together with three battalions from the Royal Norfolks, two from the Suffolks and two from the Cambridgeshires. They arrived there just as the last British troops were evacuating Malaya. Seventeen days of bloody fighting ensued, at the end of which the battered remnants of these battalions had no option but to surrender.

'You see, ladies and gentlemen, the Japanese have a very different attitude, culturally, as it were, to prisoners of war,' Vyse was saying. He peeled off his spectacles, lowered his notes, staring out at the upturned faces. They had fallen very still. There was no script for this message. 'In their culture, surrender is, well, it's a matter of grave dishonour. Something contemptible. Something to be despised. As a result, it is starting to become clear that the manner in which they are treating their POWs as well as the conditions in which they are keeping them fall way below those considered minimally acceptable within the terms of the Geneva Convention. In fact, part of the problem is that Japan doesn't even recognise the Geneva Convention. The truth, and you must forgive me, but you have a right to know this, the truth is that we are starting to receive increasingly worrying intelligence reports of hopelessly inadequate food and medical supplies, insanitary and diseased living conditions. And brutal treatment. I'm sorry but there it is, and it is no use our pretending that the situation is otherwise.'

There was more. Apparently the Japanese also believed in harsh work regimes for all prisoners, including officers. Evidently, the Singapore survivors, tens of thousands of them, had been split up and shipped like cattle to any of several possible destinations: Indo-China, Burma, Thailand, the Philippines. There they were being put to work building airstrips, bridges, dams and railways, often hacked by hand out of virgin jungle, in merciless heat and with little to survive on each day but a few handfuls of rice and occasional sips of stinking, disease-ridden water.

The young girl to Heather's right was weeping now, hunched over in her seat, sobbing softly into a grubby scrap of tissue. Heather stared at the stage. Numb. Incredulous. It was unimaginable. Unfathomable. Like a complicated mathematical theorem, its message, its implications were completely beyond the comprehension of normal beings. Nobody knew if David and Richard had even survived the initial fighting. And if they had, nobody had a clue where they might be now, and what they might be having to endure. She reached out, resting her hand lightly on the girl's back. Immediately the sobbing grew louder. Vyse was still talking; the woman in front turned in her seat. 'Pull yourself together!' She scowled. 'Blubbing like that won't do him any good, will it?'

'Come on.' Heather took the girl's arm. 'Let's go outside for a bit, shall we?'

They stood on the pavement together, the streets about them newly washed, glistening from fresh rain. Pigeons wheeled overhead beneath a piercing blue sky fringed with towering shower clouds. There was clarity about the air, a welcome freshness after the oppressive, almost trance-like stupor inside the hall. Heather inhaled deeply, waiting while the girl blew noisily on her proffered handkerchief.

'A little better now, Gladys?' she asked. 'You did say it was Gladys, didn't you?'

'Gladys, yes. Yes, a little better now, thanks.'

'Tell me about your husband. Jack, was it?'

''E's, well, 'e's not my husband, exactly. But he is the father of our little boy, Cyril. And we are going to get married, soon as possible. Or at least we was. Till this lot.' She nodded towards the entrance doors, mouth quivering again. 'It's all so horrible. The things that bloke was saying in there. My poor Jack. It ain't fair. We had so little time together.'

'Yes. I know.'

'Little Cyril, well he was a bit of an accident, like, I can't deny it. But I know Jack's a good man and would do right by us if ever he come home. But that's just it, I don't know if he *is* coming home! Nobody knows. And he's never even seen Cyril. He don't even know he exists. Perhaps never will.'

'He will, Gladys, you must keep on believing that. We all must just try to hold on. Keep on hoping. And praying—' She broke off, shamed by the patronising hollowness of her

191

words. What was the point? It was a sham. A lie. Hope wouldn't feed the baby.

Gladys, a tear rolling down her nose, was shaking her head. 'I just can't manage it no more. Can't cope. I don't know what to do. We don't get his pay because we aren't married, so we have to stay up my mum's and get by best we can on the ration. But there's only the one room and in the winter it's blooming freezing. I had a job up the munitions factory at Ransomes for a while, but my mum's bad with her chest and I couldn't leave Cyril with her, so I had to give it up.' She mopped her eyes again with Heather's handkerchief, fished a crumpled pack of cigarettes from a tatty handbag, fumbled one to her lips. After a brief hesitation she offered one to Heather. They were American. Heather took one on impulse.

'Is there anyone else?' she asked gently. Cigarettes. Nylons too. The dress might be threadbare, the shoes scuffed and holed, but the nylons were brand new. 'I mean, anyone else who might be able to help, that is.'

The girl looked away. 'I do love Jack, and that. I really do, don't get me wrong, but I just can't manage any more. I don't know what to do. I don't even know if he's dead or alive.' She glanced up at Heather. 'There's, well, there's Joey, you see. He's American. A fitter off the base at Raydon. He's from Iowa, he's so kind and ever so gentle. He brings food and sweets for Cyril, he even gets medicines and things for my mum's chest. And the cigs and nylons and tins of Spam and stuff.'

'He sounds nice. Do you like him?'

The girl nodded miserably. 'Ever so. He wants me to marry him. Wants to take Cyril and me back with him to Iowa. After the war. Mum and all.'

The meeting was breaking up, people filing into view through the glass doors. Gladys' eyes, red-rimmed, were filling once more. 'What on earth am I going to do?'

Heather dropped her cigarette beneath the toe of her shoe. 'I don't know, Gladys. What you have to. What your heart tells you to. To survive.'

He was waiting for her. Sitting there, arms folded, face up to the afternoon sunlight, on the rough wall outside her cottage when the Garretts dropped her off. He stepped forward as they pulled up, opening the door for her. Rosamund said nothing, her eyes fixed straight ahead, seeing all.

Dumbfounded, Heather stepped from the car. She seemed constantly to be introducing her parents-in-law to Americans. 'Ah, well, um, Rosamund, Gerald, this is Lieutenant, um, Hooper. He's a pilot, up at the base here. I'm sorry, Lieutenant, I don't know your first name. These are my parents-in-law, Gerald and Rosamund Garrett.' Couldn't he see? In-laws, wedding ring, husband! What on earth was he doing? And yet deep down, far within her, there was an undeniable quickening in that part of her that had been hoping, somehow, that he might come back.

'John. It's John.' Hooper ducked to the window. 'Ma'am, sir.' Gerald reached across to shake, Rosamund, tight-lipped, nodded minutely. A moment later they drove off.

'I'm sorry,' he said, watching them go. 'Last thing I wanted was to cause you any embarrassment.'

Heather sighed. 'It's all right. You weren't to know. It's, well, it is rather a difficult time just at the moment. Um, do you want to come in? Have some tea or something?'

He smiled, shook his head. He looked different. Calmer, rested, more at ease with himself. 'No. Thanks. I just came by to apologise. For storming in here yesterday like that. You must have thought you were under attack from a lunatic. It was unforgivable. And selfish. You must have plenty enough concerns of your own.'

'Nothing should be unforgivable,' she said quietly.

'No.' He smiled again. 'But thanks, anyway. I hope I didn't alarm you.'

'Not in the least. I'm flattered you felt you wanted to come and talk.'

'I don't think I could have stopped myself.'

They stood, side by side against the wall. Across the lane from her cottage, a wide field stretched gently down to a tree-lined stream half a mile away. A small group of young children were playing beside it. The wind had dropped, the shower clouds dissipated and the early evening air hung soft and still about them, scented with lavender and moist earth smells.

'What is it, John?' There was something more, she sensed. Something he'd missed out that he wanted to add. Needed to add.

They walked along a footpath that ran beside the field. After a while they reached the stream, following it until they came to a bend with a grassy bank. They sat down. Hooper split grass stems as he spoke; Heather, her cheek resting on her knees, watched the electric-blue darting of a kingfisher, listening to the soft cadences of his voice mingling with the trickle of water.

They were practically home, more than halfway across the

North Sea, coast in sight, and mission accomplished. It had gone well. One ship from the low squadron had been downed by flak on the way back out from the target, two or three others had taken hits, but managed to carry on. Englehardt's high squadron hadn't been touched, the bomb-run carried off without a hitch. All things considered, and bearing in mind the disastrous start to the day, and the shortcomings of the crew, it had been a textbook mission for them. And no fighters. They had been very lucky.

Understandably, perhaps, the crew were in high spirits. But not Hooper. He was shattered. Utterly exhausted. He felt as if he *was* the crew, as if he was operating for them, for all of them, alone and on their behalf, and had been since they'd first begun flying together. Pushing them, coaxing, compelling. Fulfilling their roles for them, forcing *Martha* to function, making it work, by sheer willpower alone. And the effort needed to sustain it, the strain of it over the past few weeks, and the lost months before, was exhausting him. Bleeding him dry. Crushing him, like a growing weight on his back, to his knees. And so he had snapped.

'Tail to pilot.'

'Yes, um, Tork. What is it?' Underwood had the controls. Hooper pulled himself straighter in his seat, lifted the oxygen mask from his face to try to rub some circulation back into his cheeks. His neck and shoulders ached, white sparks of incandescence danced before his eyes, his head hurt like the end of the world. Just like back at Brent Wallis' hospital. As though it would split in half at any moment.

'Well, sir, me and Beans have this little bet going, about which one of us gets to shoot down an enemy fighter first. I was wondering if you'd care to put a twenty in the pot. In my pot, that is, naturally.'

'Ah, no. No I wouldn't.'

'Blow it out your ass, Tork. You couldn't throw chicken-shit at a barn door and hit it. Not unless you was holding on to it with the other hand.'

'I'm in.' Via came on. 'Twenty on Torky.'

'Geraldo, my man!'

Ringwald piped up. 'What do you want to bet on him for? I bet it'll be me. I scored highest in the butts.'

'Kid! Little Kid Ringwald? Those square-head Focke-Wulf jockeys will eat you for breakfast. You leave them to me, I'll—'

'Stop!' Hooper roared suddenly, then gasped. Pain lanced down the back of his neck, the white orbs danced higher, filling his vision. He felt himself teetering on the edge of a faint. 'All of you, for God's sake, what the hell do you think you're doing? This isn't a game. Men have died today. A crew in the low squadron, men that we all know, went down. You saw it go, it could have been us, any of us, but today it just happened to be our turn to get lucky. And you're betting on it, betting on lives like it was all just some big joke.'

'Navigator to pilot—'

'No!' He should stop, he wanted to stop. But his voice, taut and tinny through his headphones, kept raging on and on. 'Okay, I'll take you on if that's what you want. Count me in. Fifty. I'll bet fifty dollars. A hundred if you like. Yes, let's make it an even hundred. But I'm putting it on the fighter. Every time. I bet a hundred bucks on the German fighter pilot. And why? Because he's better than you, better than any of you. And he's not the square-head, Lajowski, nor is he Fritz or Jerry or the Hun. He's a fighter pilot of the German Air Force, highly trained, professional and dedicated, and if you want to stay alive you'll show him some respect, because what he does is dangerous and difficult and requires more skill and courage than any of you will ever possess.' Stop. He must stop. Waves of pain were sweeping over him, a high-pitched whistling filled his head, he glimpsed sea through the side window, a mist on it, little islands of white dotting the grey-blue. Like last time. There was going to be fog again. His friends, his family, drifting down into the mist never to return. He tried to rise from his seat. The Lord is my shepherd, therefore shall I lack nothing. The shouting went on in his head. 'And here's another!' it screamed. 'I bet you fifty that none of you make it through your tour, and believe me it's a safe bet because those are the odds right now and they're getting worse every day, only you're too goddamned stupid to realise—'

'Hoop, Hoop, it's okay.' Spitzer was gripping his arm. 'It's okay, take it easy.'

He slumped back into his seat, spent. His hands flopped to his sides; he closed his eyes, crushing a tear on to his cheek which seeped hotly beneath the black rubber of his oxygen mask. After a while, much later, he felt the mask being removed, hands loosening the neck of his flying suit. He tasted hot coffee on his lips from someone's flask. 'Sorry,' he wanted to say, to them all, but the intercom was off. 'Sorry.' But it was too late. He opened his eyes; the familiar dense patchwork of greens and browns and dusty yellows slid by beneath them. He had to get away. Away from everything.

Just for an hour or so. Walk in those honey-coloured fields. Feel the earth against his skin. Talk to someone.

Fifteen minutes later, his co-pilot, Irving Underwood, teeth gritted in determination, landed *Martha*, a little untidily, but safely, on the main runway at Bedenham, and taxied her back to her hardstand.

Chapter 8

T/Sgt Marion Beans 520th BG

Dear Cheryl,

I hope you are well, I got your last letters, thanks for the latest photo, you look real cute, I put it straight in my wallet. I guess it was kind of a disapointment to here that you finaly decided to ditch living in the trailer park and head on back to your Moms in Supulpa. Still I cant say I blame you, I never did like the damn trailer nor living in OK city neither come to that. I guess that means you gave up your waitressing position at Chuckys diner too. Cant say I'm to unhappy about that and all the way those truck drivers used to sass you up all the time. All in all its a smart decision tho' it feels strange you being back at your Moms. Bit like we werent married any more. I hope it don't feel that way to you.

Me and the boys are doing fine. We just completed mission number 7 and tho' I say so myself, I say were shaking down pretty good.

7 down 18 to go — be home before you know it! The missions are going fine, Cher, you must stop worrying about that. The other day Lieutenant Hooper came down to see us in the waist during one mission, which is something he does pretty often and he says Beans old buddy I want to swap you and Herm Keissling over, left and right, because we were always getting in each others ways and our aims was off and so forth. So now Herm shoots left waist and I shoot right waist. Guess what? It's a whole deal better! We tried it in the firing butts, Lieutenant Hoop is forever having us practice in the butts, and anyway it was much better. I don't know why he didn't think of it before.

Missions are pretty good tho' we had a few tough ones. Two of the ships in Englehards squadron are gone including Dickinson's ship Looky Looky. They got hit in the tail by flak on the run-in one day and went out of control. We saw them go, they was right beside us. Lieutenant Dickinson did everything he could but the ship's tail was shot right off and they was just falling and falling, turning over and over. It was pretty sickning to see. We lost some good buddies there.

Its the flak I really hate. The German fighters is one thing. We see them coming in, those Luftwaff pilots are damn good and they come at us so fast its hard to get a bead on them. Someone in the low formation managed to hit one the other day tho'. But with the flak, well there aint a damn thing you can do except hold on and grip your teeth while the flak throws the ship all over, and pray to God you don't get a direct hit. I really hate flak much worse than the fighters. At least with those guys you can try and shoot back.

Anyway the good news is that after the 7th mission we get a 2 day pass so me and the guys are off to London to see the sites! All except Lieutenant Hooper of course, and Kid Ringwald who's got a girl in

the village. Ill write tell you all about our London siteseeing tour on
our return.

   Take care Cher honey.
   Yours for allways Marion.
   PS Say hi to your Mom for me and also my folks if you see them.

'No, look, Billy, not like that, you're over-tightening it, for God's sake, you'll strip the thread. Slacken it off, lad, go on, that's it, a little more. Good, now tighten it again, but not too much, that's it, then we can give the wheel a spin to check alignment.' Ray watched as Billy, his face a frown of concentration, his tongue between his lips, slotted the spanner on to the wheel-nut and began tensioning. 'Good, that's better. Good. See, there's no need to tighten it so much, is there?

   'Sorry, Mr H. It's the Wright Cyclones, see.'

   'The what?' Ray squinted along the bicycle's upturned wheel, spinning it with the flat of his hand. Somehow, since Maggie's outburst on the subject, the matter of Billy's leaving the forge hadn't been mentioned again.

   'The engines on the B17s. Sergeant Knyper showed me. You have to torque the nuts right down as hard as you can, and even then when he puts the big wrench on, it takes two mechanics to do the last bit together.'

   'Ah, yes, well, that's as may be. But this isn't any thundering great aeroplane engine, is it? This is Mrs Garrett's bicycle. Put two of your Sergeant Knightly's hairy great mechanics on to fixing this and they'd break it in half.'

   'Knyper, Mr H. His name's Hal Knyper. Um, he wondered if you wanted to, like, stop in. One day.'

   Ray knelt back, cupping a hand to his eyes. The wheel

clicked to a stop. They were in the open doorway to the foundry, bathed in a slanting rectangle of late afternoon sunlight. 'He what?'

'Have like a little tour around his workshop. Only if you wanted to, like. It's massive, Mr H, you should see some of the machinery and stuff. And he's very interested in your metalwork and smithing and that. I told him all about it, and the forge. He's dead keen to see it.'

'Is he.'

'Dead keen. So, like, I could take you up there, 'e could show you about the place, then we could bring him back here for a look at the forge. And tea.'

'Tea?'

Billy nodded, scratching an oily finger on his cheek.

'And who's idea was all this?'

'His! Well, the first part was. The trip round his workshop. And the bit about him being interested in smithing and that. The other bit, about the tea and that, was more mine, I suppose. Anyhow, what about it, Mr H?'

Ray began gathering tools into a tray. 'Well, it's a kind suggestion of his, maybe we could give it some thought. But, well, tea and that, I don't know, what with Mrs Howden so busy up the WVS, and old Perce a bit offish, as it were. We'll have to see. Now then, what about this other bicycle, who does it belong to?'

'Polecat. Um, Sergeant Lajowski, from *Misbehavin Martha*. You met him, remember? When he came here, that evening . . . Anyway, he says the brakes don't work and the handlebars are loose.'

Ray examined the machine. 'Well, the brakes just want

adjusting and the handlebars need a shim. Won't take five minutes.'

'That's good, then, 'cos I already charged him a crown.'

'Five shillings! In advance?'

A shadow fell across the doorway. 'Mr Howden? I'm sorry to trouble you. It's Mrs Blackstone. Area evacuee coordinator.'

Ray led her into the lounge, a small, neatly furnished room at the end of the house, with old but spotlessly clean armchairs, a faded square of Wilton on the floor and a wrought-iron fireplace with brass firedogs and brick surround. Little china animals lined the mantelpiece, books and dolls the shelves; an ancient sepia-toned family photograph stood on an upright piano against one wall, a flight of plaster ducks ascended another. It was the room for best and special occasions only, and therefore rarely used. Its floral wallpaper smelled faintly damp. Billy had only looked inside it once or twice in passing. He saw little more of it now. Mrs Blackstone stopped him in the doorway.

'Oh, Mr Howden, I do think it would be best if we went through things on our own, without young, er, William present. Purely for his benefit, of course.'

Billy clumped slowly up the stairs to the attic. That's it, he reflected, curling into a ball on his bed. The end. He screwed his eyes shut, hugging himself tightly. Clouds drifted unseen across the skylight above him. The end of the only good thing that had ever happened. Finish.

An hour later Ray called up to him. He descended once more. They were still in the lounge, Maggie and Ray. The other woman had gone. Maggie looked pale and drawn. Her eyes crinkled at him a little when he came in, but then she looked away.

'Well, lad,' Ray began, his voice very low. He wasn't looking at him either. 'I'd say you've got some explaining to do.'

The boarding house, one of dozens in identical terraced rows, was called Sea View, a blatant untruth as it stood two streets back from Lowestoft's modest esplanade. But its peeling pink exterior merged effortlessly with the tired pastels of the other boarding houses, camouflaging it into reassuring anonymity, the vacancies sign in the window was embellished with little flowers, and beneath the handwritten card next to the bell-pull saying, 'No dogs, no musicians, no Irish,' a small plaque bade visitors 'a warm welcome to our happy home'. Eldon Ringwald rang the bell and stepped back. Beside him, Claire, behatted, her Sunday overcoat tightly buttoned, the handle of her little suitcase damp in her fist, slipped her free arm through his and, chin raised, attempted in vain to banish the expression of terror from her face. The door opened. A squat, middle-aged woman in housecoat and hairnet stood, arms folded, before them.

'Lord love us,' she said, eyeing them disparagingly, like underweight sprats at the fish stall. Her voice had a hard Scottish edge to it. 'They get younger every bloody day.'

She led them into a gloomy hall, looked the other way while Eldon, after only momentary hesitation, signed the register, relieved him of one night's fee in advance, then pulled a key from a row of hooks and clumped up the narrow stairway. They followed her to a second-floor room. It was at the back of the house, smelled of polish and soap, was small and square.

The wallpaper had a seafood motif, repeating clumps of seaweed crawling with crabs, lobsters, oysters and mussels. The view from the window was of a narrow strip of over-grown garden with washing on a line and a drooping conifer at the far end. In one corner of the room was a hand-basin, an ancient chest of drawers sagged against a wall, two plain wooden chairs stationed beside it. In the centre of the room, dominating everything, stood the bed, an iron-framed double. A picture of Lyme Regis hung above it, a porcelain chamber-pot, round and squat, sat on the dusty floorboards beneath.

The landlady, hefting their room key in her hand, stood in the open doorway looking them up and down while they entered, toured, inspected briefly, then stood nervously together on a small circular rug in the centre of the floor. Then she rattled off a seemingly bottomless list of rules and regulations about the room, the blackout, noise, alcohol, mealtimes. About the bathroom and 'closet' down the corri-dor, the hot water, when they were permitted to use it and how much – 'Ye get the one bath between ye for a weekend tariff and mind you don't go filling it above the red line.' The times they had to be out of the house and the times they had to be in again. Finally, formalities exhausted, and with a last disapproving shake of the head at Claire, she handed Eldon the key and left the room. Breaths held, they listened for the clump of her foot on the stair. Then they collapsed, giggling like schoolchildren, side by side on the bed.

'You're just so damn beautiful, Claire,' he said softly, a while later. He was tracing a finger down the shadowed valley between her breasts. She was lying on her back on top of the coarse bedspread, completely naked, stiff and straight, her legs outstretched, her arms at her sides. Almost to attention. Like an inspection. The blackout was drawn, but even so, enough daylight penetrated the room to cast the pale contours of her body into stark relief. She peered down at herself self-consciously. She could clearly see where her heart banged against her chest, the stubby erectness of her nipples, the taut flatness of her belly and the dark curls beneath, the wider smoothness of her thighs. Everything. And he could see it too. She had never felt so naked in her life, so completely, tensely, open. So vulnerable. It was terrifying, and yet so exciting. The way he just sat there in his vest and shorts, staring brazenly down at her nakedness, his pale eyes glinting in the dim light, his expression serious, almost sad, yet tinged with something softer, warmer, like wonder. She gazed up at him, forcing herself to relax, and waited while his eyes, unimpeded, wide with that serious wonder, travelled her body.

And his fingers. They fluttered over her skin like tiny moths. Barely touching, sometimes leaving her altogether for brief anxious seconds, but always returning, floating, alighting here and there to brush, caress and stroke. Her hair, her whole head, her cheeks, neck and arms. Her skin prickled with sensation where the fingers touched, as though electricity flowed to it from their tips. Then they found her breasts and instantly she felt her heart quicken. She closed her eyes, inhaling deeply, surrendering to a firmer touch and a warm, melting sensation, almost like an ache, that swelled deep within her stomach. For an age, it seemed, the fingers stayed there, stroking, plucking, cupping, circling. Then, with a pang like loss, they left her once more. She held her breath, until seconds later she felt a touch on her inner thigh. Without effort, without conscious control, or decision, her whole body stirred then, her head rolled sideways on the pillow, and with a soft, child-like sigh lodged in her throat, she raised her knees slightly on the bed-spread, and then drew them apart.

'Touch me there, Eldon,' she whispered.

Billy Street, so it appeared, was not Billy Street at all. He was Albert Crossley. Mrs Blackstone, the area evacuee co-ordinator, had sat beside the unlit fireplace in the Howdens' front room and produced a thick sheaf of documents from a manila envelope. Ray and Maggie listened, pale-faced, from the sofa. Like two children caught stealing.

'Well, now, born on or about the eighteenth of the ninth 1928, the boy was registered, probably by his maternal grandparents, as Albert Harold Crossley in October of that year. He was put up for adoption almost immediately.'

'But what about his parents?' Maggie interrupted straight away. 'What about his mother?'

Mrs Blackstone, a tall, grey-haired woman of about fifty, arched her eyebrows. 'According to what little information we have on her, Billy's – Albert's – mother was only sixteen or seventeen at the time, and unmarried. She lived with her parents who ran a public house down near the docks in Tilbury. The Admiral, it was called. That's all we know, except that Tilbury is a fairly . . . well, it is a rough part of London, shall we say, and a docks, of course. The Admiral was frequented, likely, by thousands of passing sailors every year. I would hazard to suppose that Albert was most likely the unfortunate product of a brief, um, liaison between one of them and this Crossley girl. Wouldn't you?'

'Billy. He may have been born Albert, but as far as he's concerned, and we're concerned, his name is Billy.'

'As you prefer,' Mrs Blackstone replied stiffly.

'Well, we do. And furthermore, I don't like to think of him as an unfortunate product, neither.'

'No. Of course.'

Maggie cleared her throat. 'So, all right, then. Who adopted him? Some people called Street, must be.'

'Er, no. As I began to outline in my letter to you of the second—'

Maggie and Ray looked at each other. 'Letter?'

'Yes. Didn't you get it?'

The Howdens shook their heads. 'No.'

'Oh, for goodness' sake. I know there is a war on, but really the postal system is a national disgrace sometimes.' Mrs Blackstone began thumbing through the papers on her knee. 'Anyway, here we are. Albert – Billy – was fostered many times over the years, and spent a great deal of time in various children's homes and orphanages. Sadly, however, as with so many of his kind, he was never found an adoptive family.'

'His kind?'

'I beg your pardon?'

'You said his kind.'

Mrs Blackstone stiffened again. 'Mrs Howden, these are just the facts. I am simply relaying them to you as they came down to me. They are not my doing. It is an unfortunate but undeniable fact that hundreds, probably thousands of babies are born in the poorer parts of London to impoverished, uneducated and unmarried girls every year. Few of them are fortunate enough to find families to adopt them. Billy was not one of those, so he was raised by the state, for better or worse. At least he was until he was twelve.'

'Then what happened?'

Mrs Blackstone looked up at them. Their expressions were a matched pair. Blank incredulity. As though some fantastic alien monster was materialising before their very eyes. Which in a sense it was.

'He went to prison. Well, a correctional institution for young offenders. In Kent.'

'But what for?'

'For arson.'

Crew 19 left Bedenham in the early evening, catching a base bus to Ipswich station then a slow train to London Liverpool Street. Emerging uncertainly on to the cavernous station concourse, the party split into two by unspoken agreement. The three officers, Spitzer, Holland and Underwood, took a taxi straight to the West End and their private rooms with clean sheets and adjacent bathrooms at the Grosvenor Hotel.

'Lord above!' Holland exclaimed. The three, clean-shaven, showered and changed, had regrouped downstairs in the officers' mess. The bar was packed, mostly with Americans, including many women. 'All this and breakfast too, for twelve bucks?'

'Too steep for you, Dutch?' Spitzer joked. 'We could be in the Dorchester for fifteen.'

Meanwhile Beans, Via, Tork, Lajowski and Keissling, anxious not to miss a minute's 'sightseeing', also forced their way into a cab.

'Where to, lads?' the cabby chirped, as if he didn't know. There was a brief hissed conference in the rear.

'The action!'

The cabby drove them, as he did nearly all his Yank fares, to Piccadilly Circus. They all wanted to see it. Even though it wasn't a circus, the lights had been off for years, the statue of Eros had been removed for safe-keeping, and the area's legendary clubs and restaurants, strangled by rationing and the compulsory five-shilling meal tariff, were but pale reflections of their former selves, it was what they invariably asked for. As he drove, with dusk settling about the city's streets like a grime-laden shawl, he could see their faces in the rear-view mirror, pressed like eager schoolchildren's to the windows.

'St Paul's! Up there, look. Isn't that St Paul's?'

'Are you sure? Looks like a regular church to me. I thought St Paul's was like, kind of a dome.'

'No, that's West-Minster. That cathedral next to that Big Ben clock place.'

'Tork, would you get your damn elbow out of my face, I cannot see squat!'

Somewhere along a once-proud Regency façade of now drab shops and offices in High Holborn, the cab slowed to a crawl, the crew sniggering at the sight of a helmeted London bobby holding up traffic with his hand. Then they fell silent. Mountains of rubble lay, roughly cleared, at the kerbside. Workmen's lamps hung on hastily erected wooden barriers over water-filled holes and collapsing masonry. Right beside them, a whole section of building front, fifty yards or more, had been blown right out, toppling into the street like an eroding cliff. Men in dark overalls and flat tin helmets picked their way through the broken rubble, the smashed shop goods and shattered glass.

'Jerry five 'undred pounder, lads,' the cabby commented, with barely a second glance. He tipped his head towards them. 'You boys in bombers an' all then?'

At Piccadilly they paid him off and spilled out on to the street, looking around in bemused wonderment. The pavements were packed, London awash with homegoing office and shop staff, tourists, shoppers, show-goers, street vendors and milling uniforms of every colour and description. And the emerging night shift. Within seconds, as if by magic, three girls had materialised before them.

'Oi, Yanks!' they giggled. They seemed to pronounce it 'Ya-inks', their voices coarse and hard after the soft, lilting cadences of the Suffolk girls. They were dressed in tight dresses hemmed above the knee, their cheeks rouged, their lips ruby red. 'Looking for a good time, are ya? We can show you around, get you in all the posh places. Show you some sights.' They nudged one another. 'What d'ya say?'

More conferring. Eventually, Lajowski, Tork and Beans were led off in the direction of Leicester Square, arm in arm with the girls. Gerry Via remained at the kerb, Herman Keissling at his side.

'You married, Herm?' Via asked, sniffing up at the sky. Occasional fine droplets of rain fell like mist. London had a familiar mustiness to it. Grimy sidewalks, overflowing trash, kind of dirty, but alive with the feet of a million hurrying strangers. Not unlike parts of New Jersey, Via felt. Then a red bus appeared, a double-decker, just like the ones in the postcards and the habituation films they showed at base, circling round the little island in the middle of the Circus. He watched it pass, its world-famous strangeness, perversely, reminding him of home. Home. He had barely thought of it, closed it off, until now.

'You bet,' Keissling was saying. 'Four years. Blanche. Want to see a picture? We got a kid too. Elvin, see, there, he's gonna be two. Looks just like me, wouldn't you say?'

'Cute.' Via handed back the photograph.

'What about you, Gerry, you married?'

'Nope.' He glanced in the direction of the others, melting from sight among the crowds. 'Not even close. But I never paid for the company of a lady yet, and I have no intention of starting now. Shall we walk a ways?'

In gathering darkness they set off, at random, downhill. At Pall Mall they turned east into Trafalgar Square where they paused dutifully among tiers of tourists on the steps of the National Gallery to admire Nelson's Column, Admiralty Arch and the view down Whitehall. Off St Martin's they stopped at a Lyons corner house for an indeterminate and barely warmed-through dish of the day described by the eye-rolling waitress as shepherd's pie, but comprising mostly cabbage and potato.

Drifting back along the Strand they stopped outside a rowdily noisy pub. A sign in the window said: 'We welcome U.S. enlisted.' It boasted real Kentucky bourbon under the bar, and it was stiff with shouting GIs. They fought their way to a table, once again propositioned en route by English girls, cruising like starving hyena among the crew-cuts, the even-teethed smiles and the gentle, flat-vowelled ribaldry.

'Well, now I know why they call them Piccadilly

commandos!' Keissling grinned sheepishly. 'Nothing seems to stop them.' Some of the girls made a pretence at small talk, others, the desperation unmistakable in their faces behind the pasted-on smiles, dispensed with all but the bare formalities.

'Two quid, mate,' one said, leaning over the table towards Via. 'Mite', she pronounced it. Despite the lines of her face, and a dullness, a dead heaviness in her eyes, the smudged lipstick, and the spareness of her body, she still looked barely eighteen. 'Two quid. Or three quid the pair of ya. 'Ow about it?'

'What's your name?' Via asked.

'Kate.' Kite. 'What's yours?'

'Gerry. Gerry Via. How old are you, Kate?'

'Twenty-one, so are you comin' or what?'

'Not just now. Take a seat for a few minutes, Kate. Let me buy you a drink.'

'Say, listen, Gerry, buddy, it's getting late.' Keissling, glancing towards the girl, was rising from the table. 'I gotta tell you I am just completely tuckered. I think I'll head along to the USO quarters and hit the sack. I could sleep for a week.'

Half an hour later, Via left the bar, alone, and began to walk. Aimlessly at first, then more briskly, and with purpose. He found his way to the river, crossed over, turned left, crossed back again. Then, hunched into the turned-up collar of his uniform jacket, he followed the blacked-out Embankment east. Towards the City. An hour after that the air-raid warning sounded.

Heather followed the freshly powdered and perfumed Rosamund into Rosamund's sitting room precisely as their

213

allotted twenty-five minutes elapsed. Inside the room, the two men, Gerald Garrett and Sir Richard Howard Vyse, broke off their conversation and rose as one to their feet, surprise and delight arranged on their faces in the time-honoured tradition, as though the reappearance of the ladies was some totally unexpected miracle.

'Ah, look, there they are!' Gerald beamed, gesturing towards high-backed leather armchairs. 'Lovely. Come and join us here by the fire and let me fix you both a whisky and soda.'

'We're not interrupting anything important, I trust?' Rosamund recited her line dutifully. It made no difference; she'd find out everything later.

'Absolutely not, dear lady. Armament production figures and harvest statistics. Frightfully dull.' With a wet click, Sir Richard, wearing a rumpled dinner suit, returned his pipe to his mouth, patting pockets for matches. Smoke hung beneath the ornately corniced ceiling like fog. Gerald too was smoking, his usual evening panatella. Heather wondered where he got them from. He never seemed to run short.

'A record, I hear. At least in Suffolk,' Rosamund said. 'The harvest, I mean.'

'Yes, our farmers have done us proud, mercifully. But, by heavens, we need it.'

With her fingers almost completely stilled once more, Heather accepted the elegantly cut whisky tumbler from her father-in-law. His eyes, an uncharacteristic mix of kind-ness and concern, lingered questioningly on hers. She nodded a smile back, before returning her attention to the wood fire flickering in the grate. It had been that sort of an evening.

They'd dined, just the four of them, closeted in draughty splendour up one end of a candlelit table in the Garretts' darkly panelled dining room. Game pâté followed by a pheasant casserole. The pâté tasted slightly rancid, the pheasant thin and tough, but at least it was meat, albeit a rare superannuated relic of Gerald's once-abundant game shoot. A thin wedge of rock-hard Cheddar followed. But if the fare was a little bleak, the wine was nothing short of miraculous, a vintage claret pulled from a dusty case laid down, Gerald explained, the very day David had been born. Heather, eating sparingly, drank rather more of it than was her custom, half listening in reflective silence as the claret, rich, smooth and velvety, slipped past her lips, and the talk returned, time and again, to the only topic that really mattered. For Sir Richard's invitation, she knew, had been no mere guileless gesture of hospitality on the part of the Garretts. He was there to be grilled, yet again, about the plight of their son. Her husband.

Soon a muzzy glow had begun to envelop her, insulating her like a warm cocoon from the uncompromising harshness of the few available facts. And the more they talked, the more she heard of the indefatigable yet futile efforts to trace David, and the unimaginable desperation of his situation, the more her spirits sank. And the lower they sank, the more her thoughts returned, like guilty secrets, again and again, to John Hooper.

For he was real and David was not. It was as depressingly simple as that.

He came once or twice a week, usually, she soon divined,

215

after he had flown a mission. He never announced his visits, never warned her that he might be coming, nor, for that matter, that he might not. He simply arrived at her door, cap in hand, asking in his quiet American way if it was any trouble to her that he was there. Once or twice he visited when she was out. One day she returned late from preparing the schoolroom for the start of the autumn term to find him waiting, exactly as he had on that second occasion, sitting propped against her front garden wall. On others she came home to find no Hooper, but a tin of corned beef, or a thin volume of Whitman, or a hastily scrawled note lying on the step. Within a week or two she was subconsciously planning her errands for the mornings, where possible, to avoid missing him. Another week and she found herself briefing him, in a roundabout way, on her movements, her working hours, shopping habits and so on, telling him quite openly, in other words, when she was most likely to be at home.

She would make him tea, or if it was later, pour him a glass of sherry from her meagre stock. Usually both, although gratefully accepted, would remain untouched at his side until he departed. Together they would sit on a pair of David's rickety deckchairs outside the back door, overlooking her vegetable garden. Or opposite one another in her sitting room. Or, if the evening was fine, beside the stream at the bottom of the field across from her cottage.

And talk. His appetite for it was insatiable. He needed to talk and he needed to hear. It was as though conversation provided his only release from the demons that drove him through his war. That very afternoon he had sat, hunched forward on the armchair in her front room, his hands pressed between his knees, talking non-stop for an hour about his home, his childhood, his sister, growing up in Pennsylvania. But dispassionately, objectively, as though reciting facts and figures from memory. As though describing someone else's childhood. Then just as suddenly, he had switched tack and begun quizzing Heather about hers.

'You said your father was a doctor,' he began. 'What kind of medicine?'

'He's a general practitioner. Or was. Retired now.'

'Oh, right, yes. And your parents live in Lincoln, where you grew up. Tell me about that. You have a younger brother too, no?'

'Yes, Richard. He's missing, of course. As well.'

'Yes, yes, like David, I know. A year and a half. Your brother, and your husband. I thought it would be impossible to imagine loss like that.' His eyes, ringed with fatigue, lifted to hers. 'But you know, I find that I can.'

'Yes. I believe that.' A pause. She felt herself moving beneath his eyes. Without warning a distance might come over them, a cloud of concentration. As though in his head he was somewhere else, or trying to be. Then he would be back, the cloud would vanish and his gaze would soften and crinkle into a smile.

'Tell me all about that,' he would say. 'Your childhood with Richard, in Lincoln. Was it happy? Tell me everything.'

And so it went on. Long, fervent bursts of monologue followed by brief spells of reflective silence. The questions, when they came, the scrutiny, were like interrogation. Relentless, exhausting, intensely intimate, as though he was stripping away the protective layers with which she had so meticulously surrounded herself, in order to gain access to the bared core of her. Of them both. Yet not invasively, somehow, not in a malevolent or threatening way. It was not violation he was engaged in, she sensed, it was simplification.

Usually, after a couple of hours, he began to slow as fatigue finally overcame him. He rarely slept the night before a mission, she'd learned. He rose before dawn, took off with his crew from the sleeping countryside, flew through murderous hailstorms of flak and lethal rivers of fighters' bullets, then returned, homing like a bird to Suffolk, for tea and a chat. With her. War and peace. All in a day. It was as inconccivable as it was bizarre.

His silences would become protracted, so much so that she thought he might be asleep. But then suddenly he would stiffen, rise, and with formal correctness thank her, apologise and leave. Afterwards she would feel like a wrung-out dishcloth.

A third bottle of Gerald's wonderful wine appeared at the table and she felt his hand touching her shoulder as he refilled her glass. A caution? A gesture of support? Stiff upper lip, old girl? Or watch out, don't drink too much? She no longer cared. Time was running out, that's all she knew. She felt her eyelids flutter. Across the table, Sir Richard and Rosamund were conversing in low tones. They must hurry. They must try harder, all of them, David too. He *must* try harder. To exist.

For there was nothing she could do for him, not a single solitary thing, if he didn't exist.

Mission days were the worst. Lying in her bed hearing the

Fortresses fly out, hours, often, before dawn. Then waiting, a gnawing in her stomach, while the day slowly grew and ripened, and the hours dragged and dragged. Then finally, with her head cocked at her desk, or her hand frozen at the blackboard, she would hear herself shushing noisy pupils to silence, straining for the first far-off rumble of the returning bombers. At the same moment, with Pavlovian predictability, Billy Street, if he was in attendance that day, would sit up at his desk and ask her permission to visit the toilet block. Invariably she granted it. He would return to the classroom only when every one of the homecoming aeroplanes had passed safely overhead. Once at his desk she would then find herself, breath held, watching for his coded wink, or little nod, or wiggled thumbs-up, to tell her that he had identified *Misbehavin Martha* among them. About two hours later, she grew to learn, she could expect a knock at her door.

But the tension, the suspense, everything, was too much, too exhausting. She was so tired, yet at the same time so fired up. Sleep was impossible. Night after night she would throw back the covers, descending in despair to the sitting room and the armchair where he sat by the window. There, curled on it like a cat, a blanket about her shoulders, she passed the dead watches of the night in restless half-slumber, her mind in turmoil, her heart like lead. In the days that followed, punch-drunk with sleeplessness, she would find herself, her mind a complete blank, staring at the sparse shelves at the greengrocer's, or the smudged pages of her pupils' exercise books, or the mildewed walls of her cottage bathroom, utterly unable to focus on why she was there, or what she was doing.

She was sharing his burden, that's what she was doing. Helping him, providing a means to ease his pain, his fear, his suffering. She was able to help this man as surely as she was unable to help her husband. It felt wrong, yet it felt so right. And deep down the core questions heaved and stewed inside her like a witch's cauldron. What, really, was she doing? Where would it end? What were her real feelings, and how much longer could she go on denying them? There was no more time. They were destroying her.

She was standing up. Up on her feet and leaning across the table. Her head was reeling; she heard the clatter of her chair on the floor behind.

'Heather? Heather, dear! For God's sake, are you all right?'

'You've got to find him!' she screamed, her fingers like claws at Vyse's arm. 'David! You've got to, don't you see that? Find him, find my husband. Before it's too late!'

'Ray? Ray, love? Is that you?'

Ray pushed the door quietly to and tiptoed into their darkened bedroom. 'Yes, Mags, only me. Didn't want to disturb you.' He sat down on the edge of the bed and began unbuttoning his shirt.

'Is it late?' she asked.

'Yes, love. Sorry. I was downstairs.'

'Percy in?'

'Just got back. We had quite a chat.'

'Really? What about?'

'Oh, you know, the old days, old farming practices and that. His memory's amazing when you get him on to the past. He may not be able to tell you what day it is today, but he remembers every damn detail of the 1904 Ransomes plough-ing competition.'

'Did he win?'

'No. Came second to Ernie Bolsover.' Ray's dry chuckle floated in the darkness. 'That's probably why he never forgot it!'

'I'm glad, love. Glad you had a proper talk and that. It's been so long.'

Ray stood from the bed to tie his pyjamas. 'I know, in my heart of hearts, it's the senility thing. I know he's not really with us most of the time. But sometimes, you know, just occasionally, he's right there. Right here, sharp as a pin. He asked where Claire was tonight. First time he's even men-tioned her in weeks. When I said she was staying up at Deirdre Fisk's he knew exactly where I meant. Just for a minute, then he was off again about the ploughing competi-tion. As if it happened this afternoon.'

'Bless him.'

'He said something about Billy, too.' Ray peeled back the blankets and slipped into bed next to her. Immediately she drew closer, snuggling her head into his arm. 'He said, well, to use his exact words, he said that little bleeder's got destiny. Whatever the hell that means.'

'Did you speak to Billy again? Did you talk to him?'

Ray nodded in the darkness. 'Tried to.'

'What did he say?'

He'd broken down. Completely. Pleading, begging tear-fully for forgiveness. No, not forgiveness. For help. Hunched, shaking, into a ball on his bed, sobbing silently. The fervour, the fear, had been shocking. Ray drew a breath, shutting the image from his mind.

'Ray?'

'He didn't say much. The arson thing, the fire at the warehouse, he said that was an accident. A prank gone wrong. He got trapped inside, turned out he was probably lucky to escape with his life, which explains why he doesn't like the forge much, scared to death of fire. Anyway, both the other kids involved died, and since Billy already had some previous form – you know, a bit of shoplifting, petty thievery and that – he got sent down to this boys' correctional institute place down near Maidstone.'

'But it's so unfair. It was an accident, and he could only have been, what, eleven? Twelve? And those places, they're so awful. Did he say anything about it?'

'Nothing.' Ray hesitated. 'Wouldn't say.' I'd die first, Mr H, he'd vowed tearfully through gritted teeth. Before going back there. I'd rather be dead. Precious little else, but Ray had guessed the rest. Systematic bullying and victimisation from the other boys, regular and vicious beatings from the custodians, living conditions no better than those of a caged animal. He'd lasted barely a month.

'What happened to him?'

'Well, from what that Blackstone woman said, and what little else Billy himself had to say about it, turns out he absconded from the place. Then he spent upwards of three weeks living rough, scrounging food and sleeping in sheds and that, until eventually he found his way back to London and one of the orphanages he'd stayed at earlier.'

'And they let him stay?'

'No, not officially. It's none too clear exactly what. But he had a friend there, one of the matrons, an Irish girl apparently,

222

who had a soft spot for him and took him under her wing.' And then he'd had a piece of luck. Bombs began to fall on the capital. It was the end of 1939, the evacuee programme was getting under way. All London's children, including those in homes and orphanages, were to be sent to the country for safety. Billy's Irish nurse friend had simply added his name to the orphanage's list. A day or two later, he found himself on a train full of children bound for Suffolk. On the way he tore the identity label from his lapel and threw it, together with Albert Crossley, out of the window. When he arrived at Ipswich station, together with hundreds of other tired, hungry and disoriented children and inadequate numbers of harassed co-ordinators, he simply told them he had lost it.

Beyond their window the night lay still and windless. Far in the distance drifted the thunder-like rumble of anti-aircraft fire. 'Shore batteries at Felixstowe,' Ray murmured. 'Sounds like London's going to cop it again tonight, poor beggars.' Maggie said nothing, holding him closer. They lay quietly for a while.

'That children's home,' Ray went on. 'The London one where the Irish girl worked.'

'What about it?'

'It's called St Cecilia's.'

'So?'

'Guess where it is.'

'London.'

'No, what address.'

'Go on.'

'King William Street. Do you see? That's where he got the name.'

'Hmm. Clever boy. I always knew that.' Maggie's head shifted on her husband's chest. 'What are we going to do about him, Ray? What are we going to do about our Billy?'

Ray exhaled. 'I don't know. It's out of our hands now. Mrs Blackstone is going to get in touch soon as she hears from the authorities. He'll probably have to go back and serve out his sentence. Something like that.'

'He can't. You know that. He just can't. It'll kill him.'

Chapter 9

The air-raid shelter was little more than a pedestrian under-pass, a wide, low-ceilinged corridor running under the street. It was unlit, although a roving ARP warden in a black tin hat shone a masked flashlight here and there, and, despite the no-smoking signs, the red glow of cigarette tips was everywhere. The shelter, full but not overly so, held about seventy people, mostly stray audience members from the movie theatres and shows nearby. Shadowy outlines in uniform jackets and over-coats lounged against walls, squatted down on the damp concrete floor or, in one or two cases, pressed themselves urgently against one another, heads bent together, arms tightly entwined. There was the resonant nasal murmur of desultory conversation punctuated occasionally by an excla-mation of surprise or a raucous guffaw. People seemed bored, resigned, but unmoved. Near the steps at one end of the shel-ter, Spitzer, Holland and Underwood waited for the all-clear.

'How long we been down here?' Holland asked.

'Lord knows.' Spitzer checked his Hamilton watch. 'Forty-five minutes maybe.' He took a cautious step upwards towards the exit, craning his neck to the little rectangle of visible night sky. A blacked-out building seemed to yawn into the gap; above it the sky was partly obscured by cloud. But clear enough, he could see, for visual bombing. They'd heard the muffled crump of explosions, about twenty minutes earlier, felt the vibration of impact beneath their feet, and the crack of answering anti-aircraft fire. But it had all been faint, indistinct, a good way off to the east, he'd guessed.

'Terrific way to spend your hard-earned weekend pass,' Holland grumbled good-naturedly. 'Holed up in the ground like rats in a trap, while the enemy drops high explosives on your head.'

'Does have a certain irony about it, though, wouldn't you say, Dutch? Now we know a little of what it feels like to be on the receiving end. Though I don't think we've had any hits closer than a mile.'

'Close enough for me, thank you, Lieutenant.'

'Hmm. Makes you think, though, doesn't it?' Spitzer hitched his uniform trousers, squatting down beside Irv Underwood who was sitting on the bottom step, staring at his feet, his head hunched into his shoulders. 'Irv? How you doing there, old buddy?'

Underwood nodded but made no response. Then he felt Spitzer's hand on his shoulder. A wave of emotion swept over him. He desperately wanted to take it, wanted to reach up and clasp his friend's hand in his own. But he didn't have the courage. 'I'm sorry,' he whispered miserably. Spitzer's hand gripped his shoulder in response.

On the steps, Dutch was unfolding a tourist map of London. 'Where the hell are we anyway?'

They were off Regent Street. They had stayed rather longer in the bar at the Grosvenor than they intended, unwilling to relinquish the warm splendour, the cheap Manhattans and the rowdily cheerful company of their own kind, yet at the same time anxious to step out into the mysteries of the Mayfair night. The bar was so busy and convivial, studded with beautiful ladies, and very senior 8th Air Force brass. They drank rather too much, had their backs clapped by Curtis Le May – shortly to be a major general, commanding 3rd Air Division – shook hands with Dinah Shore, found it hard to tear themselves away. Eventually they reeled down the steps and into the night.

Outside, the sky was clearing. A hazy quarter-moon, taped-up vehicle lamps and the dim, low-wattage signs permitted in the entrances of bars and restaurants weakly illuminated blacked-out streets busy with nightlife. They found a restaurant in Mount Street called Nico's, where they ate a creditable pasta and drank red wine from Ruffina bottles. 'But I thought these guys were supposed to be the enemy?' Irv queried at one point, blearily examining the label on an empty bottle. Their waiter, an elderly beak-nosed man of indeterminate nationality, but with a thick Mediterranean accent, quickly brought them another.

'Who cares? I haven't eaten linguine this good since we shipped out.'

From there the three officers wandered the nightclubs,

shopfronts and bars of the West End. They too were approached by the ubiquitous Piccadilly commandos, albeit from a different battalion, it seemed, from the ones patrolling the seamier quarters for enlisted men. Loren Spitzer, lagging behind the others, found himself standing before a tall, dark-haired woman who materialised like a vision from a doorway beside him.

'Good evening, Lieutenant,' she said politely. Her accent was that delectable cultured English that all his countrymen found so irresistible. She wore evening dress, mink stole, gloves, pearls, an assured smile. She was long and slender, stunningly beautiful. 'I am not about to attempt to proposition you, Lieutenant. If, however, you feel you might like me to accompany you tonight, I would be delighted to do so, for a token fee of five pounds, which includes any service you may wish, a room for the night, and breakfast.'

Spitzer could only swallow and gape. It was incredible. London. Everything they'd heard, it was all true. 'Any old thing your dick desires,' Lajowski had related knowingly on the train up from Ipswich that afternoon. Spitzer, like the others, had feigned worldly disinterest. Back home in Boise, Jean Nash, Denise Fitzpatrick, all the nice college girls he used to date, they didn't do it. Nice girls just didn't. But over here, nice girls clearly did. And it was no big deal to them, just a harmless transaction. This young woman, a hooker, standing here offering herself to him on a plate. Yet he could take her home to meet his folks and they'd think he'd bagged a duchess or something. *Five pounds with breakfast.* It was a joke catch-phrase back on base. It was even the name painted on one of the Forts in the low squadron. Now he knew it was true.

'Spitz? Hey, Spitz! What the hell you doing back there, buddy? Hurry up or we'll miss the show.'

They went to a cinema, off Golden Square. It was showing a James Stewart movie, which the three of them felt was highly appropriate, for at that moment Captain Stewart was commanding a squadron of Liberators of the 445th Bomb Group at Tibenham, not half an hour from their base. It was a late show, but the cinema was packed. They bought tickets and were fortunate to squeeze their way into a trio of seats right at the front of the dress circle.

Before the main attraction, there was a Pathé newsreel. Much of it featured war news from the different theatres of operation, and footage from the fronts. Eastern, western, the home front of course. The Atlantic and the Pacific, the precarious new Allied toe-holds in Italy, North Africa, south-east Asia. It was an unerringly optimistic review, ruthlessly selective, devoid of a single negative item. Bad news was simply omitted, downplayed or dressed up as good. Even when describing the ongoing hardships, dangers and deprivations British civilians faced day after day, the newsreader, his English voice plummy and strident, managed to sound unnervingly enthusiastic.

'. . . no time now for the little woman to worry about life's little shortages! She has home fires to keep burning, and a hubby in Tunis, busy pushing back Rommel's mighty Panzers!'

Spitzer nudged Underwood in the darkness. Irv seemed to be nodding off. 'Hey, Irv, will you get a load of this guy!'

'. . . meanwhile, the Yanks are here! And gosh-darn, aren't we pleased to see them! Never mind the gum, chum, these bomber boys know what's what. And just try stopping them! Fearlessly braving the very worst that Goering's mighty Luftwaffe can throw at them.'

It happened very quickly. One second the film, clearly from an airborne camera, grainy, jerky, black and white, showed a stick of bombs tumbling earthwards towards a smoke-covered target. The next, with the commentator's voice as enthusiastic as ever, it cut to a formation of B17s flying through puffs of dirty grey flak. Then the camera swung forward, hunting briefly from side to side, before fastening on a small, fast-moving cross turning in towards the bombers. A second later it captured the Messerschmitt fighter, banked over on its side, as it attacked the camera-carrying airplane. Then it was gone and the camera was inside the bomber, aimed at the two waist gunners firing after it.

'No!' Irv Underwood jerked suddenly in his seat, yelping loudly, like a panicked child pursued by wasps. Heads turned in surprise. He was totally oblivious, his eyes fastened to the screen, his arms scrabbling at his head.

'Irv!' Holland leaned away from the wildly thrashing co-pilot. 'Irv! Jesus, Spitzer, what the hell is wrong with him?'

The two fought to calm him, but another fighter was coming in for the attack. Underwood screamed again and tore himself free from their grasp, tumbling from his seat on to the floor, his arms clamped over his head.

'Get it away!' he pleaded, his eyes wild with terror. All around them spectators gaped in astonishment. Holland and Spitzer shushed and struggled to control him. The newsreel moved on to a different story. Something about King George visiting a munitions factory in Coventry. Still Underwood struggled. 'For God's sake,' he kept begging, again and again, 'for God's sake. Please get it away!'

Gerry Via was miles from them, off the Southwark Bridge Road, lost, but until that moment largely unconcerned about it, when the first bombs began to fall. It was a residential area, as far as he could tell, no nightclubs or restaurants, few shops or office blocks, just row upon row of blacked-out houses. To him, many looked derelict, or abandoned, and apart from the occasional shadowy figure, the ever-present pigeons, and a couple of scrawny cats, there were few signs of life. It was empty, run down, and a little threatening. Not a part of London you see much of in the guidebooks and habituation shows, he reflected, wondering how on earth he would find his way back to Piccadilly Circus, and the others.

He had just stopped, on a little traffic island, right in the middle of a road, searching in vain for a landmark, a street sign, or better yet one of those friendly London bobbies, always pictured in the guidebooks giving directions to tourists, when the eerie drone of air-raid sirens began to swell in the gloom around him. A curtain twitched at a window directly across from him, a young face briefly showing, then it was gone. Within seconds there were a series of dull crumps, some distance away, and a brief flicker of orange far beyond some rooftops. Then came the irregular unsynchronised thrumming of approaching German bombers. Fascinated, he watched fingers of harsh white light spring skywards, as searchlights began raking the night for the intruders. Then, from somewhere down near the river, the steady boom, boom, boom of an anti-aircraft battery opened up. Then another, then a third.

It was amazing. One moment, a deserted street, silent and empty as a grave. The next, it was like the fourth of July. He'd attended compulsory air-raid training back at Bedenham, of course; everyone had. He'd even been there when the base had been attacked a couple of times, usually by some hit-and-run loner taking a wrong turning on his way home. Nobody took much notice; most people didn't even bother getting out of bed when the sirens went.

But this was something else. The noise was incredible, the roaring thrum of hundreds of bombers' engines, interspersed with the pounding flash and crack of anti-aircraft guns, what the Limeys called ack-ack, with their glowing tracer shells arcing thousands of feet into the night. Searchlights, more and more by the minute, criss-crossed the sky, hunting their targets. And then there were the bombs, falling everywhere now, a continuous unrhythmic tattoo of heavy, concussive thuds that you heard inside your head, and felt deep in your guts. Like an artillery barrage. What was it the Londoners called it? The Blitz. Short for Blitzkrieg, German for lightning-war. It sounded like some monstrous unseen giant stomping across the city.

And it was getting closer. He watched in detached fascination as a stick fell nearby, erupting not three blocks away. He recoiled, gasping at the flash, an image, a church, lit from behind, seared on to his eyes. A second later, the blast from the explosion reached him, rocking him on his heels. Then there was another, much bigger, much closer, ear-poppingly loud. He felt its shock, its heat pass right through him, like a wave, the ground shuddering beneath his feet. At the same instant, a house at the end of the street jumped between its neighbours, literally sprang upwards and outwards amid a huge cloud of blood-red dust and smoke. The cloud rose, lifting into the sky before him. There it hung, like a vast, filthy curtain, before sinking slowly to the rubble-strewn ground, where it spread, rolling, wave-like, down the road towards him. As it cleared, he saw that the bombed house had gone. Vanished. Even though its neighbours appeared untouched. He wondered, with an involuntary shiver, if anyone had been inside.

It was only then that the danger of his own situation struck him. He was in the open. Standing there, one hand still shielding his eyes from the flash, gawking like a jackass in the middle of the goddamn street. Nowhere to go, nowhere to hide. Paralysed into inaction. Transfixed, yet again, like a rabbit in headlights. He forced himself to look round, forced himself to move, stumbling backwards, away from the bombs. More were falling, all around him; the noise was deafening, numbing. He couldn't think, couldn't act. He turned, tried to run, but the ground shook beneath his feet, his legs felt like jelly, heavy and cumbersome. It was slow motion. Running through mud. There were more and more explosions, gaining on him from behind, each one nearer, each more powerful than the last. Terror welled in him. Soon, his arms and legs pumping, he was in full flight, sprinting, as though from ravenous wolves, from the very dogs of hell, desperate and directionless. He heard the harsh ringing of feet on asphalt, the hoarse gasps of his own panicked breathing. Then there was a long, whistling shriek from somewhere behind him, and an instant of silence. Then a blinding flash lit the whole street, a blast of heat and shock followed, and a monstrous explosion lifted him, bodily, arms and legs flailing, high into the air. As if he were flying, floating, in space. Then everything went black.

'Did you ever see anything the like of it in all your born days?' Marion Beans, hands on hips, stepped gingerly on to the station platform, Lajowski and Tork on either side. The platform, an east-bound Central Line station on London's Underground, was packed, completely filled from one end to the other. Awash. Spread out before them, covering every available yard from the curving tiled wall right to the platform's gaping edge, was a sea of people. Old and young, large and small, sound and infirm. Mothers with babies, snoring old men and gossiping crones. Busmen, bellboys, barmaids, bricklayers. Sailors and shopgirls, soldiers and students, sweethearts and schoolchildren. And they were on the ground, almost all of them, sitting, reclining or lying fully prone. Some were congregated in complete family groups: grandparents, aunts and uncles, parents, children. Others sat singly or in pairs. Nearby, a dozen youths played cards in a circle. Another, older group, farther along the platform, sang pub songs. Some had brought baggage with them, keepsakes and valuables, even small items of furniture, as if going on a journey. They read newspapers, held huddled conversations, argued, told jokes or just slept. They ate sandwiches, drank beer from bottles and soup from Thermos flasks. Or simply stared emptily at the peeling posters adorning the condensation-drenched walls. One or two, despite the

234

absence of even the slightest scrap of privacy, wrapped themselves in each other's arms beneath a blanket or overcoat, closed their senses to the seething masses around them, and surrendered to their passion. Running in and out of it all, like the last trickles of water through a dried-up river, streamed curling lines of children, dozens at a time, screaming with excitement, their arms spread wide like wings.

'Jesus. It's like – well, it's like something out of the Bible.' Lajowski stared around incredulously. Al Tork nodded. Although the precise context escaped him, he knew what Lajowski meant. Something about multitudes coming down from the mountain, and the gathering host. He wrinkled his nose. The gathered host's smell was not good: sweat, grime, bad tobacco and heavily over-subscribed toilets. Even the noise that rose from it sounded biblical, like a sort of rapidly spoken mass prayer, or chant. It resonated back and forth along the tube-like concourse, merging and melting into a single, indistinct, background burble. It reminded him of the noise inside the rearing shed on his parents' goose farm.

'Yanks! Look, Yanks!' In a moment a posse of children had surrounded them, a toothily grinning circle of grubby round faces, while a dozen unseen fingers plucked at their uniform buttons and stole into their pockets.

'Gum chum!' They began right away. 'Give us the gum chum!'

With a shrug, the three emptied their uniforms of what edibles they had. Hushed suddenly, the children grabbed at their hands like starving chicks. Beans, winking at the others, gently retrieved his open wallet from one wide-eyed boy's sweet-stained grasp. 'Can you believe this?' he murmured.

Tork shook his head. 'I had absolutely no idea. It's like those refugee camp films we get on the newsreel, in Holland and Belgium and places. Kind of pitiful to see. But then again, it's kind of cheery, don't you think? Nobody seems to give much of a damn.' He leaned towards an old man sitting on a bench nearby. 'Excuse me, sir. But how long do you have to stay down here in the subway like this?'

'We don't 'ave to stay at all, mate.' The old man grinned.

Tork looked confused. 'Then why—'

'Listen, son. When you're copping two or three raids a night, you soon get brassed off tramping up and down them bloody escalators. Damn sight less bother to stay put. More sociable, too, wouldn't you say? Dead cosy.'

Tork looked round. 'Dead . . . er, yes, sir, I kind of see your point. But don't they have, you know, like real bomb-shelters for you to use?'

The old man shrugged. 'If you want. But down here's safe as houses. Safer. We're more than ninety feet below ground, did you know? And it's a bloody sight warmer, too, 'specially in the winter. Far better than freezing yer bollocks off in one of them miserable municipal shelters, or some poxy Anderson nonsense dug in your back yard. No, lad, we'd rather be down 'ere any day, wouldn't we, Vera?' He nudged his dozing wife. 'By the way, son, couldn't spare us a couple of them fancy Yank cigarettes of yours, could you?'

Beans, his head turning this way and that, was moving slowly up the platform. Lajowski set off in the opposite direction, threading his way carefully among the litter of bodies. A few of them, the younger women especially, glanced up at him. Mostly, however, he was ignored. After a while, he came to the circle of card players. They looked about fifteen or sixteen years old. 'So, what's the game, fellas?'

'Beggar's bluff, mate. Want to play? Cost you a tanner in.'

'Sure, ah, beggar's bluff. Can't say I know it, but what the hell. Tanner in, did you say?'

Beans emerged from the gents' toilet a few minutes later to find a child, the small boy that had attempted to appropriate his wallet, barring his path. 'Say there, buddy,' he said absently. He peered down the platform. Tork and Lajowski were nowhere to be seen. Maybe the raid was ending. He'd better get going.

'Got any gum chum?' the boy said, his voice little more than a plaintive whisper. Beans stopped. The boy was staring up at him. He was very short, and very young, perhaps just three. His face was thin and pale, with watchful dark eyes. He wore a threadbare wool jumper and too large shorts. His bare legs were like brittle white sticks.

'No, ah, no, sorry. Your buddies clean cleared me out.'

'Got any chum gum?' There were tears welling. It was all he knew. Seek out the big, smiling men in the smart green uniforms, utter the magic spell, or something like it, and wonderful sweet things were sure to follow.

'No, like I said, I . . . oh, Christ.' Beans began checking through his pockets once more, the small boy's eyes following closely. 'Look, where's your mom, kid? Why don't we go and track her down? Maybe she's got something.' Still the boy stood, motionless, before him, mouthing his spell like a mantra. There was a dullness to his gaze, an emptiness. He looked half starved. Beans looked around. No one in the immediate vicinity seemed remotely interested in the child.

The fantastic notion, the incredible possibility that the boy might actually live down there, like some kind of orphaned subterranean stray, crossed his mind. He searched harder.

'No. Goddamn it, nothing! Can you believe that.' The boy's face fell again. 'Look, bud, I'd really like to help out, but . . .' His hand found his wallet once more, he pulled it out, opened it. There was nearly eight pounds in cash still left. Flustered, he plucked a ten-shilling note. Folding it between his fingers he bent to the boy. 'Look, take this. This'll buy you all the candy you can eat, and then some.'

But the boy wasn't looking at the money. He was looking at the wallet. At the round, blond-haired young woman's face that smiled out at him from it. His lips stopped chanting, the hunger in his eyes receded, and his thin fingers reached forward slowly, moving to touch the sun-kissed face.

When Via awoke it was dark, and cold, and deathly quiet. His cheeks were wet. He lay still for a moment, blinking. Was he dead? Was he wounded? His head hurt, quite a bit, and he felt dizzy, a little nauseous, but nothing else. He struggled slowly to a half-sitting position, checking himself for injuries. The street was completely silent, empty, exactly as if nothing had happened. No bombs, no ack-ack, nothing. The raid was over. But for how long? Ten minutes? Three hours? No injuries, he concluded, pulling himself more upright; none serious, that is. Damn miracle. There was a needle-sharp pain, high on his forehead. He must have struck it on the pavement when he was thrown by the blast. He reached up, fingering it carefully. It was a big bruise, a real egg, with a small gash on it, sticky with blood. The blood was drying.

And his cheeks. They too had been wet; he hadn't imagined it. So he had been crying. Fear? He remembered the raw rush of panic, his screaming, terrified flight as the bombs, falling nearer and nearer, pursued him down the street.

But no, they weren't tears of fear.

It was Dave Greenbaum. Big, smiling Kentucky Dave. Lying in his arms, with his wide-open face slack and smiling no more, and his bright eyes dulling, while his blood, his life, flowed from him like a river, out across the floor in *Martha*'s waist. And all the while he, Gerry Via, ship's nominated medic, just looked on, transfixed, and did nothing. Except stare, and feel afraid, and pray to God that Dave would hurry up and die.

It was the femoral artery, he'd learned later. The base paramedics told him, after they'd lifted Dave's lifeless body from the ship and carried it to the hospital for post-mortem. He'd waited outside. Skulked there all evening, alone and unseen, until they came and told him. Severed femoral, they said simply. Dave had bled to death. They acted kind, but their faces told him all he had to know. The death had been needless. And later that same night he'd stolen into the reading room in the drop-in centre, where they kept all the newspapers and magazines and current affairs materials, and also all the technical manuals and self-help books. He'd looked it up in one of the medical manuals. Femoral: the main artery of the lower limb, continuation of the external iliac artery, it enters the front of the thigh halfway along the fold of the groin. You can't miss it, can even see it, plain as day; he'd stripped off there and then on the floor of the reading room, locating his own femoral in seconds. Book said you can even take the pulse using it. So all he'd had to do, to stop Dave from dying, was slip off one glove, feel down the groin-fold until he got to where the blood was spurting, and just pinch off the severed artery with his fingers until they got back on the ground. Nothing else required. No stitching, no suturing, no digging out of bullets or shrapnel, no complicated bandaging or setting of smashed bones. Simple. He could have done it with his eyes closed.

Yet he hadn't. He hadn't done a single goddamn thing. He hadn't even been able to talk to Dave in his final minutes. Offer his fading friend one crumb of comfort. He'd just sat there, staring into those wide, questioning eyes, wishing he'd hurry up and die.

He rose unsteadily to his feet, brushed the dirt from his uniform and began to walk, retracing his steps back along the street. It looked the same. Yet not. It was pocked with holes and craters, bricks and rubble were strewn everywhere, broken glass crunched beneath his feet. To either side, tattered curtains billowed from black sockets where windows had blown out, front doors hung drunkenly from hinges, huge ragged holes gaped where sections of roofs and walls had been gouged, as though by a giant, axe-wielding hand. Reaching the end of the road, he paused for breath. The little traffic island, the one he had been standing on when the bombs began falling, was gone. In its place a perfectly circular twenty-foot crater yawned. Peering in, he could see water spewing into it from a fractured main.

'Oi! You! Get the bloody hell away from there, right now!' A shout, loud and authoritarian, echoed from the corner. Two men, tin hats and dark boiler-suits, were standing against a van. Via approached them.

'Are you hurt?' the second one said, glancing at Via's forehead.

'What? Ah, no, no. It's nothing. A scratch. What's going on?'

'Well, as a wild guess, I'd say the street got bombed.' The first man nudged his mate. 'Wouldn't you, Reg?'

'We're waiting for back-up, before going in for survivors,' the second man added.

'Survivors?' The slivers of light at the curtains, the hurrying, shadowy figures, the pale face at the window. Yet it was so deathly, palpably silent. 'There are people in there? Alive? But why wait? Shouldn't we be trying to get them out?'

'Yanks.' The first man rolled his eyes, then began counting off on his fingers. 'In case you hadn't noticed, chummy, there's a mighty strong pong of gas around here. The Gas Board boys need to get it turned off, up the road there at the main. Next, you can bet your boots there's bombs in the middle of that lot that didn't go off, plus a few of the delayed fuse variety thrown in for good measure. The whole bloody road could go up any second. So we need a bomb-disposal crew to take a shufti before we can go in and start poking around. Next, we can count ourselves bloody lucky that there's no fire. Yet. But there could be, any minute, so we need fire cover, plus the fire boys' masonry shifting gear. Finally, there's injured, and there's dead. So a couple of ambulances and some medics might be handy for that, wouldn't you say?'

'But where the hell are they all? When will they be here?'

'Soon as they can,' the second man, Reg, said gently. 'It was a bad one. Everything east from here, Southwark,

Bermondsey, Wapping, Limehouse, they all got walloped. Services are pretty stretched, but there's relief on the way, from Lambeth and Westminster divisions. They'll be here when they can.'

He stayed for the rest of the night, helping. Digging, fetching, carrying, digging again. He worked tirelessly, as though driven, and without a break, clambering awkwardly among the hillocks of brick rubble, picking, hour after hour, through the smashed ornaments, the crushed pictures, the broken furniture, the shattered lives. He spoke little, except when spoken to, or to acknowledge instructions. Okay, laddie, we're done in here, you can move through to the next room, now. Or the next house. And the next.

Everywhere there was an air of calm urgency. Everyone worked steadily, and hard, but without wasteful desperation. And there was a kind of stoic cheerfulness about it, a togetherness, even occasional jocularity. One fireman reached up to a toilet dangling precariously from a blown-out wall. As he tugged at the chain the whole thing collapsed at his feet. Someone else pulled over an upturned armchair to find a cat complete with litter of kittens beneath, all alive. At such times there would be exclamations of surprise, brief peals of laughter. But soon the heads would go down again and the digging went on. And on. Then, from time to time, a shout would go up as someone shifted rubble to find a dusty human limb lying amid the debris. Sometimes the limb was attached to a dead body. Sometimes it wasn't attached to anything. Three times during the night it turned out to be attached to a living person.

'Who's the Yank?' a young nurse in overalls asked Reg, at

242

one point. Via had joined a line of firemen, straining with them to pull down a teetering wall with ropes and grappling poles.

'No idea, love. Walked out of this mess shortly after we got here, hasn't stopped since.'

A while later, around the time a thin grey dawn was breaking over the scene, she tapped him on the arm and thrust a tin mug into his hand. 'Here, have this. You look as though you could do with it.' Panting, he stopped, as though ordered, grasped the mug, knuckles bloodied, nodding gratefully. His face was grey with fatigue and brick-dust, his uniform torn and filthy. 'Look at the state of you,' she scolded, gently brushing plaster from his shoulder. He smiled, faintly, just for a second. The tea, tepid and sweet, tasted alien, yet wonderful. Calming and reviving. No wonder Brits drank it by the gallon. He stood at the shattered roadside, just for a few minutes, while it purged the dust from his throat, and warmed his empty stomach. Then he went back to work.

Suddenly, around seven in the morning, more vans and trucks pulled up at the roadside. The men and women in Via's group, about thirty in all, began to pack up.

'What's happening?' he asked.

'Day shift, laddie. We're all done here, for now, anyway.'

'But can't I stay?'

The man, it was the one who'd shouted at him the night before, shook tobacco on to a paper, rolling it deftly between stubby fingers. 'No, son, you cannot. You're done, exhausted. That's when mistakes happen, see? Accidents.' He licked the paper. 'But you did well, really you did. You can be proud of yourself.'

'Proud.'

The man punched him lightly on the shoulder, then stepped up into the cab of his truck. 'Certainly. You did a fine job. What's your name and outfit, by the way? You'll get a mention in the report. Your superiors may even get to hear about it. Eventually.'

'Excuse me.' It was the nurse who'd brought him the mug of tea. She was standing beside him. 'I'm off duty now, too. Do you fancy some breakfast?' She had brown hair, brown eyes. Her cheek was dusted with grime. She was smiling.

'I'm sorry, what did you say?'

'Breakfast? I could clean up that bruise for you, too.'

Amid a cloud of exhaust, the truck's engine barked to life. 'Name, laddie!'

Via turned to look back down the street. It felt like he was abandoning a kind of home. 'Greenbaum, sir. Technical Sergeant David O. Greenbaum. Five-twentieth Bomb Group, USAAF. Bedenham, Suffolk.'

He damn near missed the train. Liverpool Street station was seething, as usual, the destination board completely incomprehensible. He quickly gave up, elbowing his way across the concourse to the nearest barrier.

'Ipswich!' he sputtered at a harassed ticket collector. 'The goddamn Ipswich train, which track is it?'

'Eight. But you'd better get your skates on, chum, it's just pulling out.'

Five minutes later, breathless and sweating, he was squeezing his way along the gently rocking corridor when he spotted a familiar face standing at a window.

244

'Gerry! Whoa, Gerry, it's me, Keissling!'

'Oh.' Via started, as though from a dream. 'Right. Herm. You made it.'

'Only just, bud. Went to that National Gallery art place, you know it? On the big plaza with that damn great sailor's column thing in the middle. Amazing pictures, Gerry, just amazing, you should see it. Anyway, I completely lost track of the damn time and had to make a run for it. Say, what happened to your head?'

Via fingered the bandage that the nurse, Joanna Morrison, had taped to his forehead that morning. A lifetime ago. 'This? Oh, nothing. Fell down in the street. Hit my head, that's all. Damn stupid.'

'Yeah. After I left you and that Kate broad in the bar last night, I'll bet.' Keissling nudged Via in the ribs. 'Where are the rest of the guys? Did you find them yet? Did they make the train?'

'I, uh, I'm not sure. I haven't caught up with them.'

'Well, let's get going, bud! Maybe they got a compartment or something. Just wait till I see them. That National Gallery place, you've just got to see it.'

They found the rest of *Martha*'s crew. The train was packed, practically every seat occupied, together with much of the aisle and corridor space, by American servicemen returning to East Anglian bases after their weekends of rest and recreation. Many looked in worse condition than when they had set out. Keissling and Via worked their way along corridors lined with cursing recumbent bodies, carriage after carriage filled to overflowing with sleeping airmen. Eventually, they forced themselves halfway into yet another compartment. Its blinds were drawn, its sliding door appeared to be jammed. Peering around it, they caught sight of Emmett Lajowski's booted foot wedged on the other side.

'What's the damn password, assholes.' He grinned.

'Let us in or we'll break your neck?'

'That oughta do it.'

Everyone was there. They slammed the door, dumped their bags in the overhead nets and squeezed on to the bench seats, Keissling next to Lajowski, Tork and Spitzer, Via on the facing seat between Marion Beans and Dutch Holland. Irv Underwood, jammed against the window beside Holland, had his face to the glass as the train laboured slowly through London's eastern outskirts. Here and there tell-tale columns of smoke from bombed-out buildings rose into the evening sky.

They swapped air-raid stories. Tork and Lajowski related their exploits in the Underground station. Beans, uncharacteristically withdrawn, talked little, his round head turning from Tork to Lajowski as they spoke, nodding his agreement.

'And what about our 'lustrious officer corps?' Lajowski prompted, when they'd finished. 'Get stuck under anything interesting, so to speak?'

Spitzer glanced towards Underwood. His eyes were still focused sightlessly through the window, where featureless grey suburbs gave grudging way to fields of green and brown. After the raid, Irv had returned to the bar at the hotel, remaining there for most of the night. He hadn't shown up again until it was time to leave for the station. 'Nope. Sorry to disappoint, fellas. Quiet time. Cleaned up, had a meal, walked the sights a little. Went to the movies. Spent an hour in a shelter near the movie house but didn't see or hear much.' He shrugged. 'Dutch and I went walking in the park today. Saw that Speaker's Corner thing.'

'Say, I wanted to see that!' Keissling interjected. 'But I damn overslept. Left Gerry in that bar last night, went straight back to the hostel, hit the sack and slept right through. Twelve hours straight, do you believe that?' He looked round at his comrades, in case they might not. 'Guess I must have been pretty whacked.'

The compartment fell quiet, its eight occupants submerged in thought. The train rocked slowly on, rattling through a station, and across a bridge over a wide brown river bordered by glistening expanses of marble-smooth mudflats. To the west, a soft orange sun was emerging from beneath a line of dissipating clouds, dipping towards the horizon. Manningtree, the station signs said.

'This is where we cross back into Suffolk, isn't it?' someone said.

'Home on the range.'

'Feels a bit like that, don't it?'

Another silence.

'You know . . . our bombing? Our missions?' Beans began hesitantly. Some of the others looked up. Discussing operational matters in public places, even within the privacy of a closed railway compartment, was an instant court-martial offence.

'What of them?'

'Well, they are, you know, strictly, like, strategic, aren't they? You know, ball-bearing plants, ammunition factories, railheads and so on? Isn't that right? Strategic. We don't, like, we don't bomb civilians. Ordinary folks, that is. Do we?'

'Relax, Beaner. The day we start bombing civilians is the day I step down from my turret and walk away from this war.' Lajowski leaned forward, patting Beans' knee.

''S what I figured. Just making sure.'

'I wonder how Kid Ringwald made out,' Spitzer murmured. 'With that new girl of his. What's her name?'

'Claire Howden. The blacksmith's daughter. Lives up that little lane, to the left of the pub.'

'Oh, yeah, that's right. Nice girl.'

Dutch Holland looked up. 'I've been thinking about Lieutenant Broman. You know, Crew 19's first bombardier. Before me. I was wondering what he was like. And what happened to him.'

'He couldn't cut it, that's what happened to him. Couldn't cut it, so he walked clean away from it. And us.'

'Was that his fault, Emmett?' Underwood, turning from the window, spoke for the first time. 'Dan Broman was never meant to go to war. Some people just aren't, you know. It's not their fault, it's just a plain fact.'

Lajowski scowled. 'Plain fact is he still walked out on us.'

'That's as may be,' Keissling said briskly. 'But as far as I'm concerned, Crew 19's bombardier is old Dutch here, and that's that. A damn fine one he is too.'

Murmurs of agreement. Via stirred, wincing uncomfortably in his seat.

'What happened to your head, Gerry?' Tork asked. He had been studying Via curiously. 'And your uniform, for God's sakes. Looks like you been dragged through a hedge backwards.'

She'd led him to her rooms. Somewhere near Waterloo, so

she said. They walked in silence through empty Sunday morning streets, stopped to buy provisions from a kiosk, walked on once more until they came to a door next to a hardware shop. Joanna produced a key. 'It's not much, I'm afraid. I share it with a room-mate, Bridget. She's a nurse too, at St Thomas's. She won't be here, she's on days.'

'Right.' He'd followed her up the stairs to her flat, exhaustion dragging at his heels like lead. She opened the door and stood aside for him. It was three rooms: a bedroom with two single beds, a sitting and eating room with a little curtained-off kitchen, and a poky little bathroom with mildewed walls and a rust-streaked tub.

'Could I use that?' he asked, gesturing at the bath.

'Of course. I'll make tea. Give me your uniform, I'll see if I can sponge some life back into it.'

Five minutes later the bathroom door opened. He was already sinking into oblivion, deeply immersed, coarse-caked dust melting from him like a sloughed skin, the water, warm and soft, caressing his bruised and aching limbs. Barely conscious, he heard the door click shut again, heard shoes being kicked off, buttons popping undone, the whisper of falling underclothes. Then her hands were at his shoulders, easing him forwards. She was stepping into the water behind him, sliding her feet down beside his legs, pulling him down, deeper and deeper against her, his head sinking to the softness of her breasts, her arms closing over him, folding about his shoulders and chest, her lips at his neck, her fingers at the darkly haired skin of his belly.

Later, they made love in her cramped single bed. She cupped his cheeks in her hands, crossed her legs over his back, and with a frown of concentration furrowing her brow surrendered herself, eyes closed, to her desire. He watched her, watched her face, the pursing of her lips, the slight flaring of her nose, while he slid, slowly, deeply, in and out of her.

Then they'd slept. When they'd woken, he'd told her everything. About *Martha* and that first disastrous mission. Stoller, Broman, Spitzer, Irv. Dave Greenbaum. Everything. He couldn't stop himself, nor did he want to. He wanted no pity, no forgiveness, no exorcism. He just wanted it out. 'I could have saved him.' He wept. 'I could have, and I should have.'

'No. You couldn't. You didn't know how.'

'I should have known how! That's the point. It was my job to know how.'

She'd turned to him then on the bed, run her fingers through his thick black hair, still damp from the bath. 'I could teach you.'

The train lurched into darkness, entering a tunnel. Beyond the compartment, grunts of protest, scuffing of feet, the sound of passengers gathering themselves together. They were drawing into Ipswich. Via looked round the compartment.

'It's good to see you guys,' he said.

Chapter 10

Around three-quarters of the five hundred or so airfields built in the United Kingdom during the Second World War were located in the central and south-eastern portions of England. By far the highest concentration of these was in the predominantly flat and rural East Anglian counties of Essex, Norfolk and Suffolk. Bedenham, constructed by gang labour in just ten frantic months during 1942, was typical of the sixty-seven bomber bases destined for use by the 8th United States Army Air Force. Comprised of roughly a hundred bomber and escort fighter groups, the 8th's task was single-fold: mount and maintain a strategic daylight bombing campaign of unprecedented proportions aimed at inflicting unsustainable damage upon Germany's capacity to wage war.

By the autumn of 1943 that campaign was gearing up to full momentum. Missions were launched, almost on a daily basis, against shipyards, aircraft assembly lines and oil refineries. Artillery component plants, submarine repair pens, tank factories. Radar installations, weapons testing centres, secret development sites. And the essential infrastructure of communication and distribution: airfields, major roads and canals, bridges, railheads. Sometimes in formations of just thirty or forty aircraft, sometimes in vast wings of several hundred, daily the Fortresses and Liberators of the 8th, together with their fighter escorts of single-seater Mustangs and Thunderbolts, were pitted in a grinding war of numbers against a dogged and co-ordinated defence of breathtaking audacity and determination.

Losses were severe. By September, while the Russians were recapturing Smolensk, Mussolini was surrendering Italy, and a new Southeast Asia Command was being formed under Mountbatten, East Anglian B17 bomber groups like the 388th at Knettishall, the 390th at Framlingham and the 520th at Bedenham were sustaining losses as high as thirty per cent on some missions, sometimes higher. One rainswept afternoon early that autumn, a lone Fortress appeared out of the scud over Thorpe Abbotts, home of the 100th. Although it was not his base, the pilot, lost, flying on three damaged engines, and with wounded crewmen on board, wasted no time landing his wrecked aeroplane there. 'Do you know the whereabouts of my group?' Thorpe Abbotts' CO asked him over the radio. 'I've got twenty-three ships out there. They should be arriving home by now.'

'I'm sorry, sir,' the dazed pilot responded, 'but I don't think you will have anyone home from your group this day.'

It was to get worse, the attrition rate in ensuing weeks

growing to proportions close to unmanageable. New crews came and went so fast that older hands gave up trying to make friends with them. There was no point. Before you had a chance to get to know them, odds were they were already gone. In the last two weeks of September, the 520th, including *Misbehavin Martha*, racked up four more mission credits, bringing her crew's total to eleven. All four missions went to German-occupied France, and losses, although serious, were not as high as those suffered on missions to Germany. Nevertheless, they were high enough. In hut twelve, the bunk next to Al Tork's changed hands four times in a month. He began to believe it was cursed. One evening he clumped in through the door to find, yet again, that its sheets and blankets had been freshly changed, the clothes and baggage were gone, the family photos, pin-ups and personal souvenirs cleared away. Much later that night he was awakened by the arrival of the new replacement. 'Sorry to disturb you,' the man muttered, collapsing on to the bunk. At five the following morning, he, Tork and the rest of the hut were roused by the duty orderly. That day the 520th flew to attack the U-boat pens in La Pallice, enduring flak so intense it was as if the whole sky was bursting apart. *Martha* returned to Bedenham with more than forty holes in her fuselage and wings. The man in the bunk next to Tork's didn't return at all. 'I never even knew his goddamn name,' Tork cursed, pushing his own bunk across the floor. The others in *Martha*'s crew were doing the same, forming a private cordon at the end of the hut. The luckless airman meanwhile passed into folklore as The Man Who Came To Breakfast.

On 23 September they bombed a German aircraft factory

outside Paris, and on the 27th another aircraft works, all the way down in Bordeaux-Merignac. It was a long flight, ten hours, much too far for their fighter escort. So for most of the way they were completely unprotected from harrying attacks by the Messerschmitts and Focke-Wulfs. Flying number two, as usual, to Gene Englehardt's *Shack Time*, Hooper edged *Martha* in even closer than usual, until his right wingtip was just yards from *Shack Time*'s waist aperture. The fighters, their blunt noses bearing the bright red and yellow markings of the Luftwaffe's crack squadrons in France, stood off above and to the side, paralleling the formation, taking their time. Then, upon a given signal, they peeled off, often from opposing directions, and hurtled down on to the bombers at phenomenal speed, three or four at a time, wing and nose guns blinking. In an instant *Martha* and the other Fortresses were shuddering from the collective firing of their own weaponry, the air filled with tracer, shouted warnings and the stench of cordite. Hearts raced, mouths ran dry, skin prickled. Then the fighters were through and gone, circling, climbing, re-forming. For the next attack. And the next.

After each pass, the casualties. A Fortress, its engines streaming smoke, unable to maintain speed, began to slip helplessly back from the formation, there to be picked off by the waiting fighters like wolves at a crippled pack-mule. Another dropped, its wing folding up like a shot bird's, spinning endlessly round and round towards the waiting earth. A third simply blew up, leaving little evidence of its passing save an ugly brown stain on the sky and a litter of falling bodies and debris. By the time the formation was nearing Bordeaux-Merignac, a quarter of its force had gone.

'Here they come again!' Tork's voice, tense and urgent over the intercom. 'Stern attack, right side! Eight o'clock, three of them, coming in now! There! Keiss, Ringwald? Do you see them?'

'I see them!' the two chorused simultaneously. Keissling swung his waist gun rearwards, wrenched back the charging handle and squinted out along the barrel. The leading fighter, a Focke-Wulf 190, grew rapidly in his sights. 'Come on in, big fella.' He forced himself to wait, his sing-song catch-all on his lips. 'Short bursts, short bursts, come on come on come on.' Beneath his feet, eighteen-year-old Eldon Ringwald, his head bent to his sights, depressed the pedal to swing the ball turret towards the oncoming fighter, then on, past it, right through it, in a single steady sweep, until his guns were ahead of it, leading it, by a hundred yards or more. This time, he breathed. This time. He waited a second longer, held his breath and squeezed the triggers. At the same moment Keissling and Tork opened up from the waist and tail positions. Instantly something, a section of cowling, a piece of canopy, flew off the fighter, spinning into its slipstream, and a second later a thin plume of white smoke appeared from its engine. It broke off, veered away, rolling over to expose its oil-streaked underside. As it passed abeam, Lajowski opened up from the top turret; three, four, high-speed bursts of half a second each, his tracer shells arcing across and into the fighter's belly. A second later it exploded into a ball of orange flame. He lifted his head from the sights, gaping in astonishment. In the nose, Holland and Spitzer, their boots skidding, ankle deep, on hundreds of spent shell cases from their own guns, followed the flaming wreck as it fell. 'They got it.'

Spitzer could scarcely believe his eyes. 'Good God, they got it.'

'Incoming!' A shrill voice from the right waist. 'Two more, look, over there, Jesus!'

'Where, Beans! We need height and range. Quickly now.' Hooper.

'Ah, two, no, no, three o'clock! And high. Thousand yards.'

'I got 'em! They're coming in on *Morning Glory*.'

'Fort going down from the middle squadron. Looks like Patterson's ship.'

'Never mind that now, concentrate on those two on *Morning Glory*.'

'Here they come!'

'Short bursts, everyone! Short bursts.' Short bursting them to death.

Three days later, on 30 September, *Martha* flew her eleventh mission, attacking the airfield at Vannes on the Atlantic coast of the Brest peninsula. The flak, though intense over the target, was not as bad as La Pallice had been, and their fighters were able to provide escort cover for eighty per cent of the route. Apart from an instant of disquiet for Gerry Via when a florin-sized piece of flak shrapnel burst up through the floor of the radio room, passed between his knees and punched on out through the roof, by the crew's own re-modulated standards the trip was a milk-run.

Slowly, imperceptibly, they were beginning to think, and act, as a single ten-faceted unit, rather than ten disparate ones. They were also, instinctively, drawing closer to one another, and at the same time further apart from everyone else. They socialised less with other crews, even those they'd known a long time. At around the same time that the six enlisted members of *Martha*'s crew were pushing their bunks together at one end of their hut, two of her officers, Holland and Underwood, were arranging to swap with two officers in Hooper and Spitzer's hut, so that the four of them could hut together. When they landed after missions, Hal Knyper often had to wait twenty minutes or more before he could board *Martha* to begin working on repairs or snags.

'What the hell is it you do in there?' he finally asked Underwood one day.

Irv shrugged. 'We talk.' Sometimes, at Hooper's suggestion, Hal, as the indispensable eleventh member of *Martha*'s crew, was invited on board to join them.

Scott Finginger too noticed the changes. Debriefing them after the Bordeaux-Merignac raid, he noted that the earlier mistrust and bickering was giving way to a sense of common purpose. That the fact a German fighter had been shot down was more important to them, collectively, than which one of them had actually hit it. That their aggression was being directed more at the enemy than at each other. That the false bravado was gone, the feistiness, the in-fighting.

Almost.

'Say, Cap, right waist here.'

'What is it, Beans?' They were on the way back from Vannes, descending through tiny islands of cottonball cumulus towards a Sussex coast glinting in late afternoon sunshine.

'Well, sir, I was reading *Stars and Stripes* the other day—'

The inevitable chorus of catcalls. 'Who you kidding, fat boy! We all know you can't read.'

'Shove it up your ass, Tork, I was too.'

'But Beanbag, there's words in *Stars and Stripes*, it's not just pictures.'

'And no topless girls.'

'Listen, I *was* reading it, you assholes!'

'Okay, quiet down, now, everyone. Beans, is this really important?'

'Well, yes, Cap. I believe so.'

'Right. Then, what is it?'

'Well, as I was saying, I was sitting there reading *Stars and Stripes* when I come across this piece about the German Air Force and one of the big-shot Luft-waff generals who's in charge of it.'

'What about him?'

'Well, sir, his name, get this, is General Herman Keissling. Exactly the same name as our very own Herm Keiss here. Now, don't you think that's kind of suspicious?'

Hooper sighed. 'Sergeant. I think you'll find that the Luftwaffe general's name is Kesselring, not Keissling.'

'Oh. Right. Got you. Thank you, sir.'

A pause.

'Left waist to pilot.'

'Yes, Keissling, what now?'

'Sir, did you know that when Sergeant Beans was an itty baby, his mom and pop wanted to call him Marlon. But when they got to filling out the forms, they couldn't spell, being simple country folk and all. And so they spelled it Marion by mistake.'

'Okay, everyone, now that's quite enough of that. Let's just cut out the backchat on the intercom.'

Another pause.

'Radio to pilot.'

'Via. Yes. Now what is it?'

'Fighting in the waist.'

'And so America, are you listening, Donald Westrup, was then of course a very different America from the United States we know today. In fact, there were no united states in 1773. There were thirteen loosely organised colonies that mistrusted each other almost as much as they mistrusted George III, sitting back here collecting their taxes. Nevertheless, Shirley Fry and Dolly Makepeace, although these thirteen colonies argued and feuded amongst themselves, they did all have one thing in common – they wanted independence from the English throne and my goodness they were determined to get it. You must remember there was no such thing as the telegraph then, and no fast steamers carrying mail to and fro across the Atlantic. In those days it could take two months to get a single message from London to Virginia. Trying to govern effectively on that basis was practically impossible. Not surprisingly, the colonies became more and more unruly and unruleable, Lennie Savidge, for goodness' sake just blow it, please, especially Massachusetts which became a focal point for the colonists and their demands. And so, on that fateful day of 16 December 1773, it all finally came to a head right there in Boston when a gang of angry and frustrated colonists disguised themselves as natives, went down to the harbour and did what, Billy Street?'

'Not here, miss.'

'What? Again? But where is he?'

'Dunno, miss, up the air base prob'ly.'

'Len said Rube said he's being carted off to a Borstal place in Maidstone.'

'What? Is this true, Ruby?' Heather searched out Ruby Moody's head, shrouded in brown curls, off to one side of the classroom. Then the floor shook. A lone Fortress thundered low overhead, its engines throbbing discordantly.

'Slow-time, miss,' Ruby murmured unhappily. 'Nothing to worry about.'

'I'm sorry, what's that?' Heather was watching the ceiling. Hooper. Where on earth was he?

'It's when they change a worn-out engine. Billy said they have to fly round and round with the new engine going slowly, to bed it in, or something. Makes a peculiar noise. It's called slow-time. Nothing to worry about.'

'Oh, I see. Thank you.' Heather felt colour rising in her cheeks before the rows of smirking faces. Nothing to worry about. The whole class knew. And if the whole class knew, then the whole village knew too. But knew what? That was the absurdity, there was nothing to know. Was there? 'But, Ruby, what about Billy? What's this about a Borstal?'

'Don't know. He don't tell me much of anything any more. Spends all his time up on the base or doing the cycles with Mr Howden.' Ruby looked close to tears.

'I 'eard he's having it off with one of them Yank Red Cross bints up the base.'

'Any more of that sort of talk, Stanley Bolsover, and you'll be standing in the corridor outside Mr Needham's office.

And perhaps you would be so kind as to tell everyone what happened in Boston harbour on 16 December 1773?'

'Oh, erm, Battle a Trafalgar? Was it?'

She hadn't heard from Hooper for days and days. As though he was trying to avoid her, a prospect that consumed her with dread whenever she dared consider it. As though she could only deal with it, with what they were, only manage it, as long as it went on. If it stopped, God only knew what might happen. Apart from the teaching, it was the only piece of sanity in her life. Now, nothing. Days. It was worse than she would ever have imagined possible.

They'd attended a choral evensong together the previous Sunday. That was the last time she'd seen him. Hoop had managed to borrow Scott Finginger's Jeep for a few hours and they'd driven north through misty drizzle, passing fields already dusted with the first green haze of sprouting autumn corn, and others heavy with ripening beet. After half an hour they topped a low crest above a valley not far from the sea. A river was spread out before them, a majestic sweeping panorama of water meadows, reed-beds and wide muddy shores. Alone on a heathy knoll beside its banks, rising nobly from a tiny cluster of cottages at its feet, towered a huge church. Hooper lurched the Jeep to a stop. 'Good God, look at that!'

'Blythburgh,' Heather explained, watching him. 'One of the largest churches, and many say the most beautiful, in Suffolk. People know it locally as the cathedral on the marshes. Wonderful, isn't it?'

'Magnificent. But what is it doing out here in the middle of nowhere?'

'This was an important port once, in the Middle Ages. A major centre for trading, commerce, shipbuilding and so on. They built the church on the back of it.' She was trying hard not to sound like a schoolteacher.

'What happened?'

'The river silted up, became unnavigable. It's the story of this whole coastline. The town just died, over the centuries. Now there's only the church remaining, and a few cottages.'

He shook his head, standing at the roadside beside the Jeep. A bus laboured noisily up the hill behind them. The minutes ticked by, yet still he remained, gazing down at the church's solitary grandeur. Finally Heather nudged him from his reverie.

'"It's difficult to make sense of man's unending need to create war when he is also able to create a place like this." Who said that?'

'Hmm? Sorry, I have no idea. Sounds pretentious.'

'You did. The evening we first met. The little church at Iken, remember?'

'Not really. But it figures.'

'John. We'll miss the service.'

'I shouldn't be doing this. I don't have the right. It's wrong. And completely unfair on you.'

'Shouldn't be doing what? You're not doing anything. We're not.'

'No?' He turned to her then, stared right in at her, his dark eyes hunting across her face.

After the service they drove to a nearby pub. It was large, low ceilinged, empty, he noted thankfully, of American servicemen. They sat in a corner by the window drinking halves of bitter. Outside a hazy dusk was descending over the river.

'Have you heard from home?' she asked, sensing his disquiet. During the service the choir had sung Charles Stanford's haunting arrangement of the twenty-third psalm. He'd sat there, unmoving, hunched on the pew beside her, deeply submerged in thought. But not in prayer. It's gone, he'd confided, during one of their earlier talks. Prayer. An integral part of my life for so long. Now suddenly it is meaningless, bears no relevance to what I have become.

'Home? Sure, plenty.' No mail for weeks, then four letters in a day, all together. One from each of them.

'How are they?'

'Good. Fine. Thank you.' It was like corresponding with aliens from another planet. Alden, his father, chatty but remote, discussing local politics, college staffroom trivia and the lamentable state of the front porch. Not a word about the war, about the tens of thousands of Americans fighting and dying in it. About his son's part in it. His mother, similar, as though the two of them had conferred before putting pen to paper. More news of distant relations and unremembered friends, a businesslike update on church matters, and anxious fretting over her husband's stomach ulcer. 'It's the worry, you know, John,' she chided, near the end. His fault.

And then, Jo-Beth, a scrawling blast of precocious energy, yet angry, hungry, insistent. 'John, I love your letters, but please, more, you've got to tell me more, damn it! It's scary, you sound so different, but how do you feel? How the hell does being in a war feel? I can't even imagine it. Do you need to have hate in your heart? What about the ordinary people of Germany? Do you have to hate them too? Help me, speak to me, for God's sake keep writing!'

'And you, Heather? Anything at all?'

She shook her head. Over at the bar the landlord threw them a glance, conversing in low tones with two locals leaning across from him. It was the only time they were ever uncomfortable with one another, she reflected. The only time. Even when people looked, or whispered, it didn't matter. But when they, the two of them, forced each other to confront their other selves, their other, non-existent realities, then everything quickly went wrong, fell apart, their rapport collapsing like sandcastles in the rain. He, withdrawn, lost, unspeaking. She, wrapped in shame, angry and confused.

'I'm sorry. Heather? I didn't mean to intrude. Are you all right?'

She nodded grimly. 'Is this wrong, John? Do you really believe what you said earlier, that what we are doing is wrong?'

He sighed. 'Heather. If I feel secretly relieved that you've received no news from a husband who is lost out there somewhere, maybe fighting for his very life, I guess it might count as wrong. Wouldn't you say?'

'God, why do you have to be so uncompromisingly honest all the time!'

'Because if we can't be honest with each other, then we shouldn't be doing this at all.'

'We're not *doing* anything! That's the whole point. And anyway, all this "we". It's not fair you telling us what we

264

should and shouldn't be doing, you're not the one with the entire village watching your every move! You don't have to go home to your missing husband's house every night, sleep in his bed, have his mother breathing down your neck twenty-four hours a day.' The trio at the bar had turned to listen. She broke off in exasperation, pushing back her chair. 'You don't even have a bloody mother-in-law!' There was a catch in her throat. She picked up her bag, hurrying for the ladies'.

'I've got a bloody mother-in-law, missus,' she heard one of the men at the bar call after her. 'He can 'ave her with pleasure.'

Hooper waited by the Jeep, face raised to the sky. The drizzle had stopped. Feeding swallows scythed through the air above him, sooty black, dozens of them, their shrill calls piercing the dusk, resonating from the far bank of the river. It was madness, putting her through all this. Cruel madness. And she was right, the risk was all hers, the pressure, the strain. It must be stopped, one way or another. The certainty clutched, like a cold hand, at his heart. She was all he had. Away from the bombs and the killing. All that mattered. The fourth letter was from Susan. I'm releasing you, John, her neatly sloping handwriting said. Releasing you from our troth. It meant nothing; he'd felt nothing. Heather was all. Then the pub door was opening and she was coming towards him, hurrying, running, one hand to her face, her eyes round and fearful. Instinctively, without conscious thought, without decision, he reached out for her. In a second she was in his arms, falling against him, clutching at his back. 'I'm so sorry!' she sobbed. 'I'm so sorry.'

He held her like that, tightly enveloped within his arms, his cheek to her head, one hand on her hair, not moving, not speaking. Until the crying stopped and she grew still and calm, until dusk gave way to darkness, and the swallows vanished into the night.

'Battery switches and inverters?'

'Ah, now then, okay, the battery switches seem to be in the on position.'

'They seem to be? Or they are?'

'They're on. Definitely on.'

'Fuel booster pump pressure?'

'Booster . . . Hold on, over here somewhere. Yeah, there we go, it's good.'

'Carburettor coolers open?'

'Carburettor cool— Damn, where the hell . . . Okay, I got it, I think they're open.'

'Lajowski.' Hal Knyper, standing behind the pilot's seat, lowered the checklist, pinching the bridge of his nose between an oil-stained finger and thumb. Billy, in his green airman's coveralls and cap, looked on from the co-pilot's seat. 'Listen, bud, when I call out one of the checks, it's no damn use going "ah" and "um" and "maybe over here somewhere", you got to know exactly where everything is and come back straight away with the correct response. So, like, when I ask for fuel booster pump and pressure, you throw the pump switch, look at the pressure on the dial there, make sure it's good, and come straight back with "On and check", okay?'

'Yeah, Hal, got it. Sorry about that. Do you want to run through it again?'

'Later. I'm going outside to help Wayman finish fixing the supercharger on number two engine. In a couple of minutes we'll need to start it up for a ground check. Do you think you can manage that?' He dropped the checklist on Billy's lap. 'Get Private Street here to practise it with you.'

A moment later they heard the crunch of Knyper's boots on the tarmac beneath the nose hatch. Lajowski sighed. 'Okay, lucky charm kid, I guess we'd better take it from the top.'

Billy stared at the checklist. 'Um, Polecat, look, I don't have my glasses . . .'

'You wear glasses? I never seen them.'

'Yes. No, well I would've, but my dad couldn't afford—'

'You don't read. You don't. Do you?'

'Yes, I do. But not very well. Checklists and things.' His hand reached out to the half-wheel of the co-pilot's control column, fingers lightly brushing the silver-winged Boeing emblem at its centre. 'Sorry.'

Lajowski was studying him, lips pursed. Then his hand clapped him on the knee. 'And I can't tell a carburettor supercharger from the goddamn air intake regulator, so what the hell!'

'Indicator.'

'What's that, kid?'

'It's the carburettor air intake indicator. And that's the supercharger regulator. There, look, in front of the throttles.'

'It is? Damn, you're right. How d'you know that?'

'I watched Hal. Doing engine runs on the ground. Loads of times.' He leaned forward, peering through the sidescreen. Hal, standing on a wheeled scaffold, had his head buried inside the number two engine cowling. 'Why's he making you do this?'

'He's not. It's Hooper's idea. He said we should all get to know each other's jobs on the ship, so if one of us gets injured, there's others can take his place. Like a back-up. Makes a lot of sense. So he's got us running around all over. Dutch Holland's got Herm Keissling's eyes glued to his bombsight, Gerry Via spends all his time with his nose buried in a heap of medical manuals. Lieutenant Spitzer, get this, he's teaching Kid Ringwald some navigating, and I get to be flight engineer, which is the most important back-up of all.'

'How come you got that?'

'First off, I'm the smartest. Second, I'm the nearest, what with my turret being situated right here behind the flight deck. Third, my dad runs an auto repair shop back home in Brooklyn. Fourth—' He broke off, gazing around the cockpit.

'Fourth, what?'

'Fourth, well. That day, that first mission, when poor Rudy, our original pilot, got his head blown— Well, when Lieutenant Stoller got killed, that is.'

'I know. I was here.'

'You were? Oh, yes. You were, too. Well, when it happened, I was up there in my turret. I heard the bang, ducked down here on to the flight deck. It was the worst sight imaginable. Rudy, he . . . well, he was gone and the whole place was just covered in his blood and his brains and that. Lieutenant Underwood, he was covered in it too, head to toe. He was kind of in shock, he couldn't move, couldn't speak. The ship was all leaned over on its side and going into a dive, so I just grabbed the controls and hung on, best I could, until Spitzer got here. Probably just a few minutes, but it seemed like for ever, Billy, and I do mean for ever. Like all of time just came to a stop. I decided then and there that if I ever had to do something like that again, I oughta find out first how the hell I was supposed to do it.'

'Polecat?'

'Huh? What is it, kid?'

'Do you want to come to tea?'

There was a shrill whistle from outside. They looked up. Hal Knyper was standing back from the engine, making rotating motions with his hand. 'Do you think there's any chance you ladies could get the number two engine started now?' he called. 'Only if it's convenient, of course.'

Later, after the engine run, Billy joined Hal on the scaffold, helping him replace the cowlings. A fitter on a ladder was painting an eleventh bomb stencil on to *Martha*'s nose, just below the cockpit window. Beyond it, Lajowski could be seen, studying his checklists. After a while two bicycles rolled up and Beans and Via boarded. 'I'm radio back-up,' Beans said importantly. 'Geraldo's showing me round the equipment.' A few minutes later an open-backed truck came grinding by. Hooper, Underwood and Tork jumped out.

'How's it going, Hal?' Hooper asked, pausing beneath the scaffold. Underwood and Tork were hoisting themselves through *Martha*'s nose hatch.

'It would be going a hell of a lot better if folks left us in peace to get on with the damn job. It's like Grand Central Station here, for God's sakes.'

'Sorry. We need to run some procedures, we'll try and stay out of your hair.'

Knyper's wrench slipped. It flew from his hand, spinning to the ground at Hooper's feet. Billy watched as blood welled at the mechanic's knuckles. 'Jesus!' Knyper pulled a filthy rag from his pocket, wrapping the cut fingers.

'Hal? Are you okay? Do you want Via to take a look at that?'

'No, shit, it ain't nothing. Hoop, what the hell is all this about?'

'It's about staying alive, Hal, that's all. Beating the odds.' He took his cap off, running fingers through his dark hair. He was standing at the foot of the scaffold, staring at the ground, his voice quiet and level. 'The other day, remember, when we got back from Vannes. That was *Gotcha*'s twenty-fifth mission, you know, from the low squadron? Done, finished, they can all go home.'

'So? They made it. I was at the party. *Martha*'s going to make it too.'

Hooper was shaking his head. 'I did some checking. *Gotcha*'s crew were among the first to be deployed here with the 520th. They are also the first to get through a complete tour of twenty-five missions. There will be no more. Not from that group. Of the original thirty ships deployed here last year, she's the only one left. Sure, some have gone elsewhere, some have been scrapped and replaced, some of the crews have been redeployed, some have been shot down and are in captivity, but when all is said and done, it's one in thirty, Hal.

'That's just numbers, Hoop. As you say, ships get moved, crews redeployed—'

'No. Loss rates on missions were averaging six per cent last few months. Now it's higher. Six per cent per mission.

Doesn't sound a lot. But multiply twenty-five missions by a six per cent loss rate?'

'Hundred and fifty per cent,' Billy said quickly.

'You've got it. Rate of losses for a full tour of twenty-five missions is one hundred and fifty per cent. And climbing. Shitty odds. I have to shorten them. Last week, a ship from the 95th got hit just before the IP and had to turn back for home, on its own, its pilot injured and the navigator killed. That left the co-pilot to fly the ship and no one to navigate. They lost their way over the sea, flew round in big circles for three hours, ran out of gas and crashed into the ocean. No survivors, just because nobody knew how to plot a course for home. Another ship, flak shell came right up through the flight deck floor, killed both pilots. Bombardier managed to fly the crate home, just about. But he couldn't land, didn't know how. Control tower tried to talk him down on the radio, but he stalled in on the approach, crashed and burned. No survivors again.'

'Hoop. You're going to survive. Don't ask me how, but I just know you will.'

Hooper looked up in surprise. 'This isn't about me, Hal.' He pointed towards *Martha*. 'This is about them.'

Ten minutes later a Jeep came speeding around the perimeter towards the hardstand. 'Now what?' Knyper muttered irritably. The Jeep braked to a halt.

'Bill Street! Thought I'd track you down here.' It was Major Finginger. 'I found these two ladies at the front gate. They're looking for you.'

'Hello, Billy.' Ruby squinted coyly up at him. Beside her sat Heather Garrett.

'Oh, er, hello, Rube. Mrs G. Um, would you like to come to tea later?'

'How kind.' Heather stepped from the Jeep. 'Scott, thank you for the lift.'

'No problem.' Finginger touched his cap. 'Ah, is everything all right?'

'Fine, thank you. Oh, Sergeant Knyper, how nice to see you again. I wonder, could you possibly spare Billy for a few minutes? Just for a chat.'

'Jesus!' Hal was staring back along the perimeter track. Another Jeep, smarter, a darker polished green, with a little flag fluttering on the wing, was pulling up at the Fortress on the next hardstand. A squat figure climbed out, began talking to the mechanics there.

'What is it?' Ruby asked.

Finginger peered back along the track. 'My God, it is. It's him!'

'Jesus!' Knyper swore again. He seemed rooted to the spot. The figure had already finished talking and was reboarding his Jeep. 'Shit, girls, quick, you'd better get out of sight. Jump on board *Martha*, fast as you can, use the waist door round the other side. Billy, stay put, keep your head down and don't say a damn thing!'

'But what—'

'Nothing! Don't say nothing!'

The Jeep sped around the track, skidding to a halt beneath them. A short man of about fifty sprang out, wearing a crisp uniform heavy with medal ribbons. He had a high forehead, cleft chin, dark, predator's eyes.

'Major!' he barked, throwing a salute in Finginger's

direction. 'Good to see you Intelligence boys getting out on the flight line once in a while. Sergeant! How's this ship?'

'Well, sir, she's just fine. Sir.' Knyper raised bloodily bandaged knuckles in a semblance of a salute. 'Thank you, sir.'

'Excellent. Got everything you need?'

'Yes, thank you, sir. Pretty much.'

'Good work. What about you, Private? Need anything?'

'What? I, um, well, no—'

'Excellent! That's what I like to hear. Keep up the good work, men, you're doing a fine job, the 8th is mighty proud of you. Mighty proud!' He climbed back into his Jeep and sped off towards the next hardstand.

Faces pressed up against *Martha*'s flight deck window. Beans' round head, upside down, appeared below the belly hatch. Irv Underwood was leaning out through the waist aperture. 'Was that who I think it was?'

Finginger was scratching the flak scar above his eye. 'That it was, by heavens. Genuine General Jimmy, no less.'

'Who?' Billy asked.

'General James H. Doolittle. Supreme Commander of the 8th Air Force.'

Finginger dropped the four of them at the main gate. Billy and Ruby hurried on ahead, Hooper and Heather strolling behind.

'Do you think that Billy's . . . What is her name, Mrs Howden? Do you think Mrs Howden knows he's invited my entire crew for tea?' he asked. There was an alert on; the MP at the gate had nodded discreetly towards the signal board as they passed through the barrier. Big mission tomorrow. An

ME. Everyone back on base by nightfall. Something clicked over in his head. He felt a familiar numbness stirring deep in his stomach. The clock, once again, was running.

'Heaven knows. I doubt it. Their daughter's involved too, or something. Either way, it won't be easy, feeding everyone.'

'Don't worry too much about that. I saw Lajowski and Beans making for the commissary earlier. The boys won't be coming empty-handed.'

'I'm sure!' They walked on in silence. A chill October wind stirred fallen leaves at their feet. Heather thrust her hands into her overcoat.

Hooper turned up his collar. 'Is the kid in some kind of trouble? Billy? Was that why you came on base?'

'Yes, he is. And, well, yes it was. Partly.' She hesitated, searching, seemingly, for prepared words. 'John, this isn't an inquisition or anything. But why have you stopped coming to visit? Is it that you would prefer not to see me? I do understand if that's the case.'

'Of course it isn't the case! My God, Heather, I want to see you more than you can imagine.' He swung round, walking backwards in front of her. 'Our evenings, our talks together, they're more important to me than you'll ever know. Coming to see you, after a mission, say, well it's like a bathe in a stream, a pitcher of cool beer, a warm sandy beach. All rolled into one!' Her chin was down, but he saw the trace of a smile breaking across her lips. 'It is a wonderful oasis of reality in an unreal world.'

'Then what's the problem?'

'The problem is that it is completely one-sided. The gain is all mine, there's nothing in it for you. Nothing but trouble, that is. I hadn't thought, hadn't begun to realise just how difficult a position you were in. How much pressure you were under. I can't allow that to go on. It's unbelievably selfish. I gain, you lose.'

'I gain too.' she said quietly. They stopped to face each other in the lane. 'John. For better or for worse, I made vows to someone who two years ago next month, and through no fault of his own, completely, and perhaps permanently, removed himself from my life. If David ever does comes back, then, well, I'm his, no matter what happens. That's the purpose and meaning of vows, I believe. If he doesn't, then God knows what I'll do, probably go home to Lincoln, which is where I should have stayed in the first place. But in the meantime, I'm nothing, neither wife nor widow, a sort of half-person, a shadow. Being friends with you isn't going to change that, but believe me, it makes the whole mad situation much, much easier to bear. If that's wrong, then so be it. I don't care.'

'Okay.' His face was clouded with uncertainty. 'I see. Very well put.'

They resumed walking. 'John, I've got a suggestion. Why don't we just take it one day at a time. Forget last Sunday, it never happened. If you want to come and see me, to talk, then come. If you don't, don't. If either of us begins to feel, you know, pressured or uncomfortable or it all gets too much, with the gossip or whatever, we'll simply put a stop to it. Just like that. What do you say?'

'One day at a time, and just like that. Think it'll work?'

She nudged his arm. 'I'm willing to give it a try if you are.'

By the time they reached the Howdens' house, Billy's party was already in full swing. A heap of bicycles lay outside the gate, and Scott Finginger's Jeep was parked outside the forge. Maggie opened the door to them, looking slightly flustered. Her eyes bounced from Hooper to Heather, just for a second, before the door was thrown wide. 'Mrs Garrett! What a wonderful surprise. And you must be Lieutenant Cooper. Do, please, come in. I've heard so much about you from Billy and Hal.' She ushered them into a little hall. 'Ray! Love? Two more chairs! Claire, quickly, more cups and saucers! Run and get Granny Cowell's from the box under my bed.' Obediently, like newlyweds visiting relatives, they followed her into the living room.

Hooper surveyed the room. It was getting late, they should be going soon. He was sitting on the Howdens' piano stool, holding a plate with a home-made jam tart on it. It was his third. He didn't really feel like eating, but each time he managed to finish one tart, Mrs Howden instantly gave him another. The room was filled with animated chatter and peals of laughter. Spontaneous and free of care, it rang in his head like music. His crew, most of them, were sitting or reclining on the floor, Billy and his friend Ruby in their midst. Billy was telling his General Doolittle story again. Every so often one of the crew would spring to his feet, to fetch another dish from the kitchen, gather up empty plates or relieve Mrs Howden of her huge brown teapot. Each time she came in, those on chairs would rise, insisting she sit and rest and join in. Giggling like a schoolgirl, she would comply for a minute, before jumping up again to fill someone's cup or go and make more sandwiches.

Irv Underwood was squatting on the floor in one corner, talking to an old man in an armchair, Mr Howden's father. He had wispy white hair that waved when he moved his head, and was carefully sinking dentures into a piece of carrot cake the boys had brought with them. It wasn't clear whether he was listening to Irv, but he seemed to be enjoying himself none the less, breaking into gummy grins every now and then, slapping his knee. Irv knelt at his side, smiling and talking. Irv. Each mission, at briefing, at breakfast, he looked like death. Like a sick ghost. White-faced, trembling and sweating, he hauled himself, every nerve screaming, through mission preparation and then up into that co-pilot's seat. His fear was so great that you could smell it. Yet he never complained, he never cried off. Never gave in to his terror. As far as Hooper was concerned he was the bravest man on the squadron.

Mr Howden, Ray, was talking to Hal Knyper. Hal seemed to know the Howdens well. From their hand gestures, he guessed they were discussing matters mechanical. Ray, lips pursed, listened while Hal talked, then suddenly his weathered face broke into a nodding smile of understanding. Beside them Spitzer and Finginger were talking to Heather. Spitzer was inches shorter than either of them, his smiling face swivelling from one to the other. Eternally patient, eternally optimistic. Hooper recalled how he had helped him, in his quiet, determinedly supportive way, through the early days with the crew. Through the paralysing headaches, the memory lapses, the fragmentary blackouts. The nightmares. Never a single questioning word.

'You gotta have good people, you see, Hoop old buddy,' Gene Englehardt had told him, over and over, in the officers' bar late at night. Gene liked to drink. 'Two double doubles!' he'd shout, firing up one of his cigars. It was Gene's way. Fly hard, fight hard, party hard. Pass out for an hour, get up at dawn and do it all again. 'Good people! If you got that, then believe me, buddy, you're halfway home already!'

Good people. Lajowski came reversing in through the door, a plate in each hand. He seemed to be a part of the household, too. 'Emmett, dear,' Mrs Howden called to him. 'Why don't you put that one on the piano, near Lieutenant Cooper, sorry, Hooper! And give the other one to the boys on the floor. Eldon. Eldon? Where is that boy?'

He was in the kitchen, Hooper had learned from a winking Marion Beans. Washing up. With the daughter, Claire. He'd had no idea, not the first inkling, but the moment he saw them together, he realised something profound was passing between them. It was a surprise and a worry. Ringwald. Kid, the rest of the crew called him, Babyface, sometimes. The youngest, yet with a maturity far surpassing his years. He never gabbled on the intercom, never riled anyone up, never caused trouble. On the contrary, he was quick to intervene, expert at defusing disputes before they blew up. And also a warrior. One of the best on board, cool under pressure, patient and skilled. Hooper had known immediately it was Ringwald's ball turret guns that had hit that first Focke-Wulf. He was a natural at it. Peacemaker, warrior, now a lover. All at eighteen. It was barely comprehensible.

There was more. The door opened once again and Claire came in, bearing a cake on a tray. A picture had been iced on to it, a Flying Fortress, complete with wheels and propellers.

There were exclamations of appreciation, scattered applause, wisecracks.

'Say, Hal, number four engine's iced up. Could you check it out?'

'Notice the ball turret, folks, bigger than all the others!'

'I have something to say.' Ringwald was standing by the door, Claire, still holding the cake, at his side. The room fell quiet. They looked like frightened children. 'Everyone was invited here today because, well, with Mr and Mrs Howden's permission, of course, Claire and me would like to become engaged. To get married. After the war.'

Just like that. A fractional silence, a window-frame rattling in the wind. Maggie's hand went to her mouth, then there was an explosion of cheers, catcalls and whistles. The crew got to their feet as one, crowding around Ringwald, clapping him on the back, punching his shoulder. The old man slapped his knee, the others applauded. Hooper, swallowing, joined in; it seemed appropriate. The odds, he kept thinking, the odds. Maggie was shaking her head, her cheeks between her hands; her husband, eyebrows arched, seemed in shock. Overcome with longing, Hoop sought Heather's eyes, found them, held them. They were waiting for him. She smiled, and his heart lurched. One day at a time. Simple. Absurd. Finginger was standing beside her. Poor faithful Finginger, waiting patiently on the sidelines. He too was looking at Hooper, gesturing pointedly at his watch. 'We have to get going,' Finginger said, reaching to shake Ray Howden's hand. 'Many congratulations on your happy news.' Heather, her eyes still resting on his, soft and warm from across the room. At her feet, Billy's friend, Ruby, planting a fat kiss on Billy's cheek. Maggie, tearful, pushing past the boys to embrace her daughter, and to take Ringwald's bemused face in her hands. We have to go. To blood and bombs and thunder and death beyond description.

'No! Wait!' Maggie cried. 'A song first. Just one. One quick song, then you can go. Who knows something we can all sing?'

He turned on the stool, something lost rising, coming back to him, surfacing from his subconscious, from a different past. He saw his hands lift the lid, his fingers reaching for the keys. In a moment he began, uncertainly at first, then with growing fluency. Within seconds a voice, ancient, thin, reedy but unwavering, was singing the opening lines. The old man, Percy, rising from his chair, straightening, chin held high. 'Pack up all my cares and woes, here I go, singing low, bye-bye blackbird. Where somebody waits for me, sugar's sweet, so is she, bye-bye blackbird.'

Other voices joined the old man's, softly, sweetly, respectfully. Like a hymn. Like an anthem. 'No one here can love or understand me, all those hard-luck stories they all hand me. So make my bed and light the light, I'll be home late tonight. Blackbird, bye-bye.'

Chapter 11

It was the worst week in the history of the 8th.

'Navigator to pilot.'

'Go ahead, Spitz.'

'That's our coastline there, just visible fifteen miles ahead. Our ETA back at base is twenty-seven minutes past the hour. I guess we made it.'

'I guess so. We're just descending through thirteen thousand feet, be able to take off oxygen masks in a few minutes. Well done, everybody, that was a rough one.'

'Amen to that.'

'Man, that flak was worse than anything I ever seen.'

'Bremen. I don't care if I don't hear that name again for as long as I live.'

'Let's hope that's a long time.'

'Too right. Say, nice going today, Torky.'

'Yeah, Al, you did a real great job back there today, buddy.'

'Thanks, guys.' Al Tork, his rear end numb with cold, shifted uncomfortably on his bicycle-saddle-shaped seat. He unhooked his hard rubber oxygen mask, sucking deeply on the thin air. His face felt as though the mask had been welded there, the flesh of his cheeks dented and sore, his nose dead, his throat parched, and hoarse from shouting. Thirteen thousand feet and descending. Good enough, he could breathe without the damn thing now. He left it dangling at his neck, swung his guns off to one side, slumped against his compartment's curved wall and closed his eyes. Tail gun. Tail-ass Charlie, the Brits called it. Like stuffing a rat down the end of a cigar tube, then making it turn somersaults.

But he wouldn't be anywhere else.

Bremen. It began in the usual way. The flicker of overhead lights, the rough shake of the shoulder, 'Good morning, fellas, oh-five-thirty, you are flying today.' Everything normal, everything standard issue. Until the briefing. He sits at the back, resting up with the boys. All around them the new crews are toughing it out, wisecracking, goofing off, all swank and swagger. Yet all the while their fear is as plain as day, the chinks in their armour-plating wide enough to drive a truck through. It's not their fault. Two hundred and seventy airmen are sitting there in the briefing room. How are they supposed to know sixty of them won't be coming back in the afternoon? They'd learn soon enough. Or they'd simply disappear. It was all just a question of the numbers. You watched them arrive on base. For the first few days they'd be so full of it, so cocky, it turned your stomach. You could spot them by the noise, and the activity. Setting up volleyball games on the grass outside their huts, running everywhere like kids in school, filling the air with their excited shouts and rebel yells. Sidling up to you in the sergeants' bar. How many missions you got, buddy? What's flying through flak really like? Did you kill any fighters yet?

They can't wait. But after a couple of weeks, if they're still there, the volleyball nets are hanging as limp as yesterday's laundry, the shouts and catcalls gone, dried up like a summer creek. Inside the huts their voices are low and muted, the only sports activities hide the eyeballs and horizontal PT. That and poker. Everywhere, poker. The cards. The numbers, the odds. Get lucky, be lucky, stay lucky. Beat the numbers. It becomes an obsession.

Hoop and the other officers, Irv, Spitz and Dutch, sit up front for the briefings. It's not that they don't want to sit back with the crew, they all know that. It's just that he doesn't want them to miss the slightest little detail. He's right. The other day, a ship takes off for a mission. It's cloudy, a heavy overcast all the way up to twelve thousand feet. Climbing up and up through soup so thick you couldn't see your wingtips, this ship takes off, then makes the wrong heading for the RP. Blind as a bat, it flies into a bomber stream coming the other way, and collides head-on with one of them. Full fuel, full bomb load, it's a massive explosion. Windows break on the ground. Two crews killed. Twenty guys. All for not copying the details down correctly at the briefing. Two land girls working in the fields on the ground, so the story went, heard the bang. Next thing they know it is literally raining body parts. One girl hears a thud, looks down and falls over in a faint. Some poor guy's head is staring up at her from the dirt. She swore to God later that his lips were still moving.

It's Bremen. The mission. The name means nothing, but when S-2 twitches back the curtain and everyone sees the ribbon stretching on and on into Germany, the older hands know it's going to be tough, and long. And big. The biggest ME to date, Intelligence says, standing up front on the dais. Seven hundred bombers, plus their escorts, flying in three waves. It's an armada.

Finally they get airborne. It's a cold, clear day. That's a relief; assembling seven hundred ships through cloud is a recipe for disaster. Today the sky is as clear as mountain water, but full to overflowing. Forts and Liberators in every direction as far as the eye can see, while above them the little fighter escorts scurry to and fro like dogs herding sheep. The 520th forms up into the division with all the other groups, then the whole shooting match splits into three separate wings, and their wing, two hundred ships, heads straight out across the North Sea towards Germany. Thick, cloud-like trails of vapour stream back for miles across the freezing sky from their engines, like vast come-and-get-me signs.

And they do come, but not immediately. They wait. Meanwhile, all is quiet. That's the nature of the beast: hours of anxious waiting, interrupted by minutes of raw-nerved, adrenalin-charged terror. On the order from the flight deck, everyone tests their guns. Back there in the tail Tork just gives it two half-second bursts; everything works fine. Save the ammo. He looks round his compartment. It's completely cut off from the rest of the ship. Quieter, too. Like another world. Just the wind-like rushing of the slipstream, the creak-ing of the airframe and the muffled rumble of the Cyclones.

It's cramped, about the size of a motorcycle sidecar, or smaller. A little painted sign above his head says, 'Al's Hut'. His rosary swings from its hook at his side. There's four pictures taped to the curved metal walls. All ladies. Ava Gardner, his mother, the Virgin Mary, and Charlene, perched on the hood of his pick-up back in Greenboro. He smooths them with his gloved thumb; they're a little crinkled with damp. Sometimes it gets so cold at height, the metal walls of the fuselage sweat moisture which then freezes into a coating of ice. When they begin to descend again, it thaws and runs, wetting everything.

Pee tube. Does he need to use the pee tube? Now's the time, before any action starts. No. He can wait, he knows it's just tension. Learned the hard way how his empty bladder plays tricks. Shuffling on his back up the tunnel to the waist, his blue walk-around oxygen bottle clutched awkwardly to his chest. Past Beans and Keiss, sniggering there at their guns, through Gerry's radio room and finally on into the bomb bay. It is freezing cold in there, and draughty, the noise from the engines mind-numbing. Standing there surrounded by rattling five-hundred-pound bombs, fumbling in minus thirty degrees at three layers of zippers. And after all that, nine times out of ten it's just a dribble, and the wind blows it all over your hands and clothes anyway. Complete waste of time. Once though, early on, he met poor old Dutch Holland in there, holding one of his grocery sacks brimful of puke. 'Spitz thinks it's the smell that makes me keep throwing up,' Dutch yelled above the thundering engines. 'Suggests I try jettisoning it out of the side vent.' Tork helped open the vent while Dutch pushed the soggy

285

sack out into the slipstream. 'Seems to have worked!' He grinned, pale as a sheet, and headed off back towards the nose. Tork clambered aft once more. When he came into the waist he saw that Beans, speechless for once, was covered all down his front with freezing puke. It had gone out the vent, then come straight back in again through the waist aperture.

The first fighters appear soon after they cross the enemy coast. They keep coming all the way to the IP, the run-in to the target, the turn for home, the rally point, and all the way back out to the coast and beyond. There are so many attacks Tork stops counting, stops praying, stops thinking. He's an automaton, a machine. On. Off. When they come at him he switches on, when they break away he turns off again. The 520th, with Englehardt's squadron on top, is flying almost at the back of the entire formation. Most of the attacks are coming from the rear. He's the busiest man in the 8th. The fighters hang back, and a little above, weaving from side to side at about a thousand yards, just out of range. Minutes at a time, trying to sucker you into wasting ammunition. To his left, the tail gunner in the next ship, *Toledo Toots*, a rookie, is doing just that. Tork watches helplessly as long bursts of tracer spray back from the man's guns, only to drop short of the waiting fighters. A useless waste.

Then, when they're ready, the Luftwaffe boys suddenly stop weaving, fall into single line astern and come slicing in. He switches to On, yanking back the charging handles on his two .fifty-calibre guns, chambering rounds into each. Then all hell breaks loose. He watches them come, picks one out, leads, waits, shoots, picks another. Then another, then the sky is full of them and the world goes mad. It's total chaos, a free for all. He keeps firing short bursts, but still his guns get so hot he can see the blast-tubes shimmer. Everyone's shouting, everyone's firing. He sights on one fighter, a twin-engined Messerschmitt 110, leads on it, fires two short bursts, and one of its engines explodes. A second later the whole wing comes off and the thing goes into violent pirouetting spin. Then another fighter, lower, a 109, comes in half rolling on to its back as it shoots. Beautiful flying. It barrels through, unscathed, cannon blinking. Nobody gets close to it. Seconds later its victim, a Fort from the middle formation, starts dropping back, pouring flames. To his left a sudden flash as *Toledo Toots* takes a hit; he watches, mesmerised, as it staggers in the air, like a little stumble. Then there's another flash and the midsection just explodes, bursts right open. Hanging there in the sky next to him, the ship breaks clean in two. He sees the ball turret fall clear, plummeting earthwards like a dropped stone, its gunner still trapped inside. As the two halves of the ship separate, bodies tumble out; he sees them falling from the gaping rear section, arms and legs flailing. The two waist gunners, the radio operator, three human beings tumbling over and over, like falling rag dolls. On the wings, the four engines are still running, smooth and steady, as the front half noses over, like slow motion, into a dive. Up front, the pilots, oblivious, are still fighting the controls, still hauling elevators and kicking on rudders that aren't there any more. They don't know the entire back half of the ship is gone. That they're all dying, that four of their friends are already gone. And a fifth is going. The tail gunner. He's still there in the separated tail section. It's floating, almost gently, over on to its side and down. Tork can see him. He's still shooting, still spraying his tracer uselessly all over the sky, as if nothing had happened.

Then suddenly a Focke-Wulf rears up out of nowhere, from right beneath him, no more than three hundred yards back. It has a black and white checkerboard nose, the pilot weaving it from side to side, shooting furiously. Tork swings on to him, starts thumbing the buttons as the German passes in and out of his line of fire. Short bursts, short bursts, backwards and forwards, again and again. They keep shooting at each other; he can see the pilot's masked face, see the fighter's tracer shells leaving its wings to come flashing past his head. Too high, he reflected dispassionately, thumbing the buttons again and again. The man was shooting too high. Good, but not good enough. Then the German's engine was on fire. Just pale smoke first, then suddenly there's a big orange puff and sheets of thick black oil are streaming back over the nose cowling and up the windshield. In a second he has his canopy back and he's standing up in his seat, trying to bail out. Tork can see him, pulling and fumbling at his straps and buckles. He keeps shooting. Then the man just tucks himself into a ball and dives out of his flaming cockpit, head first over the side, his maps and papers trailing after him like litter.

It goes on and on. After a while time ceases to have meaning, and the world contracts into a single seamless interval of shuddering guns, thunder, smoke and shouting. At some point he hears over the intercom that they've reached the IP and are commencing the bomb run. It is meaningless to him, signifying only that, apart from the fighters, the sky is now also thickly pocked with thousands of exploding flak shells.

He thinks of nothing, keeps his head down and the charging handles cocked. Stretching out for miles behind, unrolling before his eyes like a bizarre aerial tapestry, a smoke-covered industrial landscape, the grey glint of a river, a slow-moving barge, burning buildings, impact craters. Crawling across the tapestry, like the remnants of a crushed army, an overlay of limping, crippled bombers, smoking wrecks, falling debris, drifting parachutes.

Later the voice in his head says they're turning for home. Home. Greensboro. Warm, North Carolina nights, and cold beer on the porch with Charlene. Don't think. Watch. And shoot. He is soaked with perspiration. His compartment, awash with spent shells, is filled with cordite smoke, his guns stink of hot metal and burning oil. The rosary beads swing beside his head. A fighter streaks by, left to right, banked over hard, a perfect silhouette. He swings after it, maximum deflection, the guns shake in his hands, it rolls on its side and vanishes.

Later he pulls back the charging handles only to find his ammunition chutes are empty. 'I'm out!' he croaks. Hooper sends Gerry Via down to the tail with fresh belts. Gerry scrambles down the tunnel to him, leans in from behind, passes the ammunition and a canteen of water. 'Hang in there, Torky!' he yells, massaging his shoulders. 'We'll soon be out of this.' Tork nods, drinking hungrily, hands back the canteen, loads up the fresh belts and pulls back the charging handles.

'Did you hear the ME this morning? My God, I never heard anything like it in my life. There must have been hundreds of them up there.'

'You should try getting up a bit earlier, young lady. Of course we heard it, you couldn't miss it, the whole house was shaking from about five-thirty onwards.' Ray kicked his boots on to the back-door step and padded to the kitchen sink, rolling his sleeves. 'And watch the blasphemy, if you don't mind. We won't have the Lord's name taken in vain here.'

Maggie turned from the cooking range, depositing breakfast plates on the table. Stale bread beneath an off-white blob of watery powdered egg. Billy, knife and fork at the ready, set to with his customary zeal. Beside him, Percy, frowning, bent forward until his nose was practically touching the plate. 'Bugger me,' he muttered, sniffing suspiciously.

'Dad! Don't you start.'

'Go on, Perce,' Billy whispered. 'It's good for us. Eat up, now.'

Ray tipped the cat off his chair and sat down. 'Could do with some help out there in the forge today, Billy,' he said quietly.

'No!' Maggie turned from the range. Her hair, an unevenly streaked rust colour from home-brewed henna, was secured in a bun beneath a net. She was wearing her blue and maroon WVS uniform beneath her apron, the wide-brimmed hat waiting on a hook behind the door. 'Billy promised Mrs Garrett he'd be in school every day this week, didn't you, love?'

'Well, I—'

'Mag, I've got two horses to shoe this morning, two more this afternoon, everywhere you turn there's heaps of broken bicycles waiting to be fixed, and to top it all Harold Knyper says he's sending one of his boys over with yet another truck-load this afternoon.'

'Well, perhaps you should think about hiring an assistant.'

'I've got an assistant!'

'Not while he's supposed to be at school, you haven't.' She began pinning on her hat. 'Now then, I'm up the old folks' home the morning, then I've got a wool-drive meeting in the village hall this afternoon. There's the last of the bread, half a tin of Spam and some damsons off the tree for your lunch. I'll be home teatime.'

'Do you remember bacon?' Claire said, staring wistfully at her plate. 'That real, crispy bacon, and real fried eggs, with them brown crunchy bits at the edges. And real sausages, and ketchup.'

'And you can just stop right there with your complaining, madam,' Maggie went on. 'The entire family gave over their egg ration for a month, I would remind you, and most of their butter, to make cakes and pastries for your engagement party. And get a move on, girl! You'll be late for work. You too, Billy.'

'Mum, I wasn't complaining, just remembering. What's wrong with that?'

'Couldn't scrape out the egg saucepan could I, Mrs H?'

'It was not an engagement party.'

'What?' Everyone turned to Ray. He had his head down, munching steadily.

'Ray, love, couldn't this wait—'

'You're not getting engaged. Not now.'

'But Dad, you can't do this. We are engaged!'

'No you're not and yes I can. You're too young, the pair of you.'

'Them bloody woods,' Percy grumbled, pushing back his chair. 'Up the back. Empty like the graveyard. Not so much

291

as a mouse in 'em.' He shuffled towards the hall door. 'Some bugger's scaring them. Not so much as a bloody mouse.'

'Dad! Mum, say something!'

Maggie opened her mouth, but Ray cut her off. 'Your mother agrees with me, Claire,' he said. 'Eldon, well, he's a good boy, we can see, and we do like him and all that. But he's eighteen years old for heaven's sake, and you're only seventeen. Not only that, he's a foreigner. Over here for a few months to do his war service, then he's going home, thousands of miles to America, where you can be sure his mind'll soon be on other matters. This kind of thing, local girls getting hooked up with Yanks, it's going on the length and breadth of the county. Hundreds, so I hear, thousands. And too many of them are getting left in the lurch, like, and into, you know, trouble. And that. They come over here, worm their way into impressionable young girls' lives and beds with their sweet talk and fancy presents, then bugger off home and forget them. You're too young and there's an end to it.'

'Um, Sergeant Ringwald, Mr H. Hal says there's a good chance he'll get put up for a commission when he finishes his tour, be made an officer, like lieutenant—'

'They're too bloody young!'

'And what about us?' Maggie was standing at the back door, proud and erect in her uniform. Her gloved hands were loosely clasped, her hat-brim low on her eyes. She looked three inches taller. And twenty years younger.

'What?' There was a disturbance, muttering and swearing, coming from the hall. 'What do you mean, what about us?'

'I stood outside my dad's shop on Market Hill, and watched you and your brothers march off to Norwich to join the infantry, remember? I'm coming back, Maggie Cowell, you called out. Coming back and we'll be married. Remember that, Ray? I was seventeen, you were eighteen. It was four years before you were back home for good. In all that time, I never doubted you meant every word of what you said. Not for a moment.'

'Mr and Mrs Howden?'

The hall door opened. It was Mrs Blackstone, the evacuee co-ordinator. 'I'm so sorry, we did knock. The old gentleman there opened the door for us.' She entered the kitchen. Instantly, Billy's face went slack, his eyes, his whole body, slumping in defeat. Following immediately behind her was a uniformed policeman.

'Albert Harold Crossley?' The policeman cleared his throat in the sudden silence, began reading from a folded paper. 'This warrant, issued yesterday by the Home Office to the Suffolk Constabulary, Framlingham, authorises and requires me to take you into custody for absenting yourself without permission from the Sir Reginald Haslam Young Men's Correctional Institution, Deal Road, Maidstone, Kent. You are required therefore to come with me to Framlingham police station, where arrangements have been made for your accompanied return to the aforementioned correctional institution forthwith.' He looked round uncertainly. 'Well, get a move on, lad. I haven't got all day.'

The day after Bremen, it was German East Prussia, the Focke-Wulf aircraft assembly plant in Marienberg, on the southern shores of the Baltic. A phenomenal distance, practically all the way to Russia, it was the longest mission ever undertaken by the 8th, stretching every aircraft's fuel reserves to the absolute limits. Yet despite more clear weather, the miles of come-and-get-me contrails behind the bombers, and hour upon hour spent flying ever deeper into enemy territory, the journey was eerily quiet. No fighters, little flak. The formations proceeded unmolested to the target, dropped their bombs with more than the usual precision, swung north over the Polish port of Danzig, then west for home.

It was not until they had crossed the Baltic, crossed Denmark, skirted the Danish shore batteries, were well out into the North Sea and, bemused but relieved, starting to relax at last, that the German fighters finally pounced. Four bombers from the 520th fell in as many minutes. One of them was from the high squadron, *Evening Evelyn*, one of Gene Englehardt's original seven. As it fell, sinking towards the sea with two engines out and its left wing burning furiously, Hooper could see Gene peering anxiously down through his side window.

'Goddamn it!' Beans cursed helplessly over the intercom. 'That's Herbie Bloomfield and the boys. Jesus!'

'Maybe they'll be able to ditch,' Ringwald said hopefully.

'Not a chance. Look at them, she's a flamer. For God's sake, guys, jump!'

As though by a miracle, in that instant they saw a parachute mushrooming astern of the doomed bomber. Then another, then a third.

'Yo! Go, boys! Come on, Herb, everybody out!'

Without warning, Hooper reached out and yanked back on

Martha's throttles, cutting the engines to idle. At the same time, he banked her hard over to the left, lowering the nose until she was settled into a steep spiralling descent.

'Hoop?' Irv Underwood queried.

'We're going down after them.'

As they watched, a fourth parachute appeared. Underwood's voice was unnaturally loud in the engineless hush. 'John, I understand, really I do, why you're doing this. But quite apart from the fact that we don't have the fuel to spare, you and I both know they've had it.'

'Not necessarily.' Hooper banked the steeply gliding *Martha* over even more, further tightening the turn. While her idling engines popped and crackled, the soft rushing of the slipstream grew slightly louder.

'The water temperature is zero. They're wearing heavy flying kit. They're more than a hundred miles from the nearest shore. Even if they hit the water uninjured, they'll freeze to death in minutes.'

'Do you think I don't know that!' Hooper's eyes flashed angrily. He reached for his intercom switch. 'Keissling, go forward into the radio room. Unstow the dinghy bag and get it into the bomb bay. Be careful not to inflate it or else we'll never get it out. Dutch, open the bomb bay doors. Via, I want you to get a first-aid kit together and lash it securely to the dinghy bag.' He broke off and they all watched in awed silence as *Evelyn*, cartwheeling, exploded into the sea below their left wingtip. A curtain of spray towered high into the air from the impact point. As it subsided, they quickly picked out the four parachutes drifting down towards a huge, spreading ring of white. 'Spitz, I need a position fix. As accurate as you can make it. Pass it to Via, so he can signal the Brit Air–Sea Rescue people. The rest of you, keep your eyes peeled for fighters.'

But it was hopeless. As carefully as they could, they threw out their dinghy. It splashed into the sea three hundred yards from the frantically waving airmen. Circling low over their heads, *Martha*'s crew could then do nothing except watch as the final drama played out. Mercifully it was brief. Two of the swimmers had stopped struggling almost as soon as they hit the water, their bulky, fur-lined leather flying suits and heavy over-boots dragging them beneath the freezing waves before they'd even inflated their life vests. The remaining two managed to disentangle themselves from their parachutes and strike out towards the dinghy. Quickly, however, their strokes grew weaker, as waterlogged clothing and freezing water overcame their efforts. Soon, only one remained, reaching doggedly onward while the waves broke over him and the wind pushed the dinghy further and further from his grasp. Then he too, as though recognising the futility of his struggle, suddenly stopped, like a run-down clockwork toy. He rolled slowly over on to his back. Hooper, all of them, saw one of his arms raised towards them in a feeble final wave. Then his face was turning into the sea.

Martha flew home in silence. After landing, as they were taxiing around the perimeter track, the engines, one by one, sputtered to a stop from lack of fuel. They had to wait for a tow-truck to pull them the last two hundred yards to their hardstand.

The next morning, 10 October, and for the third time in as many days, they, together with the other remaining operational crews from the 520th, were roused at dawn. Drunk with strain and sleeplessness, they assembled in the briefing room. 'Münster,' the briefing officer announced, pulling back the curtain.

Seven hours later they were back. As they clumped wearily into his office, Scott Finginger, in common with many of his 8th Air Force intelligence colleagues that day, took one look at their faces, reached into the bottom drawer of his desk and produced a bottle of bourbon.

'Here,' he said, handing it to Lajowski. 'You look as if you could do with it.' Halfway through the mission, he'd learned, at exactly the time the formations were due over the target, a brief Morse code message had been picked up at Group Headquarters in Bury St Edmunds. It was from the mission commander's aircraft, and had been tapped out unusually slowly by the radio operator. As if he was having to muster all his concentration to hold himself steady. As if his sole pre-occupation was to send this message clearly and accurately. As if his life depended on it.

DIVISION UNDER SEVERE REPEAT SEVERE ATTACK STOP IMPERATIVE GET IMMEDIATE ESCORT STOP REPEAT IMPERATIVE END

Despite repeated call-back requests, nothing more was heard.

'We were cut to goddamn ribbons!' Lajowski, cheeks flushed, waved the bottle angrily towards Finginger. 'All of us! The 100th had the low formation and were literally shot to pieces. I didn't see a single ship of theirs come out from the target. And the 390th. It was a massacre, a turkey shoot!'

'What about the flak?' Finginger asked quietly, trying to calm them.

'Flak was bad enough. But it wasn't the flak. It was the fighters! Dozens and dozens of them, everywhere you looked.'

'How many, would you estimate?' Up and down the corridor, the 520th's surviving crews were unburdening themselves to their debriefing officers. *Martha*'s ten were slumped round his table, still partly dressed in their flying gear. Several of them were chain-smoking. Their expressions ranged from shock to disbelief to empty resignation. Hooper was standing beside the window. His eyes, sunken with fatigue, held a faraway look.

'Too many.' Underwood, licking his lips, reached for the bottle. He studied it longingly for a moment before passing it on. That's why we give you whisky, a flight surgeon had told him, weeks earlier, when the nightmare was just beginning. And why you're so young. If you were older, and thought about it, you'd never go into combat.

'Hundreds!' Beans slopped bourbon into his coffee cup. 'Well, maybe not hundreds, but I swear, much more than I ever saw before.'

'Sixty, maybe seventy,' Tork said. 'I stopped counting around then.'

'I'd estimate it could have been as many as that,' Holland confirmed.

'I see.' Finginger nodded, jotting on to his briefing pad. He rubbed nervously at his flak scar. Two hundred and fifty, in fact, was the preliminary figure coming down from HQ. Possibly more. Two fifty. It was unheard of. For the first time ever, the German pilots had very nearly succeeded in stopping an attack dead in its tracks. Less than half the bomber force were thought to have got through to the target, less than thirty per cent returning home without damage or injury. Seventy were still unaccounted for. Seventy bombers. Seven hundred men.

Loren Spitzer was watching him. 'What happened to our escorts, Major?'

'Ah, yes. I gather there was a problem. Didn't you see them?'

'Not until it was too late. There were no escorts from the IP to the drop, nor from there to the rally point and all the way back to the border. By then the damage was done. We were completely unprotected for the most dangerous sector of the mission.' Six minutes. The run-in to the target had been six agonising minutes. Flying on automatic pilot, slow, straight and level, guided by Dutch Holland and all the other bombardiers crouched over their bomb-sights, creeping across the sky towards the target. Aircraft had been shot out of the formation like pigeons from a tree.

'We're, ah, we're still awaiting a full analysis on the escort situation. Early indications are that—'

'Scott,' Hooper murmured from the window. 'It's us. Just tell us the truth.'

Finginger stared down at his pad. 'The escorts didn't make it. Their take-off was scheduled for an hour after yours. But a mist rolled in and they got grounded for another hour. By the time they got airborne, you were well on your way to the target.'

'Then why weren't we recalled?'

Because Curtis Le May never recalled a mission yet. Not in those circumstances. Because General Doolittle would never countenance such a decision in a million years. Because, no matter how bad it gets, the show that is the almighty 8th goes on, and on. Because you are expendable.

'I don't know,' he said, picking up his pencil.

'Heather. How nice.' Cool warmth flickered briefly in Rosamund's eyes. Beyond the door, fitful gusts of rain-laden wind bowled wet leaves across her neatly gravelled drive. She opened the door a little wider. 'Oh, you've brought a visitor. You'd better both come in.'

'We're sorry to drop in on you unannounced like this. Have you met Mrs Howden?'

Rosamund brightened. 'From Howden's the blacksmith's? Of course! Village hall bring-and-buy was the last time, wasn't it, Mrs Howden? Or was it the church fête? My memory! Come along inside to the drawing room. Gerald's laid a fire. We can't light it, mind you, but we can look at it.'

Ten minutes later, Maggie, sitting straight-backed on the edge of one of the leather armchairs, nervously folded her hands together on her lap. 'That's it.' She shrugged.

'Well!' Rosamund sat back. 'Good heavens above. How simply frightful for you. Unimaginable. It must have come as a dreadful shock, finding out like that. Dreadful.'

'Yes, I suppose it was. Particularly with the police coming knocking on the door, and carting him off like that.'

'Of course, of course. Ghastly. And dear Mr Howden senior. Is he all right?'

'Perce?' Maggie looked confused. 'Yes, thanks. Right enough.'

'Thank heavens. A shock like that, and at his age, goodness

knows. Tell me, Heather, wasn't this child the grubby little monster I caught trying to steal some of David's things from the cottage? You remember, one day back in the summer?'

'He wasn't stealing, Rosamund, we gave those things to him. And I think perhaps you may be missing the point. The reason we're here is to ask if you can do anything to help Billy.'

Now Rosamund was confused, turning her head from one to the other. 'Help? But I don't understand. I thought you'd be glad to be rid of the little . . . Look, I'm very sorry, I must have missed something here. I do apologise, Mrs Howden. Could you just possibly run through this once more?'

Heather went to the kitchen to brew tea. She hadn't been to the Grange for weeks, she realised, not since that last disastrous dinner with Sir Richard Howard Vyse. It smelled cold and musty, yet distantly, unwelcomely familiar. Vague, vestigial memories of other, warmer evenings plucked at her subconscious, and then were gone. It was no use pretending, she conceded, pouring water into the pot. Her preoccupations, for the present at least, lay elsewhere.

She'd seen Hooper just once in the last four days. He'd slipped out to the cottage the evening after the ME. The Bremen raid. The day Billy was arrested. He'd listened in unaffected astonishment as she'd recounted the story, promised to relay the news to Hal Knyper and the rest of the crew, asked if there was anything they could do. He was genuinely concerned for Billy, she could tell, but at the same time understandably distracted. Tense and agitated, constantly moving about the cottage, picking things up, replacing them. Bremen had been a big one, apparently. That was all he said about it. Big and bad.

'I can't stay long,' he said then, standing before her. He seemed to be studying her, every detail, absorbing her into himself. 'I'm not supposed to be off base at all. We're on ops again tomorrow. Oh-four-thirty take-off. One of those days when you have to get up before you go to bed.' He forced a smile.

'You needn't have come. Not on my account.'

'Yes. I need.'

That was three days ago. Late the next day she finally got word that *Martha* had returned, overdue but safe, from somewhere called Marienberg. Then they'd had to fly yet again, the very next day, making it three days in succession. Another ME. To Münster, this time. There was a famous cathedral there, she had pictures of it somewhere in one of her books. Something had gone badly wrong, the 8th had suffered terrible losses, but once again *Martha* came through. But the waiting, the tension, was becoming unbearable. She didn't know how much more she could endure, and still be there for him, calm and smiling, when he visited.

Maggie had told her of an old couple the Howdens knew in the village. At the suggestion of the base liaison committee, and like many of the villagers, the old couple had offered to befriend one of the American crews, and so began inviting them for Sunday lunches at their cottage. Then the crew had gone missing, shot down over France. Saddened, the old couple nevertheless agreed to get to know another crew, a replacement. Within a couple of weeks they too were lost. The couple tried once more, mainly out of courtesy to the liaison committee. When, a few weeks later, they were told that the third crew had also been killed, they flatly refused to see any more American airmen. 'I can't bear it,' the old lady had wept. 'They're just little boys.'

'I know you're seeing that American.' Heather jumped. Rosamund was standing at the kitchen door. Her arms were folded, hugging herself. She was looking at the floor. She seemed smaller, less imposing. Diminished. The brittleness was gone; her face bore a look of resignation, as though she'd lost an ally. It was worse somehow. 'I can't do anything about that. It's not my business. I would, however, request that you exercise discretion in your dealings with him. For our sake. Mine and Gerald's. We live here. And David's. He was born and brought up in this village.'

'My God, Rosamund, you make it sound like prostitution or something! There are no "dealings". And I don't need to exercise discretion. I have nothing to hide.'

'No? Are you quite sure?' Her gaze fastened on to Heather's. 'I'm sorry. But it doesn't work like that. Not in my experience. Now then, I think perhaps it would be best if you and Mrs Howden left. I'll do what I can for the Crossley boy.'

Then, finally, came Schweinfurt. A huge and complex double-strike mission to attack, amongst other targets, the biggest ball-bearing factory in Europe. 'If we can knock this one out . . .' S-2 announced, pacing his stage at the front of the briefing room. We? Tork mouthed, exchanging a glance with Gerry Via. '. . . then in two months the entire German war machine grinds to a halt!'

Lajowski shrugged. It sounded reasonable enough, although it did occur to him that the 'war machine', whatever that may be, was controlled by the people waging the war, not the other way round. Knocking it out might not stop them. And if their 'machine' broke down, surely they'd just hop aboard another. Either way, he was too tired to care.

There was a delay at take-off. They had boarded as normal, Hooper and Knyper making their walk-around in milky pre-dawn half-light, while the gunners unhooked their guns, checked them, replaced them and checked them again. Spitzer and Holland, blowing the cold from their hands, busied themselves in the nose, poring over their navigation tables and bombing charts. Gerry Via, alone in his radio room, ran through the signal codes for the day: group identification codes, the recall, mission signals, the individual squadron codes. Up on the flight deck, Irv Underwood completed a weight and balance sheet, totting up how changing fuel, armament and bomb loads would affect the aircraft's weight and centre of gravity. After a while, though, the chores, the housework, no matter how many times they repeated them, were complete. One by one, the crew ran out of things to do and surrendered to their thoughts and anxieties. Hooper clambered aboard and locked the nose hatch closed.

'So,' he said, slumping into his seat. 'I guess we wait.'

Irv Underwood turned to him and forced a sickly grin. His face was pale, and shiny with sweat. 'Don't laugh, really. But I have a very bad feeling about this one.'

He was right.

'Fighters! Eleven o'clock, three more of them! Jesus! Polecat! D'you see them? Do you see them for Christ's sake!'

'Yes! Yes I see them!'

'There's two more! Watch out, they're going straight underneath! One-oh-nines. Left to right. There! Right below us!'

'Okay, I got it. I got it!'

'Wilson's ship's hit. Low formation. Fire in the waist. Jesus, look at it burn.'

A massive flash. 'What was that, for God's sakes?'

'A Focke-Wulf. Christ. It just flew straight into *Alleycat*.'

'Anybody get out?'

'From what? There ain't nothing left to get out from.'

'Ball! Ringwald! Two more, right under you, right to left, d'you see 'em?'

'No, no wait yes! I got them now. Watch out, watch out, they're veering off!'

'Tail! Torky, they're coming your way! Shoot, shoot the sons of bitches!'

'Oh my God. Look. Englehardt's hit.'

A flak shell burst directly beneath *Shack Time*. She reared, twisting in the air beside them like a lanced bull. For a moment it looked as though he'd lost all control, the bomber rolling drunkenly, gouts of black smoke belching from one engine. Hooper veered away to give him room; the other two aircraft in the high formation did the same. Six had taken off that morning. One had turned back halfway with a failed oxygen system. A second, *Split Shift*, had been seen falling from the squadron, trailing smoke, soon after the fighters appeared. Four were left.

Englehardt's voice crackled over the command radio. 'Hoop, can you see where the bastards hit us?'

'Stand by.' Hooper peered upward at the blackened belly of

Englehardt's B17. Daylight showed through a dozen flak holes in the left wing. The left aileron was part-detached, fluttering furiously in the slipstream. The number two engine, propeller blades bent, had stopped. There was a huge, gaping rent just aft of the bomb bay. Behind it, the ball turret was a twisted mess of shattered steel and glass. 'Ah, Gene, looks like the shell burst right below the floor of the radio room.' Gene's radio operator, and his ball turret gunner, Stiltz and Benham, they couldn't have stood a chance. Underwood was nudging him, pointing. 'Yes, and you're losing gasoline. Left side Tokyo tank. It's just pouring out.'

'Right.' Gene hesitated. 'Listen, Hoop, she's handling like a plucked turkey, my navigator's hit, and I believe there's badly injured further aft. We'll have to drop out. You take over squadron lead, keep it in tight as you can, the three of you, and just make damn sure I see you all back at the ranch in a couple of hours, okay?'

'Got it.' *Martha*'s crew, together with those of the two remaining high-squadron aircraft *Danny Boy* and *Patches*, watched wordlessly as Englehardt pulled his stricken Fortress down and away for home. They all knew the odds on his making it were desperate. Alone. Unprotected. Damaged.

And Hooper's new command lasted bare minutes.

'Fighters again! Two, no three of them, six o'clock. They're coming in on *Patches*!' The three Fortresses opened up with all guns simultaneously, but *Patches* was raked, mercilessly, from tail to nose by the diving fighters. At the same time renewed bursts of ground fire began exploding in the air all around them.

'She's hit!'

'Jesus, look at it.' Slowly, almost gracefully, like a dying swan, *Patches* slipped silently over on to her back and fell from view. An instant later there was a deafening explosion and *Martha* bucked violently from a shell burst.

'What was that!'

'Shit, are we hit?'

'Quiet, everybody.' Underwood's voice. Something felt odd with the controls, a big dragging yaw to the right. Hooper, frozen, stared at the column in his hands, images popping like flashbulbs in his head. Joey Galba, his old upper gunner, tears of pain in his eyes, his fingertips shredded and bloody. Pete Kosters, his co-pilot, buckling on his flak helmet. Hoop, boy, are we in a whole heap of trouble. A singing church choir.

'Fire! Number three engine. John? Hoop! Don't do this, Hooper!'

'What?' Singing. He maketh me lie down in green pastures. Heather's eyes.

'John, we have a fire in number three!'

'Englehardt! This is Baker Group leader.' It was Group Commander, way out at the head of the formation, calling over the command radio. 'Englehardt, for God's sake pull your squadron together, man!'

Underwood looked over at *Danny Boy*. 'We are together, sir,' he replied calmly over the radio. 'Englehardt's gone. There's only two of us left.'

'What? Jesus.'

'Irv, hit the fire button, number three engine.' Hooper was back, his free hand racing around the cockpit, shutting the burning engine down. 'Get it feathered, quick as you can, the drag is killing us.'

Irv palmed the button, watching with detached curiosity through his window as the feathered propeller slowed to a stop. Now that the moment had come, he couldn't believe how calm he felt. Flame licked back across the wing from the engine's cowling. 'Prop's feathered, but she's still burning.'

'Right. We'll have to dive.' Hooper had heard about it. Nothing more than that. Rumours. Booze talk. Gene talk. You stuff the airplane into a near-vertical dive, accelerate until just before the wings fall off. The airspeed snuffs out the fire. As simple as that. Like blowing out a candle. He peered past Irv's window. Ten feet away the number three engine was an inferno, roaring like a blow-torch. He could actually hear it. His eye flicked to the bail-out button on the pilot's console. Jump? Or burn? Nine men floating, vanishing through soft white mist. For ever. Not this time. He pushed forward on the column.

Martha's nose sagged groundward. 'Hooper to *Danny Boy*. Jack, listen, we're going down. You peel off and join up with middle formation.'

'Okay, Hoop. Good luck, buddy.' *Danny Boy*'s crew looked on forlornly. Not *Martha*. Not Hooper and the boys. They were practically legendary.

'Hooper to crew, we're diving to try to kill the fire in number three. Call in, all of you, one by one. Report any damage or injury.' *Martha*, steeply angled, was accelerating fast. He glanced at the indicator: two hundred mph and rising.

The crew called in on the intercom. One by one. All except ball turret. Kid Ringwald. Hooper glanced at Underwood. Englehardt's ball turret, nothing left but a blackened stump of shattered glass and metal. Two hundred and fifty miles per hour. They were down to eleven thousand feet, the control column shaking so violently it felt as though it would come off in his hands. 'Ringwald?' Then Gerry Via's voice came shouting above the shrieking slipstream.

'I'm on it!'

Martha pulled out of the dive at three hundred miles an hour – thirty more than the B17's specified design limit, and at barely a thousand feet above the ground. The fire was out. The dead engine still trailed a plume of grey smoke, the wing behind it was scorched and blackened, but the flames were gone.

'Kid's okay!' Via's voice. 'His intercom's out, but he's fine and kicking.'

They took stock. Apart from the dead engine and some minor collateral damage from shell fragments, *Martha* was intact. But the mission was over. On reduced power and with the added drag from the dead engine, she could never regain the formation. Hooper dropped down even lower. They were flying over open farmland, board-flat and criss-crossed with dykes and water-filled ditches.

'Spitz, where the heck are we?'

'North of Osnabrück. Near the Dutch border.'

'Can you plot us a route out of here?'

They dumped their unarmed bombs into a waterlogged field. Then, still flying barely above treetop level, and flat out on the three good engines, they raced northwards towards the coast near Groningen, turning west at the last minute for the sea. They almost made it unnoticed.

It was a lone Messerschmitt 109, one of the newer 'G' models, sleek, fast and heavily armed. And its pilot was out to prove something.

For ten minutes he ducked and weaved, just in, just out of range, eight hundred yards behind them. Probing their defences, inspecting the damage, assessing, waiting.

'Can you hit him, Torky?' Beans asked.

'Not a chance. He's smart. Waste of time trying.'

'What the hell is he doing?' Lajowski cursed, watching from the top turret.

'Waiting for reinforcements,' Underwood answered. 'He won't attack alone.'

Silence descended on the intercom. Hooper inched *Martha* yet lower. The terrain was completely flat. Sand dunes began to appear, shocked faces, a woman and a child, flashed by, barely yards beneath them. Ahead gleamed a wide strip of blue-grey sea. 'I can't allow this,' he was saying, over and over. 'I can't. I won't.'

Thundering down the beach and out over slate-grey waves, he reached out to the throttle quadrant, pulling back power to the engines. *Martha* began to slow. At the same time he began moving the mixture lever to the number two engine, pushing it in and out. Instantly it began misfiring. There was a series of loud reports, black smoke exploding from the exhaust.

'What the hell are you doing?' Underwood was staring in astonishment.

'Irv, I can't allow this to happen. We've come too far.' He kept pumping the mixture lever; the number two engine belched smoke, misfiring noisily. 'He'll think we're losing another engine. Go ahead now and shut it down.'

'But what—'

'Just do it, Irv. Feather number two prop, then shut down

310

the engine.' He reached for his intercom switch. 'Listen up, everyone. I want you to let go your guns, just let them go and leave them hanging down. Via, tell Ringwald to do the same with the ball turret, tell him to leave his guns pointing straight down at the sea.'

'Ah, waist to pilot, I—'

'DO IT! All of you! Right now. Except Lajowski. Bring the upper turret round until your guns are at nine o'clock. Then wait.'

The number two propeller sputtered to a stop. Now *Martha* was flying on the two outer engines alone. 'Lower the undercarriage, Irv.'

'Hooper, that's the surrender signal . . .'

'I know that! Just do as I say and put the goddamn wheels down!'

It worked. After a minute or two, Tork reported that the fighter was approaching for a closer look. Hooper, nursing *Martha* along at minimum flying speed, flaps and wheels lowered as though for landing, rocked the wings gently from side to side, for further encouragement.

None was needed. The Messerschmitt drew right alongside, to Hooper's left. It was barely twenty yards away, brand new, its fresh mottled paintwork spotlessly clean, its spinner bright yellow. The pilot pulled off his mask. They could see his face. He had fair hair, and a wide grin. He looked very young. He waved at them cheerily, made circular motions with one finger, then pointed back the way they'd come.

'He wants us to follow him back to his base,' Underwood said, watching the little fighter. It was mesmerising, so small, like a toy. Yet so deadly. The enemy. Face to face at last. It was not as he'd imagined it. 'Thinks he's bagged a whole B17.'

Hooper nodded, slowly, at the young face. It was still smiling. Then he closed his eyes. And gave the word.

'Lajowski.'

He walked for hours. In the darkness. In the rain. It soaked right through the shoulders of his coat, to touch his skin. His shoes became wet through, his feet numb with cold. He didn't care, he didn't notice. It was a turning point, a crossing over, a point of no return. And there was no way back. Nothing could ever be the same again. Nothing. There was no health in him, no life in the world to come, and no redemption. It didn't matter. It had gone beyond mattering.

But it did hurt. Deep inside, like grief, like loss. Whatever had been left, whatever small, battered shreds of his former self remained, were finally gone. The transformation was complete. Now there was nothing to do but see it through to its logical conclusion. It was a pang of sadness, nothing more. Like losing a distant friend.

He stood outside her door, the rain gurgling down the gleaming black lane behind him, drumming on the sodden cloth of his cap. Five minutes? An hour? Then he began to knock.

'I killed a man today,' he said, when she opened. 'He was just a boy.'

She reached out to him. 'Please, come inside.'

'I'm so afraid.'

'I know.' She folded the soft fingers of her hands about his, like closing lily petals, and drew him into the hall.

Chapter 12

Schweinfurt cost the 8th USAAF six hundred men. In a single day. The same number, seasoned commentators were quick to point out, as had been ordered into another valley of death, on a different October day, eighty-nine years earlier. Other Charge of the Light Brigade comparisons were soon drawn. Sacrifice, recklessness, heroism; waste. Following so closely after Bremen and Münster, the 8th's cumulative loss rate for that week was patently more than could be sustained. A halt was unavoidable, a brief interlude of respite, to recover, regroup, re-equip. And re-man. Even Curtis Le May gave in. Telephoning around, checking readiness and status, one base commander after another told him stories of decimation on a scale that beggared comprehension.

At Bedenham, the 520th was like a ghost town. The morning after Schweinfurt, Colonel Lassiter told Le May that by pooling all his uninjured flyers together, dividing them into scratch crews, and sharing them out among the remaining serviceable aircraft, the 520th might be able to put four Fortresses in the air that day. Not a single bomber had come through the week without some damage, or injuries to crew members. It was the same story on every base. Or worse. Le May, unusually subdued, stood them all down.

Later during the morning Lassiter, unable to sit still any longer, left his office and drove his Jeep out across the rain-puddled apron to the flight line. Written-off aircraft littered the hardstands like whale corpses on a beach. Salvage crews swarmed over them, stripping them to their frames for re-usable components. Once picked clean, the empty hulks were then towed or dragged to the boneyard, a scrap metal compound behind number two hangar. Village children played there, among the bullet holes and bloodstains.

Shack Time would end up there later in the day. Gene Englehardt had nursed his crippled bomber home, with his navigator injured, and both his ball turret gunner and the radio operator dead at their positions. Arriving overhead, he'd found he was unable to lower the aircraft's undercar-riage, and had been forced to belly-flop on to the grass next to the runway. *Shack Time* was totalled. Later, Lassiter found his squadron commander drunk in the deserted officers' bar. He bought him a drink, then sent him to bed. Gun shots were heard. Rumour had it that for most of the night Gene had just lain there, repeatedly emptying his service revolver into the ceiling.

Misbehavin Martha, last of Bedenham's old F-type war horses, was also unserviceable. Lassiter pulled his Jeep up at her hardstand. A sergeant mechanic and his team were riveting aluminium patches over a row of holes down the left wing. Similar patches scarred the skin of her fuselage. Her number three engine was little more than an ugly lump of heat-blackened scrap iron. A broad swath of scorched metalwork trailed back from it across the wing. Everywhere, her drab olive-green paintwork was flaking and smut-streaked. Oil dripped into pools on the concrete beneath the remaining engines.

The mechanic was ambling towards the Jeep. 'How goes it, Sergeant?' Lassiter asked.

Knyper cupped filthy fingers around his cigarette lighter. 'That, I have to say, Colonel, is one seriously battle-weary old bus. I don't know whether to fix it, or put a frame around it and hang it on the wall.'

Something had happened. No one knew what exactly, except that *Martha* had arrived home early, mission aborted. One engine, still smoking, was dead, but mercifully her crew were uninjured. Yet something had happened. Flicking through the debriefing reports that morning, Lassiter had found *Martha*'s abnormally short, pregnant with omissions. He'd telephoned the debriefing officer.

'I don't know, Colonel,' Finginger had told him. 'Nobody had anything to say. Hit by flak before they got to the target, returned home on three engines. End of story. Lieutenant Underwood filed the report.'

'Hooper?'

'He didn't show up to the debriefing.'

It was too much, Lassiter reflected, leaning over the wheel of his Jeep. Knyper was offering him a cigarette. He'd been trying to quit. Nearly a month. He reached out and took it, bending to Knyper's lighter. These young men. What was being asked of them was too much. The flight surgeon had been to see him. One or two men were beginning to refuse to fly, he reported. Point blank. Shoot me if you want, they said. They meant it. A quick end, a court-martial, a dishonourable discharge, anything was preferable to the daily, nerve-screaming torture that was operational combat. Anything.

Lassiter looked over at *Martha*. The new G-type Fortresses were starting to arrive at the bases. There were already a few dispersed around Bedenham's perimeter, their gleaming silver skins glinting in the weak sunlight. More were promised. Hundreds. Faster, more powerful, better armed, better equipped. We're entering a new phase in this war, Charlie, Le May had told him. A new era. The gloves are coming off, and then we're going to turn some tables.

Lassiter looked at Knyper. 'Fix it, if you can, Sergeant. She's the last of the originals.'

Hal raised an eyebrow at his base commander. 'I can write her off if you want, Colonel. It's just paperwork. The new G-type Forts are a heck of a lot better.'

'I know. But this one's special. Kind of symbolic, of the way things used to be. Before everything changed. Patch her up. Good as you can.'

'Well then, Billy. So, how are you keeping, lad?'

'Crossley. You have to call me Crossley. Nobody uses first names, it's not allowed. Anyway, my name's not Billy, it's Albert.'

Ray shrugged. 'It's Billy to us.' He looked around the

room, shivering involuntarily. It was small, grey-painted brick, with a concrete floor and a single barred window high in one wall. They sat at a plain wooden table. The room was unheated, and smelled of damp and disinfectant. As though someone had recently been sick in there. 'How's the food? Are you getting enough? I brought you a bag of things, couple of tins, some blackberry tarts Maggie made from off the bushes out in the lane. Not much, I'm afraid. Something, though.'

'Thanks.' Billy's head was down. 'But I won't prob'ly never see 'em. We're not allowed food presents.'

'Ah. Yes.' Ray had been relieved of the package, carefully wrapped by Maggie, and enclosing letters of encouragement from them both, by the duty officer inside the main entrance. Even Claire had written. 'Well. Never mind, eh? Maybe later on.'

Billy said nothing, just stared down at his hands lying on the table. His knuckles were skinned. When the guard had brought him in, Ray had immediately noticed a fading yellow bruise on one cheek. Billy's eyes, round and wary, had met his momentarily, then moved away.

He shouldn't have come. It was hopeless, clearly a mistake, and upsetting for Billy. For them both. The journey had been a nightmare, an endless succession of delayed trains and buses that never turned up. He'd left Bedenham at six that morning, finally arriving in Maidstone at two in the afternoon. At that rate, he'd be lucky to get home before midnight.

And all for ten minutes. The detention centre was awful, like a prison. Worse. Bars on everything, uniformed guards, jangling keys, young boys' echoing shouts. Filthy language, obscene, high-pitched screams. It made the hairs stand up on his neck. And the stench. Boiled cabbage, stale tobacco, urine. It made you want to gag.

'Visiting's Thursdays,' a rheumy-eyed officer had growled through a hatch in the front door, when Ray had finally arrived. 'Come back then.'

'Can't,' Ray had said quickly. 'Shift work. On a bomber base.'

'Ten minutes, then. That's your lot. And you can leave the package with me.'

Billy. He looked completely different. Ray tried not to appear shocked when they led him in, but he was scarcely recognisable. Physically the same, of course; a little thinner perhaps, and sort of holding himself in more. But inside, it was as though a light had gone out. The spirit. The heart. It was gone, like a snuffed candle. In its place a wall had arisen, a barrier. Billy, the cheerful, mischief-loving Billy Street of old, with the bottomless cheek, wicked grin and a hundred bright ideas a day, was no more. Like the new identity he'd created so carefully for himself, cloaked himself in; gone.

Maggie was right. It was killing him.

'Hal Knyper came round. He sends his best.'

'Oh. Right.'

'He says – what was it? – he says you've got to hang in. Keep your head down and hang in. It's something to do with baseball. Says he'll write again soon as he can.'

'All right.' People wrote him letters. He kept them stuffed beneath his mattress. Took them out to stare at, when he could bear to. Sitting alone on his bed surrounded by the screaming and the stench and the savagery, his mouth

319

working, his round face crunched into a frown, while the loops and squiggles writhed and twisted, his head felt like bursting, and the pages blurred with frustration in his hands.

'They're very busy up there on the base. Had a rough time of it lately, so the word goes in the village. Some shocking losses. Oh, but Hal says the boys from your plane are all a-okay. In fact, come to think of it, tomorrow evening we've got that Eldon coming round for supper. Something to look forward to, I suppose. Expect he'll bring Emmett Lajinski with him again. Inseparable, those two. What is it they call him?'

Polecat. Because his name's Polish. Even though he isn't. Polecat Lajowski. Sitting side by side with him in *Martha*'s cockpit, running through the checklists, his nose filled with the scent of high-octane gasoline, dew-laden grass and gun oil. The whine, cough and splutter of a starting Cyclone. Hal, his cigarette parked behind his ear, the sweat starting on his brow, torquing down cylinder-head nuts. General Doolittle, arriving in his Jeep. 'What about you, Private? Need anything?' Street B. Private First Class.

Dead. Killed in action.

'Beryl Moody's girl stopped in. Ruby? Said for me to say hello. Asked especially.' Say something, Billy. Speak to me, for God's sake. 'If you ask me, I'd say she's a bit sweet on you.'

'Maybe it would be better if you was to go now, Mr H.'

'Is that what you want, lad?'

He looked up at last, his face crumpling. 'No!'

A thump on the door. 'Time's up, Crossley. Out you come, the both of you.'

'Christ!' Suddenly Ray was on his feet. He flung open the

door. 'Listen! I haven't spent the entire day travelling halfway across the bloody country to be ordered about by the likes of you! Now, you'll bugger off and give me another couple of minutes with my boy here, or else your governor is going to be getting a letter from my MP about your bloody manners. Do I make myself clear?'

The guard took a step back, blinking at Ray in astonishment. 'Right. All right then. Two minutes.'

'Thank you!' Ray slammed the door. Turning, he saw the tears starting in Billy's eyes.

'I can't, Mr H, I can't . . .' It was all he managed. With one arm crooked, like a little child's, across his eyes, he broke into anguished sobs. Ray, swallowing, stepped to his side.

'Here, now, none of that.' He reached out hesitantly, resting his hand on Billy's back. In a moment Billy was hugging him, burying his face in Ray's jacket. Clutching at him as though drowning.

'I can't do it! I know I can't!'

'Yes. Yes, you can. You must.' Shushing softly, Ray held on to him, lightly at first, then more strongly, one hand rubbing at his back. Slowly the spasms subsided. After a while, he eased him back on to his chair, plucking a handkerchief from his pocket. 'Listen, Billy, listen to me now. Maggie and Mrs Garrett went to see Brigadier Garrett and his wife, you know, up the Grange. They've got influence. They're going to look into all this and see what's what. I've already spoke with Mrs Blackstone and she's promised to get back to me with as much as she can. I've also talked to Ted Bolsover's brother-in-law. He's a solicitor, in Fram. Retired now, but he knows his oats. He says nothing's cut and dried, there's things called exceptional circumstances, thinks possibly you weren't represented properly at your court case.'

'It's no use, Mr H. I'm stuck here.'

'No, you're not, we'll find a way somehow. But for now you've got to do like Hal says. Keep your head down and hang on. You've just got to.'

They parted in the corridor outside. Ray, fists clenched, watched Billy being led away, dwarfed by the key-jangling warder beside him. 'You'll be all right, lad!' Ray called suddenly, but he didn't look back. 'Billy! You will. You'll be all right.'

'Do you really think he'll be all right, miss?'

Heather dropped the pile of exercise books into her bicycle basket. 'Yes, Ruby, I'm sure of it. He's a strong boy, and very resourceful. Try not to worry.'

With a furtive glance around the empty playground, Ruby produced an envelope. 'I wrote him this. It's a letter. But I don't know where to send it.'

'Well, perhaps I could address it for you, if you like. And post it for you, too.'

Ruby stared down at the letter forlornly. 'All them stories he made up. About his rich dad. And his mum getting blown up and that. I knew they was just stories, I knew it. He'd never really lie to me. Would he, miss?'

'No he wouldn't, and I believe he knew that you knew it, too, Ruby. I believe he only made those things up to try to draw a line over his past, and because he was afraid we might – you might – be disappointed in him if we found out.'

'Disappointed? But how could I be disappointed, miss? I

love him. I really love him.' She looked up at Heather, her freckled face wide with anguish. 'What on earth am I going to do?'

'Well, Ruby, I think that if someone, someone we really care about, is in trouble or danger or in pain, we should try our best to find ways to help them, if we can. Sometimes it's very hard, because no matter how much we try, it turns out that there is nothing we can do to help them. Other times, it is necessary to make very difficult choices, to find ways to help them. And that can be particularly hard, because in the end, we have to make those choices alone . . .'

'Miss?'

Heather pulled her bicycle roughly from the rack. 'Write, Ruby. Write to him as often as you can. I'll get the address for you.'

'But he don't read too good. Does he?'

'He is much more able than he believes, Ruby. You must make him read. Make him understand. Tell him how you feel, tell him to be strong, that you will stand by him through this difficult time, and that none of us feel he has let us down or betrayed us in any way. Tell him you love him and he has nothing to be ashamed of.'

She pedalled slowly through the village. The previous night's rain had all but dried, but a dank autumn mist hung like a veil over the roofs and gardens. The air lay still, the trees unmoving. And there was something else. There was no noise. No puttering motor vehicles, no children's squeals, no neighbours chatting over garden fences. No aeroplanes. It was eerie. She could scarcely recall a time when she hadn't been able to detect the rumble of an engine, somewhere in the sky. Or away on the base. It was as if the whole of Suffolk were holding its breath.

He wasn't at the cottage, but his cap and overcoat were on the hook where she'd hung them the night before. She called softly, checking upstairs and out in the back yard where they used to sit. Then, donning wellington boots, she walked across the lane and into the fields.

He was right at the bottom, down by the stream, sitting on a tree stump staring into the little river. It gurgled by busily, swelled by the night's downpour. He turned as she neared, rose, smiled, reached out his hands towards hers. Kissed her. 'It's very good to see you,' he said.

That evening they stayed in the cottage. Hoop lit a fire in the little grate in the sitting room, while Heather made a sort of kedgeree. She'd had the haddock a week, it was a little dry, and tough, but the egg was real, and in the end, sitting face to face on the floor by the fire to eat, it didn't matter.

'Tell me about your day. School. The children.' Normal things. Not war and bombs and killing.

She told him, soft smiles playing across her face as she recalled an amusing detail, a moment of hilarity, an incident of no consequence. She understood. It was a part of his need. He'd talk when he was ready.

'What about Billy?' he asked, resting his chin on one knee. She'd reached the part about Ruby, and her letter, in the playground.

'It's very sad. The classroom just isn't the same without him. Not that he was there all of the time, I have to admit, but our lives are definitely poorer without him.'

'How do you mean?'

'Well, he was always planning great schemes. Money-making ideas mainly. I remember once, soon after he arrived here, he managed to persuade Mr Needham, he's our principal, to keep breeding rabbits in a cage on the school vegetable patch. He said we'd be able to sell the offspring to the butcher to raise money for a school telescope.

'What happened?'

'Within a week the rabbits escaped. They ate all Mr Needham's vegetables, foxes ate the rabbits and that was the end of that.'

'The telescope?'

She shook her head. 'Still waiting. Billy had some vague idea about opening an arts and crafts stall on the road outside, but I think Mr Needham had lost interest. Billy too, really. The base was just opening by then. That was it for Billy. It was where he wanted to be. Did you know he used to slip me all the news, about *Martha*, and your missions? When you'd got home safely, that sort of thing.'

Hooper nodded. Beyond the window, from far out in the darkness across the fields, drifted the plaintive lowing of cattle. 'I reported back this morning. We've been stood down. Three days.'

'Good. You've all earned it.'

'The boys are out on a weekend pass. Most of them have gone to London.'

'I expect they'll manage to find ways to have a good time.'

'I expect they will.' Hooper smiled reflectively. 'Gene's alive. My squadron commander, Gene Englehardt, remember?'

'I remember. From the dance. Thank goodness.'

'Yes. He lost his ship, and two crew members, but he got back in one piece, thank God. He's kind of a linchpin at the 520th. If he breaks, we all break. Sort of Bronco Bill, Charles Lindbergh and Errol Flynn all rolled into one. Sure, he's loud and cocky and fearless, and he drinks too much and swears too much and flies a B17 standing on his head. But the kids, the new guys especially, they all look up to him. It gives them something to aim for. As though, if they can be like him, just a little, then nothing can touch them. Do you know what I mean?'

'You must be very fond of him.'

'We're completely different.' Hoop gazed into the flames. 'But, when I arrived here, from my old base, he made me believe I could do this. Within a couple of minutes of meeting him. As though there was never any doubt in his mind.'

'And in your mind?'

'Then? God knows!' He smiled, turning to look into her eyes. They sparkled like gems in the flickering light. Her cheeks were flushed from the flames, her lips dark and full. 'But I do remember you. At that dance. You were the most beautiful thing I had ever seen in my life. I just knew I had to hold you, then and there, in my arms. Just once.'

'Yes. It was a strange evening for me too. Poor Scott, I doubt I was very good company for him. Do you think he knows?'

'He's an intelligence officer. It's his job to know.' He leaned forward. She closed her eyes. Their lips met.

He held her naked body to his, watching her face in the pale moonlight, feeling the heat of her breath on his cheek. He shifted slightly on the bed, sank deeper. With a soft outbreath of surprise, she opened her eyes, smiled briefly, then closed them again, the smile fading with her rising desire. His mouth closed over the soft swell of her breast, one hand caressing her hair, her face, her arms, her flanks. She sighed, arching her body higher to him, watching his lips at her nipple. He moved his head between her breasts, inhaling, drinking the moist scent of her skin, his thighs quickening between hers. Fingers moved beneath the sheets, gripping at his back, his spine and his buttocks. He groaned, moving his head once more, to seal his lips over hers.

'Coffee.' Joanna Morrison placed the cup on the bedside table. Via stirred from sleep.

'What time is it?'

'A little after seven a.m. I have to go to work.'

'Wait.' Via hauled himself to a sitting position. 'Give me a minute and I'll walk with you.' He picked up the cup, blinking at Joanna who slipped a bathrobe from her shoulders, stooping to pull on underclothes. He sipped, recoiled. 'Did you say this was coffee?'

'Camp. With a dash of condensed milk. Haven't seen the real thing for weeks, and I'm out of tea. Do you like it?'

'Very, uh, interesting, Jo, but coffee it ain't.' He dressed quickly; five minutes later they were on the streets of Waterloo. It was Saturday, still early. A stiff breeze spiralled litter high into the air. To their right, a mournful blare sounded as a tug pushed a raft of barges upriver against a falling tide. Joanna, a nurse's cape about her shoulders, slipped an arm through Via's.

'Now then. Have you been studying your books like a good boy?'

'I have. As it happens.'

'We'll make a medic of you yet.' She hesitated. 'Would you like to come up to the ward? You could meet some of the patients. Talk to them.'

She'd told him about it. A mixed general ward. Toothless ancients waiting to die, bank clerks with burst appendixes, a sailor with terminal cancer, youngsters with bomb-shattered limbs. He felt a shiver of apprehension. Reading about it was one thing, meeting it face to face quite another. 'Sure. I'd like that.'

Her arm squeezed tighter. 'It was lovely to see you again.'

'You make it sound like it's over already.'

'Well, I suppose it is, isn't it? Oh, I know you're staying tonight and everything. But tomorrow you go back to Suffolk. You probably won't get another pass for ages. In a few weeks you'll have finished your tour of duty, and then you'll be on your way home. Isn't that how it works?'

'Well, yes. I guess.' Something nagged at his subconscious. 'But I have to tell you, somehow I don't feel that good about it.'

'What do you mean?'

'It's like, well, it feels like a drop-in war. Drop in on good old England for a few months, fly your twenty-five, then drop the hell out again. Back to the States, pick up your life where you left off. No rationing, no blackouts, no queuing three hours for a loaf of bread. No bombs falling. As if the whole war was just a far-off dream. It don't feel quite right, somehow.' He pulled her closer. They were nearing the entrance to St Thomas's. 'Don't feel quite right leaving you, neither.'

'Oh, I wouldn't worry about that. I knew it would have to be like this. I've known for years, really. Relationships. In wartime, they're temporary things. Drop-in, like your drop-in war. We're both grown up enough to understand that, aren't we?'

'Yeah, I guess. But is that how you'd want it to be? Between us. If you had the choice?'

She considered. 'No, but it's the nature of war. Nothing lasts.'

Thirty miles away to the south, Herman Keissling and Marion Beans were standing outside Maidstone railway station.

'Now what?' They looked around uncertainly. Beans approached what looked like a nineteen twenties-vintage taxi-cab. A huge neoprene gas bag was strapped to its roof, its driver asleep at his wheel. Beans tapped on the window, and pulled a scrap of paper from his pocket. 'The Haslam kids' detention place, I guess, sir. Do you know it?'

They rode in silence for a while. 'You heard from Cheryl?' Keissling asked.

'Sure. Every week. Regular as clockwork.'

'How's she doing?'

'Hates it. Never stops bitching. She's at her mom's. But at least she keeps writing, though, which is the main thing, and there's something . . .'

'What?'

'Her letters. Sure she complains all the time, but over the months, I don't know, it's like we're really talking at last.

Listening and talking. Like I never really knew her before. Before I got posted over here and we had to spend all this time apart. Doesn't make any sense, does it?'

'Yes, it does.' Keissling was staring down at an object in his lap. It was a large and ornate doll, with long blond locks and pink cheeks. She was expensively dressed in the red and gold uniform of a Beefeater. 'Blanche is suing for divorce.'

'You're kidding! Why?'

'I got this to send her. She loves dolls. Thought it might make things better.' He paused. 'Do you remember the last time we had a pass for London? A few weeks back? I kept going on and on about art galleries and shit?'

'Uh-huh.'

'Well, I never went to no art galleries. I did a stupid thing.'

'You went whoring, and then you wrote and told your wife.'

'No! Well, yes. But nothing happened. Nothing like that. I thought it would. I wanted it to, if I'm honest. But when it came down to it I couldn't go through with it. I picked up this girl, one of those Piccadilly commandos. She took me back to her place, and then we just talked. I paid her to. All night.'

'*Then* you wrote and told your wife all about it. Jesus, Herm, don't you get it? We're in a different world from them. There's things we'll never be able to tell them, things they could never understand even if they wanted to. What it feels like to see your buddies crash and burn up, right in front of your eyes, or have your pilot's brains blown all over you. Or to feel so scared from flak you can't stop from soiling your shorts. Or what it feels like to shoot a man dead. Or,

330

come to that, why you might just feel the need to sit up all night talking to a ten-dollar hooker.'

Fifteen minutes later they were at the door of the detention centre.

'Visiting's Thursday,' said a face at the hatch. 'Buzz off.'

'Couldn't we just have five minutes, sir? We've come a long way.'

'No, you couldn't. I'd lose my job. Who d'you want to see, anyway?'

'Bill Street. No, hold on, where's that damn paper. Crossley, is it?'

'Him again? Christ, he's more popular than the bloody Pope.' The face eyed the two Americans warily. Beans held up a grocery bag.

'We brought him some things. Gum, candy. Magazines.'

'No parcels allowed, neither.'

'There's a couple of packs of Lucky Strikes in it for you.'

'Don't smoke neither.' Yet the face still waited. Somewhere in the compound behind him a fire-bell was ringing. He didn't move, his eyes on Keissling's doll.

Hooper and Heather went to the Suffolk coast. A seaside town with a church on a hill, a long esplanade and a steep, shingly beach. They checked into a hotel on the front, were shown to a fourth-floor room with a large sash window overlooking the sea. Hooper threw it wide and for a while they sat beside it, still wrapped in their coats, just listening to the crash and suck of the waves, inhaling the fresh salt air and watching wooden fishing boats ply the waters below them. After a while she reached out, taking his hand.

'I know this is against all the rules.' She smiled. 'But supposing there was nothing else. No war, no David, no complications. Nothing but just the two of us.'

'I'd ask you to marry me,' he said straight away. 'I'd want us to be together. For ever.'

'Good. I accept, of course. Where do we live, in America?'

'No. There is nothing for me there. Here, England. Or maybe Europe somewhere. France, Italy, perhaps.'

'Sounds wonderful. What would we do?'

'I have no idea. Live together in a small house deep in the country. I get to stay at home and grow vegetables, while you go out to work, teaching kids.' Heather laughed, squeezing his hand. His face, dark eyes narrowing on the distant horizon, held a rare look of briefly imagined contentment. 'I've always liked the idea of tending garden. Ever since I was a kid. Growing things from nothing but a couple of specks of seed. It's fascinating and, well, worthwhile, somehow.'

They ate lunch in a pub, then walked arm in arm along the seafront. Despite a chill wind, and threatening grey clouds, the esplanade was busy. Families on a late holiday, older couples taking the air, servicemen on a pass. They came to a children's boating pond and sat down on a wooden bench, idly watching a small blond-haired boy play with a toy yacht. His parents were sitting nearby, deep in conversation.

'It doesn't change anything, Hoop, and it has absolutely nothing to do with us. But I should never have married David. I've known that for a long time. Even before he went to Malaysia.'

'What is he like?'

'Irrepressible. Very dashing. Funny. Rather headstrong. Wonderfully exciting. But wrong, for me. I know that now. We were wrong for each other. In more normal circumstances we'd have probably discovered that long before we ever contemplated marriage. But the circumstances weren't normal, I was silly and weak. And young. And what with all the excitement of the outbreak of war, well, it was rather like getting caught up in a whirlwind.'

'You shouldn't blame yourself.'

'Perhaps not. But I should definitely have stayed in Lincoln. I was really perfectly happy there.'

'I'm mighty glad you didn't.' He put his arm about her, drawing her close. She rested her head on his shoulder. 'I wish things could be different, Heather, you know that. But the irony is, if they were different, if there was no war, no killing, no David, we wouldn't have found each other. And I'm just so thankful that we did. Even if it's just for a short while.'

'Shush, now. That's enough.'

Hands clasped, they fell into contemplative silence, stranded upon a tiny island of timelessness. Seagulls wheeled high overhead. Passers-by ebbed and flowed around them like tide-water. The couple with the blond boy moved on into another present. Others arrived, stayed, departed. Sunlight split the clouds briefly, bathing their faces in gold, flinging a finger of shadow across an ancient sundial, high on a nearby wall.

'I just have to see these guys through. Heather. Get them safely through to the finish of their tour of duty. Nothing else matters. Not the war, not defeating the Germans, nothing.

With my first crew, it didn't happen. I let them down, something just went wrong. I've got to get it right this time. Get them through to the end. That's all there is to it.'

'By the way. I've put my name down for the ATS.'

'What did you say?' Maggie turned at the sink. Ray looked up, his accounts books spread over the kitchen table before him.

'The ATS. At the recruiting office in Fram.' Claire, her face a carefully composed study in nonchalance, flicked rapidly through the pages of her magazine. 'Apparently the Royal Artillery are putting together women's anti-aircraft batteries. They're recruiting from out of the ATS. I'm going to be eighteen in a few weeks, so I've signed up.'

There was a moment's silence. 'You. An anti-aircraft gunner.'

'That's right.'

'But, Claire, love, you don't know anything about guns.'

'That's the whole point, Mum. I'll learn. They'll train me. It's a six-week basic training course, in Scotland. Then advanced training somewhere else. Gun-laying, ballistics, that new radio tracking thing. All that.'

'Scotland?' Maggie, appalled, wiped her hands on her apron, lowering herself to a chair. Ray was staring at his books.

'Well, say something, you two!'

'But what about Eldon? Have you discussed it with him?'

'Of course, Mum. He thinks it's a terrific idea. We'll both be out there, in uniform, doing our bit for the war effort together.'

'But anti-aircraft batteries. I mean, won't you be in terrible danger? You're only a child, for goodness' sake. A young slip of a girl.'

'I'm old enough to join up and do my bit. It's what you and Dad have been going on and on about for years. People pulling together, facing up to their responsibilities. Doing their bit.'

'I agree with Eldon,' Ray said quietly.

'What?'

'It's a fine idea. Just as long as you are doing it for the right reasons.'

'What do you mean?'

He pushed his books to one side and began laying forks for supper. 'Well, love, you know how we felt about you and young Eldon getting engaged, and that. So long as this isn't just some crackpot scheme to get back at us somehow. You know, old enough to fight in a war, but not old enough to get engaged . . .'

'Dad, listen. I understand what you're saying, but it's not that. It's just, well, for so long now, years really, I never thought about the war, not properly. About why it was happening and what it meant. In fact, it didn't mean anything to me, except that there was never enough to eat and nothing worth buying down the shops. But then I met Eldon and we talked, really talked, about it. And I started reading the papers and paying more attention to the news on the wireless. And talking to other people, the woman down the recruiting office, our own boys, sailors and airmen and that. Suddenly, it sort of dawned on me that sooner or later everyone has to face up to it. Deal with it. More than that, we have to do whatever we can to get it over with, win it, as quick as we can. To stop it dragging on and on. Like the last one.'

Ray was studying his daughter. 'Apart from the training, chances are you'll get posted somewhere else. You and Eldon do both realise that?'

'Yes. We've talked about that too. It'll be hard. But we're strong. We'll manage.'

There was the sound of bicycles approaching in the darkness outside. Maggie was sniffing into a corner of her apron. 'This bloomin' family. Billy gone. Perce wandered off again, and now Claire leaving home to join up and get posted God knows where. It's falling apart. I don't think I can bear much more of it.'

'No, it's not falling apart, Mag. It's growing up, that's all. This is a family you can be proud of. Our daughter is joining the Royal Artillery. And we're going to get Billy back somehow. Wait for him to serve out his time if necessary, but we'll get him back. As for Percy—'

The back door flew open and Lajowski appeared, closely followed by Ringwald. 'He's not at the Fleece, folks. Sorry. The landlord says your father hasn't been there at all today. We asked around the locals, but it seems nobody's seen him for days.'

Maggie stood up. 'Ray. He was already gone when we got up this morning.'

'And I never heard him come in last night! Christ, I never saw him at all yesterday, come to that. He's been gone two days.'

'I'll get my coat.' Claire was already moving.

'I'm coming too.'

'No, Mag, stay here. In case he comes back. Eldon, you go with Claire. Head on down into the village. Knock on doors – Claire knows which ones. Maybe someone's seen him. Emmett, you come with me.'

They hurried up the lane, away from the village.

'You think he might be on the base?' Lajowski asked.

'Not the base, the woods behind it. He practically lives there.'

Ten minutes later they were plunging into a pitch-black wall of trees guided by the weak light of Ray's paraffin lantern. The air was pungent with the scent of rich soil and damp leaves. Overhead, a dying breeze sighed though the treetops. Beyond the canopy, a bright quarter-moon slipped in and out of fast-moving clouds. They stuck to narrow footpaths and animal tracks; occasionally Ray branched off into thicker woodland. Once or twice he took wrong turnings and had to double back. Frequently they stumbled on roots and thickets. 'Perce! Hey, Percy, it's me, Ray! Dad? Are you in here?'

Soon they were far into the woods. About a mile further on they could hear the sounds of the base: power generators, compressors, heavy machinery, as unending shifts of repair and maintenance teams worked flat out around the clock to bring the 520th to readiness. They struggled on.

At last Ray ground to a halt. He raised his lantern, peering into impenetrable gloom. Weak shadows swayed around them. 'He's not here,' he gasped. 'Damn it! We've covered most of his favourite haunts and trapping sites. Where the bloody hell is he, then?'

'Are you sure he would have come in here?' Lajowski drew up, panting.

'As sure as anywhere. What if he's fallen and broken something? Or knocked himself out?' Or wandered, mindless and alone, into oblivion.

'Listen, Mr Howden. I say I run back to base, round up a hutful of the guys, get a load of flashlights, come back and comb these woods from end to end. We'll never find him with just you and me on our own.'

Ray swallowed. 'Okay, Emmett, thanks. It makes sense. Can you find your way in the dark?'

'I'll follow my ears!' He grinned in the yellow light then turned to go.

It was then that they saw it. Ten yards away. A shadow, like a long, narrow sack, hanging from a tree.

'What in hell is that?'

Ray raised the lantern. Not a sack. A scarecrow, hanging limply. A thin, stick-like scarecrow, clad in rags. 'Oh, dear Jesus, no.' They moved towards it. Immediately Ray stumbled, tripping full length over something lying in the undergrowth. It was Percy's shopping trolley. They heard a groan.

'Perce? Dad? Is that you down there?'

A figure rustled in the bushes at his feet. Slowly it began raising itself to a sitting position, leaves and twigs falling from its wispy white hair.

'Dad. Thank God. It's me, Ray. Are you hurt? Perce?'

'You're too bloody late,' Percy grumbled. 'It's all flown away.'

Lajowski was approaching the tree. Ray followed, lantern raised.

It was a body. A man, hanging by a leather belt looped

around his neck. He was suspended from a bough, his feet just inches from the ground. His face, hideously contorted, was near black. His eyes stood out from their sockets, wide and bulging; a grossly swollen tongue, darkly purple, protruded from lips pulled back over black gums. His teeth were filthy, he had several weeks' growth of beard, his hair was long and unkempt. His clothes, however, torn and ragged as they were, were nevertheless recognisable. He wore a sheepskin flying suit.

'My God, it's a flyer, Emmett. From off the base.'

'I know.' Lajowski turned away, sinking to his knees. Nearby, Percy looked on in silence. 'It's Lieutenant Broman.'

'Who?'

'Dan Broman. He used to be our bombardier.'

Chapter 13

In November the weather turned abruptly, revealing, like a malevolent twin brother, the other face of an English autumn. Crisp, anti-cyclonic days of quiet skies, gentle breezes and sun-kissed afternoons tinged with autumn golds were rudely shouldered aside by a succession of tightly coiled depressions that rolled across Europe from the Atlantic like an advancing army. Thick, smothering blankets of rain-laden cloud, stretching from ground level to twenty thousand feet, enveloped East Anglia, turning runways into lakes, tin huts into noisy leaking buckets and grassy aprons into sucking bogs. The rain was incessant and all-pervading, whipped across the unprotected flatlands by treacherous, gusty winds. Missions were cancelled. Time after time, crews were roused before dawn from their mildew-smelling blankets, herded beneath the drumming roof of the briefing room, trucked, tense and bleary, through the oil-black rain to their waiting aircraft, only to have the mission scrubbed at the last minute on account of the weather.

When they did fly, inevitably the accident rate shot up. Aircraft failed to attain flying speed on water-laden runways, and crashed off the end. Others, landing too fast or too long, found that wet brakes and inadequately treaded tyres wouldn't stop them. Bombers queuing for take-off in pre-dawn darkness taxied into parked vehicles, or into each other, or took wrong turnings and sank to their axles in mud. Mid-air collisions between bombers assembling in cloud became commonplace. There was no warning. With a heart-stopping jolt, crewmen would feel their aircraft jerk suddenly, like a truck bouncing over a fallen tree-limb. That was a near miss, one aircraft flying through the propeller wash of another. If you felt it, you were still alive. Any closer and the sky would echo with the ominous dull boom of collision, and a short while later the debris and the bodies would be falling from the clouds like the rain.

Along with the tragedy there were miraculous escapes. One gale-swept afternoon, seven aircraft from a single group, attempting to land in a treacherous cross-wind, lost control, slewed off the runway and piled into each other, one after the next. In the shocked silence that ensued, dozens and dozens of men began to emerge, clambering from the twisted mountains of wreckage. Somehow no one was killed. On another base, a fully laden bomber blew up just before take-off. The explosion was so loud it was heard on two neighbouring bases. The aircraft completely disin-tegrated, its ten crewmen scattered about the blast site like confetti. But then, one by one, they picked themselves up, brushed themselves down and walked, dazed but alive, back to dispersal.

Martha and the rest of the 520th returned to operations, completing five missions in the first half of the month. Wilhelmshaven on the Friesland coast, Gelsenkirchen near Essen, twice to Düren to the west of Bonn. And Bremen again. Another four missions were scrubbed before take-off, or aborted en route, usually due to weather problems at base or over the target. To the crew, cancelled missions brought no relief. You still had to endure the dawn hand on your shoulder, the wordless breakfasts, the blood-red briefing ribbon, the kitting up, the boarding. The waiting. For most old hands, it was worse than going through with it. 'All the misery, without the mission credit' as Irv Underwood put it, handing in his parachute after yet another cancellation.

Then, for more than a week in the middle of November, the weather closed right in. *Martha*'s mission tally, stencilled beneath the pilot's side window, remained stubbornly on twenty. Yet, despite the inactivity of cancelled missions, the base was held on a state of maximum alert. Security was tightened up on the front gate, visitors and non-combatants were discouraged from entering, all leave was cancelled, nobody was allowed off base, for days on end. Nerves stretched to breaking, tempers flared. A fight was reported in a canteen, scuffles in some of the huts, a brawl in the sergeants' mess. Each evening the base cinema would fill to capacity with airmen attempting, briefly, to escape into the make-believe world of the flickering screen. Beside the screen, a red warning light was positioned to summon mission preparation officers if needed. Five nights in succession, the light came on halfway through a Betty Grable movie, and to a heartfelt groan from the rest of the audience Scott Finginger and his colleagues in Intelligence, Navigation, Meteorology and Planning rose from their seats and filed out. Later in the night the flyers would lie sleepless in their bunks, listening to the coming and going of the refuelling trucks, the armourers and the bomb-loaders. Yet in the morning, mission scrubbed. Something big was brewing.

'I had to come. I miss you so much,' Hooper said, standing in Heather's darkened doorway. She rushed to his arms, crushing him to her. They kissed. Then he pulled away.

'Can't you stay?' she pleaded.

He looked awful: thin, hollow-cheeked, his eyes red and deeply ringed. 'No. They've got MPs patrolling right around the fence. They're even going through the huts, counting heads.'

'Dear heaven. How on earth did you get out?'

He managed a grin. 'Billy's back door. Knyper showed me. Into the woods behind number one hangar. I had to see you, had to know that you're still here, that there really is another existence somewhere outside the perimeter.'

'There is, my dearest love. There is. And I'm here whenever you need me.'

Then, suddenly, the waiting was over.

It was Berlin. The big 'B'.

And then it wasn't.

In the morning the weather looked more promising. They were roused even earlier than usual, a sure sign of a longer mission, deeper penetration. Breakfast was better too, another bad sign. Waffles, pancakes and real Vermont maple syrup, to go with the fresh eggs and Canadian bacon.

343

Rookies, food trays in hand, queued in salivating amazement, but seasoned crewmen, their mouths drier, knew better, exchanging knowing glances. Briefing was packed with senior brass, another indicator, and Colonel Lassiter even made a rare go-get-'em-boys speech. The tension was palpable. But when S-2 began twitching back the curtain and everyone finally saw the ribbon stretching on and on, all the way, piercing right into Germany's heart, even those who understood the full implications felt a visceral thrill of excitement, and joined with the rookies' cheers.

Berlin. At last.

But it would be like flying into the very teeth of the dragon.

Then, as if that wasn't enough, there was a delay at start-up.

'Bombardier to pilot.'

'Yes, Dutch, it's okay. Go ahead and open the nose hatch.'

Hooper, head back in his seat, closed his eyes. Beside him, as always, Underwood stared out through the side window. To the west, stars still twinkled feebly in the blue-black firmament, while low on the eastern horizon tendrils of orange tinged the fields and hedgerows with the first pale light. All through the bomber, the crew waited quietly at their stations, while, with a nauseating smack, their ashen-faced bombardier dropped his bulging grocery sack on to the concrete beneath *Martha*'s nose.

'You missed, Dutch.'

'Hope your aim's better over Berlin.'

'There goes another five-dollar breakfast.'

'God, I hate the waiting. It's the worst.'

'Say fellas, did y'all hear about the donkey over at the 100th?'

'What donkey?'

'Well, you heard about that shuttle raid to Africa a few weeks back? Four groups bombed some place in Austria or somewhere, then flew on to North Africa, landed, refuelled, spent the night, then flew back home in the morning?'

'We heard. What about it?'

'Well, while they were there, one crew, from the 100th, they bought this donkey for ten bucks off of one of the local tribesmen or something. Anyway, they managed to load it on board their Fort and bring it back home to Thorpe Abbotts with them as a kind of squadron mascot.'

'No kidding. An African ass as a mascot. That's neat.'

'Yeah, but get this. The darn thing upped and died on them a couple of weeks later. Didn't like the weather, I guess. What do you think they did?'

'No idea.'

'Get on with it, Beaner.'

'Well, next mission, they dress it up in full flying kit – boots, sheepskins, the lot. They strap a parachute on it, then they drop it out through the bomb bay, on the run-in to the target.'

'You're a goddamn liar, Beans.'

'No, I swear it's the truth! Bud Lollings told me. Can you imagine? These German SS guys, running to capture this Yank airman parachuting down from his B17. And when they get to him and take off his oxygen mask and helmet and stuff, they find out he's an ass!'

'Beautiful.'

'I'd have given a month's pay to see their faces.'

'That is so neat.'

'Ain't it? Bud said they even hung identity tags around its neck and made sure it was carrying a wallet with a letter from a mommy donkey and pictures of a couple of baby donkeys.'

'Beautiful.'

Silence descended over the intercom once more. A breath of wind rolled across the airfield, gently rocking *Martha* on her wheels. In the next field, an early rising farmer, oblivious of the hundreds of airmen cooped aboard the nearby aeroplanes, strolled among his beet crop, pulling fleshy roots, topping them with a knife, tasting samples.

'I heard the flak over Berlin ain't nothing special.'

'You heard wrong.'

Ten minutes later the Berlin mission was cancelled.

'Waste of a fine breakfast,' Holland muttered, lowering himself to the concrete.

But the next morning the 520th returned to action with a vengeance.

'This is a short one, so it's like a double,' the intelligence officer announced at briefing. On the map behind him, a short length of ribbon stretched just across the English Channel to northern France and back. Crewmen glanced at each other, an expectant buzz washing over the hall like a warm breeze. 'Milk-run.'

They were wrong. 'Okay, listen up now. The Germans have been developing a new secret weapon. You don't have to know all the details, but let's just say it's a kind of bomb that flies. With wings, and a motor. They've started launching these things from sites hidden along the French coast here.

Reconnaissance have managed to locate two of them and today the 8th is going to blow them off the map.'

The group was split into two halves. Englehardt's squadron, including *Martha*, flew in the first wave. They reached the target in less than an hour from the RP. The flak was light, but accurate and highly concentrated, and the sky was thick with fighters. There was a mix-up on the run-in to the target. Bombers from the middle squadron released their bombs while directly overhead the low squadron. Two B17s in the low squadron were hit. There were shouts, orders, counter-orders over the radio. Confusion reigned. The bomb-run was aborted. The group had to swing away, re-form and run the gauntlet to the target a second time. Then a flak shell punched right through a brand-new G-Fortress in *Martha*'s squadron. They watched in horror as its gleaming silver fuselage crumpled, like tin foil, before tumbling from the sky. Seconds later a Focke-Wulf appeared out of nowhere, barrelling in, straight at them. At the last moment Hooper hauled *Martha* from its path. As it flashed by he glimpsed its pilot, slumped dead over his controls.

'Pilot, this is radio. I'm picking up a Boston signal.'

Boston. The code word for mission aborted. Stop what you're doing and return to base. Hooper looked around. Some aircraft were already breaking off the attack. A mile to their left a flaming Fortress exploded into the sea. Something was wrong.

'What do you make of it, Via?'

'I, uh, I'm not sure. It's not right, the letter groupings, the way the Morse is being keyed. It doesn't feel right.'

In a moment Gene's voice came over the radio. 'All aircraft, this is Charlie leader, belay that Boston, d'you hear me? Take no damn notice of it, it's bogus enemy horseshit. Hold station, close up and continue the damn attack.'

The first wave returned to Bedenham three aircraft down. Chastened, *Martha*'s crew disembarked to the hardstand, blinking in rare morning sunshine. It was still only ten-thirty.

'Man, am I glad that one's over. That was scary.'

'Too right. Give me Bremen any day.'

'I hear you, Torky. Those fighters. Madder than cornered dogs.'

'Point me at the hut, someone. I am going to sleep for a week.'

A Jeep was racing towards them. Seconds later Englehardt pulled up.

'Second wave's four ships short, Hoop. I'm going back out there with them. There's a slot for you too, if you want it.'

Hooper didn't hesitate. 'We'll do it.' He turned back towards the bomber.

'Hey, now, Lieutenant, wait there just one moment.'

'I said we're doing it, Lajowski! Get on board.'

'Hoop, listen.' Underwood rested an arm on Hooper's. 'You're bone tired. We all are. Are you sure this is the smartest idea?'

'Irv, I know.' It had started again, the pounding in his head. A dull throbbing, right at the back of his neck. And lights, incandescently bright, popping before his eyes like flashbulbs. 'We're running out of time, Irv. I can feel it. This will give us another mission credit. Two in one day. Twenty-two. It just leaves three.'

An hour later, refuelled and rebombed, they took off for Calais once more. Three hours after that they were back in Fininger's office.

'I'm sorry, guys,' he said, shrugging at them helplessly. 'There's only one mission credit.'

'What – did – you – say?' Keissling stared in disbelief.

'You don't get two mission credits. I'm sorry, I thought that had been made clear to everyone.'

'Well, it was not.' Accusatory eyes were directed towards Hooper.

'It isn't fair.' Spitzer was shaking his head. 'It isn't fair and it isn't right.'

'Major.' Lajowski leaned forward. 'Do you mean to tell me we flew back there to that target today, got blasted about the sky by some of the meanest flak I ever saw, got our asses chased to hell and back by Messerschmitts, and all for nothing?'

'Take it easy, Sergeant. I understand how you feel—'

'No you don't! One of our ships got blown clean out of the sky, for God's sakes! Ten men died. Do you understand how that feels?'

An uneasy silence descended. Fininger, pencil wiggling, studied his debriefing form.

'Maybe you should have checked, John,' Underwood said quietly. Hooper said nothing, staring as though mesmerised at the fingers of his hands lying lifeless on the table before him.

Fininger cleared his throat. 'Look, guys, I'm sorry but I don't make the rules. Why don't I look into it, speak to Colonel Lassiter. Maybe he could take it up with HQ, talk to some of the brass over at Elvedon Hall—'

'Fuck it.' Lajowski pushed back his chair, striding for the door. 'This is your doing, Hooper, you son of a bitch! You damn near got us all killed for nothing.'

'Ah, Mrs Garrett, there you are. Please, do come in, pull up a chair.'

'Thank you.' Heather closed the principal's door. Needham had called her Mrs Garrett, she noted. Not a good sign.

The headmaster began with a lengthy shuffling of papers on his desk. He was a gaunt, grey-haired man of sixty with a high forehead and close-set eyes. Through the window behind him a group of boys were kicking a football about an improvised goalpost. Heather waited, straight-backed on her chair, for the fall of the axe.

At last Needham was ready. 'Now then,' he began pleasantly. 'That's better. Tell me, is there any news on the Billy Street front?'

He was stalling, she knew, camouflaging the main issue with an exchange of pleasantries. So be it. 'I believe the Howdens have retained a solicitor to look into his case. It appears to be quite complicated and might take a while to sort out.'

'Good, good. And, er, Captain Garrett? Your husband? Any word at all?'

'Not as yet.'

'Ah. Well, you have everyone's best wishes, of course, and prayers for his safe and early return to the village.'

'Thank you.'

'Which sort of brings me to the point of this meeting, as it were.'

'Yes.'

'Yes. You see, the reason I asked you to come here this afternoon . . . . Oh dear me, this is so very difficult—'

'I am having a relationship with an American officer from the airbase. This places you in a very difficult position, as you feel it sets a bad example to the children and brings the school, the whole village in fact, into disrepute.'

Needham raised his eyebrows. 'Well, perhaps I wouldn't have put it in those exact terms, but that, certainly, in essence, is the general gist of it, yes.'

'I quite understand. Would you like me to resign my position now, to save you and the school any further embarrassment.'

'Heather, for heaven's sake, couldn't we just talk about it first?'

She lowered her head. 'Of course. I'm sorry.'

Needham pushed back his chair. 'Um, well, it's hard to know where to begin, really. But please let me say straight away that nobody wants you to resign, that's the first thing. At least I don't, and the children certainly don't. However, Bedenham is a small village, a tight-knit community, and gossip, well, you know how tongues wag, it spreads like wildfire. Whether we like it or not, the parents of our pupils, for the most part honest straightforward country folk, look to us to imbue their children with a simple sense of right and wrong, and a code of behaviour that is as uncomplicated as it is morally upright . . .'

But she wasn't listening. Right and wrong. That's what it boiled down to. What was right and what was wrong. The job she loved, everything she had worked so hard for, for so many years, was finished. One or two parents, that's all it had taken, just one or two. She'd seen them in the greengrocer's, outside the post office, at the school gate. Averted eyes, dark glances of disapproval, even barely concealed scowls. A letter or two of complaint, a small petition, one meeting with the school governors, and the deed was done, the malignancy excised like a blight-spot from a potato. Right and wrong. She'd known it must come, known how it must end. She was ready, yet despite her best intentions, her careful composure, she felt the prickling of her eyes, saw the playing children beyond the window wavering to a blur. It just wasn't fair. Overcome suddenly, profoundly fearful, she excused herself and fled to her empty classroom.

Later, she walked home, her bicycle at her side. 'Think about it,' Needham had pleaded, towards the end. 'If you could just, you know, put a stop to this . . . unfortunate situation. Quickly. Perhaps issue some sort of statement, even, to that effect. I am sure this would then all blow over and you could stay on.' Finish it, in other words. Finish it now. Or leave. But she would not. It had gone too far.

Rosamund's car was outside the cottage. Heather leaned her bicycle against the wall with a sigh and pushed open the door. It was the last straw. She was at the sitting-room window. Heather's sitting-room window. In Heather's chair, in Heather's cottage. For all she knew she had been upstairs, rifling through her cupboards, searching through her clothes, checking her bed. It didn't matter any more. Those things, the chair, the bed, even the cottage, everything, none of it belonged to her; it never had. It related to someone else. Someone who had once existed as a minor player in a brief, silly drama, but now was gone. 'I'm making some tea,' she said, moving towards the kitchen. 'Would you like some?'

'No, thank you. I came to pass on some information about the Crossley boy.'

'No, you didn't!' Suddenly she turned, colour rising in her cheeks. 'You did not! You came to pour out your contempt at the shame I have brought upon the good name of Garrett. You came to be prim and judgemental and play the grievously wounded mother of the poor wronged son. You came to lecture me about fidelity and loyalty, about corrupt morals and wickedness. You came to gloat over the fact that I've ostracised myself from the community, the fact that nobody talks to me any more or affords me any respect. The fact that I've lost my job.'

'You've lost your job?'

'Yes!' She was crying now, freely, standing in the centre of the floor, eyes wide like a little girl's, her cheeks flushed pink with tears. 'It was the most important, the most precious thing in my life and now it's gone. And do you know what? I don't care. Because what I am doing means more than any job. Means more than anything. More than a marriage that hasn't existed in years. More than sullying the good name of Garrett in the bloody fishmonger's! More than what people think of me. What I am doing is trying to save someone's life.'

'I know.'

But she didn't hear, or she was beyond comprehending. Racked with sobs, she sank, spent, into a chair. 'I'm so sorry!' she wailed. 'I never meant to hurt you.'

'I know that too.' Rosamund rose and left the room. A moment later she was back, glass of water in hand. 'Here, drink this.' She walked to the window, hugging herself, waiting for the storm to subside.

Slowly, Heather grew calmer. 'I'm sorry,' she whispered again. 'I failed you. I lost faith. Let you down.'

'No. No, you didn't.' Rosamund's back was to her, her voice quiet, resigned. 'You exercised common sense when, all around, common sense was lacking. You came to terms with the hopelessness of the situation, when I stubbornly refused to. You did what you felt you had to, when I did what I felt everyone expected of me.'

'You don't blame me?'

'No. I don't approve, of course. And I cannot condone. But blaming, being prim and judgemental, as you put it, was wrong. I see that now and apologise for it.' She turned, a faint, faraway smile on her lips. 'He is my son, you see, Heather. Being parted like this, for so long, even permanently perhaps, doesn't change that, or change anything. The bond between a mother and a son goes on for ever, no matter what happens. Do you understand what I mean?'

'I think so.'

'But it is also unique. You two were together such a short time. And so young. It is not the same, and I was wrong to expect it to be. You are right to begin to consider your own life, your own future. You must. This . . . thing, with this pilot. I cannot pretend that it doesn't shock me. And pain me. But I know it is not something you would ever have entered into lightly. I know you're not that sort of person.' The light had gone, leaving the room cold, deep in shadow. She stood, silhouetted against the window, erect, white-haired, solitary. 'I was afraid, you see. All the time. When you thought I was being strong and organised and detached and in control, I was terrified.'

'Of what?'

'I was frightened that if you gave up, then I might too.'

'Well, you mustn't. You mustn't be afraid, and you mustn't give up. You must remain hopeful.'

'Yes, perhaps. But perhaps it is also time to be realistic.'

A few days later *Martha* flew to Rjukan, in Telemark, Norway, a long, cold, fifteen-hundred-mile trek, that curved across the widest sector of the North Sea and back. The target was another secret enemy test-site, but at the briefing crews learned even less about it than they had about the V1 launch sites the week before. 'All you boys need to know,' the briefing officer told them with unusual solemnity, 'is that what those Germans are cooking up there don't bear thinking about, and so we have got to take it out, and good.'

'What the hell is heavy water, anyways?' Beans queried over the intercom three hours later. The group had climbed, circling up and up, through layer after layer of dense cloud, all the way to twenty-seven thousand feet, before breaking out into the clear. The sight that greeted them was almost biblical. Everywhere around them, bombers rose like magic, emerging from beneath the smooth white carpet, like maidenfly hatching from a lake. Where there had been one, and then a few, within minutes there were dozens, hundreds. Circling each other, higher and higher, like slow-motion dancers, forming into threes, then sevens, then the familiar boxed layers of scores and scores. Then finally the entire formation banked to the east and set out on the long haul across the sea to Norway. As they did so, the new day's sunrise appeared at last above the cloud-rim, dazzling their eyes with fire, pouring liquid gold across the snow-white layer beneath them.

'It's what you get when you swallow too much of that Limey beer.'

'Jeez, I hate that stuff. How the hell does anyone drink it?'

'I believe it has something to do with a new kind of bomb,' Holland said.

'A bomb full of water? Well, that ain't nothing new. I was making those things back in fifth grade.'

'You were never *in* fifth grade, Beanbag. You were out there in the dirt, shucking peas on your grandpappy's farm.'

'Shove it up your ass, Tork.'

'All right, quieten down, now. We've got a long day ahead of us. Go on and test your weapons.' After the stresses and strains of the last few days, it seemed to Hooper that everyone was in unusually good humour. He flicked the button once more. 'Pilot to navigator.'

'Yeah, Hoop, this is ol' Thumbs-up here, come on.'

Hooper, eyebrows raised, glanced at Underwood. But his co-pilot just shrugged, grinning. At the same time *Martha*'s guns sprang to life as each gunner test-fired his weapon. Some of the bursts went on much longer than necessary. Or normal.

'Yeah! All right, this is Kid in the ball! Everything down

here is working just fine and dandy. We are locked, loaded and ready to roll!'

'Way to go, Ringwald! Come on, you pansy-assed Luftwaff mothers, Crew 19 is ready!'

'Quiet! Everyone!' Hooper rubbed at the back of his neck. What the hell was going on? 'Pilot to navigator, have you got an ETA for the Norwegian coast yet?'

'Not as yet, Hoop old buddy, but it's a coming right up.'

Something wasn't right. Hooper tore off his headphones. 'Take it, Irv, I'm going down in the nose.'

Underwood, reaching casually for the controls, held up a gloved thumb and finger in a perfect circle. 'Gotcha.'

Hooper unclipped his oxygen hose, attached it to a walk-around bottle and ducked down from the flight deck. Forward in the nose compartment, Spitzer was leaning, slouching almost, across his little navigation table, his face resting in one hand. Beyond him, Holland was staring through *Martha*'s plexiglas nose dome. His back was to him, but Hooper could see his head was bobbing. Rhythmically, as though he was singing to himself.

Hooper plugged in his intercom. 'Spitz. Spitzer. The ETA?'

Spitzer slowly raised his head. 'Oh. Yeah. Okay. I'm on it. Right on it . . .'

'Ball to pilot.'

'Yes, Ringwald, go ahead.' He glanced forward again. Holland's head was down, not bobbing any more. And *Martha*. Was she beginning to turn?

'Lieuten'n', I have to repor . . . I'm sorry to say, hate to . . . I don't feel so good.'

At that moment there was a muffled thump from behind

357

him. Hooper turned. Lajowski's inert body had slumped to the base of his turret. At the same time he felt *Martha* sliding over on to her side.

'Jesus!' He leapt back, struggling past Lajowski's body. It took barely thirty seconds to regain the flight deck but by then *Martha* was practically inverted, rolling on to her back like a dying whale. He struggled into his seat, wedged the oxygen bottle between his thighs and seized the controls. Beside him, Underwood was limp, his arms hanging at his sides, slumped forward against his seat straps.

Within ten minutes the situation was restored. Having quickly rolled *Martha* upright once more, he snapped back the throttles, and shoved forwards on the control column, forcing the bomber's nose down into a near-vertical dive towards the waiting cloud carpet. *Martha* dropped like a rock, vanishing into the undercast. He continued to dive, flying blind, watching the airspeed build and the altimeter spin. At ten thousand feet, grunting with effort, he began to haul back, the g-forces sucking the mask down on his face. *Martha* creaked and groaned in protest. The next instant she hurtled from the base of the cloud to level off, finally, five thousand feet above the freezing waves.

One by one the crew revived. As soon as he could, Hooper sent Gerry Via round to feed them draughts of pure oxygen from a portable bottle.

'What the hell happened?' Underwood moaned, rubbing his temples. 'Feels like the worst hangover in history.'

'Oxygen starvation. The O2 supply to the whole ship failed. We all got hit. It was just lucky I was on a walk-around bottle.' Very lucky. Oxygen failure at twenty-seven thousand feet. Light-headedness, euphoria, insensibility, unconsciousness, death, in just a few minutes. Theirs wouldn't have been the first crew to succumb, fatally, to its seductive effects.

The mission was over, yet again. With no oxygen they were unable to climb above ten thousand feet, so could not regain the bomber stream. Hooper signalled Englehardt, held *Martha* low, just above the rolling, foam-capped waters, and turned for home.

They hardly spoke the entire return trip. And after landing at the deserted airfield, partly, no doubt, as a result of the hangover effects of the narcosis, the mood turned even blacker.

'Yet another goddamn no-credit mission,' Lajowski complained, lowering himself gingerly to the concrete. He was nursing a bad bruise to his forehead from his fall. Via had swathed it in white bandage. He patted his pockets for cigarettes. 'This is getting to be tedious.'

'Can your bitching just for one minute, can't you, Polecat? I'd say we're pretty damn lucky to be alive.'

'Who the hell rattled your cage, Keissling? I'm just saying that I'm getting pretty sick and tired of busting my ass for no-credit missions every day.'

'And we're getting pretty sick and tired of your bitching every day!'

'Ho, guys, easy.' Spitzer, the soft voice of reason, broke in. 'Let's not do this, all right?' They were standing in a loose circle beneath *Martha*'s nose, her engines ticking and pinging to either side of them as they cooled. The base hadn't been expecting them back so soon; transport hadn't been arranged. They could walk the half-mile back to dispersal in their cumbersome fur-lined flying clothes and boots, carrying their parachutes and their flak vests, their Mae Wests, their helmets and their bags, or they could wait for someone to send a truck.

'All I'm saying is, now that we're this close to finishing our tour, people should just be damn careful about checking important things like oxygen, or accepting half-assed no-credit missions to France.'

'Polecat, you heard Thumbs-up, this ain't going to get us anywhere.'

'Butt out, Beans!'

'Sergeant, do you have a problem with the way I command this crew?' Hooper, hands on hips, was staring at the ground at Lajowski's feet. 'It's okay, you can say what's on your mind.'

'No.' Lajowski shook his head doggedly. 'No, I can't.'

'Yes, you can.'

'Polecat, for the love of Mike, leave it, can't you? What's the point of—'

'I heard you dumped your entire last crew in the ocean and they all drowned except you. You didn't even get your feet wet.'

Underwood stepped forward. 'Sergeant, you are way out of line.'

'It's okay, Irv, let him be, it's okay.' A vehicle, at last, had detached itself from the cluster of buildings on the far side of the airfield and was crawling around the perimeter track towards them.

'You're right, Emmett. It happened. Just as you say. As far as I know. I can't tell you much about it, but it did happen, and I blame myself for it. Is there anything else you want to know? Anybody?'

'Did they kick you out the 95th for it?' It was Al Tork, squatting, pulling weeds from cracks in the concrete.

'I suppose the answer to that is kind of. They offered me a medical discharge on account of a head injury, or a transfer here. I chose the transfer.'

'Why?'

'Why? Good question. I guess I have Major Englehardt to thank for that. He told me about a rookie crew that Operations wanted to disband. He told me that despite a few problems, he had complete faith in this crew's ability to pull through. For what it's worth, so do I.'

'Yeah, but medical discharge. I mean, you could have been home free.'

'I didn't want to be home free. That would mean my crew had died for nothing. I wanted to finish my tour. Do my duty. I still do.'

'For them,' Underwood said quietly.

Hooper smiled. 'Yes, Irv. For quite a while, I suppose it was for them. But then, over time, well, it's the present that counts, isn't it? What really matters is the here and now. I've learned that recently. And things change. I've learned that too. You all taught me that. Now, all that matters to me is to get us all safely through these last four missions, and home. Nothing else.'

'Um. Five.'

'What?' Everyone turned to Keissling. He was smiling sheepishly.

'I came here straight from training, remember. When I

joined the crew, you guys had already flown one mission. So I'm one down on the rest of you. I've got five to go.'

'So have I.' Holland shrugged. 'Same thing.'

Ten minutes later the door to Scott Finginger's office burst open. Gerry Via, still in full flying kit, strode in.

'Sergeant. Good to see you made it home safely. I hear there was an oxygen problem – nothing fatal, I take it?'

'How many missions has he got?'

'I beg your pardon?'

'Hooper. How many missions?'

'Well, I have to say, Sergeant, it's not normally approved policy to discuss a flyer's combat record with someone other than—'

Via leaned over Finginger's desk. 'His last crew. At the 95th. They all died. But it wasn't their first mission, was it? How many did Hooper fly with them?'

'Eleven.'

'Jesus!' His fist hit the desk. 'I knew it, I just damn knew it!' He began pacing Finginger's floor. Something Jo Morrison had said, in London, while they were walking to the hospital. And Hooper, just now. I wanted to finish my tour, he said. I still do.

'So, that crazy son of a bitch has flown, what, thirty-two missions?'

'If you say so.'

'But why? He's finished his tour. He could be home. He should be. Weeks ago. What the hell is he still doing here?'

'I'm sorry, Sergeant, you'd have to ask him that.'

'But is it allowed? Is it within regulations?'

362

'Of course it's within regulations. Nobody is forced to go home at the end of their tour if they don't want to. It's unusual, I grant you, but it happens. I believe it's called "being a volunteer".'

'But why? With survival odds like ours. Who in their right mind would do a thing like that?' Via, head shaking in bewilderment, sank into a chair. 'He is in his right mind, isn't he?'

Finginger fished his bourbon bottle from his drawer. 'Right enough,' he said, pouring into a cup. He pushed it across. 'Do I really have to spell it out for you, Sergeant? Hooper could be a lead pilot by now, a new ship, his own squadron even. Englehardt already put him up for it a couple of times. But he keeps turning it down.'

'To stay with us? And *Martha*?'

'It's his way, I believe, of making sense of it all. And dealing with what happened before. Start all over again. From the beginning. From zero. Well, from one, that is. Like the rest of you.'

Via drained the whiskey. 'No, Major. Zero is right.'

It had been Kid Ringwald's idea. Who else? Back there on the tarmac when Keissling and Holland made their little confession about mission totals. I vote we stay together, Ringwald had said, holding his hand in the air like a little schoolkid. I vote we fly one extra mission, and all finish this thing together. To Via's astonishment, to everyone's, one by one, the hands went up. All of them.

They gathered around the Howdens' kitchen table. The newly convened Friends of Billy Street Committee. Rosamund Garrett was there, had seated herself at the head of the table as soon as she walked in. Nobody demurred. Ray and Maggie sat to either side of her, Heather and Claire beside them. Hal Knyper was at the far end. Rosamund drew up the minutes, the Howdens read out submissions on behalf of Mrs Blackstone, and their retired solicitor contact in Framlingham. Heather handed in a petition signed by every member of Billy's class. Hal produced a huge bar of Billy's favourite chocolate. Maggie fretted and made tea, while Percy snored in the corner.

'Hopeless!' Rosamund scolded disparagingly, when everyone had finished speaking. 'Thank goodness someone here is able to co-ordinate things properly. Now then, here's what I propose we should do.'

An hour later an action plan had been drawn up and agreed. The Howdens' solicitor was fired, to be replaced by the Garretts' Lincoln's Inn barrister – at Gerald's expense. The Garretts would also speak to the local Member of Parliament. 'He comes to dinner once a month anyway.' Maggie and Claire were put in charge of parcels. 'Make sure they go direct to Billy, care of the prison governor, mind you. And Recorded Delivery. We don't want those thieving guards getting their hands on them again.'

Hal offered to produce a letter of support from the USAAF.

'Can you really do that?' Rosamund asked, peering over her spectacles.

'Sure. Get Finginger to do it. He owes me. Let's see, the kid Crossley was always a, uh, cheerful, positive and helpful presence at the 520th. Always willing to lend a hand, run errands, pitch in, that kind of thing. Got a personal thank you from General Doolittle, too. What d'you say, think it might help?'

Ray was to contact Billy's old orphanage, and begin the process of tracking down his past. His records, his birth certificate. Even his mother.

'You do want to adopt him, don't you?' Rosamund asked at one point. Maggie and Ray looked at each other.

'If he'll have us.'

Eventually the meeting broke up. Heather slipped away into the night as soon as she could. The cottage was in darkness when she arrived, breathless, ten minutes later. Heart pounding, she let herself inside. He was lying on the sitting-room floor, by the dying embers of the fire. She knelt, leaned over him, kissed him lightly, her hair brushing his cheeks. Immediately he stirred, his arms reaching for her, pulling her down beside him.

They lay there, their bodies entwined, their lips touching. Not speaking, not moving, until their breathing became slow and deep. Until the fire grew cold, and the moon rose over the fields across the lane.

Chapter 14

It worked. The Billy Street relief offensive. Within three weeks, Rosamund Garrett's meticulously drawn-up and militarily executed strategy, comprising high-level lobbying, aggressive legal machinating, and a relentless barrage of letters and telephone calls to Members of Parliament, Home Office officials, social and probation services directors, and anyone else foolish enough to admit even peripheral jurisdiction, brought about a swift and sympathetic reappraisal of his case.

Billy was allowed out. Temporarily. On probation. On the strict understanding that he remain under the supervised guardianship of the Howdens, that he report to Framlingham police station weekly, and that he eventually be retried for the Southwark warehouse fire incident.

It was good enough. One cold, clear December afternoon shortly afterwards, a perceptibly thinner and taller, older-looking Billy stepped from the train to the platform at Ipswich station. He looked around in unhurried bemusement. Then there was a piercing wolf-whistle from along the platform and before he knew it, he was enveloped by well-wishers.

Ray and Maggie were there. Ray stood back, looking Billy up and down. 'Hallo, lad.' He smiled, and ruffled his hair briefly. Maggie was less reserved, sweeping him into a bosomy clinch, peppering him with kisses. She cried, then laughed, then cried again. Claire, too, had come. Arms folded, nodding, a playful half-smile on her lips.

'We've done a bit of decorating in your room, Bill,' she said. 'Made some proper curtains. Found a piece of carpet for the floor. Nailed down those nasty loose planks. Thought you'd be pleased.'

There was a small if noisy American contingent. Eldon Ringwald, of course, arm in arm with Claire. Polecat Lajowski and Hal Knyper. They cracked jokes, poked him in the ribs, punched his shoulder, stroked the non-existent stubble on his chin. Slipped candy into his pockets.

'How's *Martha*?' he asked Hal, straight away.

'Holding together. No thanks to the flight crew here.'

'The tally?'

Lajowski held up two fingers. 'Just two to go now, old buddy.'

'Hello, Billy.' Ruby was there too. Standing shyly, a little apart from the others. It had been Ray's idea. She was wearing her Sunday best, had her hair clipped back, had pinned a yellow winter rose on the lapel of her overcoat. She looked self-conscious, but determined.

'Rube. 'S good to see you. Thanks for coming. And for your letters.'

Rosamund had sent Gerald's car. It was parked outside.

'She says hello and sorry she can't be here,' Maggie explained. 'She's been such a tower, what with all the organising and letter-writing and everything. You'll have to go straight up the Grange this afternoon to say thank you. And to the other Mrs Garrett, too, your teacher. They've both done so much. They wanted to be here, but couldn't. Something come up.'

The three Americans had to report straight back. They said goodbye, then took the train to meet the base bus at Diss. Ray drove Rosamund's car back to Bedenham. On the way Billy said little, content to watch the big Suffolk skies, the winter countryside, the towns and villages, unrolling through the window, Ruby at his side. After a while his hand closed on hers. Back at Forge Cottage he went straight to his room, then to each room of the house in turn, as though checking, nose twitching like a dog's, that all was as he'd left it. Percy materialised at the back door, pink-cheeked and beery from the Fleece. 'Coming up the woods, boy?' He cackled toothlessly, as if Billy had never been away. 'There's muntjac about. Pigeon aplenty, too.'

'Expec' so, Mr H.'

'Don't you two go wandering off, now.' Maggie and Ruby were cutting sandwiches. 'Tea in a few minutes.'

He went outside. The light was already failing, the sun little more than a weak orb of pink, melting into the mist beyond the trees. Ray was in the workshop, standing beside the glowing forge, examining a wrought-iron garden gate.

'That's nice-looking,' Billy said.

'Not perfect,' Ray said, frowning at it critically. 'But it'll do. The vicar ordered it. To replace the old wooden one, on the path up to the church, you know?'

Billy nodded. 'How's the repairs?'

'Booming. As you can see.' Bicycles filled every available space. 'There's dozens more waiting outside. I had to take on one of your mates, that sniffing Lennie Savidge boy, to help with the fetching and carrying, like. Couldn't cope on my own.'

'Oh.'

'And you needn't be looking so sorry for yourself, neither. You're going to have your hands well and truly full dealing with the customers. You know, filling the orders, sorting out payment, handling the business end and all that.'

Billy stared around the forge. 'Am I staying, Mr H? You know, after the court case, and all that. After the war, even. After everything. Is this where I'm stopping? Like, home?'

'Would you like to?'

'Very much.'

Hooper arrived at Heather's later in the evening. She met him at the door, kissed him warmly, took his overcoat and cap. 'Cold out there, tonight.' He shivered. 'You English certainly know how to lay on a winter.'

'We get plenty of practice.'

He turned to her then, studying her, as always, as though for the first time. Or the last. She'd dressed up a little for him. Found an old but presentable silk blouse from her pre-war Lincoln days to wear beneath her favourite cardigan.

She'd pressed her best wool skirt, slipped on her last precious pair of undamaged stockings. A tiny string of pearls nestled at her throat, a silver bluebird brooch over her breast. Her hair was up, her eyes lightly made-up. He smiled into them. And in that moment he knew, but he said nothing.

'Something smells good. I hope you haven't been putting yourself to any trouble.' He went through to the sitting room. A little card-table stood before the fire, set for two. Silver cutlery, linen napkins, cut glasses. An open bottle of wine breathing on the hearth.

'I'm afraid not.' She followed him in. Before her eyes, his back seemed to sag, as though finally acknowledging the full weight of the load upon it. As though there was no need to pretend any more. A chill settled in her stomach, like cold lead. 'It's called Woolton pie,' she went on lightly. 'Throw anything you can find into a baking tin, cover it with a layer of pastry, put it in the oven and hope for the best.'

'Sounds delicious. Who's Woolton?'

'Food minister.'

'You don't have to do this.'

'I want to do this.'

'He's alive, isn't he? David. You've heard something.'

'Yes. Yes, he is. I heard today.'

'Heather, that is wonderful, wonderful news. And Richard?'

'Still no word. But they were in the same battalion. There are grounds for hope.'

'Of course there are. But David, what a fantastic relief. How did you hear?'

'The War Office received another list of prisoners of war

from the Japanese authorities, via the Red Cross. David's name was on it. He's in a POW camp in southern Burma somewhere.'

Rosamund had received the news first, of course. One of her contacts at the Ministry had telephoned her late in the morning. The moment Heather saw her hurrying towards the garden gate, she knew something had happened. 'Bless you, Rosamund,' she'd said, over and over, while they'd embraced. It was all she could think of. Yet she meant it.

'Strangely,' Rosamund had replied tearfully, 'just now, I find that all my thoughts are with you.'

She and Hooper ate their Woolton pie at the table by the fire. Heather put Schubert on the radiogram. Between reflective pauses, like islands on a calm sea, they talked, quietly, of other times and places.

Heather recalled a Scottish seaside holiday of her childhood. She and Richard, ten and eight, fishing for shrimp with their little nets in the rocky pools at the base of a towering granite cliff. 'I can still taste the salt and seaweed smells of those pools,' she said. 'The feel of the sand between my toes. And the heat of the sun on my back.'

Hooper nodded. They listened to the music for a while. 'I was seven when my sister came along,' he began. 'Our lives were completely separate. Happy enough, in their way, I guess, but just separate. Running along different tracks. I was no more aware of her, I suspect, than she was of me.'

'Do you regret that?'

'Yes, I do. We shared so little of our childhood. I would like to have known her then. Recently, though, we've been communicating better.'

'That's good.' Her hand stole across the table, into his. Immediately their fingers slid tightly between one another.

'John, I'm afraid. Of things changing between us. I don't want them to.'

'I know. You mustn't be afraid.'

'Will you still come?'

'Of course,' he lied. 'Whenever you want me to.'

Things had already changed. He walked slowly back through the moonlit lanes towards the base, his coat belted tightly about him, his breath misting the still night air. They'd kissed. Then blown out the candles, opened the blackout curtains and sat, wrapped together on her armchair by the window, gazing out across the white-frosted fields, her head on his chest, his arms tight about her. They'd already changed. And it had to be that way; he'd known it all along. It made no difference that David's situation was exactly the same as it had always been. It made no difference that it would remain the same for years more, until the war ended and he was released. He was alive, and that changed everything. From the moment he had managed to signal his continued existence, that delicately poised bubble of pretence in which their fragile love had germinated, and grown, and nurtured itself, ceased to exist. The one was determined by the other; they had no control over it. It was the single unspoken condition of their union.

The sense of loss was worse than he would ever have imagined it could be. It was like losing his closest friend. It *was* losing his closest friend. Arriving back on base, he went straight to the officers' bar, took a table in the corner and began ordering up doubles.

After a while the unaccustomed alcohol began to apply its anaesthetic balm. He looked around. The bar was bright and busy, noisy, full of life and male bonhomie. Some of the faces he recognised, most he did not. It was the nature of the existence they shared. The nature of everything. Fleeting.

'Mind if I join you?'

It was Gene Englehardt. He pulled out a chair, signalling to a passing waiter. Within seconds their drinks were replenished. Fast service, Hooper mused, a little blearily. One of the perks of their continued survival. They touched glasses in wordless salute. Gene drank deeply. His face was heavily lined, scored by months of sitting in the thin, freeze-dried air and unfiltered sunlight at high altitude. His skin had a pasty, sallow pallor, his once needle-sharp eyes dulled from fatigue and too much whiskey.

'Old buddy of mine from the 490th called me tonight,' he said eventually, unwrapping one of his cigars. His Southern drawl was more pronounced than usual, and a little slurred. 'Sam Banning, did you ever meet him?' Hooper shook his head. 'We went through basic together, Rapid City, Kearney, the whole shebang.'

Hooper waited. Younger faces were stealing glances at them from the bar. That's Englehardt there, talking to Hooper. The two oldest hounds in the pack.

'He's three-quarters of the way into his second tour of missions. Group lead pilot, more decorations than a goddamn Christmas tree, just heard he's up for promotion to lieutenant colonel, the works.'

'Impressive. Not too many still on operations with that kind of record.'

'You said it. He could be running the whole damn air force in a year or two, the way he's going. Curtis Le May, get this, he calls Sam for advice sometimes. Do you believe that?'

'I didn't believe Le May called anyone for advice.'

'Me either. He's quitting.'

'What?'

'Sam. He's throwing it in. That's why he phoned me. He says he just woke up this morning, and for no particular reason a voice in his head said he'd done enough and it was time to go home. So he is.'

'My God.' Hooper stared at his glass. 'Just like that?'

'Just like that.'

Underwood, Spitzer and Holland entered the bar. Spitzer caught Hooper's eye and gave a discreet thumbs-up. They'd changed, too, he realised. Completely. Older, of course; ageing in double-time. But worse, all the youthful callowness was gone, all the innocence. Erased. In five months. They too had done enough. Now they existed in a different state of grace. Within seconds they were surrounded by eager young faces, slapping their backs, dragging them to the bar, basking in the power of their knowledge and their aura of survival.

'Good people,' Englehardt mused. 'You did them proud.'

'They did it themselves.'

'See that they get through, Hoop. See that you all get through.'

'I'll do my best. Gene? What is it?'

Englehardt was tilting drunkenly across the table towards him. Hooper wondered if he was about to pass out. But the squadron commander was merely beckoning him nearer.

'They're going to screw us over, old buddy,' he murmured

in Hooper's ear. 'Doolittle, Le May, the whole goddamn 8th. They're going to screw us over and good.'

'What? Gene, what the hell are you talking about?' He was clearly drunk. Again. Babbling incoherently. But the hairs were prickling on Hooper's neck.

'You didn't get this from me. You didn't get this from anyone. But, hand on heart, Hoop, it's the truth. Doolittle is raising the mission total.'

'What?' Hooper froze. 'What did you say?'

'It's not official, but it is happening. Soon. He's upping the number of missions in a tour.'

'To what?'

'To thirty-five.' He held Hooper's eye for a moment, before slumping back. He picked up his glass. 'So I guess maybe Sam was trying to tell me something today. Maybe, in fact, he was trying to tell us both.'

Two days later they flew to Kiel.

When Hooper saw the curtain pull back, saw the line of red, and where it ended, he felt his heart falter. He stared at the map, his mind blank.

'What is it?' Irv hissed from beside him. 'Hoop?'

'Nothing. It's nothing.'

It was Kiel. Once again. But it was to be different. No Nathan Forrest. No flat formations, no bad gun oil. No foul-ups. And no sea-mist over the English coast when they came back, too, the met officer assured them.

But there was cloud. They took off early, circling up through thick, mud-coloured nimbus, their wingtips enveloped, their windshields streaming with freezing

375

rainwater. Soon, though, they were slipping in and out of higher, stratiform layers, and at fourteen thousand feet they burst into the clear, surrounded by towering, finger-like ramparts of grey, a gossamer-thin veil of icy cirrus stretching across the pale morning sky high above them.

The form-up was fuss-free, over eighty bombers coagulating to make up the high layer. The 520th was towards the rear, *Martha* in her customary slot to the left of and slightly behind Englehardt's *Shack Time II*. They headed out north over the Wash, still climbing, before curving east towards Denmark. Halfway across, the clouds beneath them began to thin and break. After a while the wide, gunmetal surface of the North Sea could be seen, stretching in every direction, five miles below.

'Happy twenty-fifth mission, everyone.' A wistful voice came over the intercom. 'I mean, those of us who are on their twenty-fifth, that is. Those of you on your twenty-fourth, well, have a nice day and thanks for nothing.'

A pause. 'Say, Polecat, by any chance are you trying to make me and Dutch feel bad about you guys flying an extra mission?'

'Herm. Would I do such a thing?'

'You bet. But you can forget it. We'd do the same for you.'

'Would you? Really, Keiss, would you?'

'Not a chance!'

Down in the nose compartment, Loren Spitzer patted Holland's back. 'They're just kidding around, Dutch!' he called.

The bombardier turned and grinned. 'I know.' His face was pink with cold above his mask. But not sickly. In fact, he rarely vomited any more, Spitzer realised. Fought his way past his sickness, somehow. Sheer willpower. He checked his watch, jotting notes into the flight log. Another hour to the Danish coast.

Standing, he poked his head up into the navigator's astrodome. Directly aft, he could see Irv and Hoop sitting in their seats on the flight deck, talking quietly. Forty feet away to the right, *Shack Time* hung, rising and falling gently beside them, as though suspended on a string. Beyond and all around, dozens more Fortresses, scores, were spread across the sky, near and far, like ships on an ocean.

Twenty-five missions. It didn't seem possible. He still remembered the first. Stoller's amused voice: 'Be my guest,' through the headphones. Broman's hunched back. Greenbaum, waving in greeting, then doubling on to the floor of the waist like a felled tree. The surprise on his face, the hot gouts of blood. The angled struggle back to the cockpit, the eerie, whistling silence there. The eight hands on the controls. It seemed like an aeon ago. And as though it was yesterday.

'Say, I got a good one.'

'Lord, here we go again.'

'No, listen, guys, this one's true! I mean it. There was this officer. An Operations major. Straight arrow, career officer, West Point, the whole crap-shoot. Trouble was he was chicken-shit scared, only had about four mission credits and was a total pain in the ass.'

'Yeah, I heard about this guy too. Over at the 388th.'

'That's him. Anyway, whenever there was a milk-run scheduled, he kept attaching himself to crews and flying with them as supernumerary, just so he could notch up mission credits, grab a few medals and get himself promoted. Trouble is he kept taking over, yelling and screaming, ordering the pilots around, aborting on missions, sending them the wrong way, interfering on the bomb-run and everything. After a while crews were starting to refuse to have him fly with them any more, everyone hated him so much.'

'Beans, we get the picture. Just get on with it, will you.'

'I am! Anyway, finally another milk-run comes up. Sure enough the chicken-shit major attaches himself to some unsuspecting crew, bumps the co-pilot down the back and settles in for the ride. Everything goes well, they drop the bombs and turn for home. But five minutes later suddenly the ship is filling with smoke and the co-pilot comes running forward saying the whole waist section is on fire. "Jeez, that sounds bad," says the pilot and hits the bail-out bell. Before you can scratch your pants the chicken-shit major jumps up, clips on his parachute and takes a nose-dive through the belly hatch. Last thing he sees is the crew waving down at him.'

'You are kidding. What about the smoke?'

'Signal flare.'

'I do not believe that story, Beans.'

'Believe it.' Irv Underwood's voice came on. 'His name was Duggan. Group Commanding the 388th got a Red Cross notification through a couple of weeks ago. He landed in a cabbage field, got roughed up by the farmer, arrested by the local police and is now in Stalag Luft-II prisoner of war camp somewhere up near the Baltic. Apparently the other POWs are trying to figure out how to send him back.'

'Be-eautiful!'

'That is a humdinger. Best yet.'

'Ain't it though?'

Silence fell. After a while Spitzer came on.

'Navigator to pilot. Enemy coast in sight.'

Ten minutes later, right on schedule, the first fighters appeared.

'One-nineties! Four of them. Three o'clock, coming high. Beaner! Ringwald?'

'Okay. We see them.' Beans, feet planted wide, hunched himself lower over the breech of his weapon, shook his shoulders looser beneath his flying suit, and, emptying his mind of all but the bead of his sights and the rapidly oncoming fighters, pulled back the charging handle.

It was ferocious and dogged and bloody, but no worse than usual. The Germans split themselves into small hunting packs of two or three and careered through the formation from all directions, dividing their fire and confusing their escorts. Soon the sky was alive with dog-fighting Mustangs and Messerschmitts, falling bombers and billowing parachutes. Inside *Martha*, the acrid tang of cordite, and voices, clipped, urgent, but calm, filled the air.

'Okay, we got one coming in, a one-one-oh, right to left, high. Polecat?'

'Got it.'

'There's another, low and slow. He's hit. Rolling clear.'

'Navigator to pilot, two minutes to the IP.'

'Roger, nav. Bomb doors coming down. Bombardier, you set?'

'Set.'

'Flak bursts up ahead, medium heavy.'

379

'Fort dropping out from low squadron. Flamer. Two 'chutes.'

'Tail here. Fighter, six o'clock, level, I'm on him. Wait. Wait! He's rolling right. He's out of control!'

A monstrous flash lit the sky outside Underwood's side window. Instinctively his arm jerked up for protection. *Martha* bucked, rolling violently to the left, shock from the blast tossing her on to her side, like a wave hitting a boat. Hooper wrenched at the controls, struggling to right her, then a shadow passed over his head, a shouted warning from Underwood breaking over his earphones. He looked up. And froze.

Directly above them, barely feet away, rolling, upside-down, right over the top of them, was *Shack Time II*. It was like looking up at a mirror image. They were so close Hooper could see right into her cockpit, see Englehardt's hands and legs on the controls, see his face, too, craning upwards, his eyes staring, unblinking, into his own. Another split second and the bomber was over the top and dropping, still inverted, down past *Martha*'s left wingtip. As it went they saw the whole rear half of the aeroplane was gone, exploded into nothing but jagged shards by the impact with the fighter. An instant later the right wing became detached. Immediately, the Fortress flipped into a tight spin, huge at first, a crazily cartwheeling, dismembered monster of a machine. Then growing smaller as it fell and fell, spinning towards the ground.

Horrified, they watched it go. There would be no getting out, they all knew that. No orderly row of parachutes blossoming behind the sinking wreck like artfully dropped flowers. Everyone from the radio room back was already dead, killed in the impact with the fighter. The five that remained were completely trapped, pinned by centrifugal force to the walls and floor of the spinning nose section. Unable to escape, for they were unable to move. *Martha*'s crew watched anyway, hoping beyond hope, transfixed with shock. *Shack Time II* spun on and on, receding, smaller and smaller, with mind-numbing slowness, like a dropped sycamore seed. Until at last the doomed men's misery came to an end in a soundless burst of red, and *Shack Time II* exploded into the ground.

Colonel Lassiter lowered the report file to the desk. 'Is that it?'

'That's it, sir. They all saw it happen.'

'Then there's no chance. Englehardt's dead, that's all there is to it.'

'Yes, sir.' Finginger reached slowly across, retrieving the file. A Jeep swept past his window, a cloud of sleety snow billowing in its wake. He scratched his scar nervously.

'Do you still keep that bottle in your desk, Major?' Lassiter asked, staring through the window. His face was grey, clouded in thought. It was barely eleven in the morning, but Finginger retrieved his bourbon without a word, slopping it into a cup.

'We're going to kill them all, Scott,' Lassiter went on, almost to himself. 'Every one of them, the way we're going. I've been in post here barely a year. Yet there is not one single crew that has come right through this period, completely and entirely untouched, without a single scratch to anyone. Not one. Did you know that?'

'Well, yes I did, Colonel.'

'Hmm. Not a record to be particularly proud of, is it?'

'I guess not. But it is for a purpose, sir. Isn't it? For a just cause.'

'Just cause?' Lassiter raised his eyebrows. 'Maybe.' He drank from his cup. 'You know what I keep thinking about, Major?'

'No, sir.'

'I keep thinking about that poor bastard Broman. You know, the bombardier who went AWOL in the summer, then turned up in the woods a couple of weeks ago.'

'Yes, sir.'

'I had to write to his family, you know. I had to write to Dan Broman's wife, and say that her missing husband, the father of their five-year-old son, lost his mind and walked off his bomber without a word. That unknown to anybody he has been living rough in the woods like a goddamn tramp. For months. And that finally even that got to be too much for him, and yet he still couldn't bear coming back to face his buddies and his superiors. And his enemy. So he hung himself from a tree. How do you tell a wife something like that? How do you tell his boy?'

Lassiter glared at him, daring him to reply. But Finginger said nothing. He didn't trust himself to.

'How do you think history will judge us, Major? The 8th, the people who died in it, the people who ran it. That's what I want to know. What do you think the orphaned children's children of the tens of thousands of young men who died here will think about this?'

'I think they'll remember the courage and dedication of

382

those who did die, sir. And why. I think they'll recognise that in a war impossible decisions have to be made, and that the men who make them try to do so with compassion in their hearts. I think they'll realise that if war has to be waged, sacrifices follow. And I hope they'll remember that there is no greater love than a man laying down his life for his fellow man.'

Lassiter regarded him, eyes narrowed. Seconds ticked by on the wall clock. Outside the door, wet boots clumped along the corridor. 'Maybe,' he said at last. He sat back, draining his whiskey. 'I guess we'll find out. Now then, where's Hooper? I need to see him.'

'I, ah, I believe he may be out and about, sir. Somewhere.'

'What? Off base?'

'Possibly, Colonel.'

'Jesus. Well, find him and send him to my office. Whether he wants to or not, he's taking over command of Englehardt's squadron.'

Finginger stirred uncomfortably. 'Sir. What you were saying, just now, about crews making it through. Hooper's crew. Well, they've just got one more mission to go to finish their tour.'

'I know that, Scott. But there's nobody else. He'll have to do it. There's an ME on tomorrow. Big one. Munich.'

'And that ship of theirs, it'll be down all day while they repair the blast damage it suffered yesterday. *Martha*. She's a wreck, sir. A flying basket case.'

'I know that too. What is your point, Major?'

Finginger drew a deep breath. 'Munich will be hard, sir. We both know that. Long and hard. Couldn't we keep *Martha*, and her crew, stood down? Just for one more day.'

'Give them a chance to finish their tour with a milk-run, you mean?'

'Give them a chance to finish their tour. Sir.'

Lassiter hesitated, his lips tightly compressed, one finger drumming on the desktop. Then he pushed back the chair, rising to his feet. 'No. Can't do it. I need Hooper's experience to lead the squadron. Find him. And send him to me.'

'Well, well! John, as I live and breathe. How the hell are you, Lieutenant?' Brent Wallis rose from behind his mahogany desk, striding, one hand extended, across the floor. 'It's damn good to see you.'

'You too, Doctor.' Hooper looked around at the panelled walls, the tall sash windows, the neat gardens, now shrunken with winter and dusted with snow. Everything was as he remembered it, although it was as if he was remembering a dream. Perhaps it was a dream, he thought. All of it. Wallis, one arm linked through his, talking ten to the dozen, led him down a dim corridor towards the bright light of the entrance doors. Perhaps everything did begin and end here. Where he had first awoken in this quiet, broken men's hospital. It was what he was here to find out.

They walked the frozen gravel paths, the stunted beds and sugar-frosted lawns, beneath the snowy branches of the giant cypress tree he'd sat under, sunning himself, all those months ago. They talked. Then they both grew cold and went back inside.

'Are you quite sure about this, John?' Wallis, shrugging on a white laboratory coat, gestured to a couch by the wall. It looked old, antique, raised at one end, like a chaise longue. A folded sheet lay on it. Hooper sat, testing the springs, as though trying a bed in a furniture store.

'Quite sure, Major.'

'I mean, you were pretty damn certain you didn't want anything to do with this the last time you were here.'

'I realise that. But that was then. Things are different now. I want to know what happened. I have to know.'

'Okay.' Wallis turned the key in the door. 'Relax. That's just so's we don't get disturbed. Now, I need to give you a physical first. And then you have to give me a good reason why.' He sat next to Hooper, slipping a stethoscope into his ears. 'Shirt off, John. Deep breaths, now.'

'Why.' Hooper exhaled. 'Well, that's a little complicated. But, to put it simply, I just want to get everything straightened out in my mind.'

'What for?'

'I guess it's a matter of getting everything in order. You know, tidying loose ends. Putting out the trash.'

'Why?' Wallis repeated, thumping fingers across Hooper's back. 'Thinking of going somewhere?'

'No, sir. Nowhere in particular.'

Eventually Wallis was finished. He sat Hooper back on the chaise longue, pulling a small wheeled trolley to his side. There was a steel dish on it. He picked up a short length of rubber, tying it around Hooper's arm, just above the elbow. Gently, he straightened out the arm, flicking at a rising vein with a finger.

'Sodium pentothal is not something to be messed around with lightly, John. I can't promise you anything. You may remember good things, you may remember bad. You may remember nothing at all. You might, I have to warn you, remember things you wished had stayed buried for ever. Do you understand me?'

'Shall we just get on with it, Major?'

Afterwards, he lay, dozing groggily for a while. Time passed. Then a nurse came, brought him hot soup and sandwiches on a tray. Wallis came and they talked while he ate. He slept a little more. When he awoke the light was just beginning to fail. But he felt refreshed and ready to get up. He dressed, took a final tour of the grounds, then Wallis walked him to the Jeep.

'Sure you feel up to driving?'

'I'm fine. Thanks, Brent.'

'Take good care of yourself, Lieutenant.'

He drove, purposefully, as fast as he dared along the slippery lanes. This time he needed no directions, no queuing for telephone calls, no quizzical looks from police sergeants. He drove straight to Orford, turned off the road on to the tracks that wound through the fields, splashing through rutted puddles, mud spurting from the lurching Jeep's wheels.

He found it first go. The field was changed, stunted winter greens poking through a blanket of dirty sleet, but the view was the same, the orientation, the lie of the land. Just as he'd seen it as his stricken airplane had broken out of the bottom of the sea-mist. And the sea. He could smell it, it was so close behind him. They had been so close, but not close enough; his navigator had been wrong. 'It's safe now, Hooper!' he'd yelled over the intercom. 'We're over land,

386

I'm sure of it!' A small mistake. Five minutes more, that's all it would have taken to save them. Five minutes. But there was no five minutes, they were at seven hundred feet, and the navigator was sure. So Hooper hit the button and let them go, drifting into the mist and the freezing waters beneath.

Then, within seconds, he too was in the fog, sinking blindly down and down. Then, desperately near, a beach, a strip of brown shingle, a river, fields, scattering cattle. There was no time to prepare, no time to do anything but cut the last of the power and hold on. The impact was shocking, a sickening metallic crump as the aeroplane flopped lifelessly into the field, bounced, smashed down again and slithered, shuddering, through the waist-high corn.

Teeth gritted, he held on uselessly to the controls, bouncing in his seat, watching dirt and corn-stalks hitting the windshield, and waiting for the bomb to go off. The five-hundred-pounder sitting, wedged in its track in the bomb bay. But the bomb didn't go off and at last the wrecked Fortress, curling, slid to a halt. He sat there, for just a second, stunned by the silence. Then his harness was off and he was struggling aft. Bowling. Babyface Danny Bowling was waiting for him in the tail.

'I can't move, Hoop!' he cried. His legs were gone, a shattered, dripping mess of steel and bone and blood-soaked leather from the flak hit. The morphine the others had given him was wearing off, he was becoming panicked, delirious with pain and shock.

'I'm coming back!' Hooper shuffled back up the tube to the waist.

'For the love of Jesus, don't leave me!' Danny screamed. Hooper, fumbling, found the first-aid box, tore it open. The metal morphine phials, like little toothpaste tubes with needles on the end. Break them open, jab them in and squeeze. He grabbed a handful. Back down the tube, Danny's tortured screams ringing in his head, hysterical with pain. He reached out, grabbed a wildly thrashing arm, scrabbled at his clothes, glimpsed flesh, plunged.

'I'm going to get you out of here,' he repeated, over and over, until Danny began to grow calm once more. But he needed help. The gunner was trapped, his lower half completely pinned beneath the wreckage of his turret. Danny's head nodded, quieter, the pain in abeyance, at least for a few minutes. But the bleeding, the shock. There was no time. 'Danny, listen to me. I'm going to get help. We're going to get you out of here, but I need to go get help now.'

'Don't go, Hoop,' he pleaded softly. 'Don't leave. Stay. Just for a minute.' And so he'd stayed. Lying, full stretch in the cramped tunnel, his arm reached forward over the gunner's shoulder, tightly gripping his hand. They'd talked. And then they'd prayed. Calmly. Quietly. The twenty-third psalm. 'The Lord is my shepherd, therefore shall I lack for nothing. He maketh me to lie down in green pastures, and leadeth me beside quiet waters . . .'

At last Danny nodded into unconsciousness. Hooper slipped his hand from the young gunner's, shuffled back up the tunnel. Reaching the waist, he kicked open the exit. Sunshine, skylarks, the smell of warm earth. There was a farm, about a mile away, up on a hill near where a distant church tower poked through trees. He began to run, awkwardly, stumbling in his heavy flying suit through the rustling corn.

Then the bomb went off.

He went on, to the little church on the sandy bluff by the river, near the farm. The thatched church where he had sat, so long ago, unable to think, unable to grieve. Where he had first met Heather.

And there, as the last of the day's winter light died in the coloured glass windows around him, he hung his head and wept for the souls of his lost comrades.

After a while he grew still. Then he became aware of a presence, standing beside him. A hand touched his shoulder.

'We've been looking for you everywhere, John.' Finginger's voice echoed softly. 'Heather said I might find you here.' The hand shook his shoulder a little. 'We have to go.'

Hooper nodded and began to rise. 'It's okay. I'm ready.'

Dear Jo-Beth

Winters come early here. They're not harsh, generally, we get much worse in Harrisburg, but they do last. A quiet comes over the countryside, people stay in more, plant and animal life retreats, it is as if the whole world is pausing, to take stock. A time for reflection.

We have little iron stoves in the huts here, there's a coal ration which doesn't go far, so we keep them stoked up with whatever we can. Chairs have been known to vanish from the mess halls, and I fear there's a certain amount of illegal tree-felling going on in the woods hereabouts. It is pretty cold, and there's a damp chill to the air that seems to get into everything, but despite the petty hardships, and the other less petty things we have been through, I wouldn't have missed being here. Not for anything.

Why? That is a little complicated. You once asked me what it was like to be in a war. Did I have to carry hate in my heart for my enemy, what did I feel about the German people. I couldn't answer those questions then. Maybe I can now.

It is like everything in time is tightly compressed, very small. Your horizons shrink, you don't think too much about the past, that saddens, nor about the future, that can be risky! The now, the today, that is the most important thing. Small matters take on enormous significance; a warm word, a tiny flower, a child's hand in yours. The kindness of strangers. Friendship. You learn to value these things highly, because when everything else is stripped away, as it is in war, it is these that sustain us, and take us forward, into the peace.

No. I do not hate the enemy, nor the German people. The pilots that fly against us do so in the face of appalling odds, with skill and bravery. The artillery gunners shooting at us from the ground are simply doing their best to protect their cities, their homes and families, their futures. The ordinary people, as always, are the victims. As are we all victims. My hatred, such as it is, is reserved for the tyranny that brought us all to this. I believe we appease despots at our peril. And because war brutalises, we are all of us, inevitably, morally the poorer for it. Nobody gains.

The enemy is intolerance. War is failure of reason. We have to stop making it.

It is Advent, little sister. A new coming. I have just one fragmentary memory of you, as a baby, being placed into my lap by our mother. We are sitting on the floor together, you are lying in my seven-year-old arms. I am slightly nervous about that. But entranced. You are quite relaxed however, staring up into my eyes, reaching your hand out towards the candles on the Christmas tree in the corner of the den. It is a treasured moment.

I will keep it with me always.

With all my love, John.

Chapter 15

Finginger met them outside the front gate at five. It was still dark, and very cold. The moon had set, the sky was a bottomless black ocean, thick with phosphorescent starlight. They clambered aboard his Jeep while he went into the hut to square it with the sleepy-looking MP on the barrier. It was a blatant breach of standing orders, they would never have made it without his help. Not even via Billy's back door. 'Are we too late?' Heather shivered anxiously. All across the blacked-out airfield came the whine and splutter of starting engines.

'No, miss. Don't worry,' Billy said from the back seat. He was wearing his mechanic's overalls and cap. Over them a crisp new leather bomber jacket, '*Misbehavin Martha*' hand-painted across the back. 'It's just the ground crews warming the engines. Soon as they're up to temperature they'll shut them down again.'

Finginger returned. 'We're in.' He grinned. 'Amazing what you can achieve with two bottles of Kentucky's finest and a persuasive tone. Here, for God's sake put this on, you'll freeze.' He passed her one of the bulky, fleece-lined flying jackets. It was incredibly heavy, smelling of gun oil and musky leather. She shrugged it on. Even above her best winter overcoat it engulfed her.

'What did you tell him?'

Scott thumbed the starter. Thin slits of light probed forward from the taped-up headlights. The tarmac glistened with frost. 'Told him you were an intelligence colonel from HQ, and that if he didn't let you in Lassiter would have him patrolling the perimeter until Easter.'

'Poor man. Thank you, Scott. I greatly appreciate it.'

'No problem. See you in the stockade!' He let out the clutch and set off.

It took nearly fifteen minutes. The base roads were thick with last-minute toing and froing. Heather was amazed at the intensity of the activity. It was like co-ordinated chaos. Lorries and trucks, fuelling bowsers, Jeeps, crew transports, motorcycles, even bicycles weaved in and out of each other in an unconducted night-ballet of movement. This was what it was all about, she realised, huddling into the jacket. This was what the three thousand American people who lived and worked here on this tiny island outpost were for. To put twenty-five bombers and their two hundred and fifty crewmen into the air every few days. This was what it took.

Gradually the traffic thinned, then they were on the perimeter and moving away from the hubbub and out towards the flight line. Shadowy outlines of aircraft began to appear from the gloom, like slumbering giants, squat and heavy on their hardstands, their flight and ground crews clustered beside them. They passed five, six, then Billy leaned forward, tapping her on the shoulder. 'There she is.'

They were all there, just preparing to board. Knyper's boys too. They came up to Billy first, pulling his cap, spinning him around to admire his new jacket, kidding about. He smiled shyly, then excused himself for a moment, and went over to the flight crew, bundled up in their fleece suits and boots, their breaths fogging the air, their arms laden with parachutes and life vests. They were pleased to see him, too. But quieter, more inwardly focused. Instinctively sensing this, he shook their hands formally, wished each of them good luck, and went back to the mechanics.

Hooper was around *Martha*'s far side, crouching beside an undercarriage leg with Knyper. When he saw Heather he hesitated, fractionally, as though not able to believe his eyes, before straightening, coming to her. He took both her hands, kissed her.

'I had to come,' she said. 'Today of all days.'

'I'm so glad you did.' He smiled. He walked her across the concrete, hand in hand, to the fence by the beet field.

'How do you feel?' she said. They turned. The first suggestions of grey were touching the night sky on the eastern horizon. Thirty yards away *Martha* stood waiting. The others were already boarding; there was a tiny glow of cockpit lighting coming from the flight deck windows. Off to one side, Finginger sat hunched over the wheel of his Jeep.

'I feel ready.'

'I wish I was coming with you.'

'You are.'

'Are we allowed to hold each other? Just for a moment.'

They clung on, a single, motionless, tightly wrapped shadow in the last of the darkness. 'I love you,' she whispered. 'God speed.'

Then it was over and he was leading her back to the Jeep. 'Take good care of her, Major.' He squeezed her hand once more, and turned away.

On board, all was quiet preparation. He reached the flight deck in time to see the Jeep disappearing along the perimeter track.

'Everything okay, Irv?'

Underwood was jotting on to a clipboard. 'Starboard Tokyo tank is down, just a tad. But it's nothing. Beans reported a sticking firing mechanism on his fifty-calibre, he's changing it for a spare right now. Dutch just confirmed bomb load is twelve five-hundred-pounders, on and locked, bomb bay doors now closed. Engine warm-up went fine. I guess we're all set.'

'Good. Intercom checked?'

'Not yet.'

Hooper pulled on his headphones. One by one the crew called in, confirming in turn that their electrically heated suits, headsets, oxygen and weapons systems were all functional.

'Ah. Listen. While you're all on,' Hooper began, when they were done. It seemed appropriate to say a few words. But now that the moment had come, his mind was a blank. 'I had wanted to say something, to you all. About what these past months have taught me. About the real meaning of loyalty and honour. Courage. Friendship. But I think that maybe now is not the time.'

'Thank the Lord for that.'

'Amen.'

'Thank you, Sergeants. Anyway, I would, however, just like to say it has been a privilege to fly with you gentlemen, and to wish us all good fortune today.

'Irv,' he said, a few minutes later. They were preparing to start engines. 'I've been meaning to ask. Why is this ship called *Martha*? I mean, who is she?'

'Rudy Stoller's daughter. She's three years old. Always getting into mischief. His wife used to write him all the time, with the latest news of all the jams she'd gotten herself into. How's Martha? we used to kid. Misbehaving again, he'd say.'

'Well.' Hooper reached for the generator button. 'This one's for her.'

'Start number one.'

'Roger, energise.'

'Mesh!'

He thumbs the switch. Out on the port wing the whine of a generator, then the number one propeller begins to turn, slowly at first, then faster. A bang, a puff of smoke, then with a roar the engine catches and the propeller whirls to an invisible grey disc. They throttle it back to idle and move on to the next.

Finginger drove her home. 'Are you sure I'm not putting you to too much trouble?' she said, as they sped through the main gate. It was light; they'd stayed to watch the take-off. Suddenly, now that its task was over, the base had fallen still.

She could hear birdsong, the bleating of sheep, faint strains of music from a radio in one of the hangars.

Finginger spread his hands. 'I'm off duty. There's nothing more to be done.'

'Except wait.'

'That's right.'

They drove slowly back through the waking village. Thin plumes of smoke were appearing at chimneys. Blackouts were coming down from windows. Early risers were sweeping frozen slush from their steps. He followed her into the cottage. It was cold and lifeless.

'I expect you'd like coffee, but I'm afraid I don't have any.'

'Tea's fine.'

They talked. Heather seemed tense, but resigned.

'So, you've been working all night?' she asked.

'That's right. Ground staff get the night shift. Operations people, planners, maps, meteorology, signals, intelligence, there's hundreds of us. We usually start work around eight or nine in the evening before a mission. Planning the routes, getting the weather, fixing bomb loads, fuel loads, so on. Every last detail. We carry on through the night and finish when the crews are woken for briefing. Then, generally, we hit the sack for a few hours' sleep, before they come back in the afternoon. Or at least we try.'

'And do you succeed?'

'Me? No. Usually not. I generally end up back at my desk catching up on paperwork. It's a good, quiet time to work.'

'He isn't coming back, Scott.'

'What?'

She was leaning against the kitchen sink, waiting for the

kettle to boil. Her overcoat was still on, she was hugging herself, staring at her feet. 'I can't explain it. But I just know. He knows. It's as if he's already decided.'

Finginger left her a while later, drove back to the base. He was exhausted, dog-tired, more than ever before. He'd go to his hut, as usual, lie down and feel the fatigue creep over him like a cold fog. But sleep would elude him, as it always did, and he'd lie there staring up at his ceiling, until they were all safely back on the ground once more.

It was pointless trying. He collected coffee and doughnuts from the canteen, went back to his office and began to work.

It was half an hour before he came to it. A message slip. Nothing more. Three lines relayed to him from an opposite number at Operations HQ in Bury St Edmunds. It had been received during the night. Dropped, along with everything else, into his overflowing in-tray. He stared at it uncomprehendingly, an icy chill settling in his stomach. Then he leapt from his chair and ran for the door.

Lassiter wasn't in his office. He wasn't in his quarters. He wasn't in the mess. Finally, skidding his Jeep to an untidy halt beneath the squat, brick box of the control tower, he sprang for the door, doubling up the stairs. Lassiter was there, arms folded, talking to the waiting controllers.

'Sorry, Major,' he shrugged, a minute or two later. He reread the note. 'But I don't get it.'

'Crew 19, sir.' Finginger struggled for calm. He was out of breath, could feel his heart banging furiously beneath his jacket. 'Hooper and the boys, in *Martha*. They flew a double mission a few weeks back. To the Pas de Calais. Attacking those V1 flying-bomb sites, remember?'

'I remember the mission, Scott. What of it?'

'They flew twice that day. Yet at the time, they were only credited with one mission. They were pretty unhappy about that. So I said I'd make a few enquiries, put a request through to HQ for clarification. Get back to them if I heard anything.'

Lassiter was still studying the paper. 'And you didn't hear anything.'

'No, sir. Nothing. I forgot the whole thing. They did too. Until now.'

'Now they've been credited with the second mission.'

'Yes, sir.'

Lassiter pursed his lips in contemplation. The other controllers looked on.

'Sir. This piece of paper. It means they've finished. It means they completed their tour of duty the day before yesterday, when they flew to Kiel.' His arm stretched out towards the windows. 'It means they should not be up there today.'

'I know what it means, Major!' Lassiter glared at him, then began pacing the wooden floor of the control room. Finginger waited.

'You are right, Scott, they should not be up there today. But there's not a damn thing I can do about it.'

'Sir, we can recall them.'

'No, we cannot!'

'But why?'

'Why? I'll tell you why. First, they're over two hours into the mission. The supers came back an hour ago, so there's no one to take their slot if they drop out. Second, Hooper's commanding the high squadron. If I pull him out, who the hell is going to take over? Third, what do you think the rest of the group is going to think when they hear a radio signal recalling just one of their number? Fourth . . .' His voice fell. He'd stopped pacing, was staring down at the note. 'Fourth, I believe, if they had the choice, they'd want it to be this way.'

Munich was a long haul, practically into the foothills of the Alps and the border with Austria, at the furthest extremes of their protective escorts' range. But the formation dog-legged its way south largely unmolested. A thick undercast obscured the ground at first, providing welcome cover from the mainly sporadic attacks of flak. And fighter activity was light, too. Occasional brief, probing raids of short duration and only minor consequence. Nothing sustained. Nothing co-ordinated. It was as if they were waiting. Watching. Drawing them in deeper, further, before springing an attack.

Martha flew at the head of a spread finger formation of five, with two more tucked in behind. Her crew were unable to resist making a little of their newly elevated status.

'Will you just look at that *Gloria* there. All over the god-damn place! It's plain shameful, these new guys, they don't have any idea how to fly a neat formation.'

'And take a look over there at *Big Boots*. Sloppy as hell. Her guns all hanging down like that. What the hell are they doing in there? Taking a nap?'

'Pitiful.'

'Disgrace to the 8th.'

Hooper kept watch on his charges with detached inter-est. He seemed withdrawn, yet restless, content to let Underwood fly *Martha*, talking even less than usual, yet constantly double-checking: instruments, position, fuel burn, flight plan. Instruments again.

'Keep her going, Irv,' he said, unclipping his straps. Spitzer had just confirmed they were drawing closer to the IP. 'I'm just going aft to check on the guys. Back in a couple of minutes.' He grabbed a portable oxygen bottle from the rack and climbed down from his seat.

Via was in his radio room, monitoring signals traffic. They exchanged a few words, then Hooper went on. 'Everything a-okay back here?' he called, stepping into the waist. Beans and Keissling looked at each other in bemusement, then nodded. Hooper knelt, unlatching the lid of the ball turret. 'You all set down here, Sergeant?' Ringwald's nodding face squinted up at him. 'Bail-out kit to hand?' Another nod. 'Good. Keep your eyes and ears wide open. Won't be long now.'

He crawled aft towards the tail. 'Everything set back here, Al?'

'Sure.' Tork turned awkwardly on his seat. 'Why, is something up?'

'Not a thing. Just making sure. We wouldn't want any foul-ups. Not today.'

'I hear you, Lieutenant! It's kind of hard to believe, wouldn't you say? That this is the last time we'll ever be doing this.'

'Yes it is. You've done outstanding work here, Sergeant. You all have.'

Ten minutes later, as predicted by the weather forecasters, small tears began to appear in the undercast. Snow-covered hills could be glimpsed. Meandering strips of black road. An arrow-straight section of railway, vanishing into a hillside. The glassy surface of an ice-covered river.

A short while after that the fighters came in.

'My God,' Holland murmured, peering through the nose dome at the circling swarms. 'Look at them. There must be a hundred or more.'

Hooper broke in over the command radio. 'All aircraft, this is *Martha*. We're coming up on the IP. Keep it in tight, watch me for heading changes, cover each other. Good luck.'

'Here they come!'

'I got five coming in at six o'clock.'

'Four more cutting through left to right.'

'I got those. Watch it, watch it!'

'Head on! A whole line of them coming in head on. Polecat, do you see them?'

'On it.'

Seconds later *Martha*'s airframe was shuddering from the collective firing of her guns. Hooper forced himself to ignore them, carefully leading his formation through a twenty-degree turn on to the bomb-run. As their wings levelled once more the familiar black islands of flak began exploding directly ahead of them.

'Pilot to bombardier, she's all yours, Dutch.'

'Roger. I have it.'

Martha lurched slightly as the automatic pilot took over. Hooper released the controls. Down below in the nose compartment, Holland, hunched low over his sights, began making fine adjustments to the squadron's heading and drift. The bomb bay doors came down, further slowing their progress. It was the worst moment. Four or five minutes flying dead straight and dead slow from the IP to the target. Behind Holland, Spitzer ducked instinctively as a fighter flashed past. Without thinking, he swung his machine-gun through the arc of its trajectory, jabbing repeatedly at the firing button. In an instant the fighter exploded into a ball of flame.

'Way to go, Spitz!'

Spitzer looked up, following the flaming wreck. The air was black with flak and smoke trails, somebody up ahead was on fire. *Martha* bucked suddenly, then there was a gut-wrenching lurch and splintering crash. He flinched, lost his footing on spent shell cases, stumbled to the floor.

'Holland's hit!' His voice crackled over the intercom. 'He's hit in the head. The nose dome's busted! Christ, there's blood everywhere!'

'Get down there, Irv!' But Underwood was already moving. It was what they'd practised. What they'd trained for. On the run-in to the target, the two pilots had no guns to fire, no airplane to fly. They were redundant. Spare. So Irv was back-up bombardier, Hooper back-up navigator.

He reached for the intercom again. 'Via! Did you get that? Holland's hit.'

'I'm on my way.'

Martha bucked again, another near miss. Engine dials were jumping. It was number four. He looked out of the window; smoke was pouring from it. He yanked back on the mixture lever, hit the number four extinguisher button. A shadow flashed past his head; he looked up, a fighter, right to left, side attack. Its wingman was following it, rolling through on to its back, guns blinking. He sensed hits, felt a series of staccato blows along *Martha*'s flanks. Then a section of instrument panel in front of him jumped and exploded, dissolving into shattered fragments. He felt a thump, a stinging blow to his right hand. He yelped, glimpsed torn flesh through a smoking rent in his glove. There was shouting in his head.

'We're hit!'

'Two more coming by under! Yours, ball, do you see them?'

'Jesus did you see that, get him! Torky yours yours yours!'

They were still flying on automatic. Straight and slow. Bomb doors gaping, six thousand pounds of high explosives hanging in the daylight. Down in the nose a freezing gale tore through the shattered glass of the nose dome. Maps and papers flew in a storm. Underwood and Spitzer were hauling Holland back from the bombardier's seat. His arms flailed weekly. He coughed, his face a mask of blood.

Via arrived. 'I've got him!' he yelled above the shrieking slipstream. 'It's okay. Irv, go!' Underwood dropped on to the sights, his left hand reaching for the bomb-release switch panel. Spitzer helped drag Holland back out of the nose compartment. 'Dutch! Dutch, can you hear me?' Via ripped open his medical kit. From the corner of his eye he saw smoke pouring from the starboard outer engine. He ignored it, bringing a compress to Holland's forehead. 'Dutch? Speak to me!'

'Waist to pilot. Hooper, this is Beans. We're hit back here.'

'Where, Beans? What damage? Can you track it down?'

'Tail to ball, can you hear me?'

'Uh, there's holes everywhere. There's smoke too. Bad smell of burning.'

'Tail here! Two more coming in. Seven o'clock level. Polecat?

'I see 'em.'

'Uh, this is Beans. Keiss is checking forward, smoke seems to be coming from radio. There's lines of holes all down the sides here. Looks like there's something flapping loose out there on the starboard wing. Aileron's hit, maybe. Shit.'

'What? What else?'

'Ball turret ain't firing.'

Suddenly *Martha* surged upwards, released from the dead weight of her bombs tumbling from their racks.

'Bombs gone!' Irv's voice. 'Doors coming up. Manual flight control, Hoop.'

'Got it!' Hooper, right glove sodden, rammed open the throttles, hauling the bomber away from the target. 'Waist! Beans, this is pilot. What about ball turret?'

'Christ.' Beans' voice again. 'Pilot. This is waist. Ringwald's hit.'

From twenty miles, and eleven thousand feet, the Alps were an unbroken jumble of gigantic, cloud-enshrouded ice-blocks. Higher peaks punctured the blanket of white that draped over their shoulders. Lower down, over the nearer foothills, the humps in the blanket sloped more smoothly. Directly below, the surface was obscured by cloud. Above, the sky stood hazy blue.

And empty. For more than fifteen minutes there had been no flak, no enemy fighters. No aircraft at all, in fact, neither friend nor foe. They were alone. They were leaving.

Hooper, his right hand hanging limply at his side, flew *Martha* with his left. She was down to three engines. Half the instrument panel was shattered. She shook, a curious, cyclic fluttering sensation transmitting itself to his feet from the damaged rudder. She was losing fuel from a ruptured wing-tank. And an arctic blast whistled through her fuselage from the smashed nose, and the countless bullet-holes that had ripped through her skin as if it were paper.

But she was still flying. Holding steady and level. The fire in number four was out. There were enough working instruments to monitor the health of the remaining three, and read off the altitude and air speed. And direction. Hooper was taking them south-west.

'You called me, Lieutenant?' Lajowski appeared breathlessly beside him. His parachute, like Hooper's, was clipped to his chest.

'What?' Hooper stirred. 'Oh, yes, I did, Emmett. How's it going back there?'

'Well, we got everybody together down in the waist. Dutch is okay. Piece of plexiglas from the nose dome must have caught him on the head. There was a lot of blood, but Gerry got it stopped. He's bandaged up, sitting pretty comfortable. Ringwald took one in the thigh and another in the upper chest somewhere, round about the shoulder. Gerry's working on him now, with Irv lending a hand. He's in a lot of pain, I guess. But conscious. Cussing like the devil. Spitz and Keiss got Torky out of the tail. He's fine, lucky as hell. Fifty-calibre went right through the fuselage, one side to the other, just behind his head. Nicked him on the neck. He was bleeding like a stuck pig, but Spitz got a compress on it, and he and Keiss got him out. Gerry's going to fix him up when he gets through with the Kid.' He looked down at Hooper's hanging arm. A dark puddle was collecting on the flight deck floor below it. 'Are you going to get that seen to?'

'In a minute.' Hooper kept checking his watch, staring down at a folded map strapped to his knee. 'Is everyone wearing their parachute?'

'Yep. We got the waist door hanging open too, just in case, like you said.' He looked around the cockpit. 'Why? Is she going down?'

'Not yet. Listen, Emmett, step up into the co-pilot's seat here.'

'Don't you want me to go fetch Irv?'

'No, Sergeant. Via needs him. Now, listen to me. I know you can do this because you've done it before, and Hal told me you've been spending time learning your way around the cockpit, like we agreed.'

'Yeah, some. But—'

'All you have to do is hold her level, and steady. That's all. See that distant ridge of mountains poking up through the clouds there? Keep them where they are, ahead and to your left. Nothing more.' He began to climb from his seat. 'I'll be right back.'

Lajowski's hands closed uncertainly over the control column. Chin jutting, he peered ahead through the windscreen at the approaching mountains. They didn't seem so distant. Close enough to reach out and touch.

'Uh. Are those, like, the German Alps?'

'No.' Hooper dropped to the floor, clambering aft. 'Not any more.'

The waist looked like a battle field-station. Daylight showed through lines of bullet-holes in *Martha*'s sides. Open medical kits, torn packaging, bloodstained bandages littered the floor, together with discarded clothing and spent shell cases. The injured crew were sitting, propped along the walls. The others sat or crouched at their sides. They all looked up as he entered.

'It's time to go,' he called. 'We'll be fine. But we don't have much time.' He smiled encouragingly. 'Don't worry, we'll go together, meet up on the ground.'

Underwood stood. 'But, Hoop, I mean, the ship . . . And what about Ringwald, he's hit pretty bad. And how are you getting out?'

'The ship's had it. Fuel's going. We can't risk a crash-landing, not through low cloud over this kind of terrain. We'll jump, it's safest.' Parachutes, descending like apple blossom into the waiting mist. He swallowed. His right arm was completely numb, his head spinning. Lajowski was alone in the cockpit. He must hurry. 'We'll secure Ringwald's rip-cord to the ship when he jumps, and send Gerry Via straight out after him. The rest of you follow on his heels. I mean it. Keep it tight. Lajowski and me will jump from the nose hatch. We'll be right behind you.'

He helped them prepare, organising them into a line beside the gaping waist door. Gerry Via stood, one arm around Ringwald, who, pale but conscious, managed to grin weakly at Hooper. Next came the other injured, Holland and Tork, followed by Keissling, Underwood and Spitzer. Marion Beans was at the back. Right at the last moment, barely seconds to go, he turned to Hooper, eyes wide with fear, his mouth working, but speechless.

'What? Sergeant, what is it?'

Wordlessly, lips trembling, Beans lifted the parachute pack on his chest. There were tears in his eyes.

'What?' Hooper looked. 'What is it?' Then he saw. A hole. A rough tear. The size of a finger. It went in through the bottom corner of the pack and out of the side. A tiny fold of scorched silk protruded from the exit hole.

Hooper hesitated, his eyes on Beans'. The parachute was useless. A death-trap. Despair washed over him, just for a second. How much more? The others were ready. In the cockpit Lajowski still waited.

Then his face broke into a smile. He clapped Beans on the shoulder.

'No problem, Sergeant, it's probably nothing.' He began quickly unclipping his own pack. 'But best not to risk it. Here, take mine. I'll go with the spare.'

'Spare? Uh, I didn't know—'

'In the nose, under the pilot's seat.' He dropped Beans' pack to the floor, began attaching his own to the gunner's harness. 'Didn't think we'd be flying about the place without spare parachutes, did you? Via! Are you ready? Irv! Get everybody together, head south, hand yourselves in at the first place you come to. See to the injured.'

'But what about the Germans?' Underwood's voice rose above the howling slipstream. 'What about evade and escape?'

'There aren't any Germans. This is Switzerland.'

It is better this way. Far better. The relief, the peace, the release, is beyond beauty. Like a warm mountain breeze. Like weightlessness. It is over. Complete.

He sits, relaxed and comfortable in his seat at the top of his empty aeroplane. They are both spent, both finished. Spiritually, mechanically, it is the same thing. But they have accomplished with dignity that which has been asked of them, and are now free to travel the last few miles together. In peace. And as they please.

Unencumbered is how he pleases, suddenly. Empty. Stripped bare. Clean again. He pulls the headphones from his head. Then struggles to his feet, planting them wide so that he is standing, straddled between the two pilots' seats, his good hand on Martha's control column. She is easy to fly like this. Like a ship, a sailboat. She is a joy. A friend. Carefully, he lifts his right hand to his throat and pulls down on the zipper of his flying jacket.

In a while, with a little difficulty, the jacket is off. He reaches into the neck of his shirt, grasps his identity tags. He removes them, drops them into the well at his feet with the jacket. It is cold, but the cold embraces him, bears him up. He is clean again. Renewed and refreshed. Untainted. Martha coughs, shakes a little in his hand. He checks the gauges; the fuel is all but gone, the number one propeller already spinning to a stop. It is time. He is ready. He stands at the helm of his ship, feet braced, and slips down with it into the waiting clouds.

Chapter 16

The man parked the Range Rover by the gate. 'Are you two coming or what?' he asked, collecting his camel-hair overcoat from the back.

'No, Dad. We'll wait in the car, shall we?' said the girl in the back seat. She was in her early twenties, dressed in duffel coat and scarf. Curls of thick brown hair protruded from beneath a woollen cap pulled low over her ears. She glanced at the young man sitting beside her, arms folded. His expression reflected in the window, was a barely disguised scowl. 'Geoff's not feeling too good, and, well, it does look sort of cold, and muddy out there.'

'Suit yourself.' He slammed the boot and set out across the field.

The young man watched him go. 'Could somebody please tell me what the bloody hell we're doing here?'

411

The girl sighed. 'Humour him, Geoff, couldn't you? Just for a bit. We are staying with him, after all.'

'Yes and that's another thing. It's Saturday morning. I do not take kindly to being turfed out of bed in the middle of the night—'

'Half past nine.'

'Precisely. And then driven all over the countryside in the freezing cold to look at . . . what? What are we looking at? Oh yes. Holes in the ground, that's it. Forty-year-old holes in the bloody ground. And where the hell are we anyway? We're supposed to be in London, you know, Alice. Miners' march starts at two, remember?'

'We're in Essex, somewhere. And we'll make the march. He's dropping us at the station after this. Anyway, it's one hole in the ground, and it wouldn't do you any harm to show a little interest. You are supposed to be a history graduate, you know.'

'But I mean, what's in God's name is it for? What on earth is he doing?'

Alice watched the squat outline of her father receding across the field. 'He's looking for something.'

The man went carefully. His daughter was right, it was cold, freezing. And muddy, the ground soft and slippery. Sheep dung and sprout-stalks dusted with dirty frost. In no time his suede brogues were filthy, an icy wetness creeping through the leather to his socks. He pressed on, a cutting wind blowing diagonally at him as he picked his way, one hand to his hat, among the ice-covered puddles.

At last he reached the hole, roughly circular, about twenty feet wide and six deep. He approached it cautiously, peered over its rim, the wind plucking at the tails of his overcoat. Three youths were at the bottom of the hole, clad in jeans, anoraks and scarves. Their boots were sodden, thick with caked mud. They were operating a small mechanical digger. As he approached, one of them looked up.

'Oh, Mr Howden, you made it. Great.' He bent down and picked up a twisted, tubular shard of metal. 'Thought you'd want to see this. Found it this morning.' He handed it up. 'I believe it's a piece of bomb-door actuator. There's a manufacturer's plate on it. With serial number.'

Billy stood at the edge of the hole, turning the metal over and over in his hands. He was in his late fifties, squat, powerfully built, accustomed to getting his way. As he held it, the fragment deposited muddy rust-flakes over the soft leather of his gloves. He wiped a finger back and forth across the manufacturer's plate. Then he handed the shard back down to the youth.

'Keep digging,' he said, turning from view.

The controversial decision to raise the number of missions flown by bomber crews from twenty-five to thirty-five was finally approved by General Doolittle, Supreme Commander of the 8th Air Force, early in 1944. The logic behind the policy was that the more missions a crew flew, the more efficient and effective they became. At twenty-five missions they were at their most useful, so it was a waste of hard-won experience to stand them down and send them home. Also, supporters of the decision argued, a little perversely, the more experienced a crew was, the better its survival chances. Statistically speaking, the point was undeniable. Finally, with the arrival of truly long-range fighters, capable of escorting the bombers all the way to even the furthest targets, together with the relentless stepping up of the air offensive, and the turning of the tide in the war as a whole, the odds on a crew getting through began to shorten at last.

But not until the spring of '44. The autumn and winter of 1943 would go down as the blackest period in the history of the 8th. The disastrous ten-day period in October when the Bremen, Münster and Schweinfurt raids were flown all but brought it to its knees. Continued losses on that scale would have been unsustainable.

During 1944, however, the balance of air power was shifting in favour of the Allies. By June, and the D-Day landings, the 8th's role was already changing. The emphasis now was on saturation rather than precision, quantity, perhaps, rather than quality, the objective being to bring about the earliest possible end to the war, by all-out assault and without quarter. As land forces retook France, stormed up through Italy and closed in from Russia in the east, the bombing of Germany went on around the clock, the Royal Air Force by night, the US Army Air Force by day. But it was no longer a strategic campaign, it was tactical, a euphemism for wholesale obliteration. No longer were targets confined to those of specific and identifiable military worth. Human misery became an objective. Bomb people's homes, destroy their houses, their families, their very existences. Bring the war, in other words, literally crashing to their doorstep, and they would turn against the leaders who refused to end it, even in the face of certain defeat. That was the thinking. Münster had been the beginning, unofficially, as early as October 1943. The first time a

mission had deliberately encompassed more than just munitions factories, railways, aircraft production lines. As the war
entered its final months, the complete annihilation of cities
was to follow. Hamburg, Dresden, Berlin. Whether it worked
is an eternally debatable matter. Whether it was morally jus-
tifiable is another. But as one commentator put it, the time for
ideological soul-searching was not then. After six years of
war, people had just had enough, and wanted it over with.

By the beginning of 1945, the end-game had at last arrived.
The final missions of the 520th and most of East Anglia's other
US bomber stations came that spring. Instead of bombing sor-
ties, operations now often consisted of delivering spare parts
to advancing ground forces, emergency supplies to Resistance
fighters, VIPs to newly liberated cities and food parcels to
starving refugees. Offensive operations ceased altogether following Germany's surrender in May. Almost immediately a
process of withdrawal began. During June and July, the bulk of
Bedenham's base population was shipped home; the remainder
spent their days waiting, packing up, dispatching expendables
to other bases, tidying loose ends and still waiting. The aircraft
were dispersed elsewhere in the European Theatre, flown
home to the US, or, in most cases, stored and subsequently
dismantled for scrap. Bedenham became an airbase without
aeroplanes. On Thursday 2 August the order came to close the
station. All but a small caretaker skeleton staff were to leave.
That day was spent removing the last of the supplies, furniture
and equipment into storage. By the afternoon men were playing cards on bare hut floors. A final meal was served, then at
around nine in the evening the trucks and buses arrived and
the exodus began. Scott Finginger, base archivist, historian

and keeper of the faith, was one of the last to go. In his memoir of the 520th, he describes the departing convoy winding through the village of Bedenham that mild August evening. The entire population turned out to see them off, many of them waving American flags. Overwrought with emotion, he recorded that it was probably the proudest, yet saddest moment of his life.

By midnight, the 520th Bombardment Group had been officially stood down. Ten days later, Order #116 Sec.II Par #1 HQ 2AF was issued, formally terminating its existence.

Alice Howden spoke to Scott Finginger the day after her excursion to the Essex crash site in her father's car.

'Oh, er, hello there,' an American voice said, when she picked up the telephone. It was Sunday, early evening. She and Geoff were alone in the big house. 'Would that be Mrs Howden I'm talking to?'

'No. I, er, well, no, this is one of her daughters. Alice. Who's speaking, please?'

'My name is Finginger. I'm calling from Seattle. Your father wrote me a few weeks back, wanting some information about an old wartime bomber base.'

'Oh, yes! He mentioned you. You're the one who kept all the records and things from when he was at Bedenham with Granny and Grandad Howden.'

A faint chuckle floated down the line. 'That's right, kind of. Ah, is he there, by any chance? Or your mother?'

'My mother died four months ago. Sorry, I should have said.'

'Please don't apologise. I'm real sorry to hear that. Your dad didn't mention it in his letter.'

'No. He doesn't talk about it much. He's at church, by the way, goes to evensong most Sundays. He'll be back soon.'

'Oh, fine. I can call back a little later. Tell me . . . Alice, isn't it? Your mother, was her name Ruby?'

'Ruby, yes. How did you know that?'

'I met her a few times when I was stationed at Bedenham. Your dad and she were just kids then, of course. But I always had a hunch those two would end up together. When were they married, do you know?'

Alice was forming the impression Finginger was taking notes. 'Um, let me see. Helen was born in '54. Mum and Dad got married four years earlier, in 1950. No, it was the year after that. 1951.'

'1951, got it. And Helen, you say she was born in '54? She's your sister?'

'That's right. There's three of us. Helen is thirty-one, Rose twenty-nine, she's married to a farmer and lives in New Zealand. Then I'm the youngest at twenty-two.'

'And are you married?'

'Married! Me?' Alice laughed, glancing at Geoff. He was stretched out on the carpet, head propped on a cushion, watching television. He threw her a rude gesture. 'No. Definitely not married. I've just come down from Hull University.'

'Oh, yes? What was your degree?'

He was definitely taking notes. 'Economics. Um, a First.'

'Congratulations. Clearly inherited your father's business instincts, it seems.'

'I beg your pardon?'

They talked a while longer, then Geoff began to make annoyed faces from the floor. 'News is on!' he hissed. She hung up. 'What on earth was that about?' he added, without interest. On the television, an image of Margaret Thatcher followed by scenes of placard-waving miner's supporters at a rally in Hyde Park.

'Nothing much. War stuff, from when Dad was an evacuee.'

Geoff grunted. She watched the screen with him for a while, then padded barefoot to her father's study. She sat at the big leather-topped desk, scrawling a note about Finginger's call, stopping to examine a silver-framed photograph of her mother. It was from a family holiday they'd all taken to Tenerife together. In 1970, long before her illness. She was laughing. Plump and tanned, a picture of health and happiness.

Alice knew very little of her parents' time together as adolescents, even less of her father's earlier childhood. It wasn't that it was taboo. But whenever the matter had been broached, usually by Alice, he became vague and evasive. 'Nope, can't recall it, girl,' he'd quip, in his faded cockney. 'Proper life begun for me when your grandparents took me on, God bless 'em. 1943. Same year as your mother started giving me the eye!'

And now, suddenly, he wanted to dredge it all up again. Or at least parts of it. A buff folder lay on the desk, its cover bearing the same year, 1943. It was already thick with newspaper clippings, letters, photocopied pages from books. Notes compiled in his appalling handwriting. It was a therapy, she knew. A way of compartmentalising his grief. Of trying to come to terms with the death of the woman he'd loved above all else.

Although the base may have closed, the village went on, much as before, in many ways, yet fundamentally altered in others.

Culturally and sociologically, whether because of the accelerated rate of change the war years had wrought, or owing to American influence, Suffolk would never be the same. It was as though this sleepy eastern English outpost, backward-looking and slow to evolve, had been hurried suddenly, and a little rudely, into the twentieth century. At last. Fifty years after everyone else.

Change was inevitable. Young men and women no longer saw their lives and futures unfolding within the confines of the parish boundaries. They left home, went to work in the bigger towns, the cities, even abroad. America and Canada became particularly popular destinations for East Anglian émigrés. For the first time, village populations began to decline, and grow older. Better communications, better bus services, a car in most homes, brought the shops and department stores of larger towns within practicable reach. It sounded the death knell for many traditional village stores.

And agriculture, farming, the cornerstone of rural existence, began to change. Ancient, proven, but hopelessly outmoded farming practices declined, together with the last of the traditional landowners and their feudal ways. To persuade a young man to work your land, you had to pay a competitive wage, with benefits, or he would simply move to Ipswich and work at one of the agricultural machinery plants, or a shop, or an office, for half the hours and double the money. Or he might begin his own farming enterprise on one of the self-managed tenancies. Small workforces, modern machines, arsenals of new fertilisers and pesticides. And generous subsidies. It was the new ruralism. Even the horse, for centuries the plodding symbol of labour in the fields, was finally consigned to history books and country fairs.

With it went the traditional village blacksmith.

But not Ray Howden. Howden's Cycles opened in Framlingham in 1946. It was an instant success. Within a few years, Billy, by then an adopted member of the family, as well as a full partner in the business, persuaded Ray to branch out into motorbikes. Two more shops opened. When Ray and Maggie retired in the mid-fifties, Ray happily passed the business – by then six shops with repair facilities and showrooms – on to the son who had made it all possible. Billy, his instincts sharper than ever, took it to new heights. Sensing that despite his best efforts the British motorcycle industry was going the way of the plough-horse, he became one of the first to sign up for the cheaper, simpler, more reliable Japanese imports that the young men wandering his showrooms yearned for. Howden Honda was to become the biggest motorcycle dealership in eastern England. He and Ruby moved their young family into a large modern home on the outskirts of Ipswich. They joined the ranks of the new wealthy; became well known and respected. Ray and Maggie were regular visitors.

So too, although less frequently, was Claire. She fulfilled her wartime ambitions and became a member of an all-women artillery battery. After training, first in Devizes and then in Scotland, her unit was initially posted to an anti-aircraft site in Bristol, where it was credited with two enemy aircraft shot down. From there she was moved to the Solent where activity was more hectic – and hazardous. During this period, before the threat of invasion had fully receded, one of Claire's duties was to prepare and detonate the explosives that would destroy the emplacement, preventing it from falling into enemy hands. After that, she was moved slightly nearer to home, to the Essex coast where her battery was employed to counter the flying-bomb menace. She was promoted to sergeant, eventually finishing the war in charge of her own battery in Hyde Park. On VE day itself, she volunteered for duty to allow some of her junior charges to enjoy the excitement. Thus she remained, alone at her post while the celebration parties swirled noisily by, until the very end. She was nineteen and a half.

She and Eldon Ringwald never married. They both knew it wasn't to be, and called it off without fuss. After the war she returned to Bedenham for a while but quickly became restless. She moved to Norwich and married a typesetter in a printing works. They had two children before Claire began to have problems with alcoholism in the sixties, after which they separated. Long cycles of rehabilitation and relapse followed until finally she found a form of peace and contentment where she had originally left it. Moving back into Forge Cottage after an absence of nearly thirty years, she became a popular if unconventional member of the Bedenham community. Together with her Californian partner, Bob, another refugee from the sixties, she lived in happy disorder, creating huge revolving garden sculptures from scrap metal. Soon after returning there, she became reconciled with her children.

She was Alice's godmother. Hopelessly forgetful of birthdays, frequently absent from Alice's life, sometimes for years at a time, she nevertheless remained in contact as best she could. Alice was very fond of her. Nearing sixty, she was scatty, disorganised and dishevelled, but a constant source of fun, and a font of stories and wild schemes. She could also surprise.

'I'm a died-in-the-wool pacifist, as you know,' she once confided to Alice in a rare moment of reflection. Alice had driven over to Bedenham for a birthday visit. 'But I have to say my military service was an empowering experience for me, and the only time in my life, until now, that I felt both a genuine clarity of purpose and a real sense of self-worth.' Alice had tried to understand, tried to empathise. But, well, military service. War. It was completely unimaginable.

Ray died in 1970, Maggie a decade later. Alice, being only seven at the time of Ray's death, did not go to her grandfather's funeral. But at seventeen she returned with her family to Bedenham for Maggie's. It was the first and only time that she saw her father incapacitated with emotion. He stood at the graveside openly weeping, Ruby, her arms around him, at his side. 'She gave me everything,' he kept saying. 'She gave me everything.'

'Is there anything I can do?' Alice asked him, a couple of weeks after Finginger had called.

'I don't know, girl. Is there?'

'Dad!' She jabbed him on the arm. 'I meant, to help you. You know, typing, or filing or something.'

'I know, love. Just kidding. Do you really want to?' They were in the kitchen, breakfasting. Alice sipped tea while Billy slit open letters. A large package with an American postmark lay on the table.

'Well, yes. Yes, I do. As long as you don't think I'm inter-fering.'

Billy, a slight frown of concentration on his brow, scanned through a letter. Alice watched. His lips moved as he read.

'Where's the gonk?' he asked, when he'd finished.

'If you're referring to Geoff, he's gone home to Sheffield, to visit his parents.'

'Ah.' His face softened suddenly. Reaching out, he brushed her cheek with the back of his finger, just for a second. Just as he used to. 'Do you love him, Al?'

'What? I don't know! I doubt it. We're friends. He's a laugh.'

'You don't have to do this, you know.'

'Do what?'

'All this. Hanging about here. Doing the washing and the cooking and that. Keeping the old man company. I can manage, you know.'

'Of course I know! Dad, I'm here because I want to be. And yes, I am concerned about you, we all are. Helen and Rose too. But they have families of their own to worry about, while I happen to be free right now, so I'm glad to come and spend time with you.'

'Hmm. Got your passport handy?'

'What?'

'I'm going to France tomorrow. You can come too, if you like.' He picked up the packet from the table. 'But first off, assuming you really do want to help, that is, you've got some reading to do.'

She spent the rest of the day in his study. Apart from the buff 1943 file, which was in some semblance of order, there were several dusty old boxfiles, stuffed to overflowing, which most certainly were not. Odd newspaper clippings, leaflets, letters, magazine articles, everything jumbled up together. A feature on a new exhibit at Duxford Air Museum dated 1980 was clipped to a wartime ration card in the name of someone called Street. A letter of condolence from Granny Moody from around the time of Ray's death was folded between the page of a recent newspaper article, something about a team of amateur archaeologists who spent their weekends excavating aircraft crash sites.

Then there were the photographs. She found one of her father, aged around thirteen. He was standing, smiling in the sunlight outside a tin hut with a curved roof. She stared at it for a long time. There were others. A big propeller-driven aeroplane with four engines and American markings. A man in wartime uniform, an officer, wearing a cap and a parachute harness. A posed group of nine more men. They were outside, in a field somewhere: four of them standing, four kneeling, one sitting cross-legged in front. They were wearing thick, fleece-lined leather flying suits, boots and gloves. They looked very young, smiled shyly into the camera. Her age, she guessed, some even younger. Names were written against each one: Underwood, Beans, Spitzer . . .

A plate appeared at her side, upon it a roughly hewn sandwich the size of a telephone directory. 'Thought you might need it,' said Billy, picking up the photograph.

'Who are they? Is that them? Is that Crew 19?'

He raised eyebrows in mock surprise. 'You do learn fast. That expensive education wasn't a complete bloody waste of time, then.'

She read on, munching slowly.

They'd all survived, she learned during the afternoon. The nine members of Crew 19 in the photograph. They'd all survived the war, several of them keeping in touch with Billy and Ruby over the years. Letters, Christmas cards, family photos, all told their stories. But Mr Finginger's dossier, the fat packet that had arrived that morning, revealed everything. It was a remarkable document, part archive, part memoir. 'From milk-run to bloodbath in half a second,' he'd typed on the first page. He said it summed up the nature of the war these young men had fought in. Reading on, Alice at last began to see why. Before she knew it, the light was going. She reached to turn on the desk lamp. By the time she finished the manuscript, it was gone midnight.

They'd landed in a snow-filled field near St Gallen, Crew 19, after they'd parachuted from the stricken bomber. It was a few miles to the south of Lake Constance. They were all together, except Lajowski who had jumped from the nose hatch a minute later. Shedding their parachutes, they began gathering themselves into a group. After a while Lajowski appeared, struggling over a low ridge, plastered head to toe in snow.

'Where's Hooper?' Al Tork, evidently, had asked the question. Down on the ground, Gerry Via was tending to Eldon Ringwald. Snow had softened the impact of his landing. Although seriously injured and in considerable pain, the ball turret gunner was still able to manage a weak smile.

'He wouldn't want us to wait.' Irv Underwood was the one to voice it. Without fuss he took charge. He saw that they buried their parachutes, then he gathered everybody together, arranged for the two biggest crewmen, Beans and Lajowski, to carry Ringwald between them, and then struck out southwards. There followed several arduous hours of foot-slogging through the snow. As night fell, the temperature plummeted. Ringwald's condition deteriorated. He began slipping in and out of consciousness, became delirious. Fortunately they were still wearing their flying suits. They bundled him up further; Via, carefully monitoring his blood-loss, and conscious of his falling body temperature, used morphine sparingly. At last, hungry and exhausted, long after dark, they stumbled upon a road. Soon after that they came to a village.

That was the last day of their war. Switzerland was neutral but under obligation to intern combatants found on its soil. The Swiss knew how to take care of visitors, and they were particularly fond of Americans. The crew spent the first night in a Gasthaus in the village where they were fed royally and plied with schnapps. They slept between clean sheets in their own private rooms. Ringwald was taken to hospital in Zurich where a bullet was removed from his lung. Gerry Via's careful ministrations had without doubt saved his life.

Within a few days they were moved to an internment camp at Adelboden, in the very shadow of the Alps, not far from Gstaad. It was simple but comfortable, and they passed the winter going for walks, playing cards with the other inmates and reading. By way of the Red Cross, they were allowed to send cards to their families telling them they were okay, and also one to the 520th with the same information. They addressed that one to Finginger.

Under the terms of a prisoner exchange agreement for airmen, they were repatriated the following spring, arriving back in the US in time to read of the D-Day landings in June. They demobilised and went their separate ways.

Irv Underwood went back to his bank teller's job in Indianapolis. He married Linda in 1948 and they had two children, Irving Junior, and a daughter he named Martha. Similarly, Loren Spitzer resumed his accountancy training in Boise. He eventually joined a large insurance group where he rose to become a vice president in charge of finance. He never married.

After a brief spell as a civilian, John Holland, the fourth of *Martha*'s commissioned officers, resumed a career in the air force. He qualified as a navigator, became an instructor, distinguished himself in the Korean War, finally rising to the rank of lieutenant colonel. In 1959 he married a Filipino girl called Tasmin, and they had two children.

Marion Beans went straight back to Supulpa and Cheryl. Within two months she was pregnant. They moved into a small house on his father's farm where the baby, a boy whom he insisted they call Herman, was born. They went on to have three more, all sons. In time he took over management of the farm from his father. They never went back to the Oklahoma City trailer park.

Early on, his close friend Herman Keissling became a regular visitor. True to her word, Herm's wife Blanche divorced him in 1945. For the sake of his son, Herm stayed on in Akron for a while, but found life difficult. In 1950, he too re-enlisted in the air force and served in Korea, but upon his return he was again rudderless. Estranged from his son, he spent much of the sixties wandering aimlessly from job to job. He married again, but it didn't last. He ran out of money and got into trouble with the law over trying to sell his ex-wife's car. Finally, broken and penniless, he turned up on the Beanses' doorstep once more. They took him in without a murmur, their boys immediately adopting him as honorary uncle. He began working on the farm. After a while he moved into the little house where Cheryl and Marion had first lived.

Gerry Via fulfilled his destiny and became a doctor. There was some parental difficulty, because his Italian father wanted him to join the family business back in Atlantic City. But a changed Geraldo was adamant and set to work studying right away. He qualified in 1950, going on to specialise in cardiothoracic surgery. In the sixties he worked as part of a Colorado team pioneering the then radical heart bypass procedures. In time he would rise to become one of its foremost proponents and a world-respected leader in the field. He lost touch with Joanna Morrison, but did marry a nurse, Sandy, in 1952. They had two daughters.

Emmett Lajowski went back to Brooklyn where he resumed work as an auto engineer in his father's workshop. In time the business expanded enough for him to run his own. He also bought and sold used cars, trading under the name Polecat Autos. He married his secretary, Donna, in 1957. Donna was unable to have children. Every few years they would drive south for a get-together with the Beanses and Herm Keissling.

Al Tork also kept in touch. Once back in Greenboro, he realised that goose farming was not for him at about the same time that Charlene realised that Al was not for her. Nor for anyone. He'd been conscious of a nagging pull in a different direction for some months. In 1947 he was accepted into a seminary in Raleigh, and was ordained five years later.

Thereafter, he stayed in the South, taking over a difficult ministry in a run-down sector of Charleston, South Carolina. When local kids asked about his war service, he always said that God found him hunched over his sights at twenty-five thousand feet over Bremen, on that interminable October day in '43.

Kid Ringwald, fully recovered from his injuries, returned to his South Dakota farming roots. But he too found that his priorities had changed and he was unable to settle. At twenty he enrolled in college, majoring in social sciences. He passed out with straight As and was accepted into law school. From there he moved to the West Coast where he joined a San Francisco firm specialising in corporate law. He watched the campus riots and social upheavals of the sixties with appalled fascination. Before much longer he was actively campaigning against the Vietnam War. Always an admirer of John Kennedy, he joined the Democratic Party and moved into full-time politics. In his mid-forties he was elected to the Senate where he was an outspoken international civil rights activist. He married Pat in 1950, with whom he had two sons, but she died ten years later from a brain tumour. A decade after that he met and fell in love with a Senate librarian fifteen years his junior. Her name was Corinne, and they were married in 1971.

They set off early the following morning, driving down towards Dover through sluggish traffic and late March drizzle. Alice slept at first, curled on the Range Rover's front seat beside her father, a travel blanket at her chin. The night before, she'd read on into the early hours, finally falling into her bed around two, only to dream of headless pilots, rivers of blood and a claustrophobically black bedroom with the windows boarded up.

She awoke with her father nudging her. The car was trundling up a ramp on to the ferry. 'Breakfast?'

After they'd eaten, she browsed the duty-free shop, the paperback shelves and cosmetics counters before joining him on the aft observation deck. The ferry was less than half full. Serried rows of red plastic chairs, their seats puddled with rain, stood waiting for the summer rush. A pair of elderly passengers, coat-tails flapping like sailcloth, leaned into the wind, their hands to their hats. She saw her father's back, hunched over the rail. He was watching the ship's wake, an arrow-straight line of white froth, stretching back like a freshly ploughed furrow.

'You miss her very much, don't you?' she said, tentatively slipping an arm through his.

He nodded. 'Worse than I ever imagined.'

'Me too.'

She hesitated. 'Dad, is that what this is all about?'

'Perhaps it is, love. Partly.'

After Calais their mood lifted as things started to improve. Traffic was light on the A26 and they sped quickly south, passing Arras and St-Quentin. At Reims the weather began to pick up, the drizzle stopped; soon mild sunlight was breaking through the ragged cloud layer. Somewhere near Chalons they stopped to fill the car and eat lunch in a café. Billy made Alice do the talking. 'Blasted foreigners,' he complained, as if it was their fault. 'Never could understand them.'

'Dad, listen, where are we going?' she asked, unable to contain her curiosity further. They were walking back towards the car. 'Is it *Martha*? Is it looking at more holes in the ground? Has someone found a crash site in France, or something?'

'No, it's not that. We're going to see someone.' He started up, following signs back on to the southbound autoroute. 'I don't know if you remember, Al, perhaps not, we all had enough on our plate that day, but at your mum's funeral there was a woman standing on her own. Your sort of height, grey hair, mid to late sixties.'

Alice shook her head. The bleak misery of that grey November day was etched forever in her memory. Yet the details, who was there, who was not, were a misty blur.

'That was Heather Garrett, my old teacher. We didn't get to speak much, what with – well, what with everything. But she wrote a very nice letter a month or so later. Told me she lived down in the south of France and to come and visit any time.'

'Oh.' Alice pondered. 'So you've spoken to her, then?'

'Spoken? No. That's what we're going for.'

'But she does know we're coming, Dad. She is expecting us, isn't she?'

'Well, not exactly, but she did say come any time. So, like, we are.'

'But, Dad, for goodness' sake, we can't just pitch up on her doorstep, out of the blue like this! What if she's got visitors? What if she's away? What if she's gone on a round the world cruise!'

'Well, she won't of. Will she?'

Alice shook her head in exasperation. 'Dad. Your trouble, you know, is that you expect everyone to just be there, ready for you. All the time. Like one of your showroom managers. You've always been that way.'

'I know. Your mum told me often enough, God rest her soul. It's time to change all that. That's why I'm selling up.'

'You're what?'

'The company, the showrooms. I'm selling the lot.'

'Selling it?' Alice could scarcely believe her ears. 'But why? I mean, your business. You can't sell it. You and Grandad got it started, from nothing. Nothing but a bunch of broken bikes in a back shed. It's your life.'

'No, Al. Not any more. I'm going to do that early retirement thing. I'm going to spend more time with my daughters, and my grandchildren. See something of the world. Find out what's going on. You can come with me if you want.'

'I don't believe I'm hearing this.' Alice's head was in her hands. They passed a blue autoroute sign for Dijon, Lyon and Marseille. To their right, the sun, a softening yellow orb, was sinking towards green plains of new corn. 'And this is all part of it, isn't it? Paying anoraks to dig up aeroplane wrecks, making two-hour telephone calls to retired airmen halfway round the world. Driving five hundred miles to drop in on an old schoolteacher. This is part of that, right?'

'Kind of. The retirement, well, that's for me. But this is for them. So as people won't forget.'

They arrived at lunchtime the next day. Billy had no directions, just the address from Heather's letter, so the last few kilometres, the locating of the house, took nearly an hour. Alice's schoolgirl French, trying both to ask for and then to understand directions, was severely taxed. Finally they pulled off a winding country lane on to a track. Rough, flinty ground sloped away to one side, and ranks of neatly tied vines, low to the ground, green with fleshy new growth, stretched away down the hillside. A group of middle-aged labourers were fixing wire supports to posts.

'Um, I say. *Excusez moi.*' Alice leaned from the window, stumbling through her lines once more. The men looked up, exchanged glances, then one of them, dark, taller, stepped forward. '*Tout droit,*' he said quietly, pointing with his arm.

'Straight on.' Alice sighed wearily. Two minutes later they arrived.

The house was brick, old and rambling, but in good repair, with outhouses and once-formal gardens. A woman was outside the front door, training a wisteria along one wall. It was Heather.

Twenty minutes later, the obligatory tour of the house completed, she led them out on to a sheltered veranda overlooking a terraced garden, an ancient Labrador panting at her heels. 'Perhaps we won't embarrass each other by calculating how many years it has been, shall we, Billy?' she said.

'Forty-two, now you mention it. Since you upped and left, that is.'

'Dad!'

Heather laughed. 'It's all right, Alice, your father was always quick at figures. Not quite so strong with his letters, as I recall.'

'Nothing much changed there, then.'

Heather told them what they wanted to know. Unhurriedly, pausing frequently, her voice quiet and mellifluous.

After *Martha*'s loss she had indeed left Bedenham quickly, she confirmed. There was nothing more for her there, except pain and humiliation. In any case, although Needham begged her to reconsider her resignation, her work in the school could not go on under the circumstances in which she found herself. She left the village, returned to Lincoln, and never went back.

David was repatriated in 1946. She travelled to Southampton to meet him. When she did, he was beyond recognition. The war, the horror and brutality of his experiences at the hands of his Japanese captors, had broken him in two, as surely as it had killed her brother Richard, who had died in David's arms a year earlier, ravaged by disease and starvation.

They went to London for a few days, then on holiday to a cottage in Wales. He was still very ill, stick-thin, incontinent, convulsed with fevers, plagued by nightmares beyond imagining. She ministered to his needs as best she could. Fed him, bathed him, calmed his night demons. There, slowly, he told her what he could bear to of his war. In time, when she felt he was strong enough, she told him of hers; her growing despair as David's wordless absence stretched into months, then years, her descent into hopelessness and lost faith. Hooper. And Molly.

She was born at the end of August 1944. 'Yes, Billy, and you needn't look so shocked,' she chided, seeing his expression. Food was beginning to appear on the veranda table, brought by a plump elderly woman in a grey apron. 'This is Chantal,' Heather explained, talking to the woman rapidly in French. 'It is a little chilly, but I thought we might all eat lunch out here.'

'All?' Billy queried.

'That would be lovely, Heather,' Alice said. 'Please go on. What about Molly? Does she live here too?'

'Good gracious me, no. She lives in Epsom, married to a chartered surveyor. They have two teenage children. They come out for the summer holidays.'

'So, you're a grandparent.' Billy smiled.

'You too, so I hear.'

She, David and Molly settled together in Lincoln. She talked at length with David about it. She would stay with him, she proposed, look after him, love him even, be the best wife she could, as she had always promised. But in return, she asked only that he treat her daughter as their own. David, instantly taken with the dark-eyed two-year-old, gratefully accepted.

But he was a broken man, both in spirit and in body. The fire had gone from him, the irrepressibility, the drive. He worked, when he could, as a manager in a nearby insurance office. But increasingly he was on sick-leave, plagued by chest complaints and recurrent bouts of malaria. Finally, five years after his return from the jungles of Burma, he took to his bed. He never rose from it, dying of pneumonia six weeks later.

'It was a release,' she said, staring down at her hands. 'What they did to him out there, it tore the life from him. It has always been my greatest hope that somehow Molly and I brought some comfort, and happiness, to his final years.'

'I'm sure you did, miss,' Billy muttered, shaking his head.

There was a pause.

'Miss?' Alice queried. A ripple of soft laughter resonated around the veranda.

'So, after that, you upped sticks and moved out here to France, then.'

Heather dabbed a single tear from the corner of her eye. 'Not quite. That came a little later.'

The first word came from Finginger. He wrote to her in 1952 saying he was compiling notes for a memoir of his time at Bedenham, and would be eternally grateful for anything she could provide in the way of background material, from the perspective of one who lived there at the time. Also, he went on tactfully, knowing how close she had grown to the men of Crew 19, her reminiscences about them, if she cared to share any, would provide a priceless and unique insight. He concluded his letter by saying that it was his goal to locate as many 520th aircrew as possible, including those listed as missing or killed in action. As a result he was following up literally hundreds of leads, including one story about a man reportedly living in a monastic community near Interlaken, in Switzerland.

She thought nothing more of the matter until a year later, when she received a second letter from him thanking her profusely for the material she had sent, and updating her on the news of Spitzer, Underwood and the others. 'Sadly, Hal Knyper died last year,' he reported. 'Cancer of the bone. It is a terrible loss; he was a mainstay of the 520th. He leaves a wife, Mary, and two fine boys.' There was a PS. 'I have received permission to pass you this.' It was an address. Poste Restante, care of a post office in Grenoble.

Men were beginning to assemble on the veranda, the labourers Billy and Alice had seen further back along the track. The three of them rose from the table, chairs were pulled up, introductions made, tumblers of wine poured and passed.

'Well. This must be the man I once knew as Billy Street.'

He appeared around the side of the house, wiping his hands on a cloth. There was a faded scar along the back of one of them. It was the tall man with darker hair that they'd seen with the others.

Alice gasped. 'Is this . . .'

'My God, yes, it bloody well is!' Billy stepped forward, gripping Hooper's hand. 'Hello, Lieutenant, it's damn good to see you.'

Hooper smiled. 'Billy, you too. Although it's a very long time since anyone called me that.'

A typically Gallic lunch, leisurely and informal, passed slowly by. The workmen placed Alice in their midst, applauding her attempts at French, piling her plate, overfilling her glass. Billy was at the head of the table, Heather and Hooper to his either side. At their request he recounted his life to date, watching them as he spoke. They listened quietly, stopping frequently to verify dates and places with one another, or simply to exchange looks. Once, to his embarrassment, Billy stretched out his legs beneath the table to find theirs were already there, loosely interlocked with one another.

Afterwards, Heather led Alice on a tour of the gardens.

'It's just so beautiful,' Alice said.

'I've a very good gardener,' Heather replied, looking back at the veranda.

Hooper walked with Billy back along the track towards the vine field. The afternoon was mild, the track dusty, and Billy, unaccustomed to exercise and overdressed in business suit and overcoat, was soon pink-cheeked and perspiring.

'Blow me. Is this all yours?' he puffed, looking out over the vineyards.

'Only a portion of it. It's a co-operative. We find that it's more than enough for our needs.'

'I'm setting up a memorial,' Billy explained later. 'On the old base. Stan Bolsover owns the land now. He said he'd be happy to go along with the idea.'

'It's a fine one, Bill.'

'I'm putting up the cash, so there's no fundraising needed, but I do want people's ideas, and involvement. I want to build something fitting, and lasting, like. So's people can come and visit.'

'I see. What did you have in mind?'

'Well, a little museum ideally. Where the control tower used to be. I've been trying to find an old B17. Not a flying one, but one in good enough nick to put in a little hangar we could build. Been paying a gang of hairy student archaeology types to go round digging up wrecks. But all they find is bits and pieces.'

'Ah.' Hooper considered. 'I believe I know where we might find one.'

Six months later, pouring mud, rust-streaked, corroded, but intact, *Misbehavin Martha*, suspended by slings from a barge-mounted crane, was hoisted to the surface of Lake Brienz, thirty miles to the south-east of Bern, in Switzerland. Billy was there to witness the moment, as were Hooper and Heather. Scott Finginger, too, was unable to resist the sense of occasion. Silver-haired, portly, red-faced, he had flown over at the last minute. Together they stood on the dockside and watched *Martha*'s return to dry land. Despite her age and battle damage, the still, ice-cold and fresh waters of the lake had protected her from the worst ravages of time. Hooper climbed back on board through the still gaping waist door. 'Couldn't resist throwing a few switches,' he reported to Finginger in the bar of their hotel that night. 'When I tried the master switch, the instrument lights came on.'

'What happened, John?' Finginger, ever the intelligence officer, had waited forty years to close the file on *Martha*'s final mission.

'I took them away from it,' Hooper said simply. 'It's all very hazy, and not something I care to think about too much. But I just felt they'd done enough. So I flew them out of the war.'

'I can understand that. And you were right, they had done enough. You all had.'

Hooper was thoughtful. 'Quite a while after they jumped clear, *Martha* was going down. There was a thick cloud layer. We just kept drifting down and down. It was incredibly peaceful. Then suddenly, very low, she broke out of the bottom, just a few miles north of here. And the lake was sitting there, dead ahead. We just glided straight down on to it. Or so I believe. There are, you know, a lot of gaps, and so much of it all seems so dream-like now.'

Finginger nodded. There were gaps. But Heather had filled them, speaking quietly to him at the lakeside that afternoon.

The monastery was on the far side of the lake. Hooper had been found the next morning on the shore nearby. He was half-dead from exposure, his head and hand were injured, and he was without any kind of identification. They took him in. 'He stayed nearly four years,' she said. 'It was twelve months before he even spoke.'

Shipping *Martha* back to England required her to be dismantled. By the time she arrived back at Bedenham, appropriately enough on the back of a USAF low-loader from the nearby base at Bentwaters, the foundations and curved roof of her final home were in place. Years of patient restoration work lay ahead. But in the meantime, she was reassembled and mounted on supporting jacks, canted at a slight angle and with her undercarriage raised, as though in flight.

Later that summer, just in time for the fortieth anniversary of the end of the war, a jumbo jet especially chartered from Boeing landed at Stansted carrying two hundred veterans of the 520th. They spent four days being bussed all over the Suffolk countryside, revisiting old friends, haunts and memories. On the Sunday, they gathered beneath blustery but sunny skies outside the new hangar. A simple stone cross had been erected before it, and a brass plaque read: 'To the memory of the men of the 520th Bombardment Group, 8th US Army Air Force, Bedenham, England, who gave their lives in the name of freedom, 1942–1945. Their name liveth for evermore.'

A few minutes later, ten men, aged in their sixties and seventies, assembled themselves, a little shyly, but proudly, into a group in front of their old aeroplane. Shutters clicked by the hundred, eyes grew moist. In the fields around them, clouds of seagulls wheeled overhead, while a tractor clawed fresh furrows into the rich earth.